AMANDINE

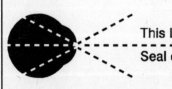

This Large Print Book carries the
Seal of Approval of N.A.V.H.

AMANDINE

MARLENA DE BLASI

WHEELER PUBLISHING
A part of Gale, Cengage Learning

GALE
CENGAGE Learning

Detroit • New York • San Francisco • New Haven, Conn • Waterville, Maine • London

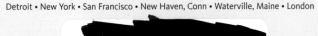

GALE
CENGAGE Learning

LIBRARY OF CONGRESS CATALOGING-IN-PUBLICATION DATA

Blasi, Marlena de.
　　Amandine / by Marlena de Blasi.
　　　　p. cm.
　　ISBN-13: 978-1-4104-3008-3 (hardcover)
　　ISBN-10: 1-4104-3008-1 (hardcover)
　　1. Nobility—Poland—Fiction. 2. Illegitimate children—Fiction.
3. Girls—Fiction. 4. Guardian and ward—Fiction. 5. Convents—
Fiction. 6. Governesses—Fiction. 7. Birthmothers—Fiction.
8. World War, 1939-1945—France—Fiction. 9. Large type
books. I. Title.
PS3604.E1225A43 2010b
813'.6—dc22　　　　　　　　　　　　　　　　　　　　2010021423

Published in 2010 by arrangement with The Ballantine Publishing Group, a division of Random House, Inc.

*To Paula and Stuart Herman
with love for then, now, and always*

*For Giuseppina Sugaroni Pettinelli,
authentic heroine, my one and only*

CONTENTS

PROLOGUE

On an evening in the autumn of 1916 on one of the estates of the noble Czartoryski family situated in the environs of Krakow, Count Antoni Czartoryski murdered the young baroness who was his lover. He then turned the pistol on himself. Count Czartoryski was survived by his wife, the Countess Valeska, and a two-year-old daughter named Andzelika.

Fourteen years later the Countess Valeska welcomed a Czartoryski nephew and his friend from their Warsaw boarding school to spend a part of their summer holidays in her Krakow palace. The friend was a young baron named Piotr Droutskoy. At the time, neither the Countess Valeska nor her nephew knew that Droutskoy was the brother of Antoni Czartoryski's lover. The countess's daughter, Andzelika, then sixteen years old, carried on a clandestine romance with Droutskoy and, as a result, remained

9

with child.

When Droutskoy's identity was discovered, the Countess Valeska, having lived through the scorn and the shame of her husband's betrayals, vowed that no child with the blood of that — to her — infamous family would she recognize as her grandchild. Andzelika, convinced that she had fallen deeply in love with Droutskoy and he with her, refused to interrupt her pregnancy. Not wishing to upset her daughter's then delicate psychological state, the Countess Valeska instead set about her plans for the eventual secret and irrevocable disposition of the child.

When Andzelika's child — a girl born with a significantly defective heart — was five months old, the Countess Valeska traveled from Krakow to a rural Roman Catholic convent near the southwestern French city of Montpellier. Great sums of money paving her way, she left the child there to be raised as a ward of the local curia. From the moment of its birth — and for some time before — the Countess Valeska had put into motion extravagant schemes to erase the child. Though she was convinced of her mission, too, she suffered for it.

■ ■ ■ ■

PART I
1931–39
MONTPELLIER

■ ■ ■ ■

CHAPTER I

Old plane trees reach limb to limb over the wide avenue and, under the parasols of yellow September leaves, a wide black Packard glides. Stippled light, rose and bronze, falls here and there upon three passengers. Funereal in their silence, there are two women and a man. One of the two women holds an infant. A small wedge of light lies across the infant's face, makes blue-black gems of its eyes. The infant is not disturbed by the light, neither closes its eyes to it nor looks away but keeps its gaze, steady and thoughtful, upon the woman who sits on the tufted gray divan across from it, her head turned to face the window. Sullen, aloof, a black-liveried chauffeur drives more slowly than he might. The only sound is the *pft, pft, pft* of tires rolling over asphalt.

I wish she would keep the creature covered. Why has she taken off its bonnet? Undone all the swaddling when we're so close to the convent? We must be coming upon it. I won't ask Jean-Pierre another time how much longer? How much longer? My neck hurts from twisting it to look away from the creature for all these hours. I can't help but see now how she's grown. I've not really looked at her since the night she was born. What possessed me to ask the nurse to bring her to me then? I'd forbidden Andzelika to see her, and yet I called for her. Seeing her was like seeing Andzelika for the first time. I reached out for her just as I'd reached for my daughter. My arms ached for her as though she were mine. She is mine. I must think of her that way. She is mine and it is I who have chosen not to keep her. Andzelika is seventeen. An unripe seventeen who mourns the boy and cares nothing for the child. Her maternal impulse benumbed, it's as though she carried it and bore it only for him. A dubious gift for he who'd run so fast and far from her. Cunning. Like all his tribe. Of all the boys and men to whom Andzelika might have given herself, why to him? What is this viperous pull between his family and mine? Were not two deaths enough to extinguish it? If only I'd understood on that first evening who he was. Fierce black eyes, fine white hand raking the great shock of his glossy hair. A bolshevik's scorn in the depth of his bow. I can hear Stas saying,

14

"*Ciotka* Valeska, Aunt Valeska, may I present my friend from the academy, Piotr Droutskoy." Yes, yes, welcome. Of course, be welcome. Your name means nothing, you mean nothing. Another knight-errant, are you? Or a blue-blooded cavalier of slender means? Yes, you'll round out the table nicely for a fortnight. I might have shot him right there in the courtyard in the fickle light of the torchières. Had I understood. Rather I welcomed him. Stas's chum. Yes, yes, please do stay. Adam scurried to take their things up to the third floor. And then he took Andzelika. The brother of Antoni's adored, whorish girl took my daughter. The brother of the enchanting baroness Urszula. Urszula. The wide Titian flanks of her twined about my husband even in death. How many nights had they slept like that? Antoni's hunting expeditions, his business in Prague, in Vienna. Visits to the farms, the villages. Always with her. Always with Urszula. Two bursts from a pistol so they could sleep like that forever. Will I never be free from the sight of her, of them?

Toussaint stood behind me as I looked from the doorway that morning, his hands iron grips upon my shoulders. What was it that he whispered then? "Even Rudolf and his baroness had the decency to cover themselves." Toussaint moved in front of me then, bent to retrieve Antoni's *kontusz* from the marble flags of the floor where it had been flung. How he'd loved that coat, symbol of his sympathy for the peasants. He'd push the split sleeves high above those of his shirt or his leather jacket and strut about, the breeze inflating the long fullness of it as he went. Toussaint covered them with the coat, the right shroud for a good *szlachta* and his beloved. I can still remember when I was his beloved.

Was it I who began the treachery? Would you have stayed faithful to me, Antoni, if I had not? Cuckolding the glorious count Czartoryski and so soon after our marriage, I was scandalous, arrogant. I would be the first between us to flash horns. Still, you were more clever than I, setting me up for it. You even put the Frenchman on your payroll for a bit, didn't you? Instructed him on approach, orchestrated the rendezvous, bought the gifts he gave to me. Yes, scandalous and arrogant, a perfect pigeon I was. Once I'd fallen you were freed for a married life of noble vendetta without noise from your soiled, wealthy wife. Who could blame you? Nimble as you were, easy as I was, the truth is that ours was nothing less than classic comportment among our kind, where the notion of fidelity has long been a fantastical diversion, a scherzo played in private and, at least as often, in public. Neither better nor worse than the others, we would have lived on that way, grown old that way, and passed on the tortured legacy of us to Andzelika as though it were a poem. That's how we would have ended. But you fell in love, Antoni.

Andzelika was two years old when you murdered your whore then put the pistol to your cheek, pulled the trigger inside your own beautiful mouth. Did you think of Andzelika, did you consider her? Your family did, yours and mine, as did kith and kin from the farthest edges of our lines. I found it strange how little mourning there was for you, how their grief was all for us, for Andzelika and me. "Poor angels," they called us. "We'll take care of you, stay close to you, protect you." Balm. And from that consolation came resolve. A double resolve. First, I would protect our daughter, my daughter. Yes, I would raise her in luxury, but I would not squander her then to the debauchery of our class. Second, I would become a better woman than I ever would have been had you lived. And that I did, Antoni. I am indeed finer without you. But in my tender mindfulness of Andzelika, in my, my — shall we call it vigilance? — over her, I failed. When, only days after his arrival, she told me — in that same half-whispered whiskey voice with which she'd uttered even her first words,

17

do you remember how we'd laugh that such a voice could come out of that tiny flower of a girl? — that she had fallen in love with Droutskoy, I looked into the grave, weepy black plums of her eyes and I smiled, told her, as though her sentiments were an illness, that the feeling would pass. Did she recall her "love" for the violin master and then for the ravishing blond boy who'd worked in the kitchens last summer? I was insensible to the eloquence of her sixteen-year-old's delicate, coltish beauty, to its power to goad, to delight a boy who would be a man. Yes, insensible, too, to the violence, the wonder of passion. First passion. Hers, his. I held Andzelika to me, Antoni, and kissed her forehead, promised a week or two at Baden-Baden or would she prefer Merano? Yes, Merano and then a few days in Venice, how would Mummy's darling girl like that? Good night, darling girl. Good night, *matka.* He found his way to her bed or she to his. For all those weeks, or was it just once? I've never asked her. One morning he was gone. Not even Stas knew where.

Toussaint found him easily enough, his inquiries illuminating the boy's parentage. Hideous parentage. Did he know? Did the boy know who we were? Had he been sent by his family to vindicate the fleshly little wench who was his sister? Schadenfreude. Is that what

18

brought him to us?

It's nearly over now. The boy is gone, Toussaint saw to that. And now with the creature soon to be gone, Andzelika will go on with her life. Andzelika and I will go on, uninjured. As though it never happened. As though they never happened, neither the boy nor the creature. No trace. No trace at all of this Droutskoy bastard. Andzelika will know nothing, nothing at all of what I have done, what I shall do today. From your hellish place, can you understand why?

Still averting her gaze from the infant, the woman, exhausted by her reverie, rests her thin shoulders against the divan, head tilted back. In supplication? She closes her eyes, and they move under the nearly transparent lids as if she were dreaming. She feels the infant's gaze.

For what I have done, for what I shall do today, forgive me, Andzelika. How indifferent you have been to anything but news of the boy. I'd thought she would fight to see her child, to hold her child, yet she stays rapt in her besotted illusion. She waits for him. In these past five months since its birth, she has made no more than trifling demands about it. Once she asked (as though he were due on the evening train from Warsaw and we two were in the glad habit of speaking about the baby and about him), "Do you think Piotr will be pleased with her, Mother?" I looked down to finger the mass of dark red peonies lying in the basket hung over my arm.

Andzelika trusts me to care for the child. When we left Krakow nearly two weeks ago, I told her I was taking it from the hospital where it was born and where it had remained — too weak to be moved, I'd said — to a clinic in Switzerland. To save it. Surgery for its imperfect heart. It's true about the infant's heart. The greater truth is that I have decided against surgery. Against saving it. Rather I shall save my daughter. In any case, its survival beyond its first year, even with intervention, is improbable, say the doctors. So be it. God's will be done. No credentialed orphanage would have it. Despite all Toussaint's gilded offers to see to the disposal of the creature through private and reputable adoption channels, there were no takers. And into unscrupulous hands I would never place her. I can hide her, deny her, leave her to the Fates but never to the blackguards.

The woman abruptly opens her eyes, jerks her head forward.

Ah, let me look at you, let me dare to look at you. How beautiful you are. My long fingers. Andzelika's long fingers. Her eyes. How you stare at me. Ah, a smile? Is that a smile for your *babcia?* Not even your smile will loosen my resolve. Such incubus would have been saved if only Andzelika had accepted the procedure. Swift, private. But I had to acquiesce. So fragile, Andzelika. But why, why have I gone to such trouble over this tiny damaged thing? The machinations, the endless signing of checks, the strangling doubts, a sea voyage, days of this fiendish hush among us in this automobile. I'll stare right back at you, you beautiful little beast. There, how do you like it? You see, there is no chink in my armor against you. No chink. A small chink. Too small. Do you think you know me? You shall never know me.

CHAPTER II

The thirteenth-century convent of St.-Hilaire and its prestigious adjunct boarding school for *les jeunes filles de la noblesse* are situated above a small village in southwestern France, scant kilometers from the city of Montpellier on the river Lez. Though the convent offers no official asylum for orphans or abandoned children, more than once a swaddled infant has been left near its doors in a basket, in a wooden fruit crate with nearly legible notes pinned to its wrappings, a few francs folded in newsprint tucked inside. The good sisters would then set about to place the child. A few days, a few weeks it wanted, the baby barely interrupting the hushed strides of their anchoritic life of work, prayer, and meditation. Yet this afternoon an infant will be delivered to the care of the good sisters in a very different manner.

The Packard moves through the great iron

gates, stops under the portico of the front entrance to the convent. The chauffeur steps out quickly to open the door to a robust uniformed nurse, who holds the infant, its layers of white and rose-colored robes spilling richly onto the folds of her dark blue cape. From the auto then steps a tall, lean man, smoothing the breast of a long, velvet-collared coat, adjusting his homburg, running his gloved hands over his thin white mustaches. Finally, another woman descends from the auto. This one is perhaps forty, her egregious beauty still fresh save the darkness around her large, soft black eyes, eyes like those of a deer, and the *triste* clench of chastely rouged lips. She wears a short silver fox jacket over a gray faille suit, a cloche she's pulled low to her brow. She is Contessa Valeska Czartoryska.

The countess takes the chauffeur's arm, and they proceed ahead of the others. The doors under the ivied portico open before the bell is pulled and by a shuffling hunch-back priest in a soutane mutilated by greedily snuffed suppers the party is led quickly inside. The priest leads the nurse and her charge directly from the receiving room through double white-enameled doors, which he closes behind them without a sound.

An old nun appears, the starched white wings of her headdress juddering as she walks, the wimple pressing into the flaccid flesh of her face. Saying nothing, she nods, leads the countess — who is still holding the arm of the chauffeur — into the temperate discomfort of the drawing room. The man in the homburg follows. The countess and the old nun sit across from one another. The man, homburg in one hand, the other pulling more violently at his white mustaches, sits somewhat distant from them. The chauffeur withdraws. There have been no introductions. Though the countess knows very well the status and character of the old nun, who is called Mater Paul, the nun knows nothing of the countess. Not her name, her title, her nationality.

The countess begins to speak and, as she does, the man with the homburg translates her words into French — softly, and with great facility — for the benefit of the old nun.

"I won't take too much of your time, Mater Paul. I believe that you understand my exigency. And also what I'm willing to pay for that exigency to be carried out. I trust the curia has instructed you sufficiently."

"I understand, madame. I understand

very well."

The man translates for the countess, though she hardly waits for him to finish before she speaks again. As though she has no need of him, as though his service is a fool's errand. Still, they keep to the game.

"Tell me then, what it is that you understand?"

As the man poses the question to Mater Paul in French, the old nun pulls a handkerchief from beneath the wide sleeve of her habit, presses it to her upper lip. To her forehead. The language the woman speaks is thoroughly unintelligible to the nun. She'd suspected that she'd be meeting with a foreigner, but somehow she'd thought an Englishwoman, a German, a Belgian. This language sounds somehow like Russian or some other Slavic tongue. Something exotic. Decidedly not European. In any language, it is clear that the woman commands. Yet it is *she,* Mater Paul, who commands this house. This school. The offering is large, though. Formidable. She cannot risk it by reminding the woman of her own position. Rather Mater Paul breathes deeply, spreads large, misshapen hands over the rough brown cloth of her robes, fixes pluvial eyes upon the soft black ones of the benefactress. She is prepared.

"From this day forward you shall never again see or hear of this child. Even should it be you who inquires, insists, legally or otherwise, to see her or be informed of her. This includes all persons connected with you or your family, or who claim connection to you or your family or the child as well as any advocate retained by you or your family or any representative of the State. Essentially, the child shall no longer exist once you leave this room. She shall be given a legal identity that will never be revealed to you or any of the parties whom I've already mentioned. The only fact that shall appear on her invented records is her birth date: May 3, 1931. No records, absolutely no original records or copies of original records pertaining to the child will be filed here. Of course, madame, I cannot speak for the documents already archived in the civil offices in the place where the child was born. I assume there are similar laws about registering births wherever it is that you come from. I cannot be responsible for them."

The countess knows that the old nun hopes there will be some slip, some fleeting indication of whence they come. Curious old wench.

"Nor do I *expect* you to be responsible for them, Mater Paul. Proceed. What about the child herself?"

"Since neither I nor anyone else here knows of the circumstances of her birth — neither place nor parentage — I shall, perforce, inform her of her 'invented' birth, of the sad events that left her an orphan. There will be no physical evidences of her history. No photos or letters that might later be traced or upon which she might attempt verification. Nothing. The child will have no past save a contrivance, a fable."

"And who will it be who tells her the *fable,* Mater Paul?"

"I, of course. I will be the one."

"And should your death occur before the time the child can comprehend it, who shall be entrusted to tell the story?"

"As has been requested, it will be Sister Solange to whom the duty will pass."

"Yes. Little Solange. And should I have a change of heart, Mater, should I, some weeks or months or even years hence, have a change of heart and return here to retrieve this child, to take it back — do you understand, Mater? — what shall you do to prevent me or my representatives?"

"I would do what I do, what we do, should anyone seek, anyone at all seek entry, unwelcomed, into this place. I would see that you were prevented. The authorities would be summoned. The police. The inviolable impedimenta of the curia would be employed, madame. Of that I can assure you. The child shall never be surrendered to you. To anyone. From the moment it was carried through our doors, it became our legal, spiritual ward."

"Very good, Mater."

The countess looks away from the old nun and gazes about the room as though she's only just noticed where she is. And why. She sees the terra-cotta tiles of the floor worn and waxed to the same brown as the nun's robes, the cold white walls, the empty hearth. She is quiet for too long to suit the nun, who wants only the passing of the promised funds and the woman's swift departure. From half-downcast eyes, the nun peruses the woman in the fox jacket, thin, silken legs crossed just above the knee, the edges of gray lace garters showing from beneath her skirt. Yes, women like her don't have to marry Jesus.

"And what assurance do I have, Mater Paul, that the funds which I have in my purse and the subsequent and untraceable funds which shall be transferred to the coffers of the curia," she asks with a backward tilt of her cloched head, "twice each year until, *until they are deposited no longer,* what assurance do I have that the child will be cared for, educated, raised, *treated* as I have instructed?"

"You have my word, madame. Just as the funds sent to the curia for the purpose of restoring the apartment for the child and her nurse here in the convent were dispersed and the furnishings acquired from the shops and the *antiquaires* in Montpellier were put into place according to Madame's wishes, so shall these 'subsequent' funds be dispersed according to Madame's wishes. I repeat, *you have my word.*"

The countess with the soft black eyes smiles for the first time.

"You'll forgive me, Mater Paul, but, as much as I shall consider the inexorability of your word, I have also established, shall we call it, a *fail-safe.* Here within these walls, Mater. A person who knows what to look for, what criteria to use in judging the execution of your *word.* This person knows how to *effect* things should effecting be necessary. Even you, especially you, shall never know who this person is. I've become something of an expert in espionage over these past few months, a trader in the discreet market of buying and selling confidences. Double confidences. Yes, I've prepared thoroughly for the child's welfare,

Mater. At least half her blood is good. Half her blood comes from me and mine, Mater."

CHAPTER III

When the lady has gone away and Paul has placed the thick, white sealed packet into the wall safe in her office, where it will stay until the bishop's emissary comes to retrieve it, she climbs the twisting stone steps to the convent living quarters. To the cells fronted by thick oak doors that face either side of the dark corridor. Always silent, usually empty at this time of day but for the house-keeping nuns, who move about with baskets of rags and brushes and tins of sulfur-smelling wax, brown glass bottles of lemon oil, today blithe laughter seeps from under the last door on the corridor.

Once the convent storage room, the long reach of the lady with the soft black eyes had brought local artisans to work at polishing the sprawling gray flags of its floor, reglazing long, lead-paned windows, scraping away layer upon layer of *papier peint* — all these the last traces of the epoch when

31

the convent was the courtly villa of a high-born Spanish family from Biarritz.

Paul throws open the door, waits on the threshold for it to swing wide, sharply claps her hands to gain the attention of a group of twittering nuns tightly gathered in one part of the room. Their glee unaffected by her command, Paul claps her hands again, shouts *"silence,"* and this time the nuns break ranks, make room for her, flail their hands in a gesture of invitation.

Plump and tawny as a russet apple, the well-made young woman who sits in their midst wears the coarse, dark dress of a peasant, short leather boots, thick black stockings and, from beneath a black kerchief knotted — perhaps too fetchingly for Paul's taste — above her forehead, tight blond curls fall. An ex-Benedictine postulant arrived at the convent from her *Champenois* village several months earlier, she is called Solange. In her arms, she holds the infant, her head bent adoringly to it. Behind Solange stands a stout, red-cheeked young woman smelling of starch and soap and wearing a long white pinafore over a much-mended black dress. She will be *nourrice,* wet nurse, to the infant.

Furnishings and accoutrements packed in unmarked cartons and trunks have been carefully arranged by Solange upon the freshly waxed floors, upon a handsome collection of lush red and yellow Turkey rugs. There is a white iron cradle wrought fine as lace and fitted in hand-embroidered sheets and coverlets and, alongside it, a white-chintz-draped baldachin, a bath table, a tiny antiquated rocking chair with a white velvet cushion, a wide, plush divan with down-filled yellow pillows, an armoire hung with a baby girl's clothes, a tall gold and white Empire chest, a small library case — still empty and with cartons of children's books and classics piled near it, a black-lacquered writing desk with crystal-knobbed drawers. There is a little chair, which, when its switch is wound, swings slowly to the melody of "Clair de Lune." A stately blue leather, chrome-trimmed perambulator sits under the windows. Yellow flames flap in the hearth of a black marble fireplace. All these compose a nursery and bedroom for the child and Solange. Too, there is an alcove where the *nourrice* will occasionally sleep.

Paul stays apart, shouts, "I believed you'd all understood, you and the rest of your sisters, that, though I'd acquiesced, respectfully acquiesced to the curia's request that this foundling, that this child, this child and her nurse, be permitted refuge here, I did

33

not acquiesce to your being party to it. These two are neither guests nor visitors but a homeless pair placed in our beneficent custody who shall be offered a form of patronage that I alone shall dictate. They will be *confined,* as much as possible, here, in these rooms, in this nymphet's Gomorrah. Our sisters shall feed them, wash their clothing, scrub and clean this apartment. Except for the garden, and there only at appointed hours, they are not welcome — save upon my invitation — to venture outside these rooms. This house, and you who are privileged to live and work and pray in it, this house and you shall remain spiritually unsullied by this *contamination.* Sister Solange, only sister Solange shall be near the child. Spread the word among your sisters as I shall do yet again. You may go now."

Paul's words are close-range rifle shots. A covey of wounded birds, the nuns disperse. Solange has begun to weep, and then the child starts to cry. Solange turns the child away from Paul, muffles its earnest sobs against her breast.

Paul walks about the room, swings the chair to and fro, notices the switch and turns it, stands there watching, listening to the soft tinkling of Debussy. She moves to

34

the armoire, fondles the hem of a small pink dress. "All this while children in the villages sleep on cornhusk pallets and wear wooden shoes."

Solange nuzzles the baby, who is once again serene. "And they drink their mothers' milk, Mater. Don't begrudge her. She pays her way, after all. That should soothe the discomfort of satin booties and a small pink dress."

"Apropos of mothers' milk, why must the *nourrice* join the household? Certainly her milk can be expelled, brought here each day for you to *dispense* it. Why —"

"It's not certain that the baby will require the *nourrice,* Mater. Jean-Baptiste has arranged things with her in the eventuality that she will be needed. He thinks that our own fresh goats' milk will be sufficient to nourish her. It along with a supplement of foods I shall prepare for her according to his instructions. Vegetable and cereal paps and —"

"You needn't share your gastronomic plans for it. I'll speak to Jean-Baptiste myself, advise that he limit the encroachment of strangers as best he can."

Paul has yet to look at the child, but now she approaches her, held in Solange's embrace. At a distance Paul stops. Craning

35

her neck so as to see the child better, she stays still for a long time.

"Have you never seen such a small creature, Mater? Come closer to her. She is quite curious, looks about at everything, everyone, and she cries *almost* never."

"You've had her in your arms for barely an hour. How do you know if she cries?"

"I've been caring for the babies in my family since I was eight years old, Mater, learned early on to understand their characters, their needs. What makes them peaceful, what they fear. I think it would be good for her to see you, to accustom herself to you, don't you? And you, to her?"

"Didn't you hear what I said to the others? She's your charge, the living embodiment of your duty. I'll have nothing to do with her, nor will I permit the pallid thing to shake the foundations of all I've worked to build here."

"Mater, it will be impossible, it *would be* unjust, that this tiny soul pass its infancy and its childhood exiled in these rooms. However lovely they may be. She will require more than the attention that I shall give her. She must hear other voices, see other faces, be held and caressed by the others in her family. Mater, we *are* her family now."

"She is not, I repeat, she is not of *this* family any more than you are. That her own abandoned her is no reason that I should want her. Take her in I must — and, yes, be paid for it I shall — but that I should want her, no one can ask of me."

"Can't you look upon her presence here as an interlude, a blessed interlude? You know that when she turns five, she'll go to board in the school, come here only as the other students do, to dine, to perform their house tasks."

"You know about her, *her frailty.* I don't imagine she'll last as long as that."

"Don't say that, Mater, you mustn't ever say that again. I'll take the best care of her, and Jean-Baptiste will see her weekly. Come to bless her, Mater. Come to pray over her, to welcome her home."

"No. I shall not welcome her. I shall tolerate her. And you. And, if I must, that toothless cow who'll suckle her. That's all I shall do."

"I shall ask for an audience with the curia myself, inform them of your, pardon me, Mater, your uncharitableness. I shall ask that another convent be found for us. I shall . . ."

Solange turns her back to Paul, moves the sleeping baby from her arms up onto her shoulder, and begins unwittingly to jostle and rock her. As though she thinks the baby has understood Paul. As though she would comfort her.

"You shall do no such thing. And if you did, you'd not be heard."

"Mater, perhaps you forget, I am a lay sister here. The rules governing my life are not those of the others. I intend to follow, to the letter, those rules that pertain to me. Beyond my adherence to those, I am free. I assure you that if and when I am convinced that your treatment of the child — or of me — is cruel, I shall not stay quiet. Neither I nor Amandine shall be your prisoner, Mater."

"Amandine?"

"Yes, I've named her."

The only sound is the baby's sucking upon the place between Solange's neck and shoulder.

Without lifting her head from where it rests on the baby's back, Solange asks, "Why do you fear her, Mater? What can make a woman of God, a bride of Jesus, what can make you fear a baby?"

"Why do you mistake a simple lack of interest for fear?"

"It can be nothing else but fear, Mater. Fear with a mask of anger. A common-enough device. My father taught me something of that when we would see a *sanglier* or a wild dog on our walks through the woods. 'They're growling and baring their teeth because they're frightened of you,' he'd say. Isn't it true that you growl and bare your teeth today because you are frightened of this baby?"

Solange places the sleeping Amandine in the cradle, makes a long business of covering her, patting her, bending to touch her lips to the baby's head, and all the while Paul looks on. Hands trembling, the nun adjusts her cincture, once again takes her handkerchief from under the sleeve of her habit and, once again, presses it to her upper lip. She prepares for battle. Solange stands then, turns to look at Paul. Both search to parry. Both know the contest has begun.

"Since my arrival here three months ago, I have thought you cold, inaccessible, bitter toward me, but I was certain that, once the baby arrived, once you saw her, held her, you would, you would *soften.* I believed that instinctual affection, if nothing else, would take over. And if not that, your calling, your vows, your Christian love, surely those would prevail. I've never known anyone made like you, Mater. I've never known anyone who couldn't look into the face of a baby."

"You don't know anything of me, of my life and my work. You're nothing but a child yourself. A brazen child. I'd rather expected you to be more docile."

"I think one of the reasons that it was I who was brought here is that I am *not* docile, Mater."

CHAPTER IV

Is it not enough that I must take in the bastard child or grand-child or whomever it may be to that aging demimondaine but, too, the bishop, His Eminence Fabrice, asks me to extend my tolerance to include a lapsed postulant, freshly fallen from grace? Why couldn't I have been privy to the child's parentage? Could it be his? I think not. Had he sired the thing, he'd have arranged for its disposal in some farther away post. And so whose is she? Who is this child? The ostentation of its trappings, the ceremony of its arrival, the saber rattling over its care, all these are made of mockery. And who is the little farm girl? Perhaps it's she who is his. His daughter. His paramour. I was his paramour.

How effortlessly you took me, dear Fabrice. A sweet from a proffered tray. Or was it I who took you? Supreme vendetta against my father, who'd said, "Don't bother packing too much, a dress for evening, one for daytime strolls along the sea." No cottage by the sea, only the burnt-milk stench of sorrowful halls. The good sisters of the Carmelites. "I'm doing this for you, my dear," he'd said.

Yes, I was his dear, my father's darling dear, plain as dirt save my beautiful hair. Lovely hair piled and massed like cream, white-blond waves of it caught in the stones of Maman's marcasite clips. It might have been enough, my hair, Papa, it might have done for Jean-Jacques, it might have done for him or for the one who came from Béziers with the wood, the one who kept his eyes on me while he drank the marc. *"Bonsoir,* Mademoiselle Annick. *Bonsoir."* My hair might have been enough. And for you, Papa, wasn't I enough for you?

Twelve-forty-five — no sooner, no later — pluck the radishes with the greenest leaves from the wet, black earth. Ten beauties into the lap of my apron. In the kitchen, shake the clinging dirt into the sink, rinse them under the cold-water tap, dry them on the blue and white towel, lay them, one by one — roots and stems untrimmed — onto the Charbonnier footed plate with the rust-colored flowers. Three prints of butter to the side, the *salière* in the middle. From the baker's boy, from the deep, narrow basket tied to his bicycle, I would choose *un baton ben cuit,* hold it to my lips to catch the broken blisters of its crust, open my hand, which clutched the two sous for him. *Bonjour.*

"Annick, Annick. *Pour vous,*" the baker's boy would shout then as I was already running back into the house.

Straddling the bicycle, his feet flat on the road, he'd pull two barely burnt croissants from the pockets of his smock, hold them in his fists like pheasants by their feet. I would turn round, take his gifts. *"Merci, Émile. À demain."* For Émile, too, my hair might have been enough. But back to your lunch. Tie the *baton* about its middle with the pale blue napkin, lay it above your fork. Five minutes before I call you, no more than five, draw wine from the barrel. A full balloon, cool, clear, smelling of apples and thyme. *"Papa, Papa. Déjeuner, Papa."* I was plain and you were poor, Papa, too poor to buy a husband for me with a dowry, but my hair might have been enough.

"How close are we to the sea, Papa? I think I can see it, Papa. Is that it, is that the sea lying there beyond the hills? It is, it is. Ah, I can smell the sea in the breeze now, Papa." You pulled short the reins, turned the carriage down a smaller road. Not even a road. Away from the sea. "But, Papa, where are you going?" Like a whip, your hand. The first time you'd raised it to me. "I'm doing this for you."

"But will they take my hair, Papa? Tell them not to take my hair."

Malicious laughter when we should have been asleep. "Would you like to join us, Annick?" They sniggered, my fellow novices, even as they wrapped it about my skirts, that heavy, sweat-smelling templar's cloak, and as they folded the pointed hood low over my face. Twittering upon their pallets, then, "You'll not be a novice for long, Annick." One pull of the bell's rope, my heart wingbeat on quiet water, head bowed, hands folded, mincingly I would follow the old monk through the black satin darkness to your private chapel, Fabrice. How old were we then, Your Excellency? You, the young, brilliant monseigneur, I, a month, two months under the veil, how old were we? How peccant were we, fiendishness spicing the lust? "I'm doing this for you, my dear papa," I said under my breath. Mother of God, pray for us all.

And when I could no longer acquit my own shamelessness and tried to quit you, you cajoled me. You and then the abbess. "We all have our private misfortunes, dear. Deceit and betrayal are blood rights from our pagan forebears. You will recall the escapades of the gods. And as for we brides of Jesus, though He soothes our souls, our flesh He leaves yearning. Besides, the pressure of virginity is distracting. Better to give it up. All the better to give it up to Fabrice. He'll be bishop someday. Mark my words."

Later still, my desire for you finally spent, I'd come to tell you. "Never again," I'd said, and how you laughed, wiping the tears with your surplice, saying, "Little boys are my true delight. A lesser divertissement, I took you because you were so solemn about the business. I did it for you, my dear."

Even scorned I remained devoted. For all the years since that epoch I have responded to your every call. To every call from His Eminence, each and every request from my old, liverish *bon viveur.* My own Daedalus. How cannily has your great bulbous nose taken on the same violaceous tint as your robes, Excellency. How well you've done. The school, the community, legacy of my work for your glory. My reward? A five-year mission to safeguard a damaged, bastard infant.

"Ah, Philippe, you startled me. Just on my way downstairs. What are you doing here?" Paul searches for her handkerchief. Philippe, Père Philippe, is the old priest who earlier answered the door to the countess and her entourage.

"I came to look for you. I've been standing here for some time, but you were so far away, your thoughts so far away, that I stayed quiet, waited . . . ," Philippe tells her.

Paul nods toward the nursery, says, "Things will want adjusting. I was thinking about all that is bound to change now."

"Change for the better, I would think. Maybe even more for you and me than for the rest. Come to walk with me in the garden, Paul."

"I can't right now. I must telephone the bishop and —"

"He'll wait. I don't know why, can't fathom why this has disturbed you so. You're pale as death, Paul. The way you were when a new postulant caught Fabrice's eye. Is it that? Are you envious of the baby?"

"First fear, now envy. Of what shall I next be accused today? Old fool you are, Philippe. It's only that having an infant and her nurse in residence is not something that *fits,* that seems at all *fitting . . .*"

"You *are* envious. And if I'm an old fool, you're a fool only three years younger. How much of our lives have we lived together? You and Fabrice and I, the last surviving —"

"Yes, but he survives far better than you and I, Philippe. He thrives while we wither, while we still tremble and fetch at his bidding."

"It's the way things arranged themselves. It might well have been I who'd been promoted and exalted in his place. I was the academician, after all, yet he won favor with *affability.* What can it matter now that we're so close to the end? I'm grateful to him that he sent me here to you. To you and the sisters, to live out my time in this place, in this pleasant enough place. He might have packed me off to some decrepit retreat for shabby, venial clerics rather than here. Ah, I tell you, Paul, in his way, he's done well by both of us. In his way, he's always done well by us. And what you don't see now is that his accepting whatever proposal was made to him to take over the care of this infant . . . What you don't see is that, by this, he gives us a last chance."

"What sort of last chance?"

"To be *typical,* I suppose that's the word. To be *ordinary.* I think our calling —"

"*Your* calling, perhaps. I have yet to hear my call, Philippe."

"That's what I wanted to say. Even *with* a calling, celibate life is neither typical nor ordinary, and yet typical and ordinary *are we.* Many of us, most of us Benedicks and Jesuits and vestals. No matter the troop, celibate life makes for a monstrous aberration, a nunnish battle with the flesh, but

47

more with the heart. I think we are meant to love someone other than God. Pardon my blasphemy. In a way, I think we're meant to love someone more than God. Denied that, denied the anguish of a personal love, the yearning, the up-close and singular purpose it gives to a life, we religious, we, all of us, become, in some way, *deviant*. At best, we grow old awkwardly, pushing against the grain till the last. Calling it piety."

"I have had a *personal* love, and it has denied me no anguish, Philippe."

"What did you expect? That he would leave old Mother Church and set up with you? It was never an option, Paul. You, and all the others before and after you, were respites. Lusty respites from the drone. The desired, the beloved drone, you were a titillating interruption from the sway of that, a deep draft of cold air. You and the others were his particular expression of deviance. One of his expressions."

"What are you trying to do with all this talk, Philippe? Are you out to comfort me, to torment me? I can't tell which."

"I'm trying to tell you to let loose your rancor. Especially toward a five-month-old infant. Paul, look at me. Do you see how wasted I am? I am a mirror of you. Why should we not take this singular opportunity, surely it's a last opportunity, to live, to live like others do? Yes, let's you and I be *grand-mère* and *grand-père* to this child. While we can. Let's pretend. God knows how proficient we've become at deceit. You more than I, Paul. Let's pretend. Who knows but that the fraud will turn about, become the truth. Wouldn't that be the miracle of our, of our *winter?* That we might actually *feel* something spontaneously rather than by rote. Nothing so much would change. You will carry out your tasks and I mine, but in between, we could, God help us, we could try to love her."

CHAPTER V

At greater speed than he drove on the way
to the convent of St.-Hilaire, the chauffeur
retreats down the same lime tree avenue,
his passengers — the Countess Czartoryska,
the nurse, and the man with the thin white
mustaches — composing a hardly less
muted group than they did an hour before.
Before having delivered their charge to its
destination. Before consigning the infant.
The baby is gone. Its gaze, though — the
serene blue-black gaze of a lamb consenting
to sacrifice — the power of that gaze flits
about the Packard's lush gray saloon. The
nurse's arms hang loosely, awkwardly in her
lap, or so they seem to the countess, who
looks then at the man with the thin white
mustaches, this Toussaint with the twitch in
his jaw, the homburg pitched far back on
his forehead now, eyes closed — calculating
his take, his deed? How odious accomplices
become afterward, the countess thinks. And

what is this pain, this heaviness about my own arms? Is it like the pain, the ghostly pain of a limb amputated? Is it she that I feel? Pray that filthy old priest shall never hold her, less that sweating bitch of a nun. Oh God what have I done? Against the pain, the countess crosses her arms about her breast, each hand clutching the long, soft fur on the sleeves of her jacket. She squeezes shut her eyes, and yet the pain and the lamb's gaze remain.

It's done. It's gone. How much longer until the station? The privacy of my compartment. Please let us not be late for that train. I must be alone. I must think. This part is done, and now I must concentrate on Andzelika. On how I shall present the events to her. I must be so careful, weigh and study every word before I say it, construct a case for each part of the lie. I shall be quite forthcoming. I shall embrace her, tell her without delay. The baby has died. Before surgery could be attempted, she died of heart failure, just as the birthing doctors had predicted she would. Predicted she *might,* but Andzelika need not know the relatively favorable odds they proposed. I shall emphasize that the doctors in Switzerland offered scant hope of saving her, assured me that, should the surgery keep her alive, it would be, at best, in a life of extreme debilitation. I shall describe the symptoms under

51

which the child would have suffered. I shall say that all agreed the early demise was "for the best." When she asks, if she asks, why I did not arrange for the child to be brought to Poland, to be placed in the family mausoleum, I shall explain that the birth and the death of the child must remain our private business. She will understand that. I shall promise to take her to Switzerland someday so that she might visit the place where the baby is buried. I shall tell her of the services, the words of the priest: "Infants who die are angels called back to God so as not to be desecrated by time on earth." Yes, that's what I'll tell her the priest said. I read that somewhere, I think that's how it went. In time, I shall convince her that such a visit would serve nothing. She will have got on with her life by then. She'll have put all this — the child, the man — aside. I shall see to that as I have seen to all of it. The death certificate, where did I put it? Perhaps Toussaint has it still. I shall remind him to give it to me when we're on the train. Ah, how tired I am. Have I thought of everything? Dear old Józef, how I wish you were here to counsel me. To help me finish the job.

Józef, my confessor, my friend, may God rest your magnificent soul. Strange that you would have died — how long was it? — only days after that last meeting. Yes, as though your great heart could contain not one more secret, as though this business of counseling me about the placement of the child was your last act of benevolence. Can you see me, Józef? Can you hear me? Surely a bishop of Mother Church can see and hear from his heavenly resting place. I did do the right thing, didn't I, Józef?

She'll be safe. Doubly safe. Your Solange. The old abbess in her white-winged cornet. And should either of them fail her, there is your friend the bishop called Fabrice. Yes, His Eminence Fabrice. Yes, it's done. It's gone. I've cast the lovely little beast upon all those caring hands. Greedy hands. Oh, Józef, can you hear me? That last day, that last meeting of ours, you were exasperated with me, almost embittered. How was it that you began?

"Let it stay with us. With me and with the Urszulines. I will baptize it. They will feed it, swaddle it, and let it be. I will bless its soul, and should God choose to claim it, I shall help it to die in sainted peace. Oh, Valeska, it will be better this way. Trust that all your and Toussaint's machinations to find just the 'right' situation for the child, trust that all came to nothing because it is not God's will. My dear Valeska, it's hardly murder that I'm suggesting but salvation. This child is both unwanted and mortally ill. What hope has she? Let her be. Let her go."

"I can't. I won't. It's true that she is unwanted, that I don't want her. It's also true that I love her. I *do* love her, Józef. I wish to provide a chance for her. Every chance. To be cared for as I would care for her. Were that possible."

"You don't want her, yet you seek some blissful life for her, some good fay to suckle her, to love her as you would. *Were that possible.* Ah, dear Valeska, how strange a path takes your love. You have not been spared suffering in the past, and yet I fear that you, with your margrave's will, now seek another occasion for it. Perhaps the greatest one yet."

"What sufferance can compare with that which Antoni bequeathed me?"

"That of denying your child."

"You will remember that she is not my child."

"All the heavier your cross. You are taking Andzelika's child from her."

"And by doing that I am saving Andzelika. By removing the child, by *erasing* the child, I am saving Andzelika a life of degradation and shame. I'll not have all of Krakow saying, 'she is, after all, her father's daughter.' No scarlet letter for Andzelika, Józef. I'll not have her sacrificed to her bastard, conceived with the brother of her father's whore. That I shall not

54

do. Daughter of an assassin suicide, Andzelika has lived since she was two years old with the legacy of her noble sire, kept her child's fierce dignity amidst whispers and ridicule from everyone outside our family. And when she was older, from many who are part of it. What juicy, dripping flesh to chew on would Andzelika and her child be. I want it away. Far, far away, Józef. Carefully placed, then irrevocably lost to us."

How long did we two stay silent then? The clicking of the nuncio's boots up and down the corridor during the short intervals when his ravening ear was not pressed to the door.

"There is a family in France. In the region of Champagne. Is that remote enough for you, my dear? Far enough away from Krakow is it? They are the family of my sister's husband. Janka's husband."

"Tell me about them, Józef."

"She was late in marrying, Janka was, late in finding her love.

"Laurent Besson. They met in Prague, where she lived, barely eating, almost never keeping warm, so she might study violin, study her music and live and walk and be in the only place on earth where she said she was meant to live. Yes, in Prague. Laurent had come from Champagne on a pilgrimage with his church. Only for a few days. They met on the Charles Bridge. Of course, it would be the bridge. And, of course, it would be winter. It was dusk and, in her mother's beaver coat, Janka played Prokofiev. People on their way home from work surrounded her, placed fir branches or small faggots of kindling at her feet. Janka would have a fire that evening. They left small cherry tarts and poppy-seed cakes, black bread, a wedge of good white cabbage, some part of whatever they were carrying home for supper. Some even had a coin to drop onto the purple velvet of her open violin case. Laurent stood among the crowd. He unfastened a gold cross from around his neck, placed it in the case. When she finished playing all she knew of Prokofiev and then of Stravinsky, she took her bows, shook hands with her audience. Laurent stepped up to her, took her hand, and kissed it. 'I am Laurent Bresson from Champagne. I am in love with you. Will you be my bride?'

"After looking at him for a long time, Janka bent to finish the business of closing up her performance. She stood up then, slung the violin case across her chest, took Laurent's arm, said, 'First you will take me to supper.'

"I trust he did indeed take her to supper that evening, since they married soon afterward. They lived on the farm in Champagne with who knows how many others in an already epic family. They birthed five daughters. Through the years Janka and I wrote to one another faithfully, her letters helping me to feel the place she'd always saved for me in her French life. Of course I traveled to Avise, to their small town, when I could, not letting more than a year or two pass between visits. And when I became ill that first time, Janka — a three-month-old daughter cradled in a red carpet bag strapped across her chest just as she once carried her violin — came back to Krakow, arranged herself and her baby in a maid's room in the presbytery, and cared for me day and night. And when I'd gained my strength, she insisted that I travel back to France with her and little Magda, spend the summer in further recuperation. She convinced me easily. Nearly a year I stayed. I baptized Magda, performed a marriage or two, as I recall. Learned about grape growing and winemaking and how good it feels to work hard and eat well and sleep a child's sleep. Surely I'd thought more than once about making it my permanent refuge.

"It's a good story, don't you think, Valeska? Even with the uncomplicated protagonists. Not many intrigues, not much patrimony over which one of them might grind his teeth. Not a single murder that I can recall. And if there were betrayals, I never knew about them, save the ones of poaching wild rabbits or the rights to a certain chestnut grove. Or so I believed back then. In any case, my dear, I tell you all this because of Magda's daughter. Magda's Solange. Just past seventeen, she's come home some weeks ago after a novitiate year and one as a postulant at Beaune. Says she's not meant to be a nun, that she would rather live and work on the farm with her family. Janka is now the clan's old matriarch, and she would lovingly take in and care for your child. With the help of her daughter and her granddaughter. With the help of Magda and Solange. They would take her as their own."

"What would you tell them? Would they take her knowing nothing about her?"

"They would need know only that she is without a home."

"Had I forgotten there were such people, Józef, or is it that I never knew there were?" From a thin silver case in her purse, Valeska takes a cigarette and — as a man might — holds it between thumb and forefinger. The bishop pulls a long match from a box on the desk, strikes it once on the roughened patch of a marble ashtray, lights Valeska's cigarette without rising from his chair. She does not thank him but says, "As much as you are offering, I want more, Józef. I want the child to be educated."

"Children are educated very well in rural France, my dear."

"No, no, I don't intend her to be schooled at home or in a public lycée. A convent education, the niceties, the advantages of a fine Catholic boarding school, just as I had, as Andzelika had."

"Valeska, Valeska, listen to yourself. Will you even choose the stuff of her dresses, dictate — from some stifled place behind the drapes — how she'll arrange her hair? She is congenitally ill, mortally ill, yet you imagine her reading Virgil. Hold her to you or surrender her. You cannot do both. Not even you can do both."

"Hush, Józef. Why must you always speak like a priest? Like a good priest. What about Montpellier?"

"What about it? You are mad if you're thinking to send her where Andzelika herself was schooled."

"Why? Andzelika's, mine, our names will never be spoken. Through your connections with the curia there, you shall ask a favor. A paid-for favor. Your wish is to place an infant in the care of the good Carmelites there. You'll say that the infant's identity and place of birth are to remain unrevealed, that, in exchange for a certain donation, the infant and its nurse are to be given refuge in the convent under

59

the auspices of the curia. Something like that. You could accomplish all that quite easily, Józef. I know you could."

"And who is to be the child's nurse?"

"Why your Solange, of course. Don't you see? If what you've told me is true, Solange would be devoted to the infant, and if this devotion were to be carried out within the very convent where Andzelika herself was so content for six years . . . Was it six? Yes, aged six through twelve she was, and how she cried when I insisted that she transfer to the Carmelites in Krakow. A selfish move on my part because I'd missed her so. I'd only sent her away because I believed that if she stayed far from our 'society,' if she remained distant from people who knew about our 'misfortunes,' then we, she and I could pretend to retrieve her childhood. Unstained, unburdened. Yes, with Solange as her nurse and the curia her protectorate, that's how I shall walk away from the child."

"Do you truly think that no one among the good Carmelites of Montpellier will remember you? Or will you simply send the child by messenger?"

"The abbess in Andzelika's time was a virago called Paul. Do you know her?"

"Not personally. I know of her. Know that she has been the bishop's champion and servant since his ordination. And before that I would guess. A lifetime of collaboration, shall we say."

"So then you are acquainted with this bishop at Montpellier?"

"More than that. Fabrice is his name. Our ecclesiastical paths have been crossing since we were very young men. We've always admired one another. But this Paul, this Carmelite abbess, surely you met with her during Andzelika's residence."

"Actually I never did. I never once visited Andzelika at the convent. All that was during the epoch of my 'mourning.' I traveled very little. It was my sister and her husband — Yolanda and Casimir — who performed the parental duties as far as the school was concerned. They accompanied little Andzelika there, brought her home twice a year for visits, went to fetch her when I could no longer abide her absence. Yes, it's this Paul to whom I'll take the child. And if Solange, your Solange, could be installed there to care for her until she is of school age, perhaps take on the role of guardian after that . . . until she was grown, until she married or —"

"Uproot a French farm girl who has just run away from convent life, you will bid her reenter another order — what is it, a thousand kilometers distant from her home? — so she may

61

devote herself to your responsibilities —"

"As a lay sister, Józef, as a lay sister. With a lay sister's rights and freedoms. I would make it worth her while. I would help the family, too."

"How deeply dyed is that margravine in you, Valeska. My telling you the story of Janka and Laurent, of their family, it was meant to demonstrate the otherness of them. They cannot be bought."

"Everyone knows that everyone else has a price. It wants cunning to divine the price and a greater cunning to offer it so that the one being bought saves face. The Carmelites shall be even more pliant than your Janka and her kin. A check-strewn path through the curia. Yes, I'm certain that you, — that I — could place the child at Montpellier."

Chapter VI

Who couldn't love you? Whoever you are. Perhaps I loved you even before today, perhaps I've loved you from that moment, that first moment when Grand-mère told me about a child without a home. Surrounded as I was by all my family, I was a child without a home. I began to think about you, about what you'd be like, how it would feel to hold you. Who are you, from where do you come? And what shall I tell you when you begin to ask those questions of me? I shall tell you what Paul has told me, that you were left as a newborn, an unidentified newborn, at the doors of the convent, your date of birth estimated, your parentage unknown. You were registered, then, as a ward of the curia. All of it true, of course. As far as I know.

Women are often left alone to bear their children. Was that how it was with your mother? And if it was? So be it. You were hers. Why did she leave you, Amandine? Was she sick, was she poor? It should be she who holds you now rather than I. Sweet child, I am sorry for you that I am not she. And if not she, why is it I who holds you? Why was I invited here? I still don't know. The woman with the eyes like a deer, the woman who came to the farm late last spring? Was it she? Is she your mother? Even though Grand-mère said she was not, I wonder.

That afternoon. How I wish I could recall more of it. More of her. Everyone gone to school or to the fields; there was no one in the house when she came, no one save Grand-mère, me, and the little ones napping up in the attic rooms. Grand-mère said I must stay in the kitchen. At all costs, I must stay in the kitchen. "Prepare tea, but don't bring it out until I come to knock on the kitchen door. Don't come into the parlor," she warned.

The wind shuddered the window where I stood wiping the mist from one small pane with the elbow of my sweater, lightning flashed in the dull yellow sky, and I saw her totter daintily up the road wearing a man's coat and pretty shoes, pointed shoes with double straps and high heels. I strained to see her face, but she was looking down, her kerchief pulled low so that only her mouth showed. Red lips. Pointed shoes. They spoke in Polish, she and Grand-mère. Grand-mère Janka spoke in Polish with the lady, and not a word of French did I hear from behind the kitchen door, the tea tray in my hands. So quiet were they then I'd thought the lady had gone, and so, putting down the tray, I slowly slid the tongue from the lock on the kitchen door, opened it a crack, and there they sat still, the lady in the man's coat and the pointed shoes and Grand-mère in shawls and pearls. Grand-mère turned to me, smiled. "Solange, please bring the tea."

I placed the tray on the big oak dresser, keeping my back to them. "Shall I pour the tea, Grand-mère?"

"Yes, child."

"Will Madame take sugar?" I asked, still not turning around.

"No, thank you. No sugar. A drop of milk, please."

Her voice small like a girl's, her French perfect. Trying not to look yet wanting to see her, I handed the tea and, as she took it from me, held it in one hand, she tore off her kerchief with the other. "Thank you, Solange. Let me look at you, dear. I've heard such lovely things about you."

She held out her free hand, palm up, to me, and when I took it, she closed her fingers about mine, then half let go of them before regretting it, I thought, and holding them longer. "I am happy to meet you."

Stunned by her face, such an astonishingly beautiful face, eyes like a deer, black and full of tears, I said nothing, nodded my head. It was I who let go first. I who let her hand fall from mine. I went to pour Grand-mère's tea, and when I turned to take it to her, I saw that the lady was gone. A small package, roughly wrapped, tied in butcher's twine, lay upon the arm of the chair where she'd sat.

"Where did she go? Who was she?"

"A friend of the family, child."

I picked up the package, ran to the door, flung it wide. "Madame, Madame, your —"

Halfway to the top of the road, she never turned back. A droning wind shimmied the chestnut leaves, thrashed the door against the stones. She would never turn back, the lady with the eyes like a deer.

"Why did she come here, Grand-mère?"

"She came because she needs help. Our help. Yours and mine."

"Mine? Yours and mine?"

"She has proposed a certain position for you, child. She has asked that you take on the responsibility, the caretaking of an infant. An infant girl, barely a month old, an orphan. She has proposed that —"

That this baby come to live with us?

"No. Not that. She would like you to care for the baby in another place. In a convent. She would like you to live, as an extern sister, in a Carmelite convent in the south, near Montpellier. You and the baby would live together among this Carmelite community."

"For how long? When? I don't understand why."

"Solange, there will be many things that you will not understand should you take on this work, this next part of your life. I can't say for how long it would be. I will tell you what I know. Almost all of what I know. You will consider the offer, and you will either accept or decline it. Come here, sit with me."

I knelt before her chair, took her hands in mine, kissed her fingers, reached up to turn her face to look down at mine. The blue of a dragonfly's wing, Grand-mère's eyes, blue melting into green, green hemmed in black, Grand-mère's eyes. Janka's eyes. She bent my head to the sun-smelling fiandre of her apron, rested her chin in my hair, touched it again and again with her lips. Her way of talking to me. We stayed like that for a long time. Already saying good-bye.

"The woman who was here is — let us say — connected to the Church in another country. She has a particular interest in this orphan child, and she wishes to be assured that it will be cared for devotedly. Why she has chosen to place it in the convent in the south she did not reveal. About why she has chosen you to be the child's guardian and nurse she said only that she had been told of you through the auspices of an extended member of this family."

"Someone in Poland?"

"Yes."

"Who was it?"

With her eyes, Grand-mère said she couldn't tell me. She continued.

"She knew of your time in the convent at Beaune. She knew that you'd only recently returned home. I believe it was instinct more than reason that convinced her of your worthiness, instinct being the more faithful device, the more courageous device, I think, when things matter most. We trust reason always less as we grow older, Solange, you'll learn that. You shall have occasion to feel how feckless reason can be. In any case, she traveled here to speak with me about you. To see you, if only for a moment. I think that moment was sufficient for her. She left this package as a kind of trust. A first step. It's for you to keep, to give to the child when she is older. When she's thirteen, I think she said. Yes, when she's thirteen."

"Thirteen? And she's just, did you say that she's a month old now? Are you saying that the child will be, that she is to remain under my care? Always?"

"Yes. I think that, as long as the child lives, until she is grown, she will be your charge."

"I'll be like a mother to her."

"Like a mother."

"But why in a convent? Why can't I take care of her here with you and Maman and Chloe and Blanchette? It would be better that way. I have only just left a convent, Grand-mère, and I know that sort of life is not —"

"It's not a nun's life you'll live. Certainly not a sequestered one. You and the child will be under the protection of the convent. Your work will be to care for the child, to raise it in the atmosphere of a religious house, but the freedoms of a lay sister shall be yours."

"I've never heard of such an arrangement and I —"

"I know. I, too, have never heard of such an arrangement. A most particular situation. In addition to the lodgings, the table provided by the convent, you will be given a stipend to further maintain yourself and the child. Every detail has been considered, Solange, but not every detail can be explained, most especially to your martinet's satisfaction. Now it is you who must employ instinct rather than reason. It's your turn. No matter what you do, you're bound to suffer. It's the way of things. But now, right now, you are straddling two lives, and I fear you will live neither of them. You say the convent is not for you — and yet I sense, nor is the world. This . . . shall we call it a rare chance? Yes. This rare chance of being called to Montpellier as lay sister, as nurse to this child, it may serve to reconcile discord if not to stave off sufferance. You may be able to combine the two lives rather than choose between them. You might appease your guilt, however contained, at having left the convent while affording yourself some measure of adventure. Once again, however contained. You would live the portions of the religious life that so appeal to you but without surrendering your liberty. That was it, I know. The suffocation of final vows, the inextinguishable promise. That was what you couldn't make. So much for a woman-child to consider, was it not?

"And then there's destiny, Solange. Sooner than later, make friends with the Fates and be less alone. What little more I know than you do now, what very little more that I know, I shall not tell you. If your curiosity is stronger than your compassion, the position is not meant for you. If you must know more than that this child is to be entrusted to you, refuse, Solange, send your regrets and get back to pruning vines and stirring soup. And outwitting the occasional lechery of your father. Not a bad life here after all, is it, child?"

At ease with the vague ways of her mother yet trusting her implicitly, Maman said little about it all. If Janka proposed my going to Montpellier, then it was for the good. That's what Maman told me as we bent to gather vine trimmings, sat tying faggots of them round with hemp weed.

"But Maman, I've just come home. Were not two years of my being away enough for you? Were they not penance enough to suit you?"

She didn't answer. She looked at me as if she would speak but then touched her hand to her mouth — as though to close it? — went about her work. All this silence. The convent, the farm, barely a difference save the bells. Everyone sealed shut, even if they speak, especially when they speak. No one can ever know another. I watched Maman then, sat back on my heels and watched her wrapping the hemp round and round the twigs, tying a loop knot, slicing the hemp with a rusted chestnut knife, piling the faggots into her apron.

"Let's get to the kitchen, Solange. *La joute* for this evening. From the cellar we'll need a cabbage, some potatoes, a string of sausages, two thick trenchers of ham. The chickens are dripping in the barn sink. Here, take a basket."

Maman, slow down, Maman, look at me, I wanted to tell her, but I didn't. Rather, I took the basket without even looking at her. She knew what Grand-mère knew. About suffering, I mean. Could it have been that she, too, would have liked to save me from it, and so, in her powerlessness, she was awkward? Ashamed? She turned away from me so I would love her less. Was that it? Was she warning me?

"Don't love me so much, Solange. I'm hardly worth it, I can hardly bear it, this blind devotion of yours. Worse now than before you went away. I'm only a woman, perhaps not yet a woman. I have borne three daughters, and still I am trying to find my way. How can I help you when I know so little myself? Don't love me so much."

Was that what Maman told me with her diffidence? Did she steel herself so that, once again, she could part with me, and I with her? I forgave you, Maman, for sending me away. For choosing him. But I'd come home. It was all okay. He wouldn't have come near me, Maman, and had he, I wouldn't have been afraid of him. I wouldn't have let him, Maman.

Mothers and daughters. Jealousy, envy. How is it that a mother can feel jealousy and envy even of her daughter? Maman's defense of me back then was quick, singular. That night when she followed Papa. Watched his back from behind my door. From the door opened only a chink, she watched him sit on a chair near my bed. Watched him kneel, then bend his head. His mouth. Watched him slide searching hands flat over my body. His hands under the thin blue quilt. She watched him, and I watched her. At last, she threw open the door, stood there, hands clutching her face, no words, no screeching. Stood there making sure of what she saw. By his hair, she dragged him away. I watched as she kicked him then, moved him down the narrow, dark hall with her feet. Never resisting her, she kicked him about the face, the loins, centimeter by centimeter across the stone floor. She left the heap of him outside their room. I could hear him weeping.

But after that, it was "Solange, that dress is ready to pass down to Chloe. Solange, cover your hair at table. Solange, is that rouge you're wearing?" Not he, it was I whom you watched. Not I, it was he whom you chose. You chose him. How you began to look at him, Maman, as though none of us were there. And when you both thought none of us *were* there, you would let him turn you about to face the wall, let him pull you to him from behind, bury

73

his face in the nape of your neck, separate your buttocks, press himself up against them to make a cleft of your skirt with that part of him. When I saw that, I remembered his hands from another time. A time when I saw him pick a melon from the vine. He stood there in the dirt, pushing together the sides of it, softening it, twisting it, ripping it open, raking out the seeds with his fingers, sucking and chewing at its heart, the juices dripping from his mouth, his chin, heaving down what was left. Knowing I was watching him from where I crouched, weeding potatoes, he turned to grin at me. "I was thirsty," he said. His performance had been just for me. I hated him, and I hated you more. I hated you almost as much as I loved you. I love you, Maman. I tried to stop loving you. Sometimes I feel as though I'm older than you. Like I'm the mother. The one who understands. I understand that you thought, that you hoped you could keep him if only I were away. Out of sight. Isn't that how it was? "Solange, Papa and I have been talking. About your spiritual life, I mean. About your future." And so I went. But I had come back. Did you really want me to go away again? Did you still choose him? And will you send Chloe away, too? And Blanchette? Is that how you'll keep him, Maman? Don't you understand that he's already gone?

CHAPTER VII

Buttressed, arched, pillared — a medieval church re-dressed for the Renaissance is the Carmelite convent of St.-Hilaire. Once a granary, then a fortress, it stood neglected for a century or two before its fragments were restructured into a grand villa. For these last forty years since its reformation into a religious house, it has seemed to the villagers a grotesque, a breach upon the peace. Twenty-seven brides of Jesus and their abbess pray, meditate, and work in the convent proper, while seven more cultivate the spiritual and secular educations of thirty-six girls, aged five through seventeen, in the convent school and dormitory. Retired from his offices in a nearby parish and residing alone in a remote wing of the convent, the Jesuit priest Philippe celebrates holy mass before his feminine congregation each morning at five, interprets and illumines doctrine for the teaching sisters, lectures morality to the upper classes, is father confessor, absolver of sins, and legendary estate *vigneron*.

The unshakable progress of days in the convent begins when Sister Sabine from Toulouse — eyes red from sleep, feet bare, and still adjusting skirts and veils about her short, pendulous figure — stands in the pitch-black corridor along the sisters' cells at 4:30 A.M. An accidental Spanish dancer masquerading as a nun, Sabine flings her right arm high above her head, rips the dark with the fierce click of wooden castanets, and, in a rich mannish voice, shouts: "*Ave Maria.* Rise and worship our Mother and her Son."

Situated on the plateau's northern descent is a hamlet of red-roofed, stone houses, tall and narrow as small ships and raised up in the shape of a horseshoe. Here abide the *metaires* and their families who work in the vineyards, the adjoining fields — convent lands all. Nearby are dairy barns, hay barns, granaries, winemaking sheds, a distillery, a meeting hall, a washhouse, a communal kitchen. An ocher stone chapel and a churchyard cling to a small shank of land farther below while, on the valley floor, a larger village sits along the Lez. Its quick waters lick the sorrel edges of the river-banks, where old men fish and children cheer flotillas of leaf-sailed boats. Here there are shops, civil offices, town houses, the small red marble-faced church of St.-Odile. A public park with a carousel.

As though the Carmelites' trafficking with God were a private business, the villagers and the *metaires* in the hamlet are rarely blessed with the benevolence of their holy sisters on the plateau. One might say that, in this case, benevolence, rather than descending from the top, is carted upward, pushed and pulled in wagons and bundled on muleback, along the chalk white roads from the bottom. Hunters leave birds — still warm, heads askew, piled in a brown canvas bag — haunches of venison and wild boar, while others leave strings of tiny, still-breathing river fish, foraged mushrooms and grasses, fallen chestnuts, a tin pail of wild berries. These are gifts from the farmers, often poor, and extraordinary to the convent's "half portion" of the farms' bounty: jute sacks of flour and cereals, laid reverently as holy relics in the pantries; each morning's milk from a small herd; glass bottles of double cream; cheeses, just made and dripping whey from their cloth netting; white butter spread into half-kilo wooden

77

forms; barrels of wine rolled gently down sagging paint-spattered planks into the musty gloom of the *chai.* To further sustain its table there are the convent gardens and fruit trees, its goats and sheep and chickens and geese, a rabbit hutch. Yet by some quirk of nature — even in the longest memory — there has never been a single instance of sufficiency that afforded the good sisters the means to send, say, a bushel of pears or plums back down the chalk white roads to the bottom. A token. Some say the virtue of charity has yet to take hold up on the plateau. It should be noted, though, that to stand in the convent hall among Mater Paul and her sorority on the afternoon of Epiphany, to sip tepid, watered chocolate from yellow and green faience cups, the villagers, the *metaires,* are all invited. But since the price of entry to the amusement is a small white envelope with a year's tithe for the Carmelite missions, many more stay away than attend, their own missions having urgency enough. Even so, since the *metaires,* many of the villagers, and the sisters have similarly dedicated their lives to work and prayer, one might presume their affinity. Yet it's *want* that separates them. When the good sisters' woodpile dwindles, they send word to the *metaires* to bring more. As they do about their wine. For meat and wool and fine sturdy boots, they send to the shops while the *metaires* and the less prosperous of the villagers patch and save and count and portion. Do without in their own lives of work and prayer. Thus the convent remains remote from the hamlet and the village, each place observant of its own spiritual law and cultural prescription, its own rituals marked hour by day by year.

On her way from the larder to the kitchen gardens to harvest the day's needs for vegetables and herbs, Solange carries a deep oval basket over her arm. Inside the basket, on a length of soft blue wool, Amandine sleeps. Solange walks quickly from the larder, where she'd fetched the basket — fetched the baby — from Sister Josephine. Josephine, who had carried Amandine about earlier in the morning as she'd moved from cell to cell to see to the week's fresh linen, had gone then to the larder to await Solange. Once Solange is in the garden, bending to inspect the new onions, flitting her hands through the peas, Sister Marie-Albert, the youngest and the most petite of the sisters, appears from the washhouse carrying an empty basket. Marie-Albert walks to Solange, looks furtively about, exchanges the empty basket for the one that holds the baby, hoists it hip-high, and — her doll's body slanted from its weight — lopes back toward the washhouse singing a lullaby. Setting about to dig potatoes, Solange smiles to herself. How the sisters love the child, how they quarrel over who will hold her, who will feed her. I would rather share her less, and yet I know that my taking on a full roster of duties makes me less prone to Paul's disdain. Too, Amandine benefits from each one who cares for her.

Solange looks about the land, the air scented with the last sunburst figs trickling sticky juices and maddening the bees. Beyond the garden, the fruit hangs heavy on the vines now. Everywhere the vines. At home the grapes will be less mature, she thinks, perhaps another month before the vendage. Père Philippe likes that I know so much about grape growing, winemaking, and so he teaches me about these southern grapes. Syrah, Mourvèdre, Grenache, Cinsault, Carignan. Not the grapes of my Champagne. Strange how what grows up from the earth in a given place reflects the people of that place. Here the vines grow taller, leaner, taller and leaner like the people. The vines of Champagne grow closer to the ground, thick, lush, plump. Like the plump, red-cheeked Champenois themselves. Slabs of shale piled up, pell-mell, into walls about the garden, box-edged plots of sprawling cabbages and trellised beans, clumps of lavender enclosing herbs, a patch of fat, bruised pumpkins, a hayfield, freshly shorn. Sunflowers. Then the vines. A row of cork oaks, their leaves marbled russet, lean over the hollow creek bed, narrow as a goat path. How good the earth smells, this southern earth, like corn and sheep and clay. Older, sun-leached, melancholy. This southern place. I like it here. Days pass without my thinking of home, of them. I say their names in my prayers as though they were part of my past and not still there, a two-day train journey away. I do not miss them. Or is it only that I do not miss her? Maman. Or is it that I miss her too much?

Philippe, who has been working in a far corner of the garden, approaches her, pushes back upon his forehead a broken straw hat, wipes his hands on his soutane, leaving mud streaks to mingle with dribbles of wine and long-cooked sauces. He nods to Solange. Smiles.

"Bonjour, Solange."

"Bonjour, Père Philippe."

From her sentinel's post at the chapel window, Paul watches this complicit greeting just as she has the last passing of the basket. Worrying the beads hung from her belt, Paul broods.

Even Philippe has joined them. Their little girls' game. A relay race, their baton a baby. They know that I know. Such esprit de corps, every last one of them, and nothing I say or threaten will turn them from their playing house with her, toting her about, precious chattel, gurgling, cooing. Moonstruck hens. And Philippe barely able to contain his glee for their tactics. *Imbécile ancien.* It was dear Fabrice, a single visit from His Eminence, my own Eminence, and every rule was dust.

"Ah, let me see her. Let me see our baby girl," he'd said.

A beauty queen clasping a sheaf of roses, Solange drifted slowly down the stairs, carried her to him. Rather than only look at her, he took her in his arms — a florid old uncle — walked with her up and down the salon, held her to his breast, pronounced her *"Jolie. Jolie angeau de Dieu."*

He asked that the house be called together and, still holding her, bade them kneel while he blessed them, blessed her.

"Remember, my dears, work and prayer and meditation. And now a shared ministry to this motherless child. I shall hold it a special favor to me every time one of you shows her love. Keep her among you, even in the *réfectoire,* in the chapel, during your evening work. With Père Philippe and Mater Paul as your examples, treat her as a rare gift and teach her

82

the ways of our holy life."

A rare gift, yes, I'd thought then. Rare enough. I wonder the sum the little thing represents. Sufficient to buy more land? Another château to restore to his imperial taste, at least enough for that. To keep the ways of our holy life.

Their eyes downcast, I heard them then, the collective *"Mais oui, Votre Eminence"* as he waddled away. Dear Fabrice.

Now, all these months later, still they play the game, still they pretend that the child stays in the apartment — swaddled, fed, and left to herself as I'd instructed — while Solange is about her work. The child has never stayed longer than three seconds without one hand-maiden or another. They keep the farce to save my face. Let them be, Annick, I tell myself. Heed Philippe, I say. Try to heed Philippe. You are too old, Annick who became Sister Paul, Mater Paul, too sick from plots far thicker than this.

Chapter VIII

A flawed porcelain doll, she is not beautiful, yet all the wrong pieces form a splendid whole. Another kind of loveliness, enduring, I think, beyond the perfect sort. Pale blue tendrils show through the diaphanous skin of her small, pointed face, and thick black ringlets are a coquettish frame for such solemn eyes. Great black solemn eyes, she closes them, totters or sits or lies down, arms outstretched, and waits to be embraced by the sisters, by Philippe. When Paul is anywhere near, Amandine scuttles to her, tries to hug her about the ankles, is fascinated by her headdress, I think, holds up her arms to the old nun, quietly beseeching her, but Paul, barely breaking stride, consents only *"Bonjour, Amandine."* Amandine lets her arms drop, looks up at Paul, inclines her head, nods, barely nods, just enough to tell her, I understand. I know. Somehow she knows.

Ah, how you grow, little one. One hundred twenty grams this month, nearly a year old and plump as a dove you are. A small dove, perhaps. Jean-Baptiste, dear Jean-Baptiste, so devoted to you. Friday mornings at ten, he listens to your heart, thumps his fingers about your chest, looks at the color of your skin under his lamp, takes you to the window, all the better to see its tone, feels the flesh of your legs for swelling, the pulsing mound of your abdomen. He looks into your eyes with his light. Holds you to him then, tells you how lovely you are, passes you to me to tie the strings of your undershirt, slip on your long pink knitted stockings, all the while repeating his instructions.

"Keep her warm. Keep her away from anyone who is sick. Even with a simple cold, keep her away. Feed her as she is hungry, as often as she wants, but never force her to eat or drink. Fresh air two hours a day, three when possible. Any sign that her breathing is labored, call for me immediately. Mater knows how and where to find me."

"Her surgery? When?"

"I don't know yet, Solange. We'll take her again soon to be seen by Lucien Nitchmann. He'll be seeing patients in Montpellier next month. We'll know more then."

Our exchanges are always the same. But I can see that he is less troubled now when he looks at her, listens to her. The muscles in his jaw not so prominent. As I dress

Amandine, I watch the form his brown ink scratching makes across the page in her folder. Apparent compensation of congenital myocardial insufficiency; atrial septal defect closing; weight progress within low-normal limits.

I say the words over and over again all the way back to our rooms, and Amandine giggles, thinks it's a new song I sing to her. I put her down in the cradle, sit at the desk, and write the words as best as I can remember them, as best as I can spell them. When I go to the village, I will stop by the *bibliothèque communale,* riffle through the medical encyclopedias. How often have I done this? I always swear it will be the last time, since I manage to increase only my fear and not my understanding. Better to look in Jean-Baptiste's eyes than to stare at the menacing script in the books. Better still, to look in Amandine's eyes. Yes, into your eyes, my love. Happy birthday, sweet child. Happy first birthday, Amandine.

I like it that most of the sisters spend their evening recreation time in what has come to be known as Philippe's parlor. Even in summer, he keeps a fire. After vespers and supper, after the convent girls and the teaching sisters have returned to their dormitory, there seems almost a rush among the rest of us — like a family whose company has finally gone home — to get to the next part of the evening. Some go to take a book, others their work bags, then settle down in the candlelit place. Philippe is already established in his black velvet, high-back chair when I carry in Amandine. Holding out her arms to him or flailing her hands as though fanning a flame, so anxious is she to go to him, she holds her breath until she's in his arms. Paul, too, draws up to the fire. Not in the spirit of the gathering family come to soothe the hurts of the day, she comes to assure that our happiness be flawed. Less and less does she triumph as Philippe makes you laugh aloud and you flail your feet and arms when he hoists you, tummy down, a squirming lamb upon his shoulder. He dances you about. Cheek to cheek then, he nuzzles you — your soft to his rough — and you, loving that caress, push your face into his and stay quiet, eyes closed, as though you would fix him with your stillness. He pulls cherries from the pocket of his soutane, dips one into the tiny glass of Armagnac that waits for him on the table near his chair and, by its stem, holds the dripping cherry to your lips. You lick your lips where the cherry touches them, smart, lick your lips again. Philippe tells you your mouth is "just like a tiny cherry." You flail your arms again as if to beg another drop of the lush amber stuff, and he repeats the gesture. The sisters giggle, goad you on to another lick of the cherry, ignoring Paul's harrumphing, a foiled effort to check the game.

And when Philippe places you down upon the small blue rug beside his chair, then sits, opens his book, you are content to lie on your tummy and look up at him, the thin wings of your back arching through the white batiste of your nightdress. He reads, and you stay becalmed upon your tiny blue sea, hushed save some intermittent gurgle or chuckle or the sound of your sucking to soothe your aching gums upon the cool metal of the crucifix that falls from his belt.

I was right about you, Amandine. On that first day when I held you in my arms, I told Paul that you would hardly ever cry. You are almost never cross or contrary. It makes me fearful, though, this restraint. Even when you topple in the garden or when Baptiste pricks your forearm to draw blood each month, you hold your sobs within. Squeezing shut your eyes, the tears streaming, your mouth opened in a scream, you make no sound. Cry, Amandine, screech, I howl at you, let it out, let it go. I shake you up and down in my arms as though the rough movement will dislodge the choked sound, but it does not. It terrifies me, this voiceless cry. Your distress is not that of a child who waits for rescue but that of one who understands she is alone. You are not alone. Do you hear me, child? You are not alone. I'm here with you, I'll always be here with you.

In the hours when Solange and Amandine keep to their rooms, they are serene together, a young mother with her growing daughter. Solange sings to Amandine as she bathes her, fixes little suppers for her over their fire, supplement to the good custards and cereals and paps that the kitchen sisters prepare. She tempts the child with a paper-thin slice of pink ham set to sizzle in a small black iron pan with an egg. Sometimes with figs roasted soft and warm over the embers then dusted in dark sugar and bathed in cream, and often apples stewed in a copper salver with a nugget of white butter. She sets a tablet of thick milk chocolate near the hearth to soften, feeds it to Amandine with a tiny silver spoon. When Solange sits with Amandine in her arms to read to her, the child closes the book, places her hand near Solange's mouth, signals that she prefers the stories Solange invents.

On her second birthday, Philippe gifts Amandine a miniature rosary made of seed pearls. The string of beads in her baby hands, she squats or tries to kneel with Solange of an evening, earnestly watching, imitating Solange's fingering, and making her own repetitive devotional sounds.

Though she walks daintily and with perfect balance, Amandine prefers to mimic Philippe's lurching gait and accompanies the motion with sounds alarmingly like his breathlessness. So clever is she in this guise that Solange, when she first saw it, called for Baptiste.

Amandine calls the sisters by name, addresses Paul as Mater and Philippe as Père just as she has heard the others do and, though her stutter and lisp seem normal infant noises to the rest, Paul pronounces them marks of the devil. Philippe tells her, "The household has understood that the child's presence is your burden, Paul. Now will you have the child herself understand it as well? Who, indeed, does the devil inhabit in this place?"

CHAPTER IX

"*Amandine, doucement, doucement.* Hold my hand now, don't run. You mustn't run. Amandine, stop now and look at me. You know you must not run. And I can't pick you up right now, don't you see all that I'm carrying in my other arm? Hold my hand, walk slowly. Père will wait for you. All right, now you may go alone."

Philippe holds his arms out straight as the two-year-old — willful against the rules — runs to him at startling speed, shrieking his name. Bending to catch her, he holds her to him, stands and swings her about then in his awkward fashion. Dear Philippe. His great Gallic nose, rutilant badge of the good Languedocian abbé, his soutane fluttering, the long black muffler wound about his neck, even in summer, a tail of it flopping against the hunch of his back, how vehement he seems in his ceremonial meandering about the gardens, among the vines,

91

head down, prowling in the sunstruck southern light as though bent on crucial enterprise. How late his muse came. Lisping, wan, adoring.

Through high parched grasses, the three walk down to the creek bank, to a soft, earthy rise under a walnut tree. Solange makes a pallet with a quilt for Amandine, takes out a pillow for Philippe. Dismissing the quilt, Amandine climbs into her place in Philippe's arms. Solange opens three paper-wrapped parcels — thick slices of black bread laid with butter and applesauce. As he does each afternoon, Philippe falls asleep during his telling of a story to Amandine while she continues to quietly champ at the last of her bread. She closes her eyes then and forces out a sound like Philippe's snore. The grasses sway like the swishing of a full brown skirt, and the two are prone beside them. Solange spreads the quilt over the sleeping pair and walks back to the convent. She will come to wake them before vespers.

By the time she is three, the sisters' shared care of Amandine with Solange has taken on its own rites and rituals. There is a place arranged for the child in every part of the convent, so that, for instance, when she is in the care of the cooking sisters, she is propped on a cushioned stool near the worktable. Given her own dose of bread dough or pastry, she works along with the others, rolling, shaping, chattering. An old parlor chair placed in the washhouse is where she naps in the late mornings while Marie-Albert runs yellow-striped dish towels or heavy cotton petticoats through a wringer, flings them into a basket. The sounds comfort Amandine and, should Marie-Albert interrupt her work for a moment, the child sits up, urges her to get on with things, then settles back down. On Mondays and Tuesdays, when Marie-Albert washes the sheets from the narrow beds in the sisters' cells and hangs them, taut and even, with wooden pins onto pulley lines strung in the shape of a quadrangle, Amandine likes to sit and sing inside the roofless, wet, white house with the flapping, bleach-smelling walls. Marie-Albert, conforming to the house rule which dictates that all under-clothing be hung out of the sight of any possible passersby, pins the sisters' off-white linen brassieres and pantalets to another line strung inside the house made of sheets. And since it so happens that many of the younger sisters seem to have their menses at, more or less, the same time, each month there is a long line of pantalets swaying dreamily on the line. Amandine asks Marie-Albert why her own pantalets are not hung there and so, rather than wash and dry the child's things in their rooms, Solange begins to bring Amandine's clothes to the wash-house. When Paul first sees the sisters' pantalets, along with her own and the longer, larger woolen ones of Philippe, waving beside Amandine's tiny, ruffled ones, she reaches for her handkerchief, pats her upper lip.

Amandine delights in the outdoors. She wanders about, touching, smelling, inspecting, Solange or one of the other sisters close by but not too much so. She scrutinizes a swallow's nest, windblown and landed in the herb beds, and often she gossips with the birds, standing under some branch where they perch, nodding, chirping. She answers them. They her. In the furrows beneath the vines, violets grow and, one by one, she gathers them — only the darkest blue ones will do. Lining up the gossamer stems in her trembling palm, she takes them to Solange to tie up with a blade of meadow grass. Wind it round and round, a one-loop bow, and there it is. Her nose yellowed from dipping it into wildflowers, leaves tangled in her sweaty curls, cheeks red from the labors of her forage, she is pleased. *Pour Mater,* she tells Solange.

On Saturday mornings Solange pushes the child in the upright pram down the steep chalk white road to the village, to the shops, to the park, to the library. Everywhere they go, they are greeted with affectionate curiosity. The orphan delivered to St.-Hilaire years ago in a limousine, her infant self preceded by a royal court's worth of possessions, her tiny soul baptized by the bishop himself. Yes, this Amandine, such a bright, sanguine little girl, she along with this handsome young *Champenoise* who tends to her so lovingly, they cause a quiet stir among the villagers.

"Ah, Mademoiselle Solange, let us have a look at darling Amandine. A pistachio macaroon for your *goûter?* Here, yes, you may take it, it's for you. Such wonderful eyes, this little girl. Yes, a meter of the rose-colored wool will do nicely for a spring jacket with a little cape. White cotton stockings, three pair. A box of soaps shaped like stars from Marseille, a bottle of almond oil. Your first pair of boots, can you button them? That's right, just like that. And you, Mademoiselle Solange, how well our sweet southern air agrees with you. *Au revoir. Au revoir.*"

CHAPTER X

On a morning late in April, Baptiste had performed his monthly controls on Amandine. The consultant specialist, Nitchmann, had also participated in the examination, as he did twice each year. Once they were finished, the two doctors left Solange to wash away the petroleum jelly from Amandine's tiny chest in the places where the cardiograph's wire suctions had been placed, to dress her then so she might go to play the xylophone that Baptiste kept for her in the lowest drawer of his desk. The doctors then left to walk in the garden.

Solange thought they'd stayed away too long and began to imagine — *how long their faces, how silent they were* — that their findings must be grave. Though Baptiste had always been tentative with his prognosis, frugal with his hope, Solange had begun to believe that some miracle would make the surgery unnecessary. Amandine played on the xylophone, Solange paced, allowed herself a glance into the garden each time she passed the window. Finally the two reentered, sat rather stiffly, Baptiste behind his desk, Nitchmann in a chair beside Solange.

"Amandine, please put that away now and come to sit with me, with us," said Solange.

Silently, Amandine did what she was asked.

It was Baptiste who spoke first. "Well, my lovelies. Doctor Nitchmann and I have been talking about your birthday gift, Amandine, and we were wondering if you had a particular desire. After all, a fifth birthday is quite a milestone."

While Baptiste took Amandine out into the garden so she might demonstrate under which tree she would like her new swing to be, Nitchmann sat with Solange. He told her, "The imperfections in her heart remain. Yet the heart itself — her heart — performs *normally.* Within normal limits. Let me say it another way: her heart has *dominated* its congenital defects. Overcome them. *It seems that it has overcome them.* It's not as though I've never seen this sort of compensation, because I have. But I admit that earlier on I wasn't expecting Amandine to be one of those *fois insolites,* unusual cases.

And so what does this mean? It means that you may, slowly, allow her to increase her activities. Stay alert to the signs of distress. You know them all too well. Of course we'll continue to examine her with the same frequency, but it's time that she begins to live more like the healthy child she seems to be."

A few days later Solange and Amandine are sitting in the park watching the children at play. Inured to prudence, Amandine is content to be the audience, to sit cross-legged on the grass merrily applauding the spectacle. Solange asks her, "Darling, would you like to join those little girls in the play-house?"

"Me? But you know I mustn't."

"It's okay. Baptiste said it would be okay. As long as you don't run too much. You know. As long as you take things a bit slowly. At first. Go on."

Amandine gets up, smoothes her plaid skirt, adjusts one fallen yellow sock, looks uncertainly at Solange. "Will you stay right here?"

"Yes. Right here. Go now. You may go. I'll be here waiting for you. Trust me."

Amandine nods, turns, starts off, then turns back. "But what if you're *not* here when I come back?"

"I'll be here."

"Is that what trust means?"

"Yes."

She goes, then returns again. "Do some people say they will and then they don't?"

"Yes."

"What's that called?"

"A broken trust."

Amandine stays still. Closes her eyes for a moment. "Can it be fixed? If it's broken, can a trust be fixed?"

"It depends on how badly it's broken. Now go. It's nearly time for us to be back at the convent."

CHAPTER XI

"Mater, I would like permission to begin bringing Amandine to the *réfectoire* at midday. I think she would benefit from the society of the children."

Seated at her desk, her hands full of papers, Paul looks up from her work as Solange speaks. She pauses, considers the request, its rationale. "How do you suppose a five-year-old could *benefit* from the society of thirty-six cosseted little chits? She holds the house in thrall, is that not sufficient? Would you have her endear herself to an even greater audience than that?"

"She herself will be joining the ranks of the 'cosseted little chits' next year, and I was thinking it might be a good thing for her to be introduced, little by little, into the next era of her life. Until a few months ago, she'd had so little exposure to other children. But now that she . . . I mean since Baptiste has given his approval for increased activity, she has made friends at the park and she's become really quite social. Surely she would enjoy being at table with the other girls and —"

"You have yet to grasp that 'what she would enjoy' is of no concern to me. She is not a student of the school, and hence the refectory is not open to her. It's that simple. Request denied, Sister."

The issue settled, Paul resumes shuffling her papers. Takes up her pen. Solange remains silent but makes no move to leave. Once again, Paul looks up at Solange, who seems absorbed in pulling at a loose thread in her apron. In a less harsh tone, Paul says, "I do you a favor by my refusal. Amandine is, she is *different,* and my convent girls will fathom that from the first moment she is among them. Let her be content as long as she can with her dilettante's occupations. Her piano lessons, her drawing. She might well do without the elocution lessons, though, futile bane against the devil's marking her with that lisp." With this last she regains imperiousness.

"Mater, I —"

"I must say you've done well by her training in the more homely occupations, what with her morning climb up onto the kitchen stool to put her hands into the dough or to stir a pudding. It's become quite the ritual, too, hasn't it? Her feeding the geese, the rabbits, the goats, and her traipsing about the garden after her beloved Philippe. Your dressing her up like some *maquette* in that blasphemous replica of our habits, that seems to please her mightily."

"Amandine asked for 'a dress like Père Philippe's,' and so Sister Josephine made her one from a length of stuff cut from the hem of Marie-Albert's habit. It did no harm, Mater."

"No, no harm. Despite your indulging, I admit she remains demure enough. I suspect the child is more resigned to her fate than are you, Solange."

"And what is her fate, Mater?"

"To be apart."

"I pretend neither to myself nor to her that she is the same as other children. Her health, her *circumstances* . . . But I think some of the older girls might champion her, be ready to help her along during her first days at school next year. The five- and six-year-olds will be concerned enough with their own settling in, will either ignore Amandine or nettle her as only little ones do to one another, and so I thought that the older ones might —"

"How presumptuous you are, Solange, to

think that you can anticipate and stave off that child's pain. I admit that she shall hardly be well-prepared to commence her school days, but that is your doing. Your bear-like fostering of her, yours and the others', and now you would have her schoolmates do likewise?"

"Mater, I'm only asking to bring her to sit at table with us. She's old enough now, she sits quietly, has learned some rudimentary manners."

Paul busies herself with the sheaf of papers, tapping them on her desk to even up their edges, tapping them again and again. "Why do you trouble yourself with seeking permission for this? For anything? *His Eminence* has —"

"Respect, Mater. My respect for you."

"Yes. Polite regard. Your polite regard for me in the face of my impassiveness. With the bishop's carte blanche in hand you might have taunted me."

"May I sit, Mater?"

"Yes, yes, you may sit."

"There have been times when you tempted my rudeness, Mater, and I think that without Père Philippe and some of the others to hold me back, I might have sparred with you but, you see, none of us believes that your heart is stone —"

"I permitted you to sit, Solange. The chair is not an invitation for a tête-à-tête, less is it meant to open dialogue regarding the material of my heart. Never mistake my occasional guile for a weakening of my will against your presence here. Yours and hers. If you wish to bring the child to the refectory, then you may. One day a week."

"Thank you, Mater. May I choose Friday as the day?"

"Friday. You may go now, Solange."

"Do you know what Amandine believes, Mater? She believes that *you* are her mother."

Paul looks up sharply, begins to speak, but Solange steps fast upon her words. "Yes, it's true. Yesterday when I took her to the park, two little girls whom we'd never seen before approached us. One said to Amandine, 'Come to play with us. Ask your mother if you can come with us to ride the carousel by the pond. And what's your name, by the way?'

"The little girls looked at me then, waiting for my response. And Amandine said, 'My name is Amandine, but she, she's not my mother. She's my sister. My mother is at home with all the others. With all my other sisters. I will go to ask my mother about the carousel. Solange, may we go to ask Mater if I can go to the carousel? What is a carousel, Solange?'

"The little girls began to laugh and ran to where their own mothers were sitting and watching from a nearby bench. The children pointed at Amandine and whispered and giggled and told their mothers that the little girl over there didn't know what a carousel was. I lifted her into my arms, but she struggled to be released and, red with shame, she ran away. I went after her, took her hand. As we walked I explained about the carousel, about the ponies that gallop round and round in a never-ending journey to the tune of *'Elle descend de la montagne,'* and I promised her that, one day soon, I would take her to ride a white one with a silver saddle just like the pony in the song. And then I said to her, 'Amandine, tell me about your mother.'

" '*Elle est fou.* You are so silly, Solange, to ask me about my mother since she is also your mother. And Marie-Albert's mother and Josephine's mother. And Marie-France et Jacqueline et Suzette. Mater is the mother of all my sisters just as Père Philippe is our father. But hurry now so that we can ask Mater about the carousel. *Solange, Solange, vite, vite.* I want so much to ride a white pony.'

"Of course I said nothing. Her notion seems just, doesn't it? We all live in the same house, we all pray and work together, we all call you *Mater,* we all call Philippe *Père.* I was shocked at myself, I mean that I hadn't considered this assumption. It's —"

"An easily clarified absurdity. She is precocious. It's time — it's perhaps even late — nevertheless you must, we all must, I suppose, begin to conspire, begin to explain to her, each in our own way, that she has no parents. That she is an orphan. Yes, we must begin. I would suggest that you begin and we shall all follow suit. And now, please leave me, Solange."

Solange makes no move to stand, to curtsy, rather she sits quietly, looking at Paul, who takes up her pen, begins to write, her slanted, looping hand sure and fast across the page.

"Please leave me, Solange." Now she commands.

Solange remains seated.

"Mater, I've decided to tell Amandine the truth."

Pen still in hand, Paul looks up. "What truth?"

"That she has a mother but that . . . that her mother wasn't able to —"

"What figment do you consult, child?"

106

"I disbelieve the story you told to me. That both her parents died only days after she was born. Without more information, more credible information, more details, more evidence, I can't believe it, and so I can't ask Amandine to believe it. I shall not try to convince her of what I am not convinced myself."

"Of what *are* you convinced?"

"That not knowing one's mother and so hoping one day to know her is far better for a child to contemplate than that her mother is dead. Especially when no one knows for certain that she is. You are not certain, are you, Mater?"

Paul stays silent.

"This is what I think will be best for Amandine, Mater. I will tell her that her parents, her mother, at least, is alive. I will tell her that I don't know who her parents are or where they are or why, exactly, they left her here with us, with you. I will tell her that one day her mother will come to take her home."

"You would give the child hope? Cruelty I did not expect of you. Better you tell her that you are her mother. I've always thought, should she live long enough to question her parentage, that you would claim motherhood. Natural enough, wouldn't you say?

107

And truer than your fantasy since mother-hood has more to do with fidelity than with blood. Certainly you have been faithful to her, Solange."

"I've thought of telling her that I'm her mother. I admit that. And if I was certain that her own mother would never come forth to claim her, that is what I would do. But under these conditions, that would be fair neither to Amandine nor to her mother."

"Conditions? There are no conditions. Amandine shall never know her parents. Her mother. Dead or alive, neither do *I* know the state of their being. What I *do* know is that Amandine does not exist for them."

Paul looks away from Solange. Sotto voce she says, *Essentially, the child shall no longer exist once you leave this room.* She turns back to Solange. "Yes, I think those were my lines."

"Pardon me, Mater. Your lines?"

"Be certain of this, Solange, that the child's life began on the day she was brought here. Left here. Be certain of that and save yourself and the child at least some part of the suffering already allotted to her. I admit the strangeness of it, but nevertheless it is all the truth we have."

"You thought she was going to die, didn't

108

you, Mater? You and the bishop, you thought it would be a few weeks, a few months, and she would be gone. She was taken on as a short-term investment of sorts, I understand that."

"Do you?"

"I think I do. I understand it quite enough."

"Just what do you propose to do should this child, should she —"

"Grow up? Is that what you're asking? Not so difficult to contemplate. Once her schooling here is complete, I shall help her to find her way, to proceed with a higher education if, *should* that seem indicated or to take the veil if she's inclined, to find good work out in the world. I would help her, guide her as best I can. Surely you would help her, too, Mater."

"She is not my charge."

"No. Not your charge. Your mortification. That's how you treat her, Mater, yet you see, you *know* how she's drawn to you, how she longs for your affection. And you speak to me of cruelty?"

Head bowed to her papers, the strokes of her pen sepulchral whispers, Paul says nothing.

"Was it a woman who brought Amandine here? A foreign woman. Beautiful."

"I know nothing of a *foreign woman*."

"You can tell me, Mater. I met her, you know. Saw her once. She came to our home to speak with my grandmother. I handed her tea and she pulled down her kerchief and I saw her. Amandine's eyes are like her eyes, don't you think, Mater?"

Paul stands, her fists cudgels upon the desk. She screams, "How dare you? Inventions, fool inventions, which can only leave the child in greater pain than her birthright has already dictated. How dare you? Follow your instructions, Solange. Should you choose not to, count on His Eminence to support my promise, the promise that I make to you now. You will be humiliated and sent away."

"And I make two promises to you, Mater. It is I who shall decide what to tell Amandine about her life. And should I be sent away, I will take Amandine with me."

Solange curtsies, turns, walks slowly to the door. Over her shoulder, she looks back at Paul, nods her head as though to say, *Count on it.* Softly, she closes the door behind her.

Chapter XII

"Amandine, yesterday when I asked you who your mother was, you thought I was joking, didn't you?"

Red leaves fluttering to the ground, Amandine rushes among them, trying to catch them as they fall. She makes a pile of those she's captured, reaches up for another as the wind scatters the gathered ones, which she then chases, retrieves. Solange stands a few meters distant from the leaping and screeching.

"Amandine, Paul is not your mother, she's not the mother of any of us. Not mine, not Josephine's or Marie-Albert's or Suzette's or . . . She is our spiritual mother, the person who is responsible for the well-being of all of us who live here in the convent. Can you understand that?"

Clutching leaves to her breast, Amandine walks closer to Solange. "Do you mean that she's a spirit? Is Paul a ghost?"

111

"No. Not a ghost. She is very real, and she cares for all of us as a mother would care, but she is not our *real* mother."

The two move to sit under the tree then, inside the red whirring of the leaves.

"Is she our fake mother?"

"No. It's only that each one of us has our *birth* mother. Our *own* mother. And Paul is not that kind of mother to any of us."

"Not to any of us?"

"No."

"Do you have your *own* mother?"

"Yes. I have a mother. And a father. I have two sisters and a grandmother, aunts and uncles and, last time I counted, eighteen cousins."

"Where are they? Why don't you live with them?"

"They live in another part of France. In the north. And I don't live with them because I chose to live with you."

"But why?"

"Because I wanted to. My choice to come here to be with you does not mean that I don't love my family. I love them and I love you. You are also my family."

"But I'm not your 'own' family. Am I?"

"No."

"Do I have my *own* mother? Who is she? Who is my *own* mother?"

"I don't know, darling. I don't know exactly who she is, but I do know that she loves you very much."

"You don't know who she is? Are you sure that no one here is my own mother?"

"No one here."

"Shouldn't we be going to find her then? I've been here for so long, won't she be worried by now? That I haven't come home?"

"She knows that you're well and safe here. She knows that you're with me, with Paul and Philippe and all the rest of us. She knows that, and so she's not worried."

"Oh. But can I just see her for a while? I want to see my own mother. I'm sure she would like to see me, don't you think she would?"

"Of course I do, but right now that simply isn't possible. She wants you to grow up to be a beautiful, strong girl, to learn your lessons, to be kind and good, to be obedient to me and to the sisters, to —"

"How do you know that she loves me?"

"I know because, because she cared so much about you that she —"

"Did she tell you? Did she tell you that she loved me?"

"In her way, she did."

"What way?"

"She sent a lady to tell me about you."

"She did? What did the lady say?"

"She said that there was this precious little baby whose mother wasn't able to care for her and that the mother didn't want the baby to be alone. She asked me if I would take care of the baby. For her mother. She asked me if I would give her all the love in the world in her mother's name. Just as though the mother, herself, was giving her that love. Do you understand?"

"I don't know. Who was the lady?"

"She was a woman with beautiful eyes, eyes like a deer and skin white like the moon. And she was very sad. I saw her only for a moment, a half moment."

"Why was she sad?"

"I think it was because she knew that your mother would miss you. That she would miss you, too."

"Then let's go to find the lady. She'll know where my own mother is and then we can all be together. The lady and you and my mother and me. And your own mother, too, and we can take Philippe and his own mother and Paul and all the sisters. And everybody's own mother."

Should I have explained it in another way? Should I not have explained it at all? Was Paul right? Was my telling her that her mother

114

couldn't care for her more cruel than my telling her that her mother was dead? Would it have been better to wait until she was older, more able to . . . ? I would have waited, I would gladly have put off such discourse, had the incident at the park not brought me face-to-face with her misconceptions. I had no choice. I couldn't allow her to go on thinking that Paul was her mother. Philippe, her father. How much more cruel would it have been if I'd not told her, if I'd simply let her wander about in that *nebbia,* that puerile rationale? On the first day of school, her classmates would have pitilessly dispelled her delusions. She would have come running to me for solace. "Is it true? Why didn't you tell me? Then who is my mother?" So well have I taught my little girl, she would call my omission, my silence a broken trust. She would be right. No, it's better this way. I will console her, and she will become accustomed to the truth. The truth. But is what I told her the truth, or have I corrected her misconceptions only to propose mine? An ambiguity exchanged for an abstraction. God help me. I try to forget my mother while she begins to long for hers.

"Do you know what, Père Philippe?"

115

"Tell me, beauty."

"When I was younger, I mean last week when I was younger, I used to think that you were my own father. Isn't that silly?"

"Not silly."

"Do you have your own father?"

"I did once, but he, long ago he went to live in heaven. You know, with God."

Soft rain chimes on the stones under the eaves of the washhouse windows. Inside Amandine sits with Philippe in the old parlor chair amid the smells of soap and steam. Marie-Albert whispers the beads while she cranks the wringer.

"Do you have a mother, Père?"

"Yes. Yes, I do. I did. She has also gone to heaven. I had a grandmother, too."

"Also in heaven?"

"Yes."

"What was she like? Your grandmother."

"Do you mean what did she look like?"

"Yes."

"She was tall, or so she seemed, since I was barely eight when she went away. Yes, I would say that she was tall. She always smelled like sugar. She wore a yellow dress with red roses all over it. And on Sundays she wore a brown dress, very soft. And a brown hat, I think. And she liked to kiss me, she was always kissing me. A four-kiss

kiss. Just the way Solange kisses you."

"Right cheek, left cheek, right cheek, lips."

"Yes, like that."

"Look over there, do you see how the creek looks in the rain? That was the way her hair looked, barely blue, like thin blue silk, and pinched into tight waves just like the creek water."

"I'd like to have blue hair someday."

"And perhaps someday you shall."

"I wish you were my own father."

Tears catching in the ruts in his cheeks, Philippe says, "I have the same wish."

"You do?"

"Yes. I do."

"Good."

"In fact, before God and the angels, right now, right here, I choose you as my child."

"I choose you as my father. Before God and the angels. Is it real now?"

"Absolutely real."

"It is not. I know it isn't. It isn't real, but I think it's true. Between us, it's true."

"Between us and God and the angels. Maybe it's as true as anything can be."

"Maybe. I love you, Père."

Chapter XIII

More often than was his former habit, Bishop Fabrice visits the convent. The ostensible motive is that Philippe seems less inclined to visit him at the curia in Montpellier, and though it's true that the bishop misses his old friend's company, perhaps there is yet another reason for this change in his routine.

Unannounced, His Eminence, *en entourage,* arrives just before vespers, prays with the sisterhood, and then, in a parlor off the kitchen, dines alone with Philippe, their schoolboy laughter seeping out from under the closed doors, pouring in upon the household. In visceral response, the sisters, even Paul, grow flushed and chirping, glide about the place. *The masters are at home and dining in the parlor.*

Often Fabrice arrives earlier in the day, sometime after lunch and, wearing Wellingtons under his purple skirts, follows Philippe down into the *chai,* where the two sit on tottering wooden chairs at a small table, uncorking bottles, swirling the fine old juice, swallowing and spitting as they wish, plumbing the depths of a terra-cotta urn — exclusive cache of molding, grainy cheese buried in grapewood ash — Philippe gouging crumbles of the stuff, passing it to Fabrice from the blade of a corkscrew. Weary lions languishing in their den.

The bishop always asks to see Amandine, bends to bless her, holds her on his knee for a moment, remarks on her growth, her brightness, hears her recitation of a prayer. Polite and dutiful, Amandine endures, performs, glancing — now and then — over her shoulder for Philippe. When she climbs down from the bishop's wide, princely upholstered lap, runs to the shelter of Philippe's embrace, Fabrice looks long at the pair, listens to their chatter, a half smile playing about his pendulous old mouth.

On one morning visit, Paul — always seeking greater attention than he is wont to pay her — requests a private audience with Fabrice. "Of course, Paul. At noon, while the house is in meditation. A walk in the garden? Will that please you, Paul?" She hears the chaff, understands what he does not say. *If you could be pleased, that is.* She returns to

119

her rooms, repeats her earlier everyday ablutions. Washes her face with lavender soap, presses a linen towel to her cheeks. Does she rub so vigorously only to dry them or also to bring on a blush? She brushes her teeth, holding the towel against her starched collar, her stiff white wings juddering as she moves. Once again the towel to her mouth. There is no glass in which she can see herself.

She begins, "I wish to know more about how she, how the child came to be under your protection. Under mine. Five years of dutiful silence, patience. Have I not earned some right to — ?"

"There is nothing more to know, Paul. Nothing that would line up all the pieces in the perfect row as you would have them. A brother of the Church, an old friend. The child's need for refuge was told to me by him. These things happen all the time, these *requests* among the greater clergy for extraordinary favors."

"Paid favors, of course."

"In one way or another, paid. Of course."

"This friend. He's not French."

"No. He wasn't French. But what does that — ?"

"Past tense. He's dead, then?"

"Yes. But his not having been French and

120

his no longer being alive, these are not factors that —"

"Is the child not French?"

"Why would you care, Paul? For all intents and purposes, she is thoroughly French. But if she were not, what would it matter?"

"Solange. She came to speak with me —"

"I know. Solange speaks with Philippe, and Philippe speaks with me. With her permission, of course. I know that Amandine believed you were her mother, I know what Solange has told her. Whether or not I am in accord with how Solange has proceeded to explain things to Amandine, I will respect her decisions. She has become far more than a nurse, a caretaker to the child. If there are *earned rights* about any of this, they belong to Solange. And if your next inquiry is to be about the woman who consigned the child to you —"

"So she's not yours, she's not your *issue?* Amandine."

At first Fabrice does not understand Paul's question, is about to ask her to repeat it when the light dawns. Turning to look at her, then she at him, he laughs to tears. "Hah. Dear, darling Paul, you flatter me. At seventy-seven, you imagine I've sired a child?"

"You would have been seventy-one or so . . ."

His laughter unspent, he speaks between chortles, "Even in my dotage, in yours, you're still jealous and possessive and rancorous. Oh, Paul, what a delicious wife you would have made to some man. No, she is not my *issue*."

Both are quiet then. Fabrice searches beneath his robes for his handkerchief, Paul finds hers first, hands it to him. Patting it about his rheumy eyes, touching it to the saliva about his satyr's lips, he says, "You know, we've grown to be an old married couple, you wanting more from me and I wanting more to be left to my own ways and means. That is, I want to be left alone as long as you *continue* your wanting more from me. Such a wonderful game."

"I suppose it is." She looks at him again, smiles, really smiles. Throws back her head and laughs as she has not done, has not allowed herself to do, for how long? Her voice is almost soft then.

"You have twice dismissed me, Fabrice. First from your bed, then from your schemes. I'd grown used to being necessary to you. I felt 'put aside' when you became bishop, when you left me behind to look after this gaggle of misfit hens, most of whom don't want to be here any more than I do. It was you for whom I stayed, and you knew that. You know that now."

"Yes, just like a marriage. You the good wife, long-suffering, sacrificed to her husband's ambitions. His titillations and fancies. But you, dear Paul, you've not received the usual glittering tokens of either arrival or remorse. Baubles neither to celebrate nor to beg pardon. I have rewarded and consoled you only with more work, more responsibility. It's true. I'd never thought of it this way before, but I did leave you 'at home with the children' while I moved about on business, whatever business was at hand. Your only bracelets have been fetters."

Paul takes her handkerchief from his lap, where it's fallen, loudly blows her nose. A gesture of self-pity? *Yes, only fetters,* it says. Then she says, "The latest fetter being this child. Will it never end, your misuse of me?"

"There hasn't been a question of my 'misuse' of you for forty years."

"Less than that."

"The child's presence in what you've grown to think of as 'your' home has done nothing but enhance it, and even you know that. I will abide your laments but not your bedeviling of plain truths."

Eyes like dry stones, she looks at him.

123

He shakes his head. "But, really, what could you have expected of me, Paul? That once I'd been ordained bishop I might take you as my official consort and that, you in your wimple and I in my robes, we would travel about the province together? Yes, it's true, you helped me to win my colors, but I believed you did it for me and not for what attentions might overflow to you. It was your duty to help me."

"My duty?"

"Yes."

"And your duty to me?"

"*My duty to you?* Do you mean my payment to you? The price for your seventeen-year-old virginity. Is that what you still seek? That would be prostitution, Paul. A debauch for payment."

"You know it's much more than that which you took from me."

"More than that which you gave to me, my dear."

"Are you the appointed, the official control over the child's well-being? The woman, that woman, who was she? What was she? I don't even know. She spoke of a *fail-safe.* That's the word she used. The word her interpreter used. I'll not forget, never forget the smug tilt of her pretty, pointed chin as her lackey said the words:

" 'Here within these walls, Mater. A person who knows what to look for, what criteria to use in judging the execution of your *word*. This person knows how to *effect* things should effecting be necessary. Even you, especially you, shall never know who this person is.'

"Can you truly wonder, Fabrice, why I have never accepted, shall never accept the child's presence?"

"From the beginning I've known you were a sham. That you are still. That you have no calling, that you were deposited here and left a prisoner of sorts. I've always known that. But have not forty years of even a sham life of piety, have not these marked you with sufficient humility to allow an orphan child into your midst?"

"More someone's abandoned bastard than orphan."

"And so? Does that make her less needy? Children die from abandonment. Another kind of hunger. Be they orphans or merely 'unclaimed.' Either way the child is wounded. In the case of Amandine, one must add her *condition* to the quotient."

" 'Children die from abandonment. Another kind of hunger.' At five months. At seventeen, too."

"Touché. You speak of yourself, of course.

125

At seventeen, one can hardly still be called a child, Paul. The gravity of the wound is not the same. But if you recognize that you and Amandine have shared a common fate, all the more I should think you would have embraced her. It might have helped you, Paul. It still could. No. It's too late, isn't it? I didn't know that until this moment. You prefer to pass on your pain. Not so different from the pest-infected souls who wiped their spit on doorknobs. Yes, you suffered and, by all that's heavenly, let her suffer more. That's it. You who inspire no love are envious of a child who inspires it so deeply. As I look at you, I can't help but think that your profanity, your godlessness, have made an ugly old woman of you, Paul."

The stab finds its mark. She gasps, flutters her hand about her face, feeling it, checking it — feminine impulse — as though homeliness is palpable. She recovers. "You? You can call me profane and godless when —"

"I am as proficient a priest as I am a sinner. I have given almost equal energy to both sides of my character, and the balance, the outcome of my life shall be judged by no one less than God. Good day, Paul."

CHAPTER XIV

The plash of a leaping trout in the creek, the dry rattle of the November leaves still on the vine, the chaste duet of his wheeze with her snuffling, Amandine and Philippe sleep in the bluish light under the walnut tree. Solange smiles to herself as she fusses with the quilt, already tucked in around them. *Au revoir, mes petits.*

As she does always when she and Philippe rest together, Amandine wakes before Solange returns to call them to vespers. But rather than stay quiet until Solange arrives, she gently shakes Philippe, tells him it's almost time to go and will he please finish the story. The one about the giant horseman who rides across the sky lighting up the stars with the sparks from his spurs. "Père, wake up." She shakes him harder. He must be so tired. She lies back down deep in his arms, closes her eyes tightly. Why does it hurt in my heart? Why is it thumping as though

127

I'd been running when I'm lying here so quietly? I must slow the pounding as Baptiste has taught me. Think about wildflowers and baby rabbits, just born, and about the baby Jesus in his crib. Still her heart beats a hard two-note tattoo, an unfastened shutter against the stones of the house. "Père, wake up. Have you gone away to that place where your grandmother lives? Your grandmother had blue hair and she went to live with God and now you've gone there, too, I know you have."

Fried corn cakes and duck sausages. Warm apple charlotte with cream. A good supper Josephine has prepared. As Solange hurries toward the creek, she tastes each dish. Fifteen minutes until vespers. What is that sound? An animal, some small animal wounded. Where —

A high, screeching wail. In the darkening under the walnut tree, Amandine kneels beside him, rocking on the heels of her muddy red boots, tugging at his sleeve.

CHAPTER XV

He asks to be left alone with Philippe. Fabrice does. Arriving at the convent a scant hour after Paul had telephoned the curia, he descends the long black official automobile — no badge of office, no pontifical vestments — his great girth wrapped in a simple soutane, black velvet slippers on his oddly dainty feet as though he'd been settled by his fire for the evening. A pandering retinue neither precedes nor follows him. Paul scuttles behind him. "I shall call you and the others later," he tells her.

In sconces on the walls, in black iron holders on the dresser, twelve white candles light the small spare room that was Philippe's. Over the flame of one of the candles, Fabrice warms oil, washes the breathless body of his friend, dresses him in the starched white undergarments and the black soutane laid out by the sisters. He combs Philippe's hair, shaves three days' growth of whiskers.

Amandine so loved the roughness of it that, for years now, Philippe had kept his beard in stubbles for her. Fabrice says the canonical prayers for a newly departed soul, reads from the Bible, picks up a Jesuit text that lies open on the bedside table and reads aloud from it. He pulls a chair close to the bed, then sits and talks for a long time to his friend. He kisses Philippe. Both cheeks, forehead. Kneels.

By then half a hundred people — clergy, townfolk, a contingent from the *pompes funèbres,* the press — have gathered outside the room where Philippe lies, there and in the convent salon.

Fabrice, still in his slippers, addresses them. "There will be no public funeral for our beloved Philippe. I will personally see that his wishes, expressed long ago and repeatedly to me, be honored. Now I will ask you all to leave, to pray, each of you in your own way, for the salvation of his soul, for his heavenly peace."

Many believe the bishop's directive is meant for others, certainly not for them. Fabrice confirms otherwise. He asks Paul to call the sisters from the chapel, where they have been praying. The sisters crowd inside Philippe's room, round his bed. The sorority says the beads. Paul keeps the first hour of vigil. The others will take their turns.

That night Fabrice sleeps in the convent, in the room nearest to Philippe. He shoos away the offerings of embroidered linens and towels. "It's not my wedding night, Paul. Leave me to mourn my friend." Next morning at five, it's he, still wearing his country priest's soutane, his slippers, who says mass for the sisterhood. At breakfast he announces the wishes of Philippe. All that day and into the evening, it's he who oversees the events.

The grave is dug in a patch of meadow only meters from the smallest, farthest-away vineyard. There will be no monument. No beribboned chrysanthemum pillows. No eulogies.

Solange has kept Amandine by her side every moment since she found her with Philippe under the walnut tree. Though she knows that Amandine understands what has happened, Solange does not speak of Philippe or his death. Rather she tries to comfort Amandine with the familiar rites of their life. In their rooms she lights the kindling in the hearth as she does every evening, fills the tub with warm water, handing the bottle of almond oil to the child, looking on as Amandine carefully measures out a capful and leans over the tub to pour it directly under the sputtering faucet. Amandine takes a jar then from the shelf over the tub, deftly pulls out one then another round purple capsule, throws them under the running water, replaces the jar. She looks at Solange and, as if on cue, they inhale the lilac scent. Just as they do always. Still in her muddy red boots and outdoor clothes, Amandine begins to undress, allows Solange to help. Concession to the evening's incidents. Solange bathes Amandine, washes her hair, helps her to stand up in the tub while she rinses her tangled black curls with fresh water poured from a small yellow faience bowl again and again over her head. Usually protesting this last step in the ablutions by pushing away Solange's hand, tonight Amandine holds her small, pointed chin high, closes her eyes tightly, awaits the assault. Lifting her from the tub, swinging her in a wide arc to stand on the chair beside it, Solange wraps Amandine in a large linen cloth, carries her to the fire, kisses her "fairy's wings," rubs her dry, burnishes her skin to a sheen with two quick shakes of talcum from the pale blue tin with the baby on it. Pink flannel bloomers and nightdress, long pink stockings, slippers. Supper. One of the sisters has left a basket on the table. A small covered copper pot wrapped in a yellow striped napkin. Solange spoons out bits of chicken stewed in cream. Mashes a piece of boiled carrot into the sauce. She butters bread, fills Amandine's glass with milk from a quarter-liter glass bottle. Sets down a little white porcelain pot of caramel pudding by each plate. Though neither of them has spoken a word, the slow, tinny whine of the funeral bells in the hamlet chapel fills the silence. A thrush laments somewhere among the vines. A thrush who would sing at night. Another concession. Philippe is dead.

On an afternoon a few days later, when Solange had left her resting in their rooms, Amandine pulls on her sweater, slips into her raincoat even though the weather is fine. It's the pockets of the coat, large and deep, that she needs. Boots, hat, she descends the stairs to the quiet kitchen, opens the door to the *garde-manger,* takes thick slices of black bread from the drawer where they are stored, ready to toast in the morning. She lays the bread flat on a shelf, lifts the cork from one of the large gray stone jam pots. Blackberry. With its own wooden spoon she spreads the thick, dark fruit onto the bread, folds each slice in half, pressing on them with the heel of her hand. She wraps them then in a sheet of brown paper, which she tears from the roll attached to the wall. She closes the drawer, corks the jam pot. Shuts the door on her deed.

Package in one of her pockets, she walks to the garden, directly to the herb patches. She tears basil from its bed. Sometimes by the roots, sometimes only the leaves. She hurries, knows that, if someone sees her, she will be scolded, sent back to bed. When the other pocket is full of basil, she starts off toward the vineyards. Her mission is a long way away. Though she walks slowly, her heart thumps, her breath is short. She walks to the edge of the smallest vineyard. She knows this is where he is. She heard them talking. She knows exactly where Philippe is. She tears the basil leaves, lets go of the bits here and there almost artistically over the sod where new grass has already begun to grow. She sets down the brown-paper-wrapped bread and jam on the stone with his name written on it. She can read it. Philippe. She notes that it does not say Père. She thinks it should. She looks about for wildflowers, but none are in sight. The basil will do, she thinks. He loved basil. Kept leaves in the pocket of his soutane. To chew after lunch. She liked when he smelled of basil. She takes a few steps backward to look at Philippe's new place.

"I love you. I still love you. But I wish you hadn't gone away."

"Where have you been? I was so frightened. I've been calling you. Didn't you hear me?"

"I had to go somewhere. I had to go by myself. I knew where it was."

"Where what was?"

"That place."

"What place, Amandine?"

"The one near the grapes."

"Do you mean that you walked all the way to, to where Père sleeps?"

"I know he's dead, Solange. You can say it. And I know he's under the ground. I'm not little anymore, and so you don't have to use special baby words."

CHAPTER XVI

I'm bad. Horrid things happen to me because I am horrid. I don't know why or how, but it must be true. She would never have left me if I'd been good. My mother. And Philippe never would have gone away. I understand. I didn't have to wait until I was big to understand. It's me. It's because of me that I don't have a mother and that Philippe died and that Paul can't love me and that Solange doesn't live with her family. It's all me. I'm bad.

Amandine's power to conceal flourishes with her new conscience. Her burden. She can find no reason for all that's wrong save her own wickedness. She is ashamed. Others mustn't know, mustn't ever find out how bad she is so, from now on, she will be extra good. She will be perfect.

Amandine does not speak of Philippe. When Solange asks if she would like to visit his grave again, gather wildflowers to take to him, she shakes her head no. In her prayers, she does not name him. If less *allègre* than before his passing, Amandine remains — it would seem — cheerful enough. More than to play in the garden or the park, she prefers to stay quiet with her books or to sit for hours at the pianoforte pounding out scales and arpeggios, endless repetitions of "Für Elise" with a heavy, dispassionate hand.

She is six now and ready to enter the convent school. She reads and comprehends in the third- and often fourth-grade primers, draws and paints and sings with — once again what would seem like — enthusiasm. As though she'd been attending it for years, she observes the convent school program meticulously.

Five A.M. rising, community cold-water washes while dressed, for modesty's sake, in long gray bathing shifts, hair brushing and braiding with the help of the dormitory sisters, a brisk walk to the chapel, mass, breakfast, classes, recreation, lunch in the convent refectory, rest, study, chores in the convent, the dressing bell — twenty minutes to rinse faces, rebraid hair, unlace the boots and slip into black patent ballerinas with floppy grosgrain bows at the toes, add a ruched velvet hair band, a wide Alençon lace collar — vespers, supper, prayers, lights out. Pliant, meek Amandine tells herself, The others mustn't know, mustn't ever find out how bad I am.

At St.-Hilaire the girls are coddled precisely as their parents — who pay handsomely for such gentle handling — wish them to be. Stitched by hand in an atelier in Montpellier, their winter uniforms are of dark gray wool bouclé: high-waisted dresses, velvet-collared with elbow-length puffed sleeves; the wide velvet-bordered hems reach to the ankles, just to the tops of their lace-up boots. Black wool capes and matching basques for outdoor jaunts. For summer, the same but in gray linen with white batiste trimming. In the classrooms, once the villa's sitting rooms and parlors, long, low tables and diminutive upholstered chairs have been arranged to serve as community desks. There is good furniture, mostly from the Empire and Directoire eras, carpets, threadbare but fine, heavy draperies and, according to the weather, wood fires smoldering in raised marble hearths. Hardly less elegant than the rooms arranged years before for Amandine and Solange, one might wonder that Paul had found those quarters decadent. Early proof of her resolute animus. She would be tranquil with nothing about or concerning *the child*. Nothing.

Apart from its status as a regionally approved scholastic institution, St.-Hilaire is an accredited *école d'arts d'agrément*. A finishing school. Thus, feminine skills such as comportment, elocution, etiquette, conversation, voice, and ballroom dancing are practiced under the tutelage of local *maîtres*. Perhaps the most unique studies on its rich agenda are: the art of dining, the training of the palate, a fundamental knowledge of haute cuisine as well as the traditional dishes of the Languedoc.

A swift, silent meal is breakfast; porridge, bread and jam, and small brown bowls of hot chocolate thick as pudding. At midday there is soup, cheese, and fruit. In a flurry of fish knives and sauce spoons, hot copper casseroles, covered tureens, butter molds, finger bowls, it is at the evening meal that the little French girls sit leisurely to dine.

Confit of duck and potatoes sautéed in duck fat; cabbage leaves stuffed with black bread and eggs and pinches of *quatre épices,* the plump rolls tied up in kitchen string and braised in broth and tomatoes; hefts of pâté de foie gras set down with toasted brioche and Sauternes jelly; wild mushrooms baked in cream; braised beef *chaudfroid;*

white beans cooked overnight in deep terra-cotta dishes with sausages and lamb; thick soups of dried peas and smoked bacon ladled over butter-fried *croûtes;* potato pancakes with plum jam; roast chicken stuffed with prunes; trout in brown butter; truffled turkey; apricots set in long metal pans, cut sides up, and strewn with black sugar, pinches of sea salt, a batter of cream and eggs and vanilla, and baked until bubbling and charred. How the little French girls dine.

Solange had despaired for their separation, for Amandine's leaving behind the intimacies, the established rhythms of their life together. On the façade, it seems she needn't have worried so. It is a Saturday afternoon at the end of Amandine's first week in the school, and the two are preparing for a walk into the village. Loosening the tight plaits in which the dormitory sisters have arranged Amandine's unruly hair, Solange feels anxious, perplexed by Amandine's remoteness.

How grown up she is. Flush with her own sufficiency. An act, of course.

"Do you miss me, Amandine?"

"Of course I do. But I'm fine."

"And the girls, how have you been getting

on with them?"

"Fine."

"Have you made a special friend with any one of them? I saw you holding hands with that girl called Sidò, Sidò with the blue glasses."

"We have to hold hands, walk two by two, to the chapel. When we lined up the first day, there was no one left but her and me. We're partners now. For the walk, I mean. She bites her nails, and the sisters put red stuff on them so they taste bad and so she won't bite them anymore."

"Did it work? Did she stop biting her nails?"

"No. She says the red stuff is not so bad after a while. She asked me if I wanted to taste it, but I said no."

"I see. And the classes?"

"Fine."

"Are you eating well? Finishing everything on your plate."

"Paul and all the others force us to. They stand over us, nodding their heads. And we have to change forks a lot. Spoons, too."

"I see. What chores have you been assigned?"

"Helping Marie-Albert with the lace collars. We soak them in bleach water, rinse them, then starch them in sugar water, lay them flat to dry in the sun. Marie-Albert doesn't need help to iron them, or at least I don't think she does. We get a clean one every Monday evening."

"I see."

"Have you noticed that you don't say 'I know' anymore? Now you say 'I see.' "

"I do?"

Still she has not said Philippe's name. She's angry at him for leaving her. And so soon after I'd told her about her mother. Twice impaled. Or is it three times? I think she also mourns her childhood. Whatever shards that remained of it, she has buried. Like chocolates from a satin box, she chooses her words deliberately. So amenable, she seems to respond not according to what she thinks or feels or desires but to what others do. What others would have her do. No needs of her own. I know about that particular façade for pain. Far too early for her to be employing such feminine devices.

Chapter XVII

Though each of them is six years old, the four infantine girls in the beginners' class with Amandine sob for their nannies; one swoons in open grief for a plush bear, left behind, which her mother promises to send by the post. These other four, if they read at all, read erringly, fidget, find undue glee or tragedy in equal measure. An oddity among them, Amandine is soon placed with the seven- and eight-year-olds, where she reads as well as or better than they, listens, comprehends, responds with poise and concentration. Astonished by, envious of the waifish younger girl, the older ones connive to thwart her, to push thorns, rub salt. There is much fodder for their undertaking: Amandine's lisp, her stutter, her lurching walk — a remnant of her will to emulate Philippe. When the girls are called upon to read, they effect stutter and lisp; when asked to step up to the front of the class for recitation, they hobble awkwardly. Their laughter is as brazen as a blow to the cheek. Barely wincing, Amandine takes the stings as her due, further proofs of her own wickedness. The teaching sisters threaten to send the mischievous girls to Paul and hand out demerits for poor comportment, but these *jeunes filles de la noblesse,* young daughters of the nobility — the *cosseted little chits* as Paul defined them to Solange — are thick-skinned against admonition. *Beware of Mummy and Daddy,* say their taunting eyes.

Understanding the way of things, Paul — had she the will to defend Amandine — would be impeded by her fear of displeasing. For displeasing these daughters of the Languedocian elite would result in the displeasure of their noble fathers who, in turn, would duly report such displeasure to the curia. Paul would be accused of ill-handling her assignments, of losing hold on the parents' confidence and their purse strings. All this is moot, though, since Paul has no will to defend Amandine. In fact, now that the child is a student, Paul knows that the bishop, too, will be less likely to take up her case, to let fly any whiff of favoritism. Hence Paul feels free to look the other way when the teaching sisters tell her of Amandine's plight, more so when she sees and hears it for herself. Paul, as she has been since the child was a baby, is blind to Amandine. She never addresses a word directly to her save to correct her and, even then, she speaks without *looking at her.* As Paul passes through the classrooms, she caresses a cheek, adjusts a collar, smiles now and then, but Amandine is invisible to her. The convent girls take note, take courage, intensify their sport. Amandine becomes invisible to them as well.

It is only when Amandine returns to the convent for meals and to perform her daily chores that she is addressed, asked after, touched, and only by Solange and the other convent sisters. Otherwise she draws a curtain around herself so as not to be alone among the others.

Bonne nuit, mes petites, beaux rêves. The dormitory sisters walk among the narrow white beds, here and there straightening a coverlet, patting a head. Tatters of smoke from the just-spent candles swirl about, and Amandine, covered to her chin, lies still, inhales it, gasps for it as if for breath. As though the sweet smoke is solace. She waits for the night music to begin, the adenoidal snuffles, the thin, whistling snores of the others, all of it ripping tiny holes in the smothering black. So still she lies that the thudding of her small, murmuring heart sounds like the hiss of creek water on pebbles. She closes her eyes so she can find Philippe. Yes, he's still there. She tries to find her mother then. Yes, she's there, too. Or is it her? How can I know? She changes the woman's hair, her dress, her eyes, her smile; she puts all the pieces back together again, but still, is it her? Maman, is it you?

Except in the refectory and at mass and sometimes at recreation, Amandine and Solange see one another only on weekends — Saturday at one until Sunday evening at six — when the other convent girls have been fetched by relatives from Montpellier or the towns close by. Amandine is permitted to stay Saturday nights with Solange in their rooms. Though Amandine looks forward to this time, she also knows that this weekly respite is only that, a twenty-nine-hour reprieve. An interval in what has become her real life. Things cannot be as they were before she went to live in the dormitory, before she began school. Before Philippe died. She reaches back further. She thinks about the changes and concludes that the biggest difference of all is inside of her. She no longer feels like a child. Surely not

like a grown-up either but rather lost somewhere in between. She begins to realize that
the only person with whom she is comfortable is the imaginary figure of her mother.
The figure who accompanies her everywhere, the one to whom she speaks in her
mind and sometimes out loud, the one who
soothes and counsels her, who protects her.
She waits for her mother, looks for her,
thinks she hears her voice. Especially on
Saturday afternoons at one.

It's then that Amandine sits or stands on
the edges of the group of her classmates in
their Saturday clothes, screeching in their
Saturday voices. Dragging their valises
across the stone floors, jumping about in
the dormitory hall, they wait for their
parents to arrive. Amandine listens to them
telling one another how lovely it is at home.
The younger ones cry tears of joy as they
wait, their cheeks red and flushed just as
they will be on Sunday evening, when they
will weep in sadness as they are ported back
to school. She listens as the older girls
recount the usual events of these weekends:
tea parties, pretty dresses, afternoons at the
ballet, pastries and chocolates in the cafés
with *Maman et Tante Julie.* One by one the
girls are whisked off by their mothers or
aunties or nannies while Amandine care-

fully scrutinizes each of the women, how they speak and walk. Their clothes. She especially likes one woman who always wears a dark purple suit and a hat with a long brown, green-spotted feather, which curls down across her forehead. It's a nice hat. She's very pretty. Not as pretty as my mother, though. She pays less attention to the fathers. Wearing coats with fur collars and rounded hats like tipped-over woolen bowls, they rush in saying *Vite, vite.* One father wears high boots with pants tucked inside them and a long jacket that ends at his knees. "Riding clothes," one of the older girls called this costume. Perhaps it's next week when she will come for me. I wonder if her hat will have a feather.

Solange desires to provide Amandine with some of the cultural events that are part of her classmates' life beyond the convent school and so begins to plan outings for Amandine as her classmates' parents do for them. To be able to afford these outings, Solange has begun to put aside the stipend that arrives for her via the curia each month — funds she would have spent on special foods to pique Amandine's appetite, on her clothes and books and toys before she entered the school — to use for tickets to the theater in Montpellier, to the ballet, the operetta, symphony concerts. She and Marie-Albert sew a party dress for Amandine; layers of off-white tulle for the skirt, which they attach to a long-sleeved, crocheted bodice of the same color and, from a length of midnight blue velvet, a skirt, a waistcoat, and a small drawstring pouch. Tiny fingerless gloves and a Juliet cap that Marie-Albert crochets from spools of bronze metallic thread. The ballerina slippers and the cape from her convent uniform will suffice to complete the *mise.*

Amandine submits to both the new clothes and the outings, and though she is courteous, appreciative, the curtain that she has drawn around herself is always more difficult to part, even for Solange. Unaware of the constant, quiet torture of Amandine's days in the school, Solange believes that the child's withdrawal is made of her grieving for Philippe. Of that and of yearning for her mother. She believes that it is Amandine herself who has hindered friendships among the other girls, has preferred emotional seclusion from them. And now from her.

One Saturday afternoon as Solange is brushing out Amandine's tight school-day braids, she announces that they will take the bus from the village into Montpellier, to the train station. Solange tells Amandine that she has knitted a shawl for her grandmother, that she will send the package to Reims by rail. The package will be held there until one of the family fetches it when they go to the city during a market week. Solange chatters on about the wool she used in the shawl; did Amandine remember her working on it last summer? *Dark green like pine trees with long black silk fringe. I've already wrapped it or I would show it to you again —*

"It's okay. I remember it. I remember that it was beautiful. But why don't you just deliver the shawl yourself? I mean, why don't you go to Avise?"

"Because Avise is so far away, and you have your studies and I my work."

Amandine takes the hairbrush from Solange's hand, turns to look at her. "I can't go with you, but you could go. Paul would say yes, I know she would. You could go for a while."

"But I would never go without you."

"Why? I live over there most of the time now," Amandine says, nodding her head in the direction of the school, "and on the weekends I can stay here with Marie-Albert and the others. I would be fine."

150

"But wouldn't you want to come with me to Avise someday if we could arrange things? A holiday perhaps. To see if you like it there."

"No. Never. I told you. I *can't* go. What if my mother came to get me and I wasn't here? I must always stay close to the convent. She knows where I am but I don't know where she is, and so it's I who must wait."

"I see."

"Anyhow, I didn't even know you had a grandmother and another mother, I mean your own mother, until, until you told me, you know, about Paul. So why haven't you ever gone to see them in all this time since you came here to take care of me? Why haven't you?"

"Well, some things happened many years ago between my mother and me that made me sad, and I guess I wanted to forget about her. For a while at least. I wanted to be away from her."

"You want to be away from your mother and I want to find mine. It's funny, isn't it?"

"Perhaps. Perhaps it's funny."

"Is that why you didn't make a shawl for your mother? Only for your grandmother? I mean because you wanted to forget your mother."

"Yes, I suppose that's why."

"Did it work? Did you forget about her?"

"In a way, yes."

"I don't think I could ever forget about my mother."

"I know."

"Do you think your mother has forgotten about you?"

"No. I don't think she has."

"I don't think so either. Not your mother about you nor mine about me. I don't think mothers forget much of anything."

"No. I guess not."

"So what will you do?"

"About what?"

"About your mother."

"Nothing. For now, nothing."

"Well, if sometime you'd like to talk about her — or about anything that's troubling you — I —"

"I shall remember that. And I offer the same to you. You know that, don't you? That if ever, whenever you'd like to talk about *your* mother —"

"But I don't know the words for some things. For some feelings."

"You don't have to know all the words. Maybe if you begin I can help you to find more of them. The words, I mean."

"Okay. So are you less sad now than you were before?"

"Yes. Less sad. Not sad in the same way."

"But still sad?"

"Yes."

"Is everyone in the whole world sad about something?"

"Go get your red boots now. And your hat."

"And my purse."

Letting go of Solange's hand and leaning backward to better view the Belle Epoque vault of the train station ceiling, Amandine, hands covering her ears against the screech of the stationmaster's announcements, slowly turns herself in a full circle.

"How far can you go on a train?" she asks Solange as the two stand still among the throngs.

"Very far, if one wishes. Not on a single train but on a series of them. One can go almost anywhere on a train, one destination at a time."

"Almost anywhere?"

"Yes. But not over the seas. Not over water. Not usually. One needs to take a ship for that. Or fly in an airplane."

"Train stations are my first favorite places."

153

"How quickly you've decided that. I think you might wait until you've seen a bit more of the world before —"

"I don't need to wait. I already know. And when I'm big, *bigger,* I shall ride trains everywhere."

"May I ride with you?"

"Of course."

"Where shall we go?"

"To find my mother."

"Yes, yes, of course, someday . . ."

"Where do the people get on the trains?" Amandine wants to know.

"Some of the tracks are along that wall. See the numbers above the doorways? Now look up there at the lighted board. The same numbers appear there. Do you see them?"

"Yes."

"And next to each number is a departure time, the number of a train, and its destination. The place where it's going. Look. From track number three at fourteen-forty, a train will depart for Paris."

"Track three at fourteen-forty, number 1022 to Paris."

"Perfect. That's how to read the departure board. There is the same kind of board for the trains that are arriving. The ones that are coming here from somewhere else. Here, on this side. So if we look here we can see that, let's see, what time is it right now? Ah, in seven minutes, at fourteen-ten, on track eleven, train number 3542 will arrive from Marseille."

Amandine studies first one board, then the other. Looks at Solange. Back at the boards.

"Track six at fifteen-oh-five, train number 1129 in departure for Lyon. Where is Lyon? Can we go there today?"

"Too far for today. Now come with me to deliver the package to that desk over there and —"

"And then may we go outside to see the trains?"

"Well, I guess . . . Yes, yes, we can. If we hurry we can meet the train from Marseille, don't you think? Look again at the arrival board, and then you lead the way."

"Track eleven, let's go."

As though they were indeed meeting someone, the two hurry out to the platform to stand among the small, noisy congregations who wait. Amandine moves closer to Solange, holds her hand more tightly, wiggles the other hand to move the satin rope of the midnight blue pouch farther up upon her wrist. She looks up at Solange. "Isn't it wonderful here?"

"Sssh, here it comes. You can't see it yet,

155

but you can hear it. Listen. Close your eyes and listen."

Amandine nestles her head against Solange. "It sounds like it's rushing to get to us. As though it can't wait to see us. Doesn't it sound like that to you?"

"I suppose it does. Yes, you're right, just as though —"

Amandine laughs and squeals as the snorting, spewing beast lunges into the station.

Solange shouts above the noise, "Listen now. The stationmaster will announce it —"

"Arriving from Marseille on track eleven. Track eleven arriving from Marseille."

Amandine watches as the passengers, smiling and waving, descend the metal steps from the car. She pays special attention to the women.

"May we stay to see more trains? I want to stay here until —"

"Let's go back to look at the board and see when the next one is due."

"The next and then the next and —"

"All right, two more. And then we're off to tea. Aren't you getting hungry?"

Two more. And then another until, against the leaving light on platform number six, the midnight blue pouch swinging from her wrist, her hat askew, Amandine looks up at

Solange. "I like it here."

"I do, too."

"I like the smell. It burns my nose, but I like it. I like the way the air tastes. It's like the spoon when I lick away the pudding."

"It's true, the air tastes like metal."

"I could stay here forever until her train comes. The one from . . . I wish I knew from where. Maybe it will be the next one. That's the best thing about trains. The train you're waiting for might be the next one."

"I think the sixteen-oh-three is right on time. Can you hear it?"

"Yes, I think I can. It's scary every time, but I like it, all the noise like a million horses galloping and smoke thick as fog on the creek and the sparks like the ones from the horseman's spurs in the story Philippe told me. Now the stationmaster will say it. Get ready . . ."

In perfect time with the stationmaster, Amandine and Solange scream at the top of their voices,

"Arriving from Carcassonne on track six. Track six arriving from Carcassonne."

One Sunday morning months later, when Solange is arranging the sheets on Amandine's chintz-draped bed, she picks up one of the pillows, holds it to the light, says,

157

"What is this?"

She peers more closely at what seems like a drawing of sorts on the pillow slip.

"Amandine, have you by any chance been drawing on your pillows? This one is smudged with something like —"

"It's charcoal. We use charcoal in our drawing classes. We're supposed to draw trees or flowers, but sometimes I draw faces."

"I see. But I don't think it's good to practice on the bed linens."

"I wasn't practicing. It's a drawing of my mother. Of her face. Look, if you hold it like this you can see —"

"Yes, yes, I do see. But why did you draw her on the pillow? Why not on —"

"I do it all the time at school, and Sister Geneviève never seems to mind. When she changes the linens, I just draw my mother another time on the clean one. I told Sister Geneviève it helps me to sleep. To have her near me. I knew you would scold me, and so I never did it here. But last night I couldn't sleep and I thought that if I drew her . . ."

"I understand. We'll just leave it be then. Leave it like this for next week. Okay?"

"Okay."

"But you know that if you can't sleep or if

your dreams are . . . You know you can come to sleep in my bed or call me to come sleep with you. You know that, don't you?"

"Yes. But when those things happen to me in the dormitory and you're not there . . . And besides, I'm seven now. I have to learn to be alone."

"Do you know how much I miss you, Amandine?"

"You have to learn to be alone, too."

The words sting, and Solange stands quietly looking at Amandine, who has turned away, gone to stand by the window.

"How would you like me to tell you a secret?" Solange asks.

"A secret about what?"

Solange goes to the sofa, sits down. "Come here and sit next to me. Closer." With Amandine's back nestled to her breast, her arms encircling her, Solange says, "Do you remember when I told you about the lady who came to see my grandmother? The one who came to talk about you?"

"The one with eyes like a deer?"

"Yes. She. Well, she left something for you in my care, Amandine. I am to save it for you until you're older. I'm to guard it as I would guard you, Grand-mère told me."

"What is it? Where is it?"

"I don't know what it is. I've never opened

159

the package. It's hidden away in my things. I'll show you the package if you want, but you mustn't open it. It will be for you to open when the time comes. I have written your name on a little card and attached it to the package. Otherwise it's just as it was when the lady left it."

"Oh yes, I would like to see the package."

Solange rises, goes to the armoire, opens one of the three narrow, long drawers where she keeps her underclothing. Riffling without looking, she pulls out a brown-paper-wrapped parcel tied with white string.

"Here it is. You may hold it, but don't shake it or be rough with it. Promise?"

"Promise."

As though it is a just-born baby, Amandine takes the package tenderly in her hands, looks down at it. "Did it really come from that lady?"

"It really did. And the reason why I'm telling you all this today, why I want you to know about this gift, is so that you will feel less alone. You see, this is a kind of symbol of the love your mother has for you."

"What's a symbol?"

"A symbol is a sign. An evidence of a sentiment. Of a feeling. In this case, whatever is in this package is a symbol of your mother's love. It hardly matters what the symbol is . . . It might be something old, something that was precious to her, something that was hers when she was a child, I don't know. But what does matter is that she wanted you to have it. Whatever is in this package represents the connection between you and her."

"The connection?"

"Yes. The truth that you are part of one another."

"Really part of one another?"

"Really. Whether she's here or not, what she looks like . . . all those things you, you *don't* know can never, ever change that single important fact. That she is your mother and you are her daughter."

"That's two facts."

"You're right. Two facts. Hold those truths tight to you, and I think you'll be less lonely."

"When can I open this?"

"My *grand-mère* said that the lady told her I should give it to you on your thirteenth birthday."

"Thirteen? And I'm only seven now. I'll be so old by the time I'm thirteen."

"I think not, darling girl. I think you'll be younger by then. Far younger than you are now."

"Is that how numbers really work? I mean,

do we get more little as the numbers get higher?"

"If we're lucky."

"Oh."

"Now I think it's time we went out to walk, so go get your —"

"Red boots. I know."

Chapter XVIII

Each Wednesday during recreation time the students are permitted a walk to the village, where the younger girls visit the *chocolatier,* the older ones the Monoprix for hairpins or tampons or violet water. One Wednesday, Amandine — who most often does not join in the outing — wanders off on her own, enters the newsstand, wishes the newsagent a good afternoon, looks about uncertainly.

"May I help you, mademoiselle?"

"Yes sir. I would like to see the film-star magazines."

"Ah, right here. Any particular one in mind?"

"No sir. May I just look a bit?"

"*Bien sûr, mademoiselle.* You'll let me know if I can be of assistance?"

She looks first at the covers, then selects one, leafs through it slowly. Nothing. She takes another one. Half an hour passes, and she has looked through all of them. The newsagent is working nearby, counting magazines and newspapers, cutting the string on bundles of new arrivals, arranging the shelves to accommodate them. He hums, and Amandine sways gently to his music. They are comfortable in one another's company. As he pulls his small knife upward on the string from a newspaper-wrapped bundle of magazines, Amandine tells him, "That's the one. That one, sir, may I please see it?"

On the cover of the one Amandine asks to see is a close-up photo of the actress Hedy Lamarr.

"Ah, Mademoiselle has excellent taste. *The most beautiful woman in films.* That's what she's called, you know."

Amandine smiles, shakes her head no. Takes the magazine from the newsagent, crouches down on the floor, and stares at the cover. She peruses the pages, looks back at the cover, back at the pages. Back at the cover. Amandine is crying. Slowly, she rips the cover from the rest of the pages, carries the severed cover to the counter, where the newsagent is serving other customers. When it is her turn, she says, "I don't think I have enough money to buy the whole magazine, and so I'll just take the cover. If that's all right."

She is searching the depths of her midnight blue pouch, picking out coins, laying them one at a time on the counter in front of the newsagent and, in between, running the back of her hand across her tears. He begins to explain that one doesn't buy only a magazine cover but quickly enters into Amandine's mode of reasoning.

"Well, for just the cover, it will be forty sous. More than enough here."

He hands back two of the coins to her. Pulls a handkerchief from his pocket, offers it to her, but she shakes her head. One more wipe with the back of her hand as she smiles her triumph smile at the newsagent.

"Will that be all?"

"Oh yes. All."

"Here, I'll just wrap that for you."

He carefully rolls a half sheet of newspaper around the cover, tucks in the ends, all the while looking at Amandine. He hands it to her.

"Thank you, sir. She's my mother."

"For your mother. I see. Well, I hope she'll —"

"No sir. It *is* my mother. The lady in the photo is my mother."

Back in the dormitory, Amandine asks Sister Geneviève for two pins. She tells her the reason and, that evening after prayers, Geneviève comes to Amandine's bed with a pincushion. Together they mount the Hedy Lamarr cover above Amandine's bed. They stand back to admire their handiwork, and some of the nearby girls come to look at it, too.

"It's my mother. Isn't she beautiful?"

Two of the littler girls gasp in admiration, but one of the elder ones begins to laugh. Calls to her mates to come see the photo of Amandine's "mother." Soon all the girls clamor about the bed, pointing at the photo, arranging themselves in divalike poses, pouting their lips, googling their eyes, laughing and screaming at the good joke. Still laughing, one picks up Amandine under her arms, swings her about, shouts, "You don't have a mother, and if you did she'd never look like that. She'd be short like an elf and have hair like a wild man —"

"And big, sad eyes —"

"And she'd walk like this —"

"And talk like this —"

In a circle now around her, they taunt. Over Geneviève's warnings, her hands clapping, her feet stamping, they chant a long, sniggering song, each one taking a turn to sharply pat her on the back of her head, the nape of her neck until Amandine, barefoot in her white flannel nightdress, pushes through their line, leaps onto her bed, tears the photo from the wall, runs to the door, into the hall, down the stairs.

Out into the courtyard, down the loggia, her feet barely touching down on the frozen stone of the pavement, she holds the photo to her chest, her breath coming roughly, a strange pain piercing her arms and shoulders. Anger must be worse than running is for my heart. Surely anger is worse. Better that I run away. I know it's better that I run. She slows only when she mounts the convent stairs to the sisters' cells. To her rooms. To Solange.

"What? What are you doing? Get in here, bare feet, you're all flushed and sweating —"

Solange takes Amandine in her arms, pulls a blanket from the bed, wraps it around Amandine, sits down then on the sofa before the fire and rocks her, kisses her forehead, her cheeks, rubs her icy feet until they're pink again. "Sssssh. First stop crying and understand that you're safe now. And when you're ready, you can tell me everything. Here then, what's this?"

She takes the magazine cover still clutched in Amandine's left hand.

"It's my mother. They don't believe it's

my mother and they —"

"I understand. It's okay."

Solange places the cover on the table near the sofa, looks at Amandine. "Why do you think that she is your mother?"

"Because I went to the newsstand and I looked at all the magazines and I couldn't find her in any of them, but then when I saw this photo, I began to cry. I didn't cry when I saw any of the others. Only when I saw this one. So it must be her. It must be her, Solange."

"I see."

Solange holds Amandine to her once again, and both stay quiet.

"You don't believe me either, do you?" Amandine says without raising her head from Solange's breast. "You don't believe that she's my mother."

"No. I don't believe she is. And neither do you. Your inventions, I, I should have tried to stop them long ago, but I believed them *innocent*. I knew that *you* knew they were inventions. That you'd understood the difference between make-believe and, and what's *real*. It's perfectly fine to invent and imagine, but you must come back from those thoughts. You must come back, Amandine, come back from your daydreaming and your night dreaming. You must leave the door open —"

"Leave what door open? The door to where? I make believe because there is nothing real. Nothing real that I want."

"Not to be with me?"

"Not in the way we used to be. That wasn't real either. That was also make-believe."

"That's not true. The way we used to be was *real*. The way we are right now is *real*. The way we'll always be together is *real*. *I am so sorry that I am not her, but I am me.* I'm real, and I love you."

As though she hasn't heard Solange, Amandine says, "Will you please get me some writing paper? Pretty paper with flowers in the corners. Violets or roses. Violets. And envelopes, too."

"Yes. Violets. Of course, I'll get some tomorrow."

"I have to go back now."

"No you don't. I'll go to tell Paul what has happened, though I'm certain that Geneviève has told her already. Let's get you into your bed now and . . ."

But Amandine is taking her raincoat from the armoire, slipping it on, rummaging through the shoe chest for her boots.

"I know the way back. I'm not afraid. Not of the dark or of them."

She opens the door, and Solange does nothing to stop her. She walks out, closes the door. Opens it again.

"I love you, too."

Cher Maman,
You don't know me. I mean we haven't met. Actually we did meet, but it was when I was very little and I think you were very little, too. I just thought that you might be missing me, wanting to know about me. I didn't want you to worry, and so I thought I would write to you to tell you that I'm fine. I'm well. My name is Amandine. I'm your daughter.

I'm almost eight, and I have dark hair, curly and long and mostly all the time woven into plaits by Sister Geneviève. Solange used to make my plaits when I was little, but now that I live in the dormitory, Sister Geneviève does. Solange is like a big sister and an aunt and a teacher, but mostly she is my best friend. After you and Jesus, I love Solange best. And Philippe, too. I shall tell you of Philippe when I see you. His grandmother had blue hair.

I can never quite tell the color of my eyes, which seems to change. It's something like gray but very dark and almost blue, like the sky looks at night. But not

170

exactly. Solange says they're the color of the inside of an iris, the color deep inside. But not exactly that, either. I'm not big and I'm not small for eight. Well, maybe I am a bit small.

I can read with the sixth elementary students and know my multiplication tables, and I love to write stories and read about princesses and saints but mostly about princesses. I love to listen to Solange when she tells me stories. She says they're the same stories that her mother told her. She has a mother, too. And a father and a grandmother and sisters. I think she has eighteen cousins. Do you have cousins? I mean, if you have cousins, then they are my cousins, too. Would you tell me someday about my cousins? I imagine that their names are Susie and Jeannette and Christine and Diane. I don't know too many boys' names, so I only think about girl cousins. Do I have a grandmother? I hope she's well, not growing too old before I can get to her to tell her how much I love her. Tell her please that I say prayers for her and that I will come to help her when she's old. Tell her not to worry because as soon as I find her, I won't ever leave her again. Actually, I don't know why I went away. I can't remember. Can you remember, Maman?

Maman, what's your name? In my mind, I sometimes call you Sophie, though I don't know why. Sophie. Sophie. I whisper it. It sounds like a whisper, don't you think? I feel sad that I don't know your name, but it must be a beautiful name, and you must be beautiful, too. I know you are and I know that you're good and sweet and I think you love flowers and the wind when the sun shines, yes, a cold wind under a hot sun is the best, especially a wind that makes you lose your breath and you have to walk backward with your arms outstretched and just let it carry you wherever it will. I always think that if I like something, you must like it, too. When I like something very much, I want you to see it or hear it or touch it. I want to know if it pleases you. Do you like raspberries? I've only tasted raspberries a few times, but I think there must be nothing better. Not even peas with lettuce, which I also like. And red is my favorite color. Do you wear your hair in plaits? Do you look like Hedy Lamarr? That's how you look in my dreams, exactly like Hedy Lamarr, only your name is Sophie. Do you think that I will look like you when I'm big? Will I look like Hedy Lamarr, too? I don't look much like her now, but I wonder.

Jean-Baptiste is the doctor who takes care of us. He says I'm strong as an ox, but even so he comes to check my heart on the first Friday of the month, places a cold metal cup on my chest and looks into my eyes while he listens through tubes in his ears that are attached to the metal cup. He always smiles then and shakes his head and tells me I'm a walking miracle, though I don't really know why. And then he reaches into his big leather bag and pulls out a bar of *chocolat,* says it's all the medicine I need. He always reminds me, though, not to run too fast, to climb the stairs slowly, to tell Mater Paul or Solange if I have a sore throat. But I never do. I mean I never, almost never have a sore throat. Do you get sore throats, Maman?

I can't remember all the things I wanted to tell you, and so I'll write to you again tomorrow. But I did want you to know that Sister Suzette is teaching me to play the piano. Actually, she has been giving me lessons since I was three, but now I can reach the pedals much better and I'm play-ing "Für Elise" all the way through without any errors. But something is troubling me. Since I don't know your name and I don't know where you live, I don't know how to get my letter to you. I think I'll leave my letter in the chapel, under the vase in front of Our Lady. She'll know what to do. She's a mother, too. I'm sure she'll get the letter to you. Really what I wanted to do is to tell you not to worry. I'm not lost, and I hope that you're not lost, either. I'm right here waiting for you.

Your

Amandine

Filling page after page of the notepaper with the violets in her achingly precise convent girl's calligraphy, Amandine sits cross-legged on a stone bench in the loggia during recreation, her schoolmates' jubilance unnoticed. She folds the thick packet of pages and urges them somewhat distortedly into an envelope. She licks the seal, presses down hard on it with both palms, tries to straighten the lopsided results by sitting on the envelope for a bit. The address is uncomplicated: *Pour Maman.* Having asked permission of Sister Geneviève to say a prayer in the chapel, she goes directly there.

Amandine has never before been alone in the chapel, has never thought it so grand as it seems now, painted in the thin yellow light of a February afternoon. She genuflects, blesses herself with water from the stoup, walks slowly, assuredly to the statue of *la Vierge*. She curtsies, smiles up at her. *"Bonjour, Notre Dame."*

Quickly she tries to slide the letter under the feet of the Virgin but finds it much too thick. Running her hand along the rough pedestal, she wonders if it might be just as good to leave it *beside* the Virgin's feet. No, it must be hidden. She steps up then upon the base of the pedestal, cantilevers her knees on either side of it, reaches up and takes hold of the Virgin by her stone-draped calves, tries to tip the statue backward, all the while, the letter held between her teeth. Won't budge. Stepping down, she stumbles, hits her chin on the tessellated marbles of the floor. The letter has suffered more than she, ornamented now as it is with tiny teeth marks and drips of saliva. She stands up straight, steps back a bit from the statue.

"Notre Dame, will you please see that my mother gets this letter? I would be so grateful to you. I'll just put it right there behind you so no one will see it. Please don't forget. She's been waiting for ages to hear from me. Probably a lot like it was for you when Jesus went wandering. I must go now. I'll come to say hello at vespers."

She curtsies, walks to the back of the statue, reaches up, places the letter. Gives a small caress to the back of *la Vierge*'s legs. Walks down the aisle and out into the loggia.

Each day she finds some excuse to enter the chapel, to walk to the statue, to check upon the status of her letter. It's always just where she left it. On the fourth day, when Sister Jacqueline is dusting the chapel, she finds the letter, thinks it can be no one's work but Amandine's, places it in her apron pocket to give to Solange.

Once she is alone in her rooms that evening, Solange carefully opens the letter, reads it. Reads it again. She goes to the armoire to take the brown-paper-wrapped package, unties the string, places the letter over it, reties the string to enclose it. Puts it away. She pours herself a glass of wine, thinks again for the thousandth time how right Philippe was when he said that Amandine was older than all of them. She sits down at the desk, riffles the drawers for paper, takes up her pen. For the first time in the eight years since she has left Avise, she writes a letter to her mother. Not to Janka nor to her sisters with a salutation for her mother but *to* her mother. *Cher Maman.*

On the fifth day when Amandine goes to *la Vierge* to see about her letter, it is gone. She comes round to the front of the statue, curtsies.

"Thank you again, *Notre Dame.* I was beginning to, you know, to wonder whether you had time to do things like deliver the post but well now I feel very happy-and-next-time-when-my-mother-sends-me-her-address-I-can-just-use-the-postbox-in-the-village-and-I-won't-have-to-trouble-you-I-have-to-run-see-you-tomorrow-you're-lucky-to-be-up-in-heaven-now-and-that-Jesus-is-always-with-you-so-you-don't-have-to-worry-about-him-by-the-way-I-keep-forgetting-to-ask-you-if-you've-met-Père-Phillippe-he'd-be-with-his-grandmother-who-has-blue-hair-at-least-she-used-to. *À demain, Notre Dame.*"

CHAPTER XIX

"Do you wish that I pity her?"

"Pity, no. Compassion, I would have thought. She is not the lisping refugee you would have the others think her to be but a little girl whose *predicament* has forced her to behave like a woman."

"Many of us do without the luxury of a childhood."

A week has passed since the evening Amandine escaped the dormitory and the convent girls' torment. Solange has arranged to place herself among the convent sisters assigned to cleaning duties in the school. An assignment that Paul has specifically, repeatedly denied her. Dispensing with yet another request, Solange simply inserts herself on the roster. The convent girls' contempt for Amandine shocks her. It is not Amandine who *prefers* emotional seclusion, as she had believed. After only a few moments, the stones fall into another pattern for Solange. It is they, the convent girls — with tacit endorsement from Paul and many of the teaching sisters — who rebuff her, recoil from her. Make her disappear.

Having thrown open the door to Paul's office, Solange can barely speak up from her fury. Her whisper is choked, breathless. "Do you persecute her so blithely, Mater?"

"Is that what you would call it? Persecution? How quaint."

"What would you call it, Mater? Would you have me believe you are not aware that you and the students injure her?"

"*Life has injured her.* I have only chosen not to be part of her, her — what is it that you and all the others run about trying to do? — to *deliver* her. Yes, that's it, I have chosen not to be part of her *deliverance.* All of you primping up the truth, trying to make her the heroine of a fable with a tulle dress and that absurd little purse she totes about on her wrist —"

"Oh, but she is a heroine, Mater. She has faced monsters and demons, and she has survived them. Brave beyond any one of us, she has fought the trolls and swum the swallowing seas and still she smiles and curtsies. Trembles. How can you not care for her?"

"I care for no one."

She turns her gaze from Solange, casts her

eyes down, moves the fingers of one hand round and round across the palm of the other. Without looking at Solange, she says, "Interesting now that I think of it. It's true. I care for no one. I perform my duties. It's better than caring."

Paul rises, walks to the window behind her desk, leans her forehead against the pane. "Leave me to my indifference and her to her *predicament.* As I told you long ago, it's her birthright."

"If only it were *indifference* you show her. The truth is that you work against her. Take away the pitfalls, Mater. An open field on which to make her way. That's all I ask of you."

Paul turns from the window, once again faces Solange. "I fear you ask too much."

Solange runs up the stairs to her rooms, opens the door so that it bangs against the inside wall, leaves it flung. She goes to the desk, takes a sheet from what remains in the box of the paper with the violets in the corners. She sits, fills her pen.

Your Eminence,
An urgent need for your counsel regarding the health and welfare of Amandine inspires me to ask an audience with you.

For reasons of privacy, I beg this meeting to be scheduled at the curia.

Your devoted Solange

CHAPTER XX

She seals the note, asks Marie-Albert to invent needs so she may go to post it in the village. Six spools of number 12 black thread, four meters of flannel for patching sheets. Elastic stockings for Paul. Done with her commissions, she walks to the park, sits down on the bench where she and Amandine had sat to watch the children play. She pulls the letter to the bishop from her bag, turns it over, gazes for a long time at her own finely penned script on the envelope. She places it back in the bag, asking herself if she shall or shall not send it. She tilts back her head, closes her eyes, lets a rogue breeze play about her face, her neck. She can feel that one of her plaits has come undone, pulls the elastic from the ends of it, puts it in her pocket, tries to push the loosed blond curls under her kerchief, and stays in this half sleep until the bells of St.-Odile strike six. She fairly runs then to the letter drop, crosses herself, lifts the lid, and pushes the note into the slot.

"Amen."

As Solange hurries through the village on her way back to the convent, the reflection of a woman in a shop window catches her eye. Who can it be who follows close as a shadow behind me? Dark rings under sad eyes, deep creases around the mouth, thick waist, matronly bosom, dowdy dress, cumbrous old boots, both plaits loosening now under her kerchief. She turns away, shuts her eyes and, in a graceless blind run, escapes the shadow, the preposterous image. Breathless then, her face wet with tears and sweat, she slows her pace. Approaching the next set of shop windows, she keeps her eyes forward until, at the last — barely turning her head — she dares to look. Despising, taunting, the same woman looks back at her. Weeping aloud now and mindless of the choking heat, the lace on one of her boots undone and slapping hard against her leg, she runs up the chalk white road to the convent, heaves her parcels in the vestibule of the chapel, slips sideways through the half-opened door, blesses herself, genuflects, hurries to her pew, falls heavily upon the wooden kneeler. *Domine, ad adjuvandum me festina.* Vespers have begun. As one, the

183

sorority turns to look at her. *God, make haste to help me,* she prays with them. And as they proceed in the liturgy, their voices soaring in plainsong, Solange whispers the same phrase again and again, her body swaying, barely swaying. *God, make haste to help me.*

As vespers finish, Sisters Josephine and Marie-Albert, whose places are on either side of Solange in the pew, bend toward her, whisper concern.

"Solange, how pallid you are."

"Have you fever, Solange? What is it?"

As the pews empty and the sisters walk in double file from the chapel toward the refectory, Solange breathes deeply, smoothes her dress, smiles at Josephine and Marie-Albert. "I'm fine. It was only that I was late coming back from the village. I ran up the hill. Just a bit tired, that's all."

Josephine pleads, "Why don't you go to your rooms and I'll explain to Paul, tell her that you're not well. I'll send supper to you. I'll prepare the tray myself —"

"No, no. It's better that I go in. I'm well enough now. Besides, I haven't seen Amandine at all today, and I'd like to greet her for a moment."

"At least go to wash your face, fix your

hair. Better to be late than . . . ," says Marie-Albert.

Solange tucks her hair farther under her kerchief, touches her face with one hand. "And suffer Paul's wrath for tardiness at table?"

The three laugh quietly, fold their hands, and join in the exit. They do not notice Paul, who stands to the side of the altar in silent observance.

When everyone is seated in the refectory, it's Paul rather than one of the sisters who stands to say grace. As she finishes the prayer, she does not sit, does not wish the sorority and the convent girls a smiling *bon appétit, mes petites,* as is the custom after grace. Rather, her arms crossed and tucked inside her sleeves, she remains quiet, looks about the handsome room warm with the steamy perfumes of a good supper.

"Disorder of the mind and disorder of the body are invitations to the devil. Do we all agree?"

"Oui, Mater Paul" rings out the collective response.

"Therefore you will also agree with me that Soeur Solange, rather than having prepared herself to sit at our sacred table, has seen fit, this evening, to invite the devil to join us."

The sisters sit quietly while the convent girls crane their necks to see Solange, whisper. A few laugh. Mortified, flushed, shaking, Solange, trying once again to push strands of hair under her kerchief, rises, asks, "Mater, I beg your pardon for my appearance, but you see —"

"Silence. I shall give no pardon to your transgression of modesty nor, I'm certain, shall any of your sorority nor our dear young ladies. You are not worthy to sit among us. Please leave us now and go to humble yourself before our Lord."

Solange, still standing, bows her head, then moves slowly, awkwardly among the tables until she reaches the clear area near the doorway. She turns to look at Paul who stands watching her progress. She opens her mouth as though to speak, then turns away, rushes from the room.

"And now, *mes petites, bon appétit!*"

The sisters are stunned, picking up their knives and forks as though they are foreign instruments, putting them down again. Fidgeting.

"Mater, may I please have permission to speak?"

It is Amandine who asks. A small, sober soldier standing erect at her place, hands at her sides, her tiny pointed chin tilted upward, she awaits response. The room is hushed as a tomb.

Clearing her throat, clearing it once again before she answers, Paul asks, "What have you to say?"

"I think that you are cruel, Mater Paul."

Paul chuckles as though to discount what the child says. "So you think that what I did was cruel? Is that —"

"No, Mater. I said that *you are cruel.* Everyone knows that Solange is good. Even you know that Solange is good. And everyone knows that you are not."

Her voice has grown stronger, more shrill with each word.

The silence of the others bursts into gasps, into shouts. Paul, on her feet now, her face red as meat, bends to pound her fist on the table.

In a voice half strangled, Paul begs, "Silence. Silence. Silence."

Still rooted to her place and as though she has not heard the din, Amandine is tranquil, prepared for the next parry.

"I have never in the thirty years of the life of this convent school felt the necessity to impose punishment upon either a sister or a student in this refectory. This evening I have been first forced to do one, and now, now I am forced to do the other."

187

Paul turns her back to the room, walks a few meters to a tall, dark wood armoire, its massive doors incised with intricate scrollwork. The consensus around her is that she is searching for some sort of strap or paddle or birch with which to inflict penalty upon Amandine. Rather, when she turns, she is holding what looks like a bowl. Small and made of pewter, it has a long, thin handle. She walks to where Amandine stands, picks up one of her hands, places the bowl in it.

"And now we shall soften your insolence. Your punishment is this: You shall go to each and every one of us here in this room and beg for your food. It shall be the right of each to refuse you. Or to grant you. To each you will curtsy, say, 'Though I am unworthy to eat the food our Lord has granted, I beg you to feed me.' Say it. That's right, 'I beg you to feed me.' Louder. Good. Begin."

Amandine walks to the farthest point in the room, where the older convent girls sit, begins her task. The first girl shakes her head, no. Amandine goes to the next. No. The next. No. When she has asked five girls and received five refusals, Paul says in a hoarse, harsh whisper, "And so, *mes petites,* do we begin to understand which one among us is *cruel?*"

With expectations of neither rescue nor

188

sympathy, Amandine continues her penitent's walk. Before she can finish her question at the seventh girl's place, the girl puts a small bread roll shaped like a rose into the pewter bowl. The next girl does the same. And the next. When Amandine approaches another table, Sidò, with the blue glasses and the red medicine on her nails, places both her biscuits in the bowl. The same Sidò goes to a sideboard, takes down a large wooden tray, comes back to Amandine, says, "I'll walk behind you with this. That bowl is too small. Okay?"

"Okay."

And the two proceed. Now, though, the girls don't wait for Amandine to arrive at their places but go to her with their bread, with pots of sweet white butter, small Banon goat cheeses, each wrapped in a chestnut leaf. They touch her. On the shoulder, the arm. Kiss her cheek. One of the littler girls embraces her. Another carries a great bunch of green grapes and two brown pears pulled from the centerpiece of Paul's table, lays them on the tray. Three, four convent girls are on their feet, collecting, table by table, every portable comestible, carrying them to Amandine, filling a second tray. A third. In all this time, not one of the sisters, not Paul, no one has interfered with the convent girls' enterprise of feeding Amandine. When the eldest girl in the school, a beauty called Mathilde — in a final demonstration of solidarity — walks to the high, wide dresser where the evening's desserts await, the convent girls applaud. A clafoutis of small yellow plums and a silver bowl of thick cream she places on a fourth tray, lifts it with one hand high above her shoulder, and — the applause greater now — leads the way for the other girls. The way to Paul. Complicit as a well-rehearsed troupe, they know what they will do with the food. Amandine places the pewter bowl before Paul. One by one, so do the other girls place their trays before Paul, then touch Amandine in some affectionate way and return to their tables. Standing directly in front of Paul, Amandine empties the pewter bowl of all but two rolls, takes a pair of goat cheeses from a tray, a pot of butter, grapes, a pear. Thinks again. Takes another pear.

"For Solange. The extra pear is for the devil. All the rest is for you, Mater."

The convent girls scream with laughter. Over it Paul shouts, "If you think you have endured your just punishment, I warn you to think again."

"What will you do to me, Mater? Place me in *châtiment*? I am not afraid. I have lived in your disgrace for a very long time."

Amandine curtsies to Paul, turns back to face the room, holds one hand waist high, and, like a fan, waves it back and forth to the girls.

From the room a chorus: *"Bonne nuit, Amandine."*

"I brought you supper. Not so much but . . . Is the fire going? Would you like me to stay for a while?"

"What? Why aren't you at table? Mater will have both our heads. Do they know where you've gone?"

In her nightdress and bare feet, Solange stands by the door to their rooms, startled, stuttering while Amandine places the pewter bowl on the table near the hearth, goes to fetch two glasses.

"May I drink water with wine this evening?"

"Amandine, come here and tell me what's happened."

Solange notes some change in Amandine. As though she's older. She goes to her, takes her by the shoulders, looks at her. "Tell me."

"I think it's best that Marie-Albert or Josephine or one of the others tells you. I mean, I can't remember all that happened except that I stood up, asked permission to speak. And —"

"You stood up in the refectory and asked to speak? And what did you say?"

"I was angry. I was angry at Paul for sending you away, and so I said what I thought. I said that she was cruel, and then everyone was talking, you know, kind of surprised talking I think because I said that and then Paul punished me by giving me that bowl and asking me to beg all the girls for my supper. I had to say: 'Though I am unworthy to eat the food our Lord has granted, I beg you to feed me,' and at first no one gave me anything and then Sidò gave me her bread and then everyone was giving me something and soon all the girls were screeching and clapping and Mathilde took a whole clafoutis from the sideboard and then everyone was clapping more loudly and we all brought the food to Paul. I told her she could have it, most of it, except the few things I kept. The stuff in the bowl. I told Paul it was for you, and I'm not afraid of her, Solange. I'm not afraid of her at all and it was kind of easy to say what I thought and she said that I would be punished again and I asked her if she would put me in *châtiment* and I told her that she already had put me in *châtiment* and that I'd been living in *châtiment* for so long now and it was

192

really kind of easy to tell her that and I was thinking of Philippe and of you and of my mother but mostly of you because she was so cruel to you and I don't mind if she's cruel to me because I've grown used to it but when she was cruel to you it made me feel like I wanted to stop her. I wanted to stop her so she couldn't do to you what she does to me. I just wanted her to stop and so it was easy after I began and I'm not afraid of the girls either. Not anymore. They touched me like this. On my arm. You know like a pat. Not like a slap. And Celine, do you know Celine? she's the only girl more little than I am and she reached up and kissed my cheek I think she might need my help being so small and —"

"Yes, Celine might very well need your help."

Solange smiles, lifts Amandine in her arms, begins to laugh then, laugh and laugh, and Amandine begins to laugh, too, and they dance about the room, twirling and laughing and screeching, both of them undoing Amandine's braids and shaking their unshackled hair until they fall onto the sofa, Amandine exhausted from her evening's passage and its illumination. Solange from the wonder of her. They eat the cheese then, peel the pears, butter the bread. Sip the watered wine.

CHAPTER XXI

For days and days the convent sisters, the teaching sisters talk of nothing else than the refectory scene and, in whispered reprises, they take turns playing the role of Paul, the role of Amandine. Being wise, Paul deals with its aftermath by ignoring it. Her rage she contains in cordiality. Only to old Josette, the lay sister whose labors shift from scrubbing and polishing to a kind of lady-in-waiting to Paul, only to Josette does she speak her mind. Tells her she wishes *the lot of them to burn in hell.*

And as she has always, Paul avoids the *displeasure* of the *jeunes filles de la noblesse.* Should Paul dare to waver — their lashes fluttering, eyes dancing — they would remind her to beware Mummy and Daddy. No, not even the *scent* of reprimand shall she press upon the dear little chits. Her composure elaborately contrived, Paul keeps to her office or stays longer at her turns in the garden, walks far less often among the classes, only rarely addresses any one of the convent girls. And when the whirring of her stork wings *is* to be heard in the halls, doors close, shoulders turn inward, away from her. As though *she* is invisible. Neither seeking nor avoiding her, and — neither ironically nor affectionately — it is only Amandine among the girls who does not veer from her habitual *politesse*. Amandine's wisdom, quixotic rather than self-preserving like Paul's, she, too, deals with the aftermath of the refectory scene by ignoring it. Amandine's generosity Paul perceives as parody, and every display of it pushes her toward frenzy.

In her linen shift, Paul sits on the hard, straight-back chair in her cell one evening, bending to untie her shoes. Only a small bedside lamp lights the room. Josette's signature four-tap knock interrupts her reverie.

"*Entrez, Josette.*"

"*Bonsoir, Mater.* Will you be needing something before I — ?"

"Nothing. Nothing at all. Will you sit for a while?"

She extends her hand toward the bench under the window, but Josette bends to finish the job of removing Paul's shoes, carries them to the armoire, takes out a brush and begins to clean them, stuffs them then with tissue paper, places them on the bottom shelf of the armoire. Proprietary as a mother, Josette takes Paul's nightdress from a hook, sets about removing her shift, hands her the nightdress, folds the shift neatly, puts it in an armoire drawer, opens another, takes out black slippers — the leather deeply embossed by the deformities of Paul's feet — places them on the floor before her. She checks to see there is water in the carafe by the bed, turns down the covers, looks at Paul, who has once again sat down upon the chair.

"You needn't carry on with these rituals, Josette. I can well do for myself."

"But I like to do for you, Mater."

"Yes, yes, I know. How long has it been that you've been *doing* for me, Josette? How old are you?"

"I am seventy-eight. And in February, you shall be seventy, Mater."

Josette says this as though their ages can be calculated only in reference to one another. Paul, elbows resting on her knees, fists supporting her chin, turns her head toward Josette, shakes it in wonder. At the numbers? At the audacious passage of time?

Turning from Josette, her gaze fixed beyond the room and the moment, Paul begins to weep.

"You are not well, Mater?"

Turning back to Josette, trying for a smile, "I'm well enough."

"What can I do?"

As though she has not heard Josette, Paul moves her lips, forming words, half pushing them out, half swallowing them. Devastating words. *What devil inhabits her, Josette? What keeps the breath in that child? I wish her dead and gone and never having been. May God forgive me.*

Josette steps closer in to Paul.

"What did you say, Mater? I could barely hear you."

Paul flings her arm, dismissing Josette.

"Bonne nuit, Mater."

Josette curtsies. Having heard every word, she shuffles from the room.

It is a Saturday, and Amandine is walking under the loggia from the school to meet Solange as Paul is walking toward her. Amandine stops to curtsy, and Paul, without a sound or sign, takes her roughly by the shoulders, begins to shake her. Amandine does not defend herself save to shut her eyes, and then, in something like an embrace, Paul is holding her, looking down at her. Amandine does not pull away but keeps Paul's gaze.

"Who are you?" Paul asks her.

Amandine steps away then, straightens her dress, finds Paul's eyes again.

"Who are *you,* Mater?"

As for the convent girls themselves, what impulse compelled them to displace their obeisance — if not to Paul herself to her mode of operation — and to champion the creature who was for so long their communal and preferred victim? Was it hoarded disdain for Paul, a whole apocrypha of grief? Was Candide so commanding, her words — *Everyone knows that Solange is good. And everyone knows that you are not* — so limpid as to tantalize revolt? Was it all of these? Paul wonders. Amandine wonders.

Delicious as it is for Amandine to taste the convent girls' bonhomie, to be cheered, to be touched, it is not this, not this at all that pleases her most. She reasons like this: Since she'd done nothing to earn the hostility of the convent girls in the first place, how can she be certain that hostility will not be shown her again? More, what she said and did in the refectory was not a ploy to extinguish their antipathy but a defense of Solange. So fickle are the convent girls, how can she know what word or action of hers might relight the antipathy? Further, she reasons, Paul is constant. Her hate hurts more, but Amandine can count on it. So who is the greater foe, and how can one tell? And what if one can't? The mystery swims and dives and leaps about in her, and she thinks it might continue to do so for some time. Perhaps forever. No, it is hardly the bonhomie that pleases Amandine most but rather two other spoils of the evening: The first is the thought that she might not be wicked after all and the other, a sentiment more difficult to comprehend and to name, is the beginning of her understanding of her own grit. Yes, no matter what they did or didn't do, she is well. And she will be. Hence, when the convent girls begin to beckon her into one or another social or political sanctum of their intricately drawn castes, Amandine demurs. She says no thank you when invited to smoke Gauloises with Capucine and Antoinette in the woodshed during recreation, to borrow for a whole hour one of Frédérique's special books along with a small black torch for reading under the covers, to observe the initiation rites into the circle of the menstruating girls. To the most distinguished of all the invitations — since it is usually offered only to a few select girls in the seventh form and higher — she does accept. It is to look at Mathilde's breasts. Front and side views. *Mon Dieu.*

There is combat for a place next to her in the refectory and to determine who shall link arms with her when they form a circle to say the beads of an evening. A praline on her pillow, a flower in her pocket, they pinch her cheeks in affection, try to commiserate with her about her mother, ask: "How does it feel, not knowing your own mother?" tell her: "Whoever she is, surely she's even more beautiful than Hedy Lamarr." And to celebrate her eighth birthday, they pool funds to commission from the village *pâtissier* a seven-layer mocha marjolaine, upon which they beg him to write: *"Bon anniversaire, notre jolie mignonne."*

Solange gasps, marvels at the convent girls' immoderate designs to restore Amandine to favor and, all the more, she marvels at Amandine's resistance to them. To herself, she cheers that resistance, the prudence therein.

Chapter XXII

Only six days pass before Solange has a letter in return from her mother. In the first pages, Magda is timid, formal even. But by page three she begins to speak in her real voice, the voice Solange remembers from when she was very little. Before the troubles. Magda says that talk of war is everywhere. "The *boche* will try with us, but I think we're ready. Still we are beginning to think and act like people who wait for war. We were canning peaches, your sisters and I, with Madame Borange and her girls and someone asked what would be the good of all this work only to leave the fruit to be gobbled by the *boche*. Blanchette thought we should poison a batch, arrange the jars extra cunningly somewhere in view and bury the rest. Some people have indeed buried silver and other things they think to be valuable. Just as we did during the Great War. I admit I've packed two old valises with photos even though I know we'll run them out like pigs to slaughter. The *boche*. Even though."

By page five she begins the story of Solange's father. Of his exit from the family nearly three months earlier. She says that he's gone to work in Belgium, a small farming village near the border, that he's taken up with a woman there or at least that's what she's gleaned from the gossip which trickles down from as far away as that. A woman from Charleroi or a village near there, a widow with daughters. "God help her," she writes.

No, he never came near Chloe or Blanchette. But when he'd be gone for weeks during the winter, working as a carpenter's helper up in Châtillon, well, I had suspicions. And one day, the suspicions became flesh. Her name was Margaux.

Having hitched a ride from Châtillon in a lumber truck, she'd come down to the farm looking for him. She was pretty enough, with gorgeous auburn hair all tied up in a pastiche on top of her head, small and well-made, wearing an old tweed jacket and men's trousers and, apart from envy of her hair, all I felt for her was pity as she stood in the kitchen, weeping and ranting about how her own father had warned her that her new boyfriend was *un mauvais, un charlatan.* From the first, your *père* proved him right. He took money, told tales, always vowing to Margaux that he loved her, that he'd never loved anyone before her, least of all his wife. He'd told her to be patient. He'd never mentioned his three daughters. When Margaux's father saw your *père* with another woman in the town, he confronted him. *Père* laughed at him, called his Margaux a whore. The typical condemnation of women thrown about by men like your *père.*

I made tea for Margaux, put bread and cheese on the table, though she never touched either, and then I drove her back to Châtillon. She was only a year older than you, Solange. It was three days later that I went to Reims, to the attorneys. Set the divorce in motion. On the way home, I stopped at the commissariat in the village and filed a restraining order. When your *père* came in from the vineyards that evening, two gendarmes were waiting for him. He never said a word, never tried to reason with me, never that night nor since has he asked me to reconsider. Do I regret that I waited? Yes. Am I lonely? Yes. But less lonely than when he was here.

I've cut my hair, a bob with a long fringe, and now that I no longer have to turn over the money I make selling my cheeses in the market, I've bought new clothes. A gray dress with silver buttons made from old coins and a navy blue one, with small white dots. Chloe doesn't like the navy one but Janka does. Blanchette hasn't said. I think I'll send you the navy one. Would you like that? I'm very thin but well. I'll be forty-two in November.

By the time Magda had filled up pages nine and ten, she'd told Solange more about herself, her sentiments than she had ever before. She asked Solange for forgiveness. Said she would understand if forgiveness could not be honestly granted. Said she hoped Solange would come home, bring Amandine — whom she'd long before begun to think of as a granddaughter.

How I long to hold Amandine in my arms. Surely I think of her as yours. And so I admit that part of my longing for her is so that I may have another chance to be your mother. Can you understand that, Solange? I wonder if other mothers feel that. I've wondered this same thing about Madame Borange with her brood and about my sisters with their children. I've wondered about Janka. Has she ever wished for another chance to be my mother? I wonder about you, too, Solange. Do you long for another chance to be my daughter?

The bishop has, however, not been so prompt in his response to Solange. Two weeks, perhaps nearly three, have passed since she had posted her note to him when Paul sends for her one morning as she is working in the garden. Fearing that Fabrice has informed Paul of her request for a private audience, her hands tremble as she takes the towel wet with lavender water that Sister Josephine holds out for her. She washes her face, smoothes her hair. She thinks of Amandine and smiles to herself, walks quickly to Paul's office.

"His Eminence has sent a note requesting a meeting with you at four o'clock this afternoon. In Père Philippe's parlor no less. I trust you'll see that the room is in order, that there are flowers."

"Yes, Mater."

"I've ordered *les calissons* from the village."

"Yes, of course. Though he'll likely bring his own."

Paul looks up at her with a frank, confiding smile, begins to say, "No doubt of —"

She checks her candor, is flustered by it, as is Solange. The silence is long then. Paul does some business with the papers on her desk while Solange pats her perfect plaits, bites her lips, forces them into a smile and then a purse and back again.

Failing at nonchalance, Paul openly waits for Solange to tell her more. Rather, Solange asks, "Is that all, Mater?"

"What do you suppose is the object of his desire to meet with you?"

"I don't know, Mater. Surely something to do with Amandine."

"It seems that everything in this house has to do with Amandine. I shall, of course, be available should he wish me to join the two of you."

"Of course, Mater."

"Plaits *and* a kerchief."

"Yes, Mater."

Not long past four, Fabrice arrives at the convent in much the same unceremonious manner that he did on the evening Philippe died. In his country priest's soutane and a black cap, he alights inelegantly from the

official limousine, the green of his Wellingtons thrusting out like the short, thick stems
of succulents from under his skirts. Reminding the chauffeur to carry in the pastry
boxes and wines from the boot into the
kitchens, he mounts the steps — *"bonjour,
mes petites soeurs,"* he says to the sisters
who've gathered to greet him under the
portico — passes through the door, nods to
Paul, who stands just inside it, and propels
his massive, rubber-shoed bulk down the
long corridor to the far wing, to Philippe's
rooms. Without turning around but knowing they all watch him, he shouts, "I trust
Solange is waiting."

And she is. Holding the door open for
him, curtsying, bending to kiss his ring, she
watches as he burrows himself in the depths
of Philippe's high-back chair, bends to
remove his boots, raises purple-stockinged
feet to rest on a hassock. Set near the chair
on a gilt-painted table with a black marble
top, there is a footed silver tray, a silver
candlestick set with a thick honey-colored
candle, already lit, a cut-crystal bottle, a
matching tumbler. In a long, untidy gush,
Fabrice pours out the old tawny port he
likes at this time of day, cradles the glass
between his large white hands, manicured

nails glinting in the yellow light of the candle.

"Now, my dear. Come sit by me. I hope you don't mind that I preferred to meet with you here. Though I understand your desire for privacy, there is no need for secrecy. You, as do all the other sisters, have a perfect right to seek audience with your bishop. That you shall incur Paul's wrath by exercising that right should hardly matter. I've left off caring what Paul thinks, and I would recommend the same to you. It would seem that Amandine has already done so."

Liquescent, mud brown eyes nearly swallowed in the glee-crinkled folds of his lids, he laughs. Sipping the port once, then again, he holds the glass upon the taut abundance of himself and looks hard at Solange.

Still standing, Solange smiles, nods her head, carries a small wooden chair close to where Fabrice is sprawled. She sits, folds her hands in her lap. Still smiling, she says, "It's Amandine about whom I wanted to speak, Your Eminence."

"Yes, I know."

"I've practiced the words I wish to say, the way I wish to say them, but —"

"Would it be simpler if I began?"

"Well, if, well, yes, of course, as you wish."

"I think you should take the child and leave this place."

"What? What are you — ?"

"Listen. Hear me. Neither you nor Amandine thrives here."

"How do you know — ?"

"I asked you to listen. I know of the recent events in the refectory, I know that Amandine has, shall we say, found her voice, that in her artless way she has gone toe-to-toe with Paul and held her ground. Won the admiration of her schoolmates, whatever that might be worth. More than a reason to stay, this seems like a natural ending, a victorious exit, if you will. Why should you not run from a place that nourishes neither of you? You and the child are not prisoner to Paul. Why would you stay?"

"Because it is my duty to stay, sir. Staying here to watch over Amandine is what I promised to do." She's standing now, leaning toward him, perhaps beginning to weep.

"I think it's the *watching over her* that you promised to do. That is the duty you assumed all those years ago. A duty that you have executed splendidly and that I trust you would continue to execute splendidly in any other place. Hence I repeat my question: Why would you stay?"

She moves in tight circles, turning her back to him, then facing him. "Wasn't that the agreement? That she should be schooled here . . . and — ?"

"I suppose it was. But perhaps that agreement has outlived its original intent. Perhaps those who wished to ensure Amandine's welfare would be the first to say that it is not here, not in this school, not anywhere about this place where her welfare is of particular and primary concern. You can't change that, and neither can I. Knowing that we can't change it makes us wise. And being wise, we should seek an alternative."

She backs up into her chair. "What are you saying, sir? Another convent?"

"No. I'm saying that I believe you should be on your own. A family of two. You should make a home for Amandine, for yourself. You should marry someday, Solange. You're beautiful and lovely and fine."

Awkward under his appraisal, she blushes, covers her face with her hands, looks up at him, her thoughts muddled.

A sip of port, a broad smile, the amethystine veins of his nose in high relief in the candlelight, the bishop asks, "How would you even begin? Is that what you wonder? With my help. The Church has a wide embrace, my dear. I would help you to find work, good work. An apartment in Montpellier, a little house somewhere in a village. As you prefer. Or perhaps you would choose to go to your family. It's for you to deliberate calmly and eventually to decide. I say 'deliberate calmly and eventually decide' with some reservation, though."

He looks hard at Solange, tilts the decanter over his glass again.

"The war. My mother wrote to me of it. But that was a few weeks ago, before these, before the Germans . . . I mean, no one here talks much about —"

"Hitler? Well, they should. I understand that Czechoslovakia and Poland seem the other side of the moon to you, yet they're just up the way a bit and, depending upon who steps in this Hun jackal's path, who turns the other way, depending upon the shape and force of it all, well, what I'm saying is that nothing can be the same for very long anywhere in Europe now that this has begun. It *has* begun, Solange. We've declared war on the *boche.* The die is cast. Improbable, *unthinkable* as it is, this blitzkrieg of theirs may just be beginning. What I'm trying to say is that, should the *boche* invade France, well . . . Should that happen, the south will be safer than the north, at least until . . . It will be safer here for a while."

He drinks down the port. Changes expression.

"You know I've had her papers prepared, her identity card, her passport, all is ready. *Amandine Gilberte Noiret de Crécy.* I've taken the liberty to give her my name. And my mother's as well. Gilberte, it's quite beautiful, don't you think? If I'd ever had a daughter, she would have been Gilberte Noiret de Crécy. And so Amandine will carry on. For my mother, for me. It's all quite round, quite settled. *'Amandine Gilberte Noiret de Crécy, born May 3, 1931, Montpellier, mother: unknown; father: unknown; a foundling awarded to the curia of Montpellier on the day of her birth.'* It's as good a beginning as any of us have had."

"When she began at the school, I'd registered her as Jouffroi. I'd given her my name, but I don't know if she ever had occasion to note it or to be called by it. And so Noiret de Crécy it shall be. Thank you, sir. Thank you."

"But having papers is not meant to be a reason to go from here. Surely should you decide to stay I admit that a certain truce will reign between the two of you and Paul. She'll not change. *Ma âme damnée.* She,

213

the spiritual mother of all these little birds, is herself a damned soul. Poor old bitter thing. No, she can't change any more than we can, than anyone can. Still, I suspect some subtle reformation would take hold. The worst is past."

Solange stays quiet as though clicking through her intelligence, verifying what he says, all the while pushing away words like *blitzkrieg, Hun, boche.*

"Yes, I think that, too. The worst is past. And yet what troubles Amandine, what shall continue to cause her suffering, is the incurable want of her mother. Of knowing something about her, of finding her. Can you help me with that? Help me to help her?"

"I know very little. A friend, an old and dear friend, told me what he needed. And I did as he wished. It was the sort of affair about which one asks nothing. Do you understand?"

"I think so. But this help you gave to your friend, I mean this arrangement to keep Amandine here, if I take her away, what about, about the funds that —"

"The funds, yes. The curia was paid to take in Amandine. Generous, enormously generous funds were passed to the curia upon the child's arrival here. Since then nothing has arrived from that *source* shall

214

we call it. A question of misappropriation perhaps or, more likely, someone's convenient forgetfulness about the promise of maintenance. It hardly matters."

"But my monthly stipend . . . the —"

"As I've said, you've fulfilled your duty, Solange, as have I. I promised to see that the two of you were cared for, and I have. I shall always. It's I who has seen to your checks. I, through the auspices of the curia's plenteous accounts. As long as I live, Solange — and if there is even a whit of honor among my successor, long after I'm gone — you and the child shall be under my protection. No matter where you are. No matter where you go. Now I want a nap, so begone with you."

As though she has not heard his imperative she stays in her chair.

"Why does Paul want to hurt Amandine, sir?"

"Because Amandine is the child she wanted to be."

"What?"

"In Paul's strangely ordered mind, Amandine is fortunate, *monstrously* fortunate."

"A mortally ill infant abandoned by her parents she believes is *monstrously fortunate*? An orphan whose father figure dies while she sleeps in his arms when she's not yet six

215

years old, a . . ." On her feet again, Solange weeps openly.

"Allow me to tell you Paul's story. Her mother died during her birth. A hideously vain man, her father thought of his own comfort, *his needs*. Intending a certain efficiency, I suppose, he brought in one of his village paramours to care for this newborn Annick. Did you know that was her name, Solange? Yes, Paul's real name is Annick. Interesting, isn't it, that you gave your tiny ward a name beginning with *A. Alors.* As soon as it was clear to this village woman that the father of this infant had no intention to keep, let alone marry her, she ran off and, at less than a year old, Annick was left for days and nights tied to her crib, bread and whatever else the father could spare placed in her reach. He was the village doctor, Solange. Annick's father was the village doctor, the young widower applauded for his sacrifices, his "managing" such a difficult life. Though other village women lined up in droves to aid him, the good doctor refused all save the ones he coveted and, of those, there were few who cared about the moaning, half-starved creature in the locked room down the hall.

"Please, sir, I can't bear to —"

"Come now, does it shock you to hear of

such savage behavior? In one guise or another it's rather common, you know. Yes, while the doctor was off to visit his patients, he left his baby girl in the squalor of her own soil, her own vomit, her own hunger for however long it suited him. But whether he was absent or present, the baby was alone. He never held her. Do you understand what diabolical abuse it is to deny an infant the embrace for which it yearns?"

This Fabrice says in a less belligerent voice. As though the words, the events they paint, have fatigued him. He bows his head, closes his eyes, and stays quiet until, nearly startling Solange, he snaps his head back to rest against the chair, fixes his gaze upon her, continues.

"But there was a person — a girl who must have been no more than seven or eight when Annick was born — who took it upon herself to care for the baby. She was one of five or six children of a poor village family, the eldest I think. Born handicapped — *arrière mental,* slow in comprehension and speech — she was a folkloric figure, the endearing village idiot. Another child left to her own devices, she wandered about the village and the countryside all day, sometimes returning to her home in the evening, often not. Sleeping under trees, stealing what she could from gardens and orchards, knocking on doors for succor when it rained or was cold. She got by. It wasn't as though her mother was cruel but only distracted and broken with misery and the care of the younger children. It seems that when this little girl heard about the death of the doctor's wife, about the baby, she somehow got the idea that it was she who must care for it. The doctor humored her, let her use the little thing as a kind of doll, a reward for doing his bidding. Feeding the animals and dragging coal up from the cellar, jobs he would have had to pay someone to do or do himself. When the girl had finished her work, she would run to the baby, wash it with her own spit rubbed on whatever cloth was at hand; she'd share her dubious and purloined food with it or try to nurse it as she'd seen her mother give her breast to her brothers and sisters. She would sing to it for hours, rocking it in her bony, filthy arms until both slept. She'd give it a good whack now and then, too, another lesson in child rearing learned at her mother's knee. All in all, she did the baby less harm than good, you see, for she loved the thing. An instinctive love, I suppose. She knew no one else loved it, as she knew no one loved her. She set out to defend it, to *save* it and so save

218

herself. Annick was the one mission in the little girl's life. Still is."

"What do you mean, 'still is'?"

"That little girl was called Josette."

"Josette. Josette? This Jos— ?"

"The same.

"Annick somehow survived and grew up and grew older, but even when she began to take care of herself, Josette stayed by her side. And though Annick must have surpassed Josette in intelligence by the time she was four or five, Josette thrived in her own way, her own time. With Annick's help. When Annick went to school, she began lessons for Josette. Taught her to read and write, if in a particular fashion. Helped her to take care of her physical self, shared her clothes with her. And her food. Thus the wheel turned and Josette became Annick's mission. After a while, having Josette underfoot no longer suited the doctor, and so he set different rules, banned Josette's visits, sent her away rather roughly. Still, she came back. Less often, of course, but she always found a way to come back to Annick. When the doctor signed his daughter over to the Carmelites, Josette — refusing to be left behind — arrived that same night, bag and baggage, presenting herself to the abbess as a cleaning girl. She was taken in as a lay sister — the greater truth, as a slave — and took up her vigil over her beloved Annick. And they've both been here all these years.

"It's from Josette and some from Paul — Annick — herself that I've learned much of this but far more from the doctor. It must have been fifteen years ago when he came to the convent wanting to speak with his daughter. As men like he are wont to do, he'd waited for the occasion of his last earthly days to make the visit. She refused to see him. Philippe sent him on to me, and I became the repository for the things he'd wanted to tell Annick. How sorry he was, how he'd been a weak, lonely man, how he'd believed that little Annick — by the event of her birth — had murdered his wife. The wife whom he betrayed and beat and . . . I heard his confession, told him to go home to die, absolved by God if not by his daughter."

"I'm sorry for Annick, I mean for Paul. For Josette. Dismally sorry, sir. But what has it all to do with Amandine?"

"Has the closing circle not occurred to you? Paul has avenged herself upon Amandine. The fresh white canvas of a newborn baby. It was too great a temptation for her. She would devour that infant. That infant who'd been left, abandoned, yes, but into

220

such worthy hands. With such worthy trappings. That child who conquered a mortal illness, conquered Jean-Baptiste and Philippe, every last one of the convent sisters, you, of course, and meanest of all for Paul to suffer, she conquered me. All of us besotted with her. Some want the pain to end with them, some want to pass it on. It's really that simple, my dear."

"I hardly find that *simple.* Was your telling me meant to raise my sympathy for Paul?"

"Not at all. It was my answer to your question: 'Why does Paul want to hurt Amandine?'"

"You don't know who her parents are, do you, sir?"

"I do not."

"Can you help me to find out?"

"Even if I thought that best, I know not where I should begin."

"With your friend."

"Long dead. He is long dead, as I believe is all trace of those who wished to forget her. Amandine is not the first child to have been so willfully, so determinedly *lost.*"

"But you see, sir, she is lost not only to them but to everyone. To me. To herself. They did their work too well."

"So it would seem. But she's wise and strong. She was made well. They gave her

221

that. It will be enough. The child will come around. You'll see. But this business about the war, it's real, Solange. In one place or another, you and Amandine, like all the rest of us, must endure what the powers have in store for us. You must decide where it is you prefer to be: here with us, with your family, on your own somewhere. You've a good deal to think about. Yes?"

A good deal to think about, yes, Fabrice. Revelations, counsel, mandates, affirmations all delivered blithely before the fire, his unquiet guzzlings of port, his confident, unfaltering voice. His loyalty to his friend, to this brother bishop, his pact with him to guide the path of this child. His embrace of me as the figure chosen to mother her. His preparedness to help us. To stay, to leave, he puts no conditions but trusts me to say which. I dare believe if he were younger, he would have said, "Let's go," and would be starting off with us; yes, it's almost as though he wants us to leave here in his name. To do what he didn't do. To do what Paul never did.

I shall write again to Maman. If she says we should come home, then we shall. Yes, that's it, that shall be the point of decision, Maman's word. From all she's said already, I have no fear for her wanting us but only for what more she might consider about this war. How did

Fabrice put it? "depending upon who steps in this Hun jackal's path, who turns the other way, depending upon the shape and force of it all, well, what I'm saying is that nothing can be the same for very long anywhere in Europe now that this has begun. It *has* begun, Solange."

Maman will tell me if the time is right now. If it seems right to her. But what will Amandine say and think and feel if I tell her that we are leaving? The new school year has just begun, and she is more at ease. The worst is past, Fabrice said it himself. I hesitate because it's I who am fearful. Especially at the prospect of setting up as "a family of two." Without the help of the sisters, could I take care of her? Is that why I want to take her to Avise? To Maman and Grand-mère, to Blanchette and Chloe? Would I be trying to reconstruct the convent? The shared work. Another tribe of women to love Amandine, to pet her. Fabrice trusts me. I sought his counsel, and he gave it. Now I must try to trust myself. Still, for better, for worse, this is the only home she has ever known. And I remember her fierce response when she was younger and I broached the idea of our visiting Avise. Would she feel the same way now? What is best for you, Amandine? God, make haste to help me.

■ ■ ■ ■

PART II
MAY–JUNE 1940
KRAKOW, PARIS

■ ■ ■ ■

Chapter XXIII

Krakow fell in five days. More a genuflection than a fall. The grand old medieval dame. The date was September 6, 1939. Five dementing days after nearly two million German troops stormed Polish borders from the north and from the west in tanks and planes, in trucks, on foot, all of them bent on obliterating the Polish army and, more, the Polish soul. But that had been tried before. Historical partitions and redrawings of borders, every nation that touched upon Polish land came to have its way with her, carving her up, bleeding her, trying to smother her *Polishness,* calling her Prussia or Germany or Russia or Austria. Invasions, dominions, police states, persecutions, puppet governments, change a border, change a name, *still we are Poland.* You see it wasn't the Polish military machine — ragged, deficient — that terrified the Germans in 1939, nor was it the fierce daring of the bravehearts — the only army in all of Europe who fought from the first day to the final day of that war. No, not the military machine but the moral machine. Polish loyalty thrived not in the name of a heinous butcher but in the name of the Poles' own humanity. Yes, it was their *Polishness,* that inexorable *Polishness,* which rankled the Führer's boys.

Unlike Warsaw, unlike Lwów, unlike the towns and villages along the pitiless way of the blitzkrieg, the blood and bones and bricks of Krakow suffered little. Less. No fire, no ravage, no slaughter ornamented the intrusion into what the Germans considered a city of their own. *Unser Krakau.* The Countess Czartoryska was there.

Forty-three now and perhaps more beautiful than she was on that day in Montpellier in 1931 when she brought her daughter's five-month-old baby — consigned it irrevocably — to the convent of St.-Hilaire. Life for the Countess Czartoryska had proceeded much as she'd desired. Privileges, duties, pace, rhythm, tone, marcel waves, sable jackets, and Chanel trousers. Schiaparelli gowns and canary diamonds. The theater, the opera, a window table at Jama Januszika each morning at eleven for raspberry pastries and the exchange of darting glances with a silver-bearded cellist from the Krakow Philharmonic. Sojourns to the family estates for hunt parties and balls, fire-lit picnics in the Carpathian foothills laid by caravans of servants porting silver and linen and provisions, readied to await the arrival in luxury automobiles of nobles wrapped in good Scots cashmere. A month in Paris, a few weeks at Baden, a long-standing love affair with an inconsiderable Slav prince. Life for Countess Czartoryska — as it did for all the women of her set — drifted along much as it had for the aristocracy since the sixteenth century.

And, grand egoist that she was, the countess believed that all she'd done, all she'd thought, all she'd lived for was *others*. For Andzelika, of course. Her Andzelika. But more recently also for Janusz. Prince Janusz Rudski, with whom, two years earlier, Andzelika had stood in the Sigismond chapel of Wawel Cathedral — a glory of a bride in ice blue satin, her five-meter train rippling behind her, held barely aloft by eight page boys in white velvet breeches and damask waistcoats — to take the prince as her lawfully wedded husband. Sitting as the countess is now in the second from the last pew on the left side of the Mariacki, her brown and white toeless spectator pumps — revealing perfectly enameled dark red nails — resting on the kneeler, her lighter brown silk dress kilted above bare, unsunned, perfectly taut knees, she recalls her triumph.

Truth be told, though, Janusz was all too willing to court Andzelika. Less than my wiles, it was Andzelika's beauty. Her father's ivory skin. But her eyes, black as Magyar grapes, I admit her eyes are mine. And all that hair, worn loose that day when Janusz first saw her, wasn't it? Flying behind her as she rode past him with the others in the hunt. A long pink jacket buttoned up to her chin. He'd arrived late, Janusz had, too late to ride that first day, and I remember how he paced and paced, the long, lean frame of him striding the rooms, running his fingers through his white blond hair, waiting for them to return. For her to return. Foolish child, she thought him old at thirty-one, went sashaying about in league with the two Rolnicki brothers the whole week long, but Janusz was patient. It was the mazurka on that last evening. Reckless and nimble a dancer as she was, his hands turned palms up at his waist, he circled her tauntingly, chin high, hair falling in a fringe over his forehead with each stomp of his boot until Andzelika's eyes narrowed, smiled at him, dared him. Everyone saw it. Janusz smiled back, and it was done. Were they ever apart after that for more than a day or two? I can't recall.

I feared she would tell him of her escapade, and so I begged her silence. We'd carried off the impossible feat, Andzelika and I, that of keeping a secret among our set. There were times when I began to think that even she didn't recall it, so rarely, so very rarely did she address the child. How I'd feared her an- nouncing one day her desire to visit the grave site in Switzerland, how I'd armed myself with reasons why such a journey would . . . But she never asked. When she heard that Drout- skoy had married, she sulked for a few days. Asked me, was I certain that no one had ever informed him she'd given birth to his child? Wholly certain, I told her. And that was the last time she spoke of him, of the child. As though both were part of the same bad dream she'd willed herself to forget. I know they were real, though. I know that the child was real and I have been besieged by her every day and every night for all these nine years. By now I am expert in my war with the agony of her. And then I think of Andzelika, *Princess* Andzelika, how her life would have been stained, not throttled, by the presence of the child. Who would have wanted her? Surely not Janusz.

The countess always ends her reverie just

at this point. With the same question. The same answer. Over and over again she must convince herself that her deed was in Andzelika's name. If she thinks it one more time, perhaps the lie will change color, become a truth. It never does, though. In the deepest place in her heart, she understands that it was not to protect Andzelika that she abandoned the child but for her own vendetta. Her revenge against Antoni, against that one, that single act which demonstrated that his little baroness meant more than life to him. How could anyone expect that she, Valeska, would love and embrace a child of the same blood that flowed through Antoni's own whore?

Any other man or boy, Andzelika, and I might have, I would have looked beyond my displeasure, but never to the issue of Droutskoy. And so my sins were not those of maternal ferocity but simply those of pride. My own. My only salvation is that, no matter how I try not to, I always tell myself the truth.

Untying the white kerchief that covers her head, stuffing it into the string bag hanging from her wrist, she walks out through the south-facing doors of the Mariacki into the unusually sultry late May morning.

After nine months of occupation, Krakow appears astonishingly unchanged, its architectural glories whole, a semblance of normalcy everywhere about the nearly quiet streets. People work, go to mass, light candles, pray, shop, dine, sleep, hold tight to their heritage, their ideals, to the word of Polish allies. After all, would France betray them? Would England? This too shall pass. A short war. Until then, this half life, half familiar. One must submit to the illusion that Krakow center has been transformed into a film set on which hundreds of splendid-looking jackbooted boys and men parade about in uniform, yes, *a semblance of normalcy* wants only a flash or two of a small distorting mirror. To further the cheat, though, one must ignore the neat hand-lettered signs announcing *Nur für Deutsche* — for Germans only — posted in the windows of the better restaurants and shops, choose not to hear the talk about the torturings in Montelupi Street, hurry away — head cast downward — during the *lapanki,* the random arrests that the jackbooted boys perform here and there, now and then. And at the dry, sharp crack of a pistol from the far side of the café, eyes forward and another jaded sip from the tiny crystal cup of slivovitz. Oh, one more thing. Keep far from the Podgórze, from the ghetto where the Jews have been herded. All the harum-scarum of the occupation of Krakow happens there. Mortification, hunger, the quick spray from an MG34 across the apartment doors facing onto an upper balcony just to rip the tedium of a quiet spring evening, the jackbooted boys rival one another for duty in that province beyond the pale. That place where the Jews are. Yes, by all means keep far from the Podgòrze.

The countess wanders into the Rynek Glowny, the main market square, to look at the occupiers' leavings of the day, food for the *Untermenschen:* rotting vegetables, bruised and broken fruit, the less tempting parts of a pig. It matters little, though, she thinks, fondling a hill of small, hard brown pears, since hers is an exercise in habit, this morning perusal of the marketplace. Crates and boxes and sacks of exquisite food are punctually delivered to the back door of her palace each Tuesday and Saturday. Lake fish from the north on Fridays. She walks back down Franciszkanska Street past the Nazi Partei-Haus to the Czartoryski palace to leave her few findings with the cooks, to check the progress of lunch, and then to freshen up, to rest before her ritual presiding over the one o'clock meal. They would be eight today, or was it to be nine?

Rather than friends or family, she will be dining with her German houseguests. Wehrmacht officers and their aides. Long-standing houseguests. You see, despite the desperate urgings of her daughter and other members of her family, the countess had stayed behind in Krakow when the others fled. The selfsame zeal with which she had *protected* Andzelika, she will employ to protect her home, her possessions, the pulse of her life. As though her presence could stay the very German army.

She'd waved from her bedroom window as Andzelika and Janusz, the white Bentley piled with valises, joined the nearly soundless dawn hegira from Krakow of the Rudski clan less than a day before the invasion. Hundreds, thousands had gone before them, exiting Krakow for the outlying villages and farms, for destinations beyond the borders into Romania and Yugoslavia and Czechoslovakia, unaware they raced not toward freedom but into the vile embrace of the advancing Russians. But on that last day of August 1939, it was to Paris that Andzelika and Janusz and his family were headed. Just as threatened Poles of lesser and greater nobility had done in the nineteenth century and again during the Great War, Andzelika and Janusz and the others would establish a Polish court of sorts in several of the grand hotels, entrench themselves in much the same life they'd lived in Krakow. They would wait out the war as befitted those of their station. Though the opera house was closed and air raids interrupted late suppers and there were maddening shortages of preferred wines, there was consolation that the war was far away. Just as the Krakovians who stayed behind used the distorting mirror to survive, so did those who fled. On June 3, 1940, though, when German bombs first fell on Paris, even those mirrors were shattered. Meanwhile in Krakow, just as she had done always, the countess had *arranged* things to suit her.

In early October 1939, when the Wehrmacht colonel Dietmar von Karajan and his aides banged the lion's-head knocker against its iron plate on the great carved doors of the Czartoryska palace, the countess was prepared. She'd wondered, in fact, why her home had been so long left unclaimed while, in nearly every other prestigious palace, SS and Wehrmacht officers and sometimes men of the Gestapo were already ensconced. What she didn't know was this: The colonel had seen her three weeks before, on one of the first days of the occupation. She had been walking, hurrying over the stones back from mass at the Mari-acki. As the colonel's auto passed her, their eyes met. He told the driver to stop, to have her followed, to find out who she was. With that intelligence, the colonel would secure lodgings and, perhaps, he thought, a woman. He had business in Warsaw, and when he returned, it was he himself, his aides surrounding him, who struck the lion's head against the countess's door.

She received the troupe as though she'd invited them, the colonel, a captain, and their respective entourages — nine Wehr-macht in all. Speaking easily, volubly in her convent school *Hochdeutsch,* she offered them 11:00 A.M. silver cups of amontillado and hazelnut biscuits, stepped prettily in her white faille morning dress up the stair-case to demonstrate the upper floors, the six sprawling suites where the troupe would sleep. The company of men had always suited Valeska. If there must be a war, if there must be an occupation of her city, a requisitioning of her home, let things be car-ried out with some modicum of dignity, she told the colonel with her eyes as he bent to light her cigarette.

In addition to the second and third floors,

the colonel requested full use of the receiving rooms on the first floor, including the main drawing room, the dining salon, the library. It was the countess who, desiring to save the colonel's having to ask it of her, offered to arrange herself in a small ground-floor suite — bedroom, sitting room, and small drawing room — once the domain of Antoni's aged mother. Like any fine hostess, she then set about to explain the house rules: the punctuality of meals, the quality of her kitchen and her cellars, demeanor at table — *there would be no talk of war, she'd warned* — the prohibition of any female guests unless approved by her, a midnight curfew so as not to disturb the servants, one of whom had a new baby. Each caveat the countess delivered directly into the dark blue Tartar's eyes of the colonel, and he, his hand held loosely over his mouth, fingers pulling his lips from an involuntary smile, listened as though to profound, unimagined truths. Sharp nods of the head then, from the troupe, hand kissing, assurances of the completion of their quiet, efficient encampment well before dinner. Yes, it had all suited the Countess Valeska.

Aloof as a portrait at the head of her table, flanked by her perfumed, scrupulously shined and creased guests, the colonel on her right, the countess sipped and dined with the Wehrmacht and, together, they spoke vaguely of their lives. During those first days, the countess thought to invite her female friends to dine so as to amuse the young men. But among those few who remained, there was no one who would be quite right. No one who was pretty but not too pretty, charming but not fatally so. Of course they found their own women, the paid ones from the Ukraine who sat in groups in the market bars and some of the local girls, too, love and lust or want of supper overriding patriotism from time to time. But the men were respectful and even drank in a mostly chivalric way. Some of the aides were posted outside the city several days each week and there were mandatory maneuvers each afternoon for the others, so the house was tranquil much of the time. Life proceeded.

The evenings after dinner Valeska spent in her rooms, reading, listening openly to the BBC, even though it was decreed that those radios not already confiscated be surrendered. Early on the colonel asked if it would disturb her should he play the piano sometimes. *Not at all, I play myself.* She, Chopin, he, Bach, the two played for one another and often for the others. Valeska and the colonel were hardly ever alone yet, when they were, she grew skilled at keeping him close while keeping away — a dance that the colonel enjoyed — and the only intimacy they approached was in speaking of their families. Of Andzelika and Janusz, of the colonel's wife, his adult children.

One evening the colonel enters the salon while Valeska is playing the piano, her heavy white silk shawl in his hands. He stands behind her, gently places the shawl on her shoulders. His hands linger, trembling. She slows her playing but does not stop. Even as he begins to speak, she continues to play.

"Come, let's walk a bit. I'd like to take you to a little place where I go from time to time."

"As you well know, I go out very rarely in the evening and never in the company of an occupying officer. And less to some cellar bar."

"This evening I am not an occupying officer but a man who wishes to, to 'court' you, Valeska." It is the first time he omits her title. "And what makes you think that I would take you to a cellar bar?"

"I understand it's only those — only the most degraded of those — where we *Untermenschen* are permitted."

"Allow me to show you that, for every rule, there is an exception."

The colonel has two motives for his invitation. Apart from his wanting to be with Valeska in a setting where they might better ignore his role as the occupier and hers as the invaded, he desires to tell her that many of the officers have begun to send for their families. The governor-general of Krakow, Hans Frank, having a few days earlier publicly declared: "The world will cease to exist before we Nazis depart Krakow," spurred a rush of soldiers' communications with their families who waited in the fatherland. The colonel was not one of those who wrote to his wife. Rather it was he who received a telegram from her. *"Ich freue mich Sie wiederzusehen.* I look forward to seeing you again," it said. He has yet to respond.

Estranged emotionally for much of their marriage, the colonel and his wife had long been adept at farce, of painting over sangfroid, trying to make it pass for love. For the children, for the sake of familial duty. But when the children were grown and gone and the musings of war reached him, the colonel thought to take a mistress. The Wehrmacht would make a fine one, he'd thought. And she did. Until he saw the woman with the long black eyes mincing along across the market square of Krakow. Am I in love with the countess? Never having felt love nor even mistaken it, I can hardly say. Still.

This evening he wishes to *inform* the countess of the impending arrival of some of his men's families and, more, to watch those eyes when he tells her that perhaps his wife, too, will join him. Another game, yes. But how else to know what she thinks? Over these months, he has learned to listen more to her eyes than her words.

The countess has been speaking. Something about *patriotism,* is it?

"I cannot claim expressions of fervid patriotism, Colonel, and I freely admit that I have been more than a little Neroesque in my fretting over the state of my marble floors or my hairdo while shunning the gruesome truths about the occupation of my country. But I, too, am of the race of *Untermenschen,* Colonel; I, too, am a Pole. Why would you contaminate yourself by 'courting,' as you call it, one of us? What makes you think that I would want you, Colonel? How do I know what you do when you leave here in the morning, or what you've done or are inclined to do in the name of your heinous little god? *The other name of honor is loyalty.* Isn't that the oath you swore, Colonel? In other words, shall you not do whatever is asked of you? *Whatever.* I beg you not to mistake my hospitality for anything more. I am playing house with you and your men, waiting as politely as I can for the day when you shall leave my home and my city."

The countess has brusquely removed the shawl placed by the colonel so tenderly a few moments before. It falls from her hands, and the colonel bends to retrieve it. Holding it, wishing he were holding her, he tells her quietly, "Madame, you quote the SS oath, which is not mine. The German race, like all others, births men of different characters. I would peacefully shoot myself before I could be convinced to certain acts. But you already know that, Valeska. And, as well, you know something else."

"What is it that I know, Colonel?"

"That my sentimental feelings for you are, are *requited.* Yes, that's the word I was searching for."

CHAPTER XXIV

It is toward the end of June 1940 — June 22, to be precise — a week or so after the encounter between Valeska and the colonel. Since that evening, the two have remained in genteel détente. They speak at table, play the piano for one another after dinner, but neither risks personal discourse. The colonel did, however, tell Valeska that some of his aides would be welcoming their wives and young children in Krakow, that — until other accommodations could be secured — they would be living together in her palace. As always, she was gracious, accommodating, set about to have small beds and other furniture brought up from the storage rooms, heirloom linens aired from long years' resting in cedar chests. The colonel never mentioned his own wife, his own situation. He no longer needed to do that. By her silence, she admitted that he was correct in his thinking. She cared for him. That

244

was enough for now. In time . . .

Earlier in the day, the BBC had announced the total capitulation of France to her German invaders. Street by street, house by house, the news traveled through Krakow. Shutters banged, long medieval keys were turned in the doors, and, as though in mourning, families sat together around their kitchen tables and wept. France would not rescue them. Another sweet hope strangled, left for dead. Sixty citizens of Krakow would commit suicide that evening. There were those who would later swear the number was much higher.

The colonel had sent a note to Valeska saying that he and his men would not be "at home" for lunch or dinner, and so she'd stayed most of the day in her rooms, listening for further BBC announcements and waiting for the colonel to return so that he might somehow explain to her what it meant, this French surrender.

It is sometime after ten o'clock when she hears him enter the main hall. She puts down her book, walks out to meet him. No words. He removes his hat, pulls her close, presses his dry, soft lips against her temple. Somehow, between that morning and this evening, that which had separated them is no more. *German, Pole, war, duty* — all that remains is his mouth on her skin, her thin, weeping body in his arms.

She sends him off to bathe and change, orders supper for him, takes up her shawl and goes out into the night. *A short walk, some air, so much to talk about.*

She walks up the narrow back street behind the Czartoryski palace to the market square, finds it bedecked for the grand occasion of France's fall with a great red forest of Nazi flags, hundreds upon hundreds of them, *yes, a strange red forest under the moon.* And there are bells. Every church in Krakow rings out the news. As though the bells know, the sounds they make are knells. All holed up against the flags and the bells and the news, there is not a Krakovian in sight. Standing along the edges of the square, her hand resting on one of the flagpoles, she watches the jackbooted boys at play, shouting, singing, cracking the green glass necks of French Champagne.

France has quit, and I am here to see the pageant of her funeral. All the while Andzelika is there. And, somewhere in France, is the little one also there? The little one. Is she alive? Where is she? What will become of her now? What has it been? Ten months? Is that what it took to bring the Franks to their knees? Whimpering. Heil Hitler.

There will be masses of French fleeing to God knows where. Will the convent be requisitioned? Where will they go? I shall contact Montpellier, I shall go to Montpellier, I shall see for myself, yes, Dietmar will help me. Yes, I must tell him, I will tell him this evening. No, what am I thinking? To put at peril Andzelika's gingerly built life? I must remember who she is, who she might have become had I not protected her. Ah, such a noble mother am I. Nearly as noble a mother as I am a selfish one. What was it that I decided about myself that morning while I sat in the back of the Mariacki? How did it go? . . . My sins are not those of maternal ferocity but of pride. At least I am still telling myself the truth.

Valeska stands nearer to the flagpole, one arm encircling it, resting her head against it. She tries to imagine what the child looks like now. Turned nine less than two months ago. A noise distracts her. An explosion, like fireworks. Oh, these boys think of everything. A second explosion, a third. The singing has stopped, there is silence and then another kind of screaming and then a voice, a single voice through a speaker shouts over all of it. What is it saying? Long live Poland. The Germans flee the square; she would run, too, and yet her legs are leaden. She feels faint. I need air, too many people, too hot, the shock, the news, yes, I must get back home and wait for Dietmar in the garden. He'll be down by now, surely he'll be down by now. She is falling, sliding really, her arm still clinging to the pole, trying to throw off her shawl with the other hand. What is this warmth, this wetness gushing from my side? And from my head? Just where he kissed me. She begins to laugh, a giddy, breathless laugh. Ah, so this is how it shall be? She thinks of Antoni. She thinks of the baby. She falls. Men who are living in her home see her as they run. One lifts her in his arms, the others run ahead down the alleyway, to the back entrance of the palace.

Thinking she, too, has gone to freshen up, the colonel has been playing the piano while waiting for Valeska.

Bring her to her room. Contact the medics, tell them it's I who need them.

Colonel, sir, it's, it's . . . The wounds are . . . There is chaos out there, bombs, the resistance . . .

Leave me alone with her.

Colonel Dietmar von Karajan kneels by the countess's bed. He can see the wounds now. Understands. He holds her, whispers to her. He rips the hem of the sheet to tie about her head, and he screams out to God. She opens her eyes.

Can you hear me?

Her voice is someone else's, someone far away.

He kneels once again by her, lays his head on her breast.

I beg you to listen. My daughter . . .

Your daughter will be safe . . .

You must tell my daughter. The baby did not die, the baby did not die. I left her there with . . . She did not die. I left the necklace, Andzelika's necklace. The baby did not die. Tell her. You must tell her.

CHAPTER XXV

In desolation I inform you of your mother's
sudden death on the evening of June 22,
the result of wounds suffered during a
bombing in the Rynek Glowny for which
the Armia Krajowa has claimed responsibility. The curia has undertaken arrangements. With humility I recommend that you
do not travel to Krakow during this particu-
larly uncertain moment. As there is other
urgent business about which I must speak
with you, please expect my arrival in Paris
within the next twenty-four hours. Specific
advisory to come.

Yours truly,
Dietmar von Karajan

When her maid knocks on her door sometime toward dawn, wordlessly places the
telegram in her hands while she is still prone
in her bed, Andzelika is certain it can only
be news of Janusz's death.

250

She throws down the unopened telegram, leaps from the bed, holds her maid by the shoulders, tells her, "I tried to keep him here. I tried, Bajka. I begged him to wait just a little longer. Janusz, Janusz. Open it, Bajka. Open it for me, please. I can't, I can't do it."

A deafening, strangling thrill of reprieve. And then fresh horror. Not Janusz. Janusz is not dead. It is Matka. Matka is dead. My mother is dead. How can that be?

Over the past months, Valeska had often written to Andzelika about the colonel. About him and his men, about her peaceful coexistence with them in the palace. Still it feels odd, wrong somehow, that a Wehrmacht colonel has informed her of her mother's death. *A casualty of the Polish resistance.* A telegram written in French. Perhaps it's not so, only some sort of trick, a ploy, what could it be?

Andzelika sends word to Janusz's regiment, informs him, asks that he take leave and come to her. She walks the rooms of her suite, waiting for the absurd dream to end, for her mother cannot be dead. Valeska Czartoryska, the indestructible Countess Czartoryska, *moja piekna matka*, my beautiful mother, anyone but you.

It is late in the evening of June 26 when the concierge calls to say that Colonel Dietmar von Karajan awaits her presence in the lobby.

"I beg your pardon, Princess, for arriving without further notice, but travel these days hardly permits the courtesies . . ."

The colonel bows, kisses Andzelika's hand, looks in her eyes. "I hope, Princess, that you will also pardon my presumptuousness when I say that your *tristesse* is mine."

"My mother often wrote of you. She described you well, sir."

Andzelika, having moments before been wrapped in her husband's dressing gown, smoothes the skirt of her black voile dress, pushes her toes farther into her black satin mules, wishes she'd taken time to do her hair, to bathe her swollen eyes. *A handsome man, no matter the circumstances of his presence,* she thinks.

"I cannot bear, at this moment, to hear the details from your point of view. I have been in touch via telephone with Bishop Mateusz and —"

"I have not come here to relive those moments. As you are not prepared to hear them, Princess, I am not prepared to tell them. I am here only to deliver the message your mother entrusted with me."

"My name is Andzelika, sir. My mother left a message for me? Something she said on, on that evening?"

"Something she said as she was dying."

Andzelika grips the raspberry damask arms of her chair. "Go on, Colonel."

Word for word, the colonel repeats the message. He hears Valeska saying the words in his mind as he speaks them. As though she is coaching him.

Andzelika is still as stone. Until slowly she begins to move in a rocking motion. She closes her eyes, bows her head. Andzelika weeps. Not as she has wept for her mother, not as she would weep for her husband but, for the first time, she weeps as a mother for her child.

The colonel requests of the concierge that the princess be accompanied to her rooms. The maid arrives to help Andzelika and, as the two are leaving, the colonel touches Andzelika's shoulder and nods as in good-bye.

"Colonel, will you be kind enough to join me in an hour? I must be alone now, but afterward I believe I would welcome your company. It seems that my mother has made comrades of us."

"She must have said more. Tell me once

again, word for word, where did she leave her, with whom, where is my baby?"

"I know nothing more. You must understand that your mother never spoke to me of, never, before that moment, told me of your child. Never. She spoke at length of your father, of his liaison with the baroness, his unfortunate death, their unfortunate deaths. She spoke of you and your childhood, your talents, your beauty. She spoke of your husband, of her joy in your marriage to him. But never a word about a child. Not until, not until then."

The two are sitting in the mandatory dark in the small drawing room of Andzelika's suite, the long windows open to a midnight on the Île Saint-Louis, to the whispering of the Seine against the stones of the quai d'Orléans. Bajka hovers, brings tea, sets down a bottle of Frapin and a large Baccarat snifter in front of the colonel.

"You see, had I known about the child, anything at all about the child beforehand, I might have asked her where, with whom but —"

"I understand. It's only that she has left me nothing, nothing at all with which to begin my search for my baby. My child. Nor has she left me an explanation as to why she would have 'hidden' her from me, kept her 'hidden' for all these years. Why the lies, the secrets, the mysteries? Yet I hardly need ask since my mother's life was made of maneuvers and feats of the impossible. They were her drugs, Colonel."

Having himself been witness to a few of those maneuvers and feats of the impossible, the colonel smiles, asks, "What of this necklace she mentioned? *'I left the necklace, Andzelika's necklace.'* Could it somehow be traced?"

"I've thought about it, and I think she must have meant the pendant she gave me on my thirteenth birthday. A very old Bohemian piece that belonged to her great-grandmother and was passed down from mother to daughter. She must have taken it from among my things at some point, because I recall looking for it and not finding it. I'd been fearful of asking her about it because I didn't want her to know that it was missing. She loved that piece above all. Mother had magnificent jewels, Colonel, though I doubt she displayed many of them during your 'stay' with her. But how she loved that little amethyst carved into the shape of a bottle with a lilac pearl for a stopper. That she left that, precisely that, along with whatever else she bequeathed my baby tells me much."

"That she accepted her as, as the next female in line. Is that what you mean?"

Andzelika nods. "Still, it by no means represents a clue to where she left her or how I can find her."

"Who was the child's father?"

"A boy who was a schoolmate of my cousin. Boarding school in Warsaw. I think he was a year older than I. About a year older. He didn't love me."

"Did you tell him about the child?"

"No. I never saw him after, after his visit. Mother made certain of that. She was very good at 'making certain,' Colonel. It would seem that she saw to everything. Even I didn't know how wide was her *sphere*. She must have seen to it that the boy would never contact me again — I rather doubt that took much doing — and then she went about the 'disposal' of —"

"*Disposal* is not the word, Andzelika. Surely she had her reasons."

"The child was born 'unhealthy,' with a weak heart, not given much chance of survival. That's what she told me. And then she told me that she was taking the baby to Switzerland, to a clinic. Surgery. But when she returned, she told me that the baby had died. Of course I believed her. I had no reason not to. The distillation of the story is that, Colonel."

"Surely there will be tracks to follow. You can begin with the hospital where the child — I'm sorry, I don't know the child's name . . ."

"Nor do I."

"Where the child was born, take her birth certificate to . . . And then there's the Swiss clinic . . ."

"That's assuming my mother told me the truth about this Swiss clinic, the truth about anything at all. I don't even have my child's birth certificate. I have nothing."

"Yes, but among your mother's papers, surely you'll find . . . It's only that now, now with this war, thousands and thousands of people are looking for one another, refugees, the loss of records, the broken communications, indistinguishable paths . . ."

"Of course. I understand. But I have yet another trial to face, Colonel. My husband knows nothing of this child. Nothing of my history."

"She saw to that as well, did she?"

Andzelika smiles, whispers, *"Yes."*

The two sit quietly then. Though there seems nothing left to say, neither of them wishes to be alone. It is Bajka who insists that Andzelika rest.

The colonel promises to write, gives Andzelika numbers where he can be reached. Hat in hand, he bends to kiss hers, turns to leave. Bajka has gone ahead to open the door for him and, as he approaches it, he turns. "I loved her. I love her still."

It is late on the next afternoon when Andzelika opens the doors to her husband. Never having seen him in the uniform of the Wielkopolska, the glory of him stuns her. A beautiful blond-haired cavalier in high, lustrous black boots, his crimson riding coat and white breeches taut like skin, Janusz — grave, pale — stands before her.

She is awkward in his arms, wanting his comfort yet fearing it, heartsore with the burden of her mourning. More for what she must now confess. Janusz holds her, caresses her, speaks softly to her until she can no longer bear his tenderness. Asking him to sit away from her, to listen well, she begins her story.

"As she was dying, Mother asked Colonel von Karajan to tell me something. She asked him to tell me that . . ." Andzelika stops, hides her face in her hands, looks up at Janusz, begins again. "She asked him to tell me that my baby did not die."

"What?"

"No questions, Janusz, or I shall never be able to do this. Please. Only listen. When I was sixteen, I had a brief, a very brief romance with a boy. A friend of my cousin. The two of them had come for a holiday in Krakow. I had never had a boyfriend. I was a very young sixteen, timid, fragile, I guess. I was still wearing white stockings and oxfords. I was a convent schoolgirl who fell to pieces whenever I had to speak to a boy. I was *Matka*'s little darling. And so when this boy sought me out, told me I was lovely, I —"

"You needn't explain to me, Andzelika, how an adolescent male goes about seduction."

"No, of course. After the boy left our home, I never heard from him again. I was desolate, ashamed. I think I was angry, and when I understood, when I finally understood what had happened to me — I mean that I was going to have a child — I ran to my mother, as I always did. So much of what happened right then and for a long time afterward is unclear to me, Janusz."

"Unclear?"

He is on his feet now, pacing the room, turning every once in a while to look at his wife as though to be sure it is she who sits there, she who tells him this tale.

"Unclear. Yes, truly unclear because my mother did everything, decided everything. But let me go back a moment. You see, the boy, my *amour,* well, neither Mother nor I, nor, I think, even my cousin, knew who he was. I mean about his family. None of us knew that he was the younger brother of my father's mistress. Of the baroness. He used a different name than she had used. Perhaps they were born of different fathers, I don't know. Piotr Droutskoy. That was his name. I don't think he meant to conceal anything from us; in fact, I think he might not even have known who we were. Or, in any case, I think he made no connection between us and his sister. He would have been about three or four when his sister died. When all that happened. I was two so, yes, he would have been only a bit older. But Mother found out who our guest was at about the same time I told her that we'd been lovers. That I was going to have a child. A doctor came to the palace, examined me. While I was dressing, she came into my room, took me in her arms, held me for what seemed like hours, never saying a word except 'Antoni, Antoni.' She said my father's name over and over again. A chant, a prayer. Of course I knew the story of my father and the baroness. A tidied version of it, I suspect.

But we almost never spoke of him, so I was perplexed by her invoking him, addressing her lament to him.

"Mother looked at me then, asked me if I would be willing to endure a 'procedure.' That's what she called it. A procedure that would 'make the baby go away.' Thinking only of my lover and that I could never allow what he had given me to be taken away, I refused. Vehemently so, as I recall. Vehement not because I wanted the baby itself but because that creature was part of him. Mother was wise enough to understand. She never again mentioned the procedure. She promised me a vacation at the spas. Said I should worry about nothing. Nothing at all.

"Days later, Mother announced our departure for an extended holiday, had our things packed, chattered away to family and friends about how I'd been studying too much, how it was high time we two took the grand tour. Rome, Venice, Paris, Vienna, she cooed, when all the while we were on our way to the Black Forest, to a villa on the grounds of Friedrichsbad. We stayed there for seven months. A little more. Until the baby was born. In a private hospital nearby. Another villa. All very posh and silent. I was heavily medicated during the delivery, and after that, all I remember are long sleeps, modulated voices, a constant needle in my arm. It seemed like it was days. It might have been less. I recall nurses and doctors who moved about me looking somber, Mother, who was always there, solicitous but distracted. I don't recall much else."

"Don't recall much else? Your baby? When you held her?"

"I never did."

"Why?"

"Janusz, please. If I thought anything about the baby during those first moments, those first days and nights, it was that it had been born dead and that they were all tiptoeing about trying to keep the truth from me. That's what I thought. And so I let them. I made it easy for them. I asked nothing, welcomed injection after injection, trusted my mother to take care of things as she'd always taken care of them. Finally, one morning Mother came to sit by my bed and she told me that the baby had been born with a severe heart defect, that she was perilously ill and would likely not survive the next few days. I accepted the news, of course, and was almost cheered by it after having thought her already dead. But no, *cheered* is the wrong word. The truth is that I felt nothing. I mean nothing that might be termed 'maternal.' Mother's maternalness overwhelmed any burgeoning instinct I might have felt in that direction. She was all the mother there was room for in our lives. The baby was not real to me. Only my shame was real. My shame and my hope, my belief that this boy would return to me. I can't imagine this will make sense to you, but that's all I felt. All that I remember feeling.

"A few days later we went back to the villa. Mother told me that the baby would have to remain in the hospital for further care. I accepted that just as I had all the rest. A month passed, and it was the end of May I remember when Mother said we'd be returning to Krakow. Without the baby. At this point I was once again certain that the child had died, otherwise why would we be leaving it behind? And also not once during that last month did Mother, as far as I knew, visit the hospital where the baby supposedly was. Surely she never asked me to go there with her. I stayed quiet, dutiful, and we returned to Krakow.

"It was in September that Mother announced she was returning to Germany to fetch the baby, that surgery had been arranged for her in a clinic in Switzerland.

She explained that there was new hope for the child's survival. Now, now that I know what she did subsequently, I think she was testing me that day, trying to determine my feelings about the baby. I think she was trying to decide. Should she surrender the baby or should she not? Yes, that's what she must have been struggling with, because I'd never before seen my mother with the frightened look she wore then. The terror in her eyes. But of course I didn't know what she meant to do or that I might have said something to deter her. I couldn't have known."

"Known? No, you couldn't have 'known what she meant to do,' but how many months had passed by then? Four? Five? Why didn't you — ?"

"If you have not understood by all that I've told you up to now, Janusz, you will never understand. I am simply telling you what I think and what I recall. I do not tell it to gain your sympathy."

She wants him to cross the room, to take her in his arms again, but rather he walks to the long windows, opens them wider, lights a cigarette, one booted foot resting on the small wooden stool that Bajka uses when she cleans the glass. Holding the cigarette between his thumb and index finger, palm facing inward, he inhales deeply, the red ash the only light in the room. When he turns his head to the left to blow the smoke from the corner of his mouth, a river breeze chases it back upon him, making a lissome ghost of him, the husk of a dervish wheeling his way to the other side.

"Lutèce. City of Light dark as a grave."

"What did you say?"

"Lutèce. It's what the Romans called this place. Paris without light is unthinkable."

"Are you finished with me now?"

"Does *now* refer to this evening or to forever?"

"Let's begin with this evening."

"Is the princess fatigued with all this serious talk, is that it?"

"Sarcasm doesn't suit you, Janusz."

As though he hasn't heard her, Janusz walks to the divan where Andzelika sits, bends to take her shoulders roughly in his hands. "Oh, yes, let's speak of something else, my darling. Where would you like to dine this evening? By the way, where is your daughter dining this evening, Andzelika?"

"How unjust."

"No. Just, it *is*. Just to the teeth, my princess."

"Are you saying it's what I deserve?"

"Of course I am."

"I feared you would behave badly, but I never thought you would be cruel. You know you can likely buy an annulment from the curia for this, Janusz. I'm certain the bishop will find just the right phrase in your defense, something like —"

"Be quiet, Andzelika. Your story makes me neither love you less nor regret that I married you. In fact, it's not even you I'm thinking of right now. It's certainly not myself. I'm thinking about a little nine-year-old girl who is part of you and so is also part of me. No matter who else's other blood is hers. It's bad enough that your mother didn't trust me, but that you didn't startles me. I feel cheated not that you had a lover before me but that there is a part of you, that there is a child that you kept from me."

"A child that was kept from me, as well, you will recall. I couldn't help what I did, Janusz, can't you see that?"

"No. Nor shall I ever. Sixteen is one thing, but nine years have passed also for you. If only you'd grown to be woman enough to have asked your mother a question or two. Or better, to have told me, so that, together, we might have asked the questions. But it doesn't matter now."

"What does that mean?"

"What matters is to find her."

"Then you'll help me?"

"I was hoping that you might help me."

Janusz sits then next to Andzelika, folds his arms across his chest. Both look straight ahead.

"In these past twenty-two hours, since I've known that my baby might still be alive, I have begun to invent nostalgia for her. That sort of Russian nostalgia which one feels for a person even without having known him. Who was it who went out to look for his lover's footprints in the snow even though he knew she had never walked there? Janusz, I have pictured her, imagined her in ten thousand ways. I almost fear going out into the world because I know that I shall 'see' her everywhere, in every little girl's face. I shall stop children in the street, look into their eyes, run after any one of them who seems the least bit familiar to me. I will spend the rest of my life waiting for that thud of recognition which, more than likely, will not be recognition at all but the longing for it. I shall wander through parks, study the whirling of the carousel for a rider who might be mine. Is she the blond one? No, no, there she is, the dark one over there."

Andzelika weeps softly.

"I must get back to the regiment. I promised to return in forty-eight hours. It's nearly longer than that now since I left. Trains don't run, roads don't exist."

Janusz stands, looks at his wife. "I think I can arrange to get you back to Krakow, or will your colonel friend take care of that?"

"Back to Krakow? Why? Isn't it much too dangerous to —"

"I would have thought that your desire to begin, to somehow begin the search for her would overtake any other consideration. Or do you prefer to sit here in all this gold-leafed grandeur to weep and to wait for her to find you?"

Eyelids nearly closed, all the better to see this man whom she can't quite recognize, Andzelika looks at Janusz. In the half-whispered whiskey voice she had as a little girl, she asks, "Do you always shoot at dead men, Janusz? Is that what noble cavaliers do? Do they twist their sabers into the hearts of them just for sport? Tell me, how does it feel, my love?"

"Touché. But I repeat. Krakow is where you must begin. Besides, there is nothing, absolutely nothing left either here or there that lacks the shivery element of danger."

"Now that France has surrendered, there will be —"

"Get yourself to Krakow and go through

your mother's things. Whatever she did, she didn't do it alone. She must have left some trace, names in a book, letters. Who was in her pay back then?"

"I don't know. Toussaint, I guess."

"Who is Toussaint?"

"He was her attorney, a disbarred advocate whom Mother retained for many purposes."

"Where is he? When was the last time you saw him?"

"He was an expat French who lived in Krakow. He spoke Polish like a native, so he must have lived there for a long time. I don't remember seeing him in recent years."

"Begin with him. Go to her confessor. She was very attached to the clergy at the Mariacki."

"Bishop Józef was her confessor from the time I was little. He was often a guest at the palace. He died years ago, though. I don't know if she developed the same close relationship with anyone else there."

"Who were her maids? Talk to everyone who was and is still in the household. Talk to everyone, I tell you. She would have been less careful in her own home than she would have been with the extended family. With her friends."

"Do you think the baby was left in an orphanage?"

"It's possible. But that doesn't seem to fit Valeska's style. More likely a private home. I don't know. Or a private school. A good Catholic boarding school in Switzerland."

"Boarding schools do not enroll infants."

"No, of course not. Wherever it was that she left her, surely Valeska left her granddaughter in good hands. The right hands. You know what I mean."

"The most likely thing is that Mother arranged adoption. To some minor royals who wouldn't have minded one more child roaming about the manor. Something like that."

"If she was as ill as Valeska led you to believe, she may no longer be alive, Andzelika."

"I believe she is alive."

"Good. That will help me to believe it, too. But Valeska is dead, and the chances of my lasting out the war without some *boche* spilling my brains are close to nil. That will leave you to find her. To find our child."

Andzelika forces a laugh, tries to push it forth. The tears fall again as Janusz rises, appears as though he is preparing to leave.

"Where are you going?"

"Back to the regiment. I told you that."

"Not even a night's rest?"

"On the train, if there is one. You'll

understand why I can't, why I can't embrace you now? You do understand?"

"Yes."

"*Ja robi kochaja was.* I do love you. Even more than I did when I arrived."

"I know."

Matka, what did you do with her? Where is she, Matka? Where are you, little girl?

■ ■ ■ ■

PART III
JUNE 1940
MONTPELLIER

■ ■ ■ ■

CHAPTER XXVI

Maman. Maman, Maman, where are you?

In delirium, Amandine cries out for her mother. An old woman in the gray cotton dress of a lay sister, her mouth slack, sleeps in a chair across the room from the bed where she lies. The old woman opens her eyes to the child's febrile whispers, rises, approaches the bed.

Hush, child. Sleep is what you must do. Only sleep.

Water. Please. Need water.

No water for you. Nothing. Only sleep. Now hush or I shall have to tie that old stocking across your mouth again. And tie your wrists. You don't want that, do you?

Several days earlier, two of the convent girls began to exhibit alarming symptoms, unmistakable evidences of scarlet fever. A day later eleven girls and three convent sisters were symptomatic, and all of these were isolated in the infirmary. The fact that everyone in the convent and in the school had, to some degree, been exposed to the students and the sisters who had already contracted the fever caused Jean-Baptiste to set up a makeshift secondary isolation ward in rooms adjoining the infirmary. Here he swabbed and probed and listened and looked, and those showing mild or even suspect symptoms were quarantined. Solange was among them. The students and sisters who appeared without infection were confined to the dormitory.

With so many of the sisters unable to execute their house duties, aid was solicited from among the villagers, the *metaires,* even from other religious houses nearby, people to cook and clean and help with the running and fetching. But St.-Hilaire was not the only place where the scarlet fever was registered. Public offices, hospitals, prisons, orphanages — its reach was epidemic. At the earliest moment in the drama, Jean-Baptiste had telephoned the provincial public health offices.

Yes, Doctor, of course help will be sent to St.-Hilaire, just as soon as possible, sir. The waiting list, however, you understand. Priorities, sir. If it's drugs you need, however, those can be sent. . . . I see. Well, all right then,

276

It had been for Amandine that Jean-Baptiste had requested nursing care from the public health offices. It was she who most troubled him. An attack of scarlet fever would be far more threatening to her than to a person without her congenital weaknesses, even weaknesses restored to a tenuous equilibrium. She would be safest if isolated from both the infirmary patients and those in secondary isolation.

Jean-Baptiste consulted Mater Paul about where Amandine might be kept, telling her that physical distance from the infirmary and the adjunct ward would be necessary to keep her from exposure to those who would be caretaking the others.

"Philippe's old rooms," said Paul. "They're in the extreme opposite wing of the building, so we could assign one person to see to her needs and there would be no reason for anyone else to even pass nearby."

"Yes, yes, that's the right place for her. But who is to care for her? If it weren't for her accident, she could do for herself and would only need someone to check her temperature and pulse several times a day and throughout the night, bring her meals. Give her a hand with bathing, perhaps. Essentially just keep vigilant, but with —"

"Ah, yes. Her injury. Graceless little fool that she is. Trying to pirouette in someone else's ballet shoes."

"You forgive her nothing, do you, Mater? Soon you'll be saying it was she who brought down the fever upon your house."

Paul pulls her eternal handkerchief from beneath her sleeve, pats her upper lip. Chooses to keep silent.

"The ankle was far less swollen last evening, but the ligaments are badly torn. She must rest, keep the leg elevated, and the ankle compression must be removed every three or four hours for twenty minutes or so and then rebandaged. We'll need someone who —"

"Josette. She is strong, can lift the child with ease, and, once shown a procedure, she will perform it with precision. Yes, Josette. I can personally attest to her competence. I'll call her in right away."

"Actually, I'd prefer to meet with her."

"But you've been exposed and will therefore expose Josette. If you're not concerned about that, why, I'll take on the duty of caring for Amandine myself."

"You've quite enough to do I would think —"

"Baptiste, don't you trust me to care

properly for the child?"

Baptiste's smile is brief. Perhaps insincere. He says, "Why not someone from the farms, someone who's come up to help from the hamlet?"

"But how do we know who among them has or has not been exposed? At least Josette keeps herself in a kind of isolation most of the time anyway."

"You're right, of course. I'll write instructions. Josette can read, can't she?"

"Some. But I shall review it all with her. Here, sit down and I shall go along to alert Josette."

Paul is indeed diligent in clarifying the instructions for Josette. In a larger, clearer hand, she rewrites Jean-Baptiste's notes in a leather-bound book, which she knows will please Josette, help her to feel the distinction of her role as nurse.

"Though Cook will be given a list of appropriate meals for Amandine, Josette, you must be certain that the food sent to her concurs with your list. Look here now. She must be fed small, frequent meals composed of

white rice
potato puree
stewed fruits

279

poached eggs
raw egg beaten with a touch of sugar and
  a few drops of coffee
blancmange
petit gervais
poached marrow on lightly buttered toast
the juice of an orange diluted with mineral
  water

"It is important that she take in a minimum of eight large glasses of cool water each day in addition to unlimited quantities of weak tea. Do you understand, Josette?"

In the leather-bound book, Paul has drawn columns for days of the week, hours of the day, categories of information to note. She instructs Josette to enter into the book, no matter how primitively, everything that the child eats and drinks as well as her pulse and temperature.

"And here are the warning signs you must watch for, Josette.

a flushing of the face, even a mild one
a rash on any part of her body
chills
fever
headache
vomiting

rapid pulse
a whitened tongue

"Do you understand each of these? Amandine is very verbal, to say the least, and she will certainly alert you should she feel discomfort."

Josette is peevish under Paul's fastidious delivery.

Has Paul forgotten how I, Josette, cared for her all those years ago? How I kept many a vigil with the child Annick in my arms when she was burning with fever or blue with cough? While her doctor father roved about the village, it was I who treated little Annick with herbal remedies, rubbing her chest with the poultices my mother would make of olive oil and white willow or slippery elm for my brothers and sisters. I would cover her thin, wheezing breast with a rag warmed by the fire. The most important part of the cure was my rocking her in my arms then, and the lullabies. And here, now, all this fuss over what to do for Amandine.

"And remember, Josette, no one, absolutely no one must be admitted to those rooms. Trays will be prepared and left for you by Cook or one of her helpers near the entrance to that wing. And you will leave the empty trays in the same place. Likewise

281

with linens and towels and changes of clothing for both you and Amandine. Whatever else you might order. Write what you want and leave the note on the tray. Also, tear out the day's page of entries and leave it on the last tray in the evening. We'll see that Jean-Baptiste receives it. Do you understand? And I'm certain I don't have to remind you to keep the rooms in pristine fashion. You may sleep in the room adjoining hers or on the sofa in the parlor but, wherever you are, leave the door ajar so you will hear should she call you. And use this to wake yourself every two hours during the night." Like an Olympic torch, Paul slaps the metal clock with the two large bells on either side into Josette's open palm, watches as the old woman, leather-bound book under her arm, starts haughtily on her way.

"But why can't I take care of her, Baptiste? I don't have the fever, I'm perfectly well —"

"Lie down, Solange, lie down and I'll be happy to explain things to you once again. It's true that you don't have a fever, but you were exposed to nearly all, if not all, of the students and sisters who do. Three of whom, I might add, are gravely ill and must be moved to hospital later today. As for you, your throat is speckled in white, your tongue is yellowish, your pulse rate is elevated, and you've a mild rash on your neck and shoulders. It's likely that you will be fully symptomatic by this evening, when I shall have you moved to the infirmary and begin dosing you with penicillin just as I have the others. Now do you understand why it can't be you who cares for Amandine?"

"Yes, yes. But of all people, why is it to be Josette who —"

"At first I too was uncomfortable when Paul suggested Josette but, under these conditions, she's actually the best choice. She keeps so much to herself, works quite alone at her scrubbing and cleaning, and prefers to take her meals in her room rather than in the refectory. A strange old duck, I know, but we've all witnessed her hawkish approach to her work, to whatever assignment she is given. And that's what Amandine needs right now. I must tell you that Paul was wonderfully solicitous in setting things up. Explaining the tasks to Josette, the caveats. These days will pass by quickly and, besides, I expect the provincial offices to send help at any time. As soon as they do, I'll relieve Josette. Rest, now. Save your strength."

CHAPTER XXVII

"What devil inhabits her, Josette? What keeps the breath in that child? I wish her dead and gone and never having been. May God forgive me."

These words, spoken by Paul to Josette months before — soon after what became known as the refectory event had occurred — have remained an almost constant reprise in Josette's disheveled mind, goading, spurring, obsessing her. Now this windfall of chance to act. How long has she sought retribution, some small justice for all that her beloved Annick has endured? All those years ago she'd wanted to murder Annick's father. Wandering through the woods and over the meadows when she was eight or nine and had just taken on the care of the doctor's infant daughter, Josette's favored pastime was to rhapsodize ways and means of his demise. She would stab him in his sleep or poison his tea with the yellow powder meant for rats or, better, she would take Monsieur Dufy by the hand some afternoon, lead him through the elm wood and down to the river when the doctor and Monsieur's red-haired, white-breasted wife were in dishabille on the damp blue rug in the fishermen's cottage. Let Monsieur Dufy shoot him, that would suit her fine. But Josette never did a thing to hurt Annick's father except to store up her bitterness for him. By the time Annick had become Soeur Paul and she, Josette, had joined her at the convent, she'd dug a deeper and wider place for that bitterness what with all she'd accumulated of it by then for the bishop Fabrice. Yes, the bishop's fancy for Paul so fleeting, Josette still sometimes hears the great liquorish cackles he'd send up into the unholy night while she waited outside the chapel doors for her Annick. Annick would have killed or died for him and — then and now — Josette well understands that sentiment. But what could she have done to harm a bishop? There were others, too, over the years, postulants who scoffed at Paul, lay sisters who guffawed when her back was turned, convent sisters who conspired to her discomfort. But what could she do to any of them really, they whose lives were already so full of misery? At last, this child.

■ ■ ■ ■

Metaires from the hamlet — both men and women — have come to help at St.-Hilaire. They take over kitchen duties, scrub floors and walls and stairs with a vile-smelling disinfectant, see to the laundry and the gardens. One of them carries a small, white-wrapped bundle down the stairs from the convent girls' dormitory. Her splinted, bandaged ankle held up stiff as a rudder, Amandine giggles, asks her young porter to walk faster, faster so she can feel a breeze, then bids him stop in the garden to let her stay for a while in the hot June sun.

"But Mademoiselle Amandine, they're waiting for you now. I promised. In a few days all this business of the fever will be over and your ankle will be good as new and the sun will be warmer yet, you'll see."

Under the loggia then, into the convent, down the far west wing to Père Philippe's old rooms, where Josette is folding down the linen sheets of the freshly made bed.

"There we are. Carefully now. Thank you, Monsieur Luc."

"Yes, thank you, Monsieur Luc. Will you come to visit me soon?"

"I would be happy to. In fact, my mother

has offered to stay with Mademoiselle during the nights, Sister, should she be needed. She asked me specifically to speak to Mater Paul, but I was unable to find her and —"

"Thank you, Monsieur Luc, but all the arrangements are quite in order. Please do thank your mother, though."

"Can Monsieur Luc come to visit me, Josette?"

"No visitors for you, my dear. Surely that was explained to you. No visitors. Not until this siege is over. Now Monsieur Luc has many things to do . . ."

Josette guides the young man to the threshold, nods her farewells, closes the door. Locks it. Removes the key and puts it in her pocket. Pats the pocket. Smiles at Amandine.

At last.

"Josette, did someone bring over my books, my drawing pads? I put everything in my satchel and —"

"It's all here. But first let me explain Jean-Baptiste's orders for you. The most important thing to do is to sleep. You must sleep as much as possible, lie still and be very, very quiet —"

"But, Josette, I'm not sick. It's only my ankle, but even it is much better, see? And I know how to undo the bandage without disturbing the splints and then I have to let it rest for twenty minutes and then I'll need help in putting the bandage back on though I do know how to do it, it's a little hard for me to get it even and tight but —"

"You mustn't worry about a thing. I know what to do. And even though you're not sick, as you say, we will follow exactly what Jean-Baptiste has asked of us, won't we?"

Josette walks to the large oak dresser across the room and, from the same pocket where she has put the key, she takes out a small brown glass vial. Her back to Amandine, she shakes a liquid from the vial into a glass, pours in less than an inch of water from the pitcher on the dresser, turns and, smiling, walks to the bed.

"What's that?"

"Why, your medicine, of course."

"What medicine? I haven't been taking any medicine. What's it for?"

"I am sure I don't know, dear. It's what Baptiste has prescribed. Likely it's just a vitamin potion or some such thing. Now drink this all in a single swallow. Go ahead."

Josette pulls Amandine's head back with one hand — tugging at her hair with just a touch too much force — and, with the other, tips the glass into her half willingly open mouth.

"Thank you, Josette. May I have my satchel now? I would like to study the fingering for my new piano piece. I have a paper keyboard you know and I can practice quite well with it —"

"Not right now. Now it's time to sleep."

"But it's ten-thirty, almost time . . . *pour le goûter* . . . I mean. I'm a little hungry."

"When you wake. Now lie back and close your eyes. I'll just pull the curtains and —"

"Where will you be?"

"Right here in the parlor. Just on the other side of the door. Hush, now."

"Will you wake me when they bring *le goûter?*"

"Certainly."

Passiflora, valerian, hops, lemon balm. Another of my mother's potions. This morning when I asked the herbalist for three vials rather than my usual single one, he barely blinked an eye. Mild but efficient, he said as he always did while he twisted the thin blue paper about each vial. I knew that, of course. When Annick was teething or restless or in any sort of pain, a few drops on my finger rubbed across her tongue. And then for Paul, fifteen drops in a bit of water to help her sleep. She's hardly been asking for it lately, though. Now she takes those long white pills. I took those, too, from her drawer. Way in the back on the left-hand side; she's never been able to hide much from me. I can't read the label except for b-a-r and then the ink is smudged. I wouldn't be able to read it anyway. But if these help Paul to sleep, imagine how they will help the child. I'll just mash up a piece of one in with the next dose of the potion. In a few hours. Wait to see how she fares with the thirty drops. Such a tiny mouse, she is. To have caused so much trouble. I don't want things to go too quickly, though. No, not too quickly. Ah, look at her now. See how she sleeps?

Josette checks her watch, unlocks the door, leaves the room, locks the door again from the outside, walks to the place where the trays of food and drink are to be left. The midmorning tray waits on the table. Two trays. Amandine's with a pot of tea, toasted black bread with raisins, still warm and wrapped in a yellow napkin, a small ramekin of fresh cheese. Someone has placed a blue glass plate laid with six candied violets on Amandine's tray. On Josette's tray, the same elements are there, save the violets — but in larger quantities. Practiced in such matters, Josette balances one tray upon the other, walks back to the rooms, sets down the trays, opens the door.

Closes it. Locks it from the inside, pockets the key. She sits herself at the table in front of the window, opens the curtains just enough to let in a streak of light, then slowly, deliberately, works her way through the tea and toast and cheese from both trays. She sucks on the violets, crushes the sugar crust of them between her teeth. Retraces her steps to the pickup and delivery point, and returns then to the rooms to rest herself in Philippe's old high-back chair in the parlor.

Limbs askew, breath faint, Amandine sleeps the sleep of the dead, a black and white butterfly pinioned rakishly upon a board. Hours later, when she stirs, it's to look about, to try to recall where she is and why.

I know now, I am in Père Philippe's room. Yes, the fever, I am here so that I will stay safe from the fever. How thirsty I am, mouth dry, cannot swallow. So warm. Perhaps *le goûter* has arrived by now.

"Josette. Josette. Josette."

Startled from her own sleep by Amandine's feeble call, Josette approaches the bed. "Yes, yes. I'm here. Awake already, are you?"

"I'm thirsty. Some water, please."

"No water, child. Doctor's orders. Nothing to drink. Only sleep."

"But my mouth is so dry and I'm hungry. Please. My leg, the bandage, will you take it off? It hurts, Josette, and my arms feel so heavy I can hardly reach —"

"Here, let me see the leg."

Josette pulls back the sheet, raises the bandaged leg, moves it about roughly as though priming a long-unused pump, and Amandine screams in pain. Screams until her breath catches and tears run and she wills herself to wake from the bad dream. But Josette has found a good game and so moves the leg about in the same way again while Amandine, pulling herself upright, flails stick-doll arms in futile defense. Josette laughs, and Amandine knows she is not dreaming.

"Solange. Please, call Solange. Some mistake, Josette. Please call Solange."

"You can call out all you care to for your Solange, but she can't hear you and neither can anyone else. You're mine. No mistake at all. There is only Josette. Let me see to that bandage now."

Unwrapping the ankle, then lashing the stuff round and round the tiny bones so tightly that, had there been no wound at all, the pain would have been grinding.

"There, that's what Baptiste wanted. Better, isn't it? Of course it is. And now, your medicine."

"Why, Josette, why?"

Josette walks to the oak dresser, pulls the vial from her pocket, measures out into Amandine's glass a generous forty drops of the valerian potion, perhaps a few more. From some other place in her voluminous skirts, she takes the bottle filched from Paul's drawer. Shakes out a tablet. Breaks it between her fingers, takes a shard of it and rubs it to a powder in her palm, flicks the powder into the potion. A little water then, not too much. She swishes the cocktail and takes it to Amandine. Putting the glass to the girl's lips, she pours the liquid into the dutifully open maw, moves the little pointed chin to be sure she's swallowed.

"Good girl. Now all you need to think about is sleep."

"But I'm thirsty and hungry . . ."

As she had done with *le goûter* and with the lunch, Josette does with the evening's dinner. This time, though, after collecting the trays, she pulls the small round table to the bedside, sits herself on the edge of the bed very close to Amandine. Josette sprinkles a bit of water over the sleeping child's face, her eyelids, rousing her, if only partially, so she might witness the feasting.

"Amandine, do look at this. A puree of potatoes with a poached egg on top, and when I pierce that lovely yellow yolk, see how it trickles down into the potatoes and, oh, how delicious they are mixed together, yes, yes, you must taste this, just be patient while I taste it again and then I'll spoon up some for you, yes, just wait a moment."

Willing her eyes to stay open, smelling the food, Amandine is ravenous for it yet does not ask Josette to feed her and neither does she reach to take the spoon from Josette's clutch. With no sound, no sigh, slow, hot tears fall, collect in the corners of her mouth, drip from her chin, wetting her neck and the white lace of her nightdress. Like a wind-fed fire in a hay barn, the knowing sweeps over her, the knowing that hers is a helpless rage, and so she is, in her way, serene watching Josette, watching her with the clear-mindedness of one who has understood — not that life is always bad but that, bad or good, it is mysterious. That it will always be mysterious. That life has so little to do with our will for it, and less is it linked to our own goodness or badness. However shakily goodness and badness can be defined. So if not that, if neither will nor just deserts shape life, what does? She lies there licking the salt tears and wondering. She will have to wait awhile longer to understand about the weight, the power of historical revenges and follies and Judas kisses. She will have to wait to know that we inherit life much as we do the slope of a cheek or silver in a velvet-cushioned box. And to know that it's we who then perpetuate the life we inherit — gently or ferociously, according to our natures — repeating the ancestral follies and the traitorous kisses and leaving the legacy nicely intact for those who will come after us. Like silver in a box.

And so Amandine lies there in the soiled, crumpled bed where someone means her to die, magnificent as only a stick doll with unshackled curls and a daintily pointed chin and eyes like drowned plums — the same weepy black plums that are her mother's eyes — can be magnificent, while Josette, amid her guttural swallowings, says once again, "Just one more spoonful for me and then . . ."

Amandine watches the thick black veins in Josette's hands as she runs her fingers over the plate, brings them to her mouth and sucks them dry. Still holding the plate, Josette bends her head close to Amandine, whispers something into the tight pink whorls of her tiny ear. Her spittle warm, her sibilance deafening, she asks Amandine if she's hungry, wishes her a bawdy *bon appétit,* swipes her mouth with the back of her hand, licks her lips, sets the phlegm-smeared plate down on Amandine's chest.

"Mater, Baptiste has just pronounced me fit, no symptoms after four days in isolation. I asked him if I might take over for Josette and he agreed, asked that you accompany me to relieve her. He said that Amandine should stay another day or two apart and then she, too, can be released, join the others who've returned to the dormitory. Will you go with me now, Mater?"

Marie-Albert waits as Paul considers the request, straightens the already perfectly organized elements laid out on her desk.

"Yes, I suppose Josette should be relieved, but are you certain you're not needed elsewhere? I mean Josette's usefulness is limited more than yours, isn't it?"

"Actually, I think it's Amandine who might enjoy a respite. Four days and three nights with only Josette for company, well, you understand what I intend, don't you, Mater?"

"Yes, yes, I suppose I do. Though one might look at it from the opposite view and say that four days and three nights with only Amandine for company . . . Poor old Josette. Yes, well, let's go. Just be sure to be gentle with Josette, tell her what a good job she's done. Did Baptiste tell you how she's charted the child's vital signs, marked down everything she's eaten and drunk? Absolutely perfect records she's kept."

When Paul knocks on the doors to Philippe's old suite, there is no answer. Marie-Albert knocks harder. Still no answer.

"Josette, open the door. It's Paul. And Marie-Albert. Open the door, Josette."

Josette is sleeping. Having neither washed herself during these four days nor changed her clothes, she sits, barefoot and wearing only her shift, in Philippe's high-back chair in the now putrid air of the parlor. Not speaking a word in answer to Paul's commanding voice, Josette walks quickly to Amandine's bed, hoping to find that her breathing has stopped. That the affair will be finished. But no. Not yet.

"Just a little longer, Annick," she says quietly. "If only you could have waited just a little longer."

"Josette, open this door. Do you hear me, Josette?"

In a joyful falsetto, Josette asks, "Is it you, Annick? Darling Annick? Just a little longer.

Nearly finished."

"Who is Annick? What is she saying? Use your key, Mater, I don't understand this."

"I don't carry the keys to this wing. In my desk, top right-hand drawer."

Marie-Albert is already racing away as Paul screams after her, "Get Baptiste."

Paul rattles the knob, flails her body against the door, pounds it with the heels of her hands, all the while shouting, *"Josette, Josette, Josette."*

But Josette, if she hears Paul, does not respond. Yellow-streaked, white hair falling in thin unctuous points about her shoulders, the stench of her diffused now about the bedroom; she is a crone inflamed with her last act of devotion to little Annick. A small pillow, white linen embroidered with dark green leaves and their tendrils, she holds over Amandine's face, pressing it with all her might. The job finally done, she lifts the child in her arms, turns toward the door as Marie-Albert bashes it wide against the wall.

Josette holds Amandine out to Paul. A trophy. It is Marie-Albert, though, who pushes in front of Paul, takes Amandine in her arms, carries her to the bed. Paul pushes Josette to the floor, kicks her about the face and chest while Josette repeats and repeats Paul's own words.

298

I wish her dead and gone and never having been.

"For me? You've murdered her for me?"

Paul kicks Josette again, goes to stand at the foot of the bed, shaking the bedpost as though to wake the child.

Marie-Albert lifts Amandine's head, a ripe fig lolling on its stalk, gently lays it down again, places her open hands over the tiny, cadaverous yellow face, like wax even to the touch. Her keen the plucked string of harp, Marie-Albert caresses Amandine's lips with her thumb. Lays her ear to the child's heart. So accustomed to asking permission, she looks up at Paul, then quickly bends to force her own breath into the small dried rose that is Amandine's mouth. She thrusts breath after breath into the child until the narrow, sunken chest of her begins to heave and, from the small dried rose, shallow gasps come. Amandine opens her eyes, rimmed and crusted and wet with grief.

"Marie-Albert, are you dead, too? Are we all dead? Where is Philippe and his grandmother? Blue hair. Maman, Maman, where are you? Are you dead, Maman?"

Chapter XXVIII

Pressure sixty over thirty, pulse rate one hundred fifteen but steady, temperature nearing forty. Potential complications due to heart disease. I need an intravenous solution of potassium chloride, sodium, glucose. I don't know yet, I don't know if I'll send her in. Just get the solution and the setup here.

Having alerted Les Secours from the telephone in Paul's office, Jean-Baptiste races back to Philippe's rooms, where he's left Marie-Albert to bathe Amandine with alcohol, to feed her sugared water with an eyedropper.

"What is it? What's happened to her, Baptiste? The fever? Is it the fever? What did Josette . . . ?"

"She's been starved, Marie, starved and drugged. She's dying of thirst and the effects of suffocation."

He is unwrapping the bandage, massaging the blackened flesh of Amandine's leg. He

300

listens to her heart. Listens to it again.

"Call Fabrice. Ask him to come. Sacraments."

Marie-Albert sends two village women who have been working in the kitchens to assist Jean-Baptiste while she goes to alert the bishop. Jean-Baptiste shows the village women how to care for Amandine. "Feed her like a newborn bird. Cool water, a few drops at a time. Bathe her with alcohol, bathe her again, open the windows a few centimeters. I'm going out to the portico to wait for Les Secours. Remember, like a newborn bird. And for the love of God, air the parlor."

Amandine awakes and sees the women who work quietly about her. Since they are not familiar to her, she thinks she must have arrived in heaven. She sees the needle in her arm, and her eyes follow the tubing upward to the bottle of clear liquid mounted on something that looks like a metal tree.

"What is this in my arm?"

"It's medicine, child."

"No, I don't want any more medicine, please, please . . ." She touches the needle as though to dislodge it, but one of the women stays her hand while the other caresses her forehead. Both whisper to her.

Tell her all is well.

"It's the medicine that Monsieur le Docteur has ordered for you, child."

"That's what she said. Josette said hers was medicine that Baptiste had ordered."

Her mind, misted, spinning — am I dead? am I alive? — Amandine recalls another moment, when her foes the convent girls suddenly turned, became her friends. As she did then, she wonders now, How can one tell friends from foes? And what if one can't?

Later, when the village women have gone and the first dose of the intravenous solution is finished, Baptiste removes the needle, lifts Amandine into his arms, arranges himself in Philippe's high-back chair, and rocks her gently, two of his fingers always on her stick-doll wrist. She opens her eyes to him.

"Baptiste. Also you? All of us dead?"

"We're none of us dead. We're here with you now."

"I'm not dead? I thought I was and that I could hear all of you talking but I couldn't tell if you were dead, too, or still, you know, still . . . I wanted to tell you that I was fine, that I wasn't afraid or anything, but I couldn't make the words come, my mouth so dry and my head spinning, spinning. And there was this terrible smell, a scary smell that I thought was death. And then I couldn't breathe anymore . . . no breath at all."

"You're not dead, and neither am I. I'm here with you and I promise you that —"

"I know. That she won't hurt me anymore. Isn't that what you promise?"

"That's what I promise."

"And that medicine in my arm, what was it for?"

"It was to bathe your innards, to make your pipes plump and pink again, drench you like rain does a pot of pansies left too long in the sun. You shall have more of it later."

"Like rain on a pot of pansies . . ."

"Exactly like that. And soon you'll be —"

"I'm grown up now, Baptiste. Even more than I was before. I don't know yet if I like it, but I think it's true. I think it's true that I know things, understand things that I didn't when I was, you know, before this. I think that's why I feel so cold."

"That sensation will pass, Amandine. All of this will —"

"I shall not forget what happened. I don't want to. Only children forget, Baptiste. Or pretend to."

Chapter XXIX

Baptiste arranges things for Josette according to the wishes of His Eminence. Though visibly pained, shocked by the affair, Fabrice wishes to keep its horror within the family.

No criminal charges, no announcements to the press. What would the scandal of it serve, save justice perhaps, since there is no kith, no kin to clamor for it? Better to remove the seventy-nine-year-old from society, let her live out her days, at the expense of the curia, in a private institute. In humane confinement. Better to save the curia embarrassment. Better to save the school its reputation, its income.

In a few hours it is done. Restrained as well as medicated, dressed in a clean gray shift, one of Philippe's old sweaters, and new black oxfords — Paul's own — a gift of farewell, of *adieu* that Paul brought to her room just after sunrise, Josette is guided by two orderlies through the convent halls, out the garden door, and into a waiting institute automobile. Leaning her stout black form against an ivied column, Paul stands on the front portico waiting for the automobile to move down the drive. She is a silent send-off party of one. No wimple, no cross about her neck, no beads about her waist, this morning she is less the abbess of the convent of St.-Hilaire than she is little Annick, grown old and come to see the single champion of her life ride away from her forever. For the first time since she was less than a year old, Annick/Paul will proceed without this champion, without her being across the room or down the hall or on her way through the elm woods to bring her a posy or an apronful of wild berries or half a cake stolen from the baker's boy. The first time.

Paul watches the small square auto plow the greenish light that the leaves make of the plane tree avenue. She stands there long after it has gone from sight.

Just after three o'clock on that same afternoon, Marie-Albert goes to the infirmary to tell Solange that Baptiste wishes her settled back into her own rooms. Beyond contagion, she has been three days on penicillin therapy, her symptoms mitigated. Baptiste

305

had implored Marie-Albert to say nothing to Solange of the events, to wait for him to do so. His duty, he'd said.

I shall join you in Solange's rooms just after vespers. I must tell her everything, tell her the truth but tell it carefully. I know that you understand.

As she rushes down the corridor to the infirmary, Marie-Albert has difficulty staying her tears. How can she face Solange, Solange, who believes that Amandine has been, these last four days, in the well-meaning hands of Josette? Out of harm's way.

At first there will be blank disbelief, Marie thinks, the mind revolting at what it hears as mine did at the plain sight of Amandine held out in Josette's arms. Baptiste is right, we must tell her all we know, but still she will be spared what we saw.

"Marie-Albert, how wonderful to see you. Should you be here, though? Am I past the risk of sharing this plague?"

"Baptiste says you are. And I must say you're looking well, nearly well. I have other news. Baptiste says you must leave this grand hotel and content yourself with your own rooms. How do you like that?"

"When? I'm ready this moment. Will Amandine be coming home as well? I've

306

had no news of her today, but surely, if she's not symptomatic, she will be —"

"Baptiste will be by to visit you after vespers, and we can ask him then. I'm to be your lady-in-waiting, by the way. Lovely duty, don't you think?"

"What's the matter, Marie?" Solange stops midway while trying to find her slippers under the bed, looks hard at Marie-Albert.

"What do you mean, what's the matter? Nothing at all. I, I. . . ."

Solange sits back down on the side of the bed, her head reeling from even such slight exertion.

"Marie, tell me."

"I can't right now. When Baptiste comes . . ."

"Is it Amandine? If something is wrong, I must know. You can't —"

"Amandine is well. She's fine. Let's pack up your things now and get you home."

In the same quiet, steady voice that had re-assured her for nine years, Baptiste speaks to Solange. Perched on the edge of the bed where Solange lies, Marie-Albert holds her hand, keeps her eyes fixed on Baptiste, who spares nothing of what he knows but much of what he suspects. The particulars of Josette's conduct. As he speaks, he hears the thinness of the story, the hollow parts, the inanity. How could it have happened? All of us so close while . . . He hears himself trying to find an ending, a summing-up.

"There is no further manifest damage to her heart, though we'll do another cardiogram in a day or so. Her vital signs are stable and have been since six hours after we found her, after we began therapy. The principal damage is emotional. Spiritual the better word in her case."

Solange has not spoken, neither whimpered nor wept. At some point in Baptiste's delivery, she'd begun to look toward the window and then about the room, her gaze resting here and there as though she's trying to recall having once seen that chair, that bookcase, that painting, those red rubber boots.

Baptiste rises from his chair, walks to the bed and, for the first time since he has known her, wraps Solange in his arms, holds her. She looks down at him as at an impertinent stranger. She says nothing. She is thinking of Janka and the lady with the eyes like a deer and that afternoon on the farm. And for some reason, she sees the garden, she sees Marie-Albert stepping carefully among the peas, the onions, coming toward her conspiratorily, laughing then, holding her arms out to take the deep oval basket from her, the basket with the length of soft blue wool in it where Amandine slept. Her mind wants to know: How did we get from that morning in the garden to this day?

Baptiste goes away, leaves Marie-Albert with Solange. Perhaps an hour has passed when, still not having said a word, Solange rises from the bed and walks quickly to the armoire. As she had done once before, when Amandine suffered the treacheries of the convent girls, she throws the contents upon the beds, the chairs, the rugs. Marie-Albert tries to stop her, tries to lead her back to the bed.

"Whatever you want to do, let me do it for you," she says. "You're weak and still very ill. What is it you're doing with all of this?"

"Preparing to leave."

"Yes, of course. To leave. When Baptiste returns, surely you can speak to him —"

"No need. He's already said that she's well. Physically well. Only a train ride away. Two days' journey. We'll be home. I should have gone long ago."

"To your family, is that where you'll take her?"

Solange nods her head, sits on the red and

yellow Turkey rug among their things, touching one or another of them without looking at it.

"I'm going to bathe now, to dress and to find Baptiste. Will you help me?"

"Of course I'll help you, but there's no need for you to . . . I shall go to find him. Stay in bed and I'll be right back."

Baptiste tells Solange it is imprudent for Amandine to travel, to risk fatigue. To risk worse. He shouts, he implores. He is quiet then, goes to sit on the edge of the bed. The heels of his hands gouging his eyes, he tells her, "I think you are mad. Mad with grief and shame. Just as I am. As, I believe, is Paul. All three of us holed up in our souls, sick with guilt for what, what name can I give it? For our *ingenuousness.* Yes, that's a clean-enough word. *Ingenuousness.* Each of us knew something of Josette, you more than I, but, no one ever consulted you, and so it was I, Paul and I, who decided she was the right one. The best one. But sweet Jesus, Amandine survived. Now are you resolved to try her again? Have you considered the war?"

Solange laughs quietly. "The war out there. The one in here. Yes, madness. There is no place left to hide from it."

310

"You must arrange for someone to meet you in Reims. That's the nearest station, isn't it? And then she should resume her recuperation. Not complete bed rest but very mild activity, frequent repose. That sort of thing. I'll arrange things with a colleague who sees patients in Reims once a month. He'll examine her. Keep watch over her. I'll write to him tomorrow. You'll take along her records. You must be prepared for delays in the train schedules. Discomfort. Despite your lofty dismissal of it, please understand that the news from the north is grim, Solange.

"And your news of today, was it not grim?"

"War is different."

"Is it?"

"You must know that it is. Invasion, occupation, requisition, deportation, work camps, extreme privation —"

"Extreme privation? Hunger, is that what you mean? And grotesque cruelties, too, I imagine. It all sounds familiar enough, Baptiste. Perhaps only the aggressors' costumes will change from the ones worn here. And now I wish to see Paul. Will you ask her to come here to me, or shall I go to her?"

Baptiste notes Solange's use of the name rather than the title.

"You must know that she is devastated. I have little will to protect her, yet I assure you that she did not, in any way — shall we say — assist Josette. Fabrice tells me that you know the story of Josette and Paul, the story of when they were children. As I admitted before, had I known more of it, I might have —"

"I blame no one. I have no heart for anything but to take my little girl away from here, quickly and forever away. It's neither in fear nor disgust that I'm leaving. Amandine and I will go away because this part of our lives is finished, and so to stay would be wrong. It might have been finished a while ago, longer ago than that, but I didn't understand until now. I didn't recognize the ending. I want to see Paul not to punish her but to say good-bye."

"Wait, Solange. Wait until tomorrow. Tomorrow we'll bring Amandine here. We'll bring her home and —"

"This is not our home. I don't know when it ceased to be our home, but it is no longer that."

"And your home in the north, when was the last time you heard from anyone there? Hadn't you better write, if not a letter, a telegram? Some communication seems indicated. What if they've gone? The *boche* taken over the house? It's possible there is no home up there for you. Have you thought of that?"

"They'll be there. I know my mother. My grandmother. There may be a few *boche* boarders, but my mother will be there."

Baptiste and Solange continue to look at one another but neither speaks, she seeing his white flag, he her mettle.

"And His Eminence?" Baptiste wants to know.

"I was just going to ask you if —"

"He's here. He's been here since, since earlier today."

"Why the train, my dear? My driver will take you door to door. There's the difficulty about petrol, but we still have it hoarded here and there as far as I know and, of course, the roads will not be unencumbered with either vehicles or refugees, but surely an auto ride is preferable to . . ."

As he speaks, Fabrice takes a chair from its place at the dining table, carries it across the room to Solange's bedside.

"Thank you, sir. I can't thank you enough, but Amandine has always adored the idea of a journey on a train. This is the right moment for it. This is what I want to do."

The bishop settles himself in the chair,

reaches for Solange's hand. His gaze is stern before it's tender.

"I see. You have reflected on the fact that disorder mounts every day, have you, child? Everyone from the north is on the road south, here to this so-called Free Zone."

"I have reflected, sir."

"We French are a race of self-servers, and I can tell you that the shutters will be tight up there even against a Frenchwoman and her child. *Let them do without* shall be the theme of your northern countrymen except when it comes to themselves. You mustn't think you can count on anyone, Solange. Not until you reach your mother. I am not trying to dissuade you, only to —"

"The traffic going north should be light, sir."

The wry phrase stops the bishop in mid-sentence.

"Yes, the road into enemy territory, yes, very light traffic. . . . And what if your family is among the exodus?"

"My family would never leave the farm. They didn't during the Great War and they won't now. *Boche* or not, I would rather that Amandine and I be there with them."

"Yes. Of course. And what does Amandine say about — ?"

"I haven't yet told her. I haven't yet seen

314

her since —"

"I see. Well, maybe you're right after all, Solange. To seek a fresh new hell. You've decided, then?"

"Yes, sir."

"I shall help you, Solange."

Chapter XXX

"We don't have to talk about it now. About what happened. We don't, do we?"

It is nearly eleven on a Wednesday morning, and Amandine and Solange are together in their rooms. Earlier Baptiste had taken Amandine for a walk about the gardens and for a visit to the chapel before accompanying her to Solange. Bidding them both a good day, he tells them that he will be by to check on them in the early evening. Amandine reaches up to embrace him, and he goes quickly, perhaps uncomfortably, on his way.

Both Amandine and Solange are skittish, each one worried about the other. Thinking it might be ritual they need to bring them back to where they'd been — if indeed anything ever could — they begin the bathing one.

Amandine turns the taps to fill the tub with warm water and, deft as a spa matron, goes about her business with the almond oil, the purple capsules of lilac foam, shakes open the towels, lays them over the chair. Solange helps her to undress, to step into the tub. Though Amandine remembers to inhale the lilac scent, Solange does not.

Now, holding hands and propped upright with bed cushions, they sit — side by side in fresh nightdresses — on the sofa before the spent hearth. Marie-Albert has brought them tea and a small bowl of wild strawberries.

"No. I don't think we do. Not now. When we're ready, when we desire to talk about it, then we shall. Jean-Baptiste told you that we're leaving, didn't he? He wanted to be the one to tell you, and I agreed. He thought that you would be, you know, more open with him. Tell him your true feelings about that prospect."

"He told me, and I said that I would like to go."

"Good. Then it's settled."

"And I'm not even worried about my mother, about her not being able to find me. I've left her a note."

"You've left who a note?"

"My mother."

"With *la Vierge?*"

"Yes. She's not very efficient, but still, I

trust her."

"And what did you say in the note?"

"I told her that your last name is Jouffroi and that we are going to Avise. And that I was going to learn to milk goats. I am, aren't I?"

"Absolutely."

"I wrote it on a sheet of paper that Jean-Baptiste gave to me. The kind where he writes what pills to take. I know *la Vierge* doesn't really deliver mail. Not exactly anyway. But I feel better that I wrote the note and left it with her. I just feel better. I didn't tell my mother about Josette."

"No. No, I wouldn't think you would. So, you're ready to go?"

"Ready. And I'm sort of glad that none of the girls are here. Or are some of them still — ?"

"No. All of them gone to spend the summer in one place or another. At least I think so. Won't they be surprised to find you gone when they return? But you'll write to them, they to you."

"I suppose. Mostly I'll miss Marie-Albert and Josephine and the other sisters. And Baptiste. I wish you would marry Baptiste, and then we could take him with us. I told him so, and do you know what he said?"

"No, and I'm not certain I would like to —"

"He said: 'There'll be time for that.' What does that mean exactly?"

"It's another way to say *Maybe someday.*"

"So *maybe someday* you'll marry Baptiste?"

"Enough."

"I don't know if I shall miss Mater. Will you miss her?"

"Perhaps I will. But I think *miss* might not be the right term. More she has left me a great deal to think about. More that."

"I'm a little scared about going. But not too much."

"That's one of the best things about a journey . . . being a *little* scared."

"I guess . . . it's a good kind of scary, isn't it?"

"Yes, the good kind. We'll be leaving on Saturday morning. The eight-forty-nine from Montpellier to Nîmes. We'll change trains there. If all goes well, we'll arrive in Reims sometime on Monday morning. Maybe a little later."

"How many trains will we take?"

"Four. Altogether, four."

"I want to take ten, twenty . . ."

"I promise you that there will be many train rides in our future. But for now, we'll begin with four."

"Okay."

"We have two days to prepare. Two more days plus the remainder of this one. You must rest and —"

"And you, too. We can rest together."

"Together."

Amandine lies down, her head on Solange's thighs, and closes her eyes. Solange caresses Amandine's hair, sings a quiet song until she hears the even breathing of her sleep.

"Where is Josette?"

"I thought you were sleeping."

With her eyes still closed, Amandine says, "I was pretending. Anyhow, just before I fall asleep I always think of Josette, but Baptiste says that will pass. I told him that I won't forget what happened and he said that things passing and forgetting them are not the same. He says that, even if I don't forget, I will soon stop thinking about Josette. Do you think that's true?"

"I know it's true. And to answer your question, Josette has gone away, been taken away, to a kind of hospital. A hospital that's also a prison."

"How long will she stay there?"

"She'll stay there always."

"Will they be cruel to her there?"

"No. But probably not loving, either."

"Why did she do it?"

Solange, still caressing Amandine's hair, stays quiet, then moves her hands to hold Amandine's face, to turn it up to hers. "I don't know. No one can. Not even Josette."

It is just after one that same day when there is a knock on the door. Solange rises to answer it.

"I think it's Marie-Albert with our lunch. She will stay the afternoon with us. *Bonjour, Mar—— Mater.* I was expecting —"

"Yes, I know, but I asked Marie if I might carry this up to you. Were you napping? I hope I haven't come too early."

Solange hesitates, says, "If anything, Mater, I fear you're too late."

Paul looks at Solange, takes in the quiddity of her words.

"Yes, yes, I'm sure I am. Too late."

"Here, Mater, let me take the tray."

"It's all cold food so that whenever you have appetite . . . Amandine." Paul holds out her hand to Amandine, who stands now behind Solange.

"*Bonjour,* Mater." Amandine takes Paul's hand, shakes it very formally.

"Well, you're both looking well, I must say."

"Thank you, Mater. Won't you sit?" Solange invites.

The three arrange themselves almost simultaneously in a row upon the sofa, Amandine in the middle. They smile at one another, settle into the cushions. Looking straight ahead then, all of them seem exceedingly fascinated by the spent hearth.

"I haven't seen these rooms for a very long time. It feels much like a home, a real one, I mean."

"Maybe you could come to live here, Mater, now that we're going. You could have Solange's bed because it's bigger, and then you could have one or another of the sisters come for a sleepover sometimes. The convent girls always talk about sleepovers but I've never been to one although Sidò invited me many times and —"

"Isn't that a lovely thought. Thank you."

Solange pulls Amandine's hair, grimaces at her.

"So then it's true? That you'll be leaving," Paul asks.

"Saturday," Solange confirms.

"So many changes." Paul turns to look at Solange.

Still sitting between them, sensing their breach growing, Amandine asks Paul, "Would you like to hold hands?"

She holds out hers to Paul, who takes it, looks down at her old brown hand enclosing Amandine's tiny white one.

"I like holding hands better than talking sometimes," Amandine tells her.

Amandine takes Solange's hand with her other one, then begins to swing the arms of her two charges as though they were off to see the fair. Paul begins to laugh, then catches herself, places Amandine's hand gently on the sofa, rises. "I shall leave you now. To your lunch and your rest."

"Thank you, Mater. Thank you for bringing the —"

"If only I'd thought to bring it sooner."

CHAPTER XXXI

It is Saturday morning, June 22. The sun just risen, Amandine and Solange are on their way to bid farewell to Philippe. Solange had made a pallet of the old picnic quilt, laid it inside a wheelbarrow, and then set Amandine upon it. Cleopatra on her barge. The way to Philippe's grave is long, and sometimes Amandine prefers to walk, to gather wildflowers and pretty weeds and to disappear every once in a while down a narrow path between the vines, to lie for a moment on the soft black earth.

"What are you doing? The ground is still damp. You'll need to change and all our clothes are packed."

"I'm saying good-bye to the vines."

"There are tons of vines in Champagne."

"I know, but they're not these vines."

When they arrive, they fuss a bit over the stone, Amandine polishing it with the juice from a milkweed and a fistful of leaves. Hav-

324

ing brought a small shovel and a pot of basil, they set about planting it in a great lush clump in front of the stone. A jug of water from the bar row then.

"I hope he still likes basil."

"No doubt he does."

"Marie-Albert will come to water it. She promised."

"Yes, she told me you'd made those arrangements."

"Are we ever coming back?"

"I think we will. Someday. But when we do, we won't be the same and whoever is still here won't be the same, not even the house or the land will be the same. It's okay to go back to a place as long as you understand that."

"I do. That's why he's coming with us. Philippe."

"I know. Let's start back. In an hour the bishop's auto will be waiting . . ."

The convent sisters have packed bread and cheese, a small crock of duck rillettes, dried sausages, candied fruits stuffed in a jar, honeycomb in another, gingerbread, chocolate, petits beurres, two packs, each thing wrapped in brown kitchen paper or a crisp white napkin and all of it pushed down into a market string bag. Enough for days and nights.

Amandine's *mise,* mildly eccentric, includes the red boots, her tulle skirt — once scorned, now beloved, and recently dismembered from its crocheted bodice, which had become too snug — a tartan shirtwaist, and a rose-colored sweater embroidered with darker rose fleurs-de-lis. Her hair is loose and wild. Solange wears a soft yellow cardigan closed up to the hollow in her neck with satin loops over small pearl buttons. The sweater had belonged to her mother, and when Solange was preparing her valise before departing Avise for Montpellier, Magda had brought it to her. All folded in tissue paper, Magda had laid the sweater on top of the other things in the valise, smiled, almost smiled, then turned and walked away. In all the nine years since, Solange has never worn it. With a narrow dark blue skirt — part of the *tallieur* that Janka had bought for her in Reims on her sixteenth birthday and that fits the curve of her derriere — the soft yellow sweater is beautiful. She wears the regulation patent ballerina slippers with floppy grosgrain bows at the toes, which are part of the convent girls' evening uniform since, twice yearly, the teaching sister in charge of such things ordered a pair for her. Solange, too, has left her hair loose, a mass of tight blond ringlets and waves falling beyond her shoulders. A few reddish marks from the fever are scattered on the tawny skin of her cheeks and neck.

Slung across her chest, Solange wears the purse in which she's placed the black leather portfolio Fabrice had given her, into which he'd tucked the papers he had had drawn for Amandine, those and an inordinate number of francs and letters of introduction to be presented, upon need, to the curia of any parish of Mother Church in France. Solange had placed her own papers in the portfolio as well and Baptiste's file with Amandine's records. She opens and closes the purse to touch the portfolio, the file, closes the purse, opens it again.

They climb into the backseat of the limousine with the small purple flags mounted on the windscreen while the driver sees to the string bag and their single valise, the same one Solange had carried from the farm. How little there was to pack. Books and toys and winter clothing they left in wrapped, marked boxes for eventual posting. The driver closes the door. Amandine opens it to blow a last kiss to the sisters who huddle under the portico waving, holding their balled-up handkerchiefs to their eyes, their noses.

At the same time that Fabrice's driver is delivering Amandine and Solange to the station, an aide knocks on his door. He is still abed.

"Entrez."

"Your Eminence, please forgive the intrusion, but we've just learned, just been informed . . ."

"What is it? Say it."

"France has surrendered, Your Eminence. Total capitulation, sir."

"Take the jeep, go to the station, find them. Find Alain. Tell the authorities to use the loudspeaker. Don't let them board that train. Go."

Solange asks Alain, the bishop's driver, to leave them at the main doors of the station.

"Thank you very much. No, the valise is light. And Amandine wishes to carry the string bag. We're fine, really we are. Thank you once again."

Solange hears the news as they enter the station. People are shouting in disbelief, weeping, running, screeching. Decorum, civility shut down like metal gates.

So we French have submitted to the *boche.*

Now it will be French against French here just as Fabrice says it is in the north. Look at them, how they pummel one another to get out, to get in, to be first. Step on Grand-mère's throat, the French would.

She holds Amandine tighter. She tells her, "Look at me. No matter what, you must never let go of this hand. Never. Not for a half second. Do you understand?

"The eight-forty-nine to Nîmes. Track seventeen. Do you see it up there? The fourth one down. Let's go." She takes the string bag from Amandine, settles it on her shoulder, pats the valise, the purse, holds up Amandine's hand as if in victory.

"Let's go."

■ ■ ■ ■

PART IV
JUNE 1940–
APRIL 1941
JOURNEY THROUGH
FRANCE

■ ■ ■ ■

CHAPTER XXXII

We never arrived in Nîmes that day. As it was scheduled to, our train stopped at the station in Baillargues but, once passengers had descended and others had stepped up into the cars, it was announced that the train would go no farther. To each one who waited in line to speak to the ticket agent, his response was as if from a script. "Due to the 'circumstances,' schedules are being re-arranged. Come back tomorrow, there's bound to be something. No, no lodgings here, but perhaps in the next village. A few kilometers down the D-3. The A-11. Per-haps there."

Along with three others of the stranded, Amandine and I walked to that next village. A cluster of blue-painted houses with swags of blown red roses arching the doors, it hugged the verge of the road. No bar, no hotel, no sign of welcome, or of life for that matter. Shaking their heads, speaking in quiet commiseration, our companions bode us adieu, turned and walked, single file, back toward Baillargues, leaving Amandine and me standing alone in the gold silence of noon. Not a single starched Flemish lace curtain parted.

"Wait here," I told Amandine, setting down the valise. I knocked at the first house, waited and walked on to the second, Amandine, pulling the valise along behind her, following my progress. I might well have been knocking on the lids of coffins. The fourth door opened, if only a crack.

"What is it you want?"

"The trains, madame, we were on our way to Nîmes but . . . A place to stay, madame, for my little girl and me. I can pay."

"Not nearly enough, I would think. Go away."

A road sign a few meters from where we stood pointed to Nîmes. Our lodestone, our north. Several smaller signs were posted under it. Places on the way.

"Shall we walk a little farther, my love, or shall we look for somewhere to set out a picnic? Or would you . . . ?"

How thin my voice sounded, even to me. Where had she gone, that arrogant self of a few hours ago? Buttoning up my pretty sweater, brushing out my hair. The bishop's chauffeur waiting in the drive, shining the fenders of the wide black sedan. I'd thought I was heroic, I'd thought I was grand. The war is somewhere else, the war is something else. We'll be fine. Two days and we'll be home. God, make haste to help me.

A breeze blew hot and damp and, under the shivering blossoms of chestnut trees, we walked on the road to Nîmes. Resting in the shade of roadside woods, eating cheese and bread and sipping water cupped in our hands from a faucet on the side of a barn, our pace was slow and somehow ghostly. No rhythms and rituals, no bells, no clack of the castanets, no trainman to tell us we'd arrived and could depart again on track number . . . Adrift. Terrifying. Yet not altogether so. The second day, the third.

At the station in Sommières.

"Ah, to Nîmes, mademoiselle? Left an hour ago. Tomorrow. Perhaps tomorrow."

Whenever I thought of turning back, the not-altogether-terrified part of me pleaded, Just one more day. Amandine is doing well. There is still gingerbread in the sack. If we can get to a larger town with a better train line . . . But then, when an explosion — unrelated to war, we were assured — destroyed two cars of a train a few kilometers down the track from where we waited to board it in Alès, it seemed wiser to walk, and that's what we did through much of the summer.

We saw a shepherd wielding a stick and a black dog, pirouetting, inflict order upon a disheveled band of sheep. As though there was no war. Pink clouds moved in a pewter sky, and a dark-eyed woman sat in a cart with no wheels, peeling an apple with a green-handled knife. As though there was no war at all. We saw a barn door swung open, and we looked inside, smelled hay fresh from the sun and sank our tired bodies into its comfort, heaped it over us like a quilt, slept in the solace of some nightbird's whirring. So where is the war? In the hot reddish blaze of a sinking sun we saw an ox draw a plow through a rusty-earthed field, a farmer walking beside it speaking tenderly to the beast. The man drank, sometimes, from a bottle strapped across his chest. I asked myself again, Where is this war? Don't you see how the plowing goes on so the wheat will grow? And when it's high there'll be someone to cut it down and someone to beat it and take it to the mill and the miller will drive the wheat to the baker and the baker and his son will make it into bread so that the baker's girl, with her broad, hard thighs under her blue linen dress, will pedal the tall narrow wagon stacked with baskets of still warm loaves and, pulling the rope on her bell, chant at the top of her voice: *"Le pain est arrivé. Le bon pain est arrivé."* If all that can happen, how can there be a war?

And later, when we came to another field where the wheat was already grown, we walked across it, seeing lights in a farmhouse on the far side. With our hands we made a path through the high stalks, which were already bent here and there by a corpse. Bodies laid down, shot down, past pain. We'd found the war.

We slept wherever we could. On the floor of a town hall or a church, in barns and in automobiles propped up on blocks in old garages. We managed. As for food, we did well enough. On the fourth or perhaps it was the fifth day, when we'd finally made our way to Nîmes, a grocer there asked me, "Your ration books, mademoiselle?"

"Oh, I, ah, we don't really need those because we're going home, a village near Reims, and once there, we won't need anything like that, of course, my mother, my grandmother . . . the farm . . ."

"All of France eats what the *boche* deign them to eat, and that which has been deigned can only be procured with these little pieces of paper. Even in Reims, mademoiselle. Where have you been for the past year?"

"But I have francs, you see, and I, well, we only need something —"

"Ah, of course, francs. Then perhaps you should eat them, mademoiselle."

Next morning we queued at the *mairie*. It was the first time I'd had to show Amandine's papers, and I feared that the official would find some pulsing flaw in them, that someone would try to take her from me. I should have know that Fabrice would do his work well. With no break in the rhythm of his pounding timbre, the official slid two thin sheaves of paper across the wide wooden expanse of his desk. *"Prochain."* All of France eats what the Boche deign them to eat. . . .

But even the ration coupons are often of little use. The *boche* take almost everything. According to our ages, Amandine is rated J2 and I, I am rated A. This means that she can have milk and even chocolate, should there be such. Sometimes we can get only a single egg or a dried sausage, but there are many times, too, when full rations are set before us. Margarine, bread, cheese, potatoes, biscuits, a piece of *ventrèche* with skin rough as hide. Even honey. And, once in a while, vegetables that are hardly rotting at all. There have been times when we've supplemented our supper with black market food. It's not as though one has to look very far or hard to find a supplier. A fistful of francs laid on a table in a bar and someone wanders over. *Mademoiselle desires?* From some trunk or chest or drawer or cellar, voilà. Into the string bag, back on the road. I bless Fabrice for the still fat wad of francs in my bag. No matter what, we have never been without.

And what village was it where we first saw the *boche* up close? I can't recall its name. Two weeks it was, maybe three into our wandering. We took a room at the top of a high stone building with dark green shutters and a black iron sign swinging on a rod, its cutout words showing yellow from the flame of the lantern fixed behind it. L'Auberge Fleurie. Through the open windows, the smells were good and we were hungry.

Madame didn't look up from her wiping down the zinc bar. She had hair so red it was purple in the dim light.

"Fourth floor, number six. The key is in the door."

I started to walk back to where Amandine was waiting for me when she said, "Pay now, if you don't mind."

On the wet bar I put down the small patrimony of francs she required, and we went up to wash. Later we sat side by side on a small wooden bench set against a wall in front of the table that Madame had arranged for us, set with clean white napkins, a fat, oily candle stub in an iron holder, and a blue glass bottle of sweet peas. We had a fine view of the hot, dark room ripe with old sweat and the sharp smells of aubergines and garlic rising up through a Gauloise mist. I'd learned quite a lot about the war, about my France, during that early period of our flight. Learned by listening and watching. Therefore I knew that the *boche* who sat there in front of us in Wehrmacht gray-green with their collar studs undone — raucous and unself-conscious, clinking down their belts and helmets and pistols and making a victor's noise — were likely an advance guard searching out partisan movement. Surely those *boche* suspected, knew, that the men they hunted sat at the next table, eating the same supper. Spilling down the same cool, light red wine from small stone bowls rather than glasses. The *boche* had seemed to like the wine bowls, held them to the candlelight, all the better to see them. Yes, at the next table, and at the one behind them, and at those all around them sat partisans, faces hard as those stone bowls and so unlike the fresh, rosy-cheeked ones of the big blond boys. In black basques and poor men's clothes, the partisans were quieter than the *boche,* theirs being a subtle language of codes: wine bowls raised to a certain height, a glance pitched left or right, the removing of a cap, the fumbling with a button on a shirt, a kiss on the cheek to signify "stop," a hand on a shoulder, "proceed."

And among the black basques there was sure to be a collaborator, maybe two, tipping down their wine. Collaborators who work for the masquerade at Vichy? A cell of partisans with different priorities? One with another mode of operation? Communists? Those French who would stand up to the *boche* and those who would lie down with them, sometimes the lines between the factions are smudged. The partisans are hardly of a single mind. Less the collaborators. Nor is it so that one chooses sides. One can move in and out and back in again. If he's lucky, back out once more. Often it's the way of things what with sentiments and ideology shifting according to hunger. One hunger or another. Yes, it was the night at les Fleurie when I first began to understand how the war raged within the war, the war that France was fighting with herself. The only constant among the French is that none are passive. Against the French grain to be gray. And so there they were, the *boche* and the partisans and the collaborators, eating aubergine stew at les Fleurie. And all of them looked up when the town girls stepped in, laughing. Not to eat but to show off their pumps and ankle socks, they walked in and, there being no chairs, they stood in counterfeit ease at the bar. Their kerchiefs tied in loose knots above their foreheads, their lips slicked in dark red from what must have been a single rouge pot, they were like town girls everywhere, timid, yearning, waiting to be cherished. There were no town boys, of course, for, upon capitulation, two million French soldiers — not unlike herds of cattle, fleets of trucks — had been requisitioned, taken into *boche* slavery in the fatherland. There were few young Frenchmen left in France, yet young girls must preen for someone.

I'd heard a word in les Fleurie that night. A word I'd heard often enough over those weeks. *Résistance.* Mostly I'd heard it whispered, but once I heard it shouted from the swollen, bleeding mouth of an old man who'd sat down the aisle from us on a train. A *boche* had walked past him, stopped, turned back, and said something that I didn't understand. And then the *boche* smashed the old man with his pistol butt. The old man rose from his seat, stood to his full height, which barely reached the *boche*'s shoulder, and screamed, *Je me défends. Je suis la Résistance.* The *boche* laughed, lit a cigarette, went back to his seat. Sometime later I saw the *boche* approach the man again, this time to offer him a cigarette. An olive branch. The old man hesitated, and one could see that he wanted it, perhaps craved it. He made a cutting sign with his hand, turned to look out the window. *Résistance.*

There is another word one hears now and then. *Maquis.* It's what the moorland of Corsica is called. The secret and desolate terrain of the island's interior. *Maquisards.* Those who hunt there. The *boche* would not walk so easily over France.

Nor did we. We bought a bicycle in a hamlet near Aubenas and, like most all business, the deal was clinched in a bar. The woman there had asked where we were headed and by what mode. When I told her that we were walking to the Champagne, she lifted her apron to her eyes and laughed behind it until she cried. She wheeled a bicycle out from a shed behind the bar, and Amandine began to dance around it. The woman — was her name Yvonne? — said that her father would rig up a seat for Amandine behind mine. It wasn't a beautiful thing, the bicycle. Still . . .

"Where can I find a small wagon to tow our things?"

She fed us, invited us to rest in the little room behind her kitchen from whence we heard banging and pounding in the garden and an irritated voice asking, *How large is the child? Tell me how large is she?* When we walked out, there it was. The metal scrubbed, shined, the wooden seat from what must have been a donkey cart strapped with leather thongs tight over the back wheel, a kind of stirrup was attached somehow to either side and just below it. Amandine climbed in. An adjustment or two. A small three-wheeled wagon was rigged up to trail a meter or so behind us. The whole affair was shaky. But everything else was, too.

"The price, madame?"

And that's how we became *pédaleuses.*

When we find decent roads, we go like the

wind. Not so much like the wind, really. While pushing the cycle uphill or over stones or through the woods, often I think to leave it by the wayside but then tell myself, *Perhaps I shall keep it just awhile longer.*

We rarely advance far in a day, five or six kilometers, often less. I am hard put to explain the sense of liberty I feel. Midst the *tristesse.* The more we learn about, see, hear, feel the war, the more we consent to it. To its shoals, its traps, its shelterlessness. We revise expectations to suit the burdens and are astonished by the smallest goodness. We are grateful for supper. Unaware and without intention, Amandine has instructed me. Surely I will be content to reach home. But meanwhile . . .

We arrive rather conspicuously in each of our destinations, dismounting our homemade contraption, untying our kerchiefs. We wander about the village, find the place where we shall queue next morning for food. In whatever shops are open and in some of the more prosperous-looking houses, I always ask to trade work for a place to sleep. For a little something more to eat. When someone says yes, we stay for a few days until that yearning to keep going sets in. Or until the grocer or the lady of the house or whomever we've taken up with needs our bed, our place at table. Our plate of soup. Until someone doesn't like my prowess with the laundry or the way Grand-père's eyes sparkle when he sees me.

While the weather is still fine, we often prefer to camp near a river or a creek, set up our traveling household. What with the luxury of the wagon, we've accumulated quite a battery of things, found, gifted, pilfered — a mirror to hang on a low-slung branch so we can fix our hair, *marché noir* underwear and socks, wool and knitting needles for me, books for Amandine, a can of sea salt, a torch, matches, soap for us, soap for our clothes, a thin-bottomed pot with no handle, wooden bowls, spoons, forks, a black-enameled Laguiole, a good woolen blanket, two glasses engraved with a François Guy absinthe bottle, a wooden fishing pole, a one-person *boche* tent, found wet and muddied in a stretch of beech woods that we scrubbed, dried in the sun. We have a small tin of walnut oil, which must have fallen from someone's bundles where we found it along a stony back road on the northern edges of the Gard.

We wash our clothes and ourselves in cold, sweet river water, sit on its bank to let a soft wind blow us dry while we fish for our supper. We pile up stones and make a fire. If the fishing is good, we cook the catch — mostly carp but sometimes trout — usually wrapped in leaves and buried in embers. To the tender music of an old oak's creaking limbs, we sleep under our blanket on a pallet of leaves in the *boche* tent. We wake with the birds and, if a village is close enough, sometimes the bells. By now I am less shamed by my heedless flight from the convent. I and myself, we are reconciled. I know that what was still safe back there, back then, is, by now, no longer safe. Less safe. While we've been wending north, sometimes east, even turning back south for a way until we can return to a passable northern route, they've seeped south, the *boche.*

It seems that all of France is moving. *Le grand exode.* Though the flight from north to south to outrun the *boche* is greater, we are not alone as we plod against the headwind. Northern French who'd been living in the south have family and farms and property to protect or, having fled early on from the north, are already turning back, ravaged, saying that the perils of facing the *boche* could not be worse than those wrought by six million French on the open road. Running away, running toward, all of them dispossessed of their plenty, they are frenzied, savage. The rich travel in fancy cars until the petrol is gone or the tires split, and the poor push carts and pull wagons. Of both classes, the minds and souls of those we meet are bolted fast as the doors of those still at home. For all that blood spilled in the name of *fraternité,* the French are not tribal. Not even here in the woods. Hiding a box of biscuits. Stealing a box of biscuits while one goes to bathe. And then hiding it. Shoes. A sliver of soap. An egoism fierce enough to seem like cowardice. Amandine is another kind of French.

Look at her now, splendid in her black market sundress and Philippe's broken straw fedora, wandering about the woods as if they are hers, as if all the others setting up for the night are her guests. She picks the new shoots of wild grasses, sucks their bitter green juices, chews them like salad. She gathers sorrel and *pis-en-lit* on the riverbanks, ties them in neat bundles with the stem of a weed, scent for the soup we'll stir up from river water and a potato. Soup from stones, just like in the fable. Gorging upon the freedom of this primitive vagabond life, Amandine is peaceful.

We have no plan except to pedal and walk

until we reach home. I send Maman postal cards, the official *boche*-approved ones, which have some chance to pass the censors. I can't say much but only tell her that we're well, that we're on our way. I send the same to Fabrice. Of course I can give no return address, so even if they do receive our messages, they cannot reply.

I choose our route mostly by instinct. Sometimes from the counsel of a man — *résistant? maquisard? collabò?* —who gives us passage in a truck fed on *boche* petrol. How much alike are these ruffian saboteurs. Cigarettes clenched between their front teeth, they heave our rig onto the truck bed and themselves back onto their thrones, slam their doors while we're still climbing in. Always some quaking, rattling thing, they pelt the truck over stones, take the crests of hills without touching ground, all the while cursing or singing, the cigarette, even when it's gone to ash, still clamped in place.

"How does one become a *maquisard?*" Amandine asks one of them.

"A what?"

"You know, a *résistant*. How old must one be?"

"A year older than you are."

"Oh."

"Are you eating?" the *résistant* paladin

349

asks her.

"Uh-huh."

He pulls a paper-wrapped piece of chocolate from his shirt pocket. Holds it in his open palm.

"Stay out of the Loire valley," he tells me as he swings the bicycle and the wagon back onto the ground.

"But it's the best route north."

"Not anymore. Stay east."

East or west, the farther north we go, the more flagrant is this war. How sinister the lawlessness of these *boche*. Not an army operating under resolute codes of behavior toward the conquered, they seem renegade bands, each one interpreting its duty and exercising conqueror's rights with erratic perversity. We watch from our place in a roadside wood as a colonnade of jeeps and trucks and motorcycles speed past a small, poor farm. Preferring to descend upon the fiefdom of a fat landowner? But we stop at the place they ignored and find chores and supper and tales of the *boche* told around the table. The farmers say that if people are still living and working on the great prosperous farms, the *boche* will sometimes permit the family to stay, to set up in the outbuildings or even in a part of the main house. For weeks or months, the *boche* and the farmers move about together in a stilted tableau of everyday life in the country. Other times the *boche* might give the farmers and their householders an hour or an afternoon to pack up what they can carry. Send them on their way. When it suits them, the *boche* line them up in a field and shoot them or use them, one and all, as servants. And then shoot them. Content sometimes with a single evening of pillage and rape before they move on, the *boche* confound.

Along our route we find burned farmhouses, new graves. Slaughtered animals. Silence. The *boche* take the wheat and the potatoes from the field, fruit from the trees, wine from the cellars, they take horses and petrol and autos. They take the women when they can. Mostly they can. They leave the lavender along the paths to the farmhouse doors though. And the rosebushes. Gentlemen conquistadors. And what the *boche* don't take the French keep. To themselves. *Go away.* All those hissed voices from behind the wide warped doors of the landed gentry. From behind the toile de Jouy drapes of the bourgeoisie in the towns. *Go away.*

Chapter XXXIII

There are days and days of this past year that I hardly recall while, of some, I see and feel and hear everything. The day we met Aubrac. It was still September. Toward the end, though, since the air was cool and it had that green smell of ripening corn. The leaves on the beeches were already yellow, already trembling in the soft nibbles of wind. My self-rebuke rearing itself once again, I'd thought that I should be trembling, too, for the folly I'd wrought. Our advances had been so tentative, small progresses canceled if we'd see a prettier road, heard the gushing of another river. But that day, I remember that I was too tired to pedal and so walked the bicycle while Amandine slept and snored in her wooden chair, Philippe's hat having slid down to the bridge of her nose. She slept, and I looked back upon our procession across France. Phantom trains, *résistants'* trucks, a rickety bicycle, our feet. Our own kind of march. I saw a tower ahead — a church? the *mairie?* — in the village where we would stay the night. Almost there. Find a place for us. Wash, eat, sleep. Absorbing thoughts of hot water and bread and wine shattered when, spitting up stones, a small truck sped toward us. I moved us into the ditch, stayed still, waited for it to pass, and, when it did, it swerved to the side, stopped. A man stepped down, leaving the door swung wide.

"Bonjour, bonjour."

Loping in quick strides over the few meters that separated us, blue cotton trousers and shirt, a corduroy jacket buttoned high on his chest, thick, dark hair mostly covered by his basque, eyes slits of steel blue fire. He wanted to know, "Are you near your destination?"

"Yes, the village ahead."

"Do you know it?"

"No, but I'm certain we can —"

"I am going to Le Puy-en-Velay. An hour or so north. You'll have a better chance there."

"But the Loire, I've been told it's —"

"You were told correctly, *ma petite.* Just as it is everywhere else in France. Dangerous. Do you have papers?"

353

"Yes."

"Are you Jews?"

"No."

By this time Amandine had come to stand next to me, her forehead printed in cross-hatchings from Philippe's hat, her eyes round and dark. Intrigued by this rare social encounter, she'd wanted to please the gentleman and so asked me, "Are you sure we're not Jews?"

"Very sure."

Looking at me and then at Amandine, back at me, the man said, "Well, if you were, I could take you to a safe house."

"We're not running from anything really. Just trying to get home."

"And where is that?"

"Reims."

Like the woman in Aubenas, he laughed. He laughed so long and hard that Amandine began to laugh, and then I did.

"*J'adore les femmes françaises.* All of you kin to Sainte Jeanne. There are more *boche* up there than there are in Germany. No French left in Reims, haven't you heard? From a quarter of a million last year, now three or four thousand, fewer every day."

"It's not to the city that we're going. To a small village in the countryside. My family will not have fled. They're there."

Wiping his eyes with the sleeve of his jacket, he said, "And the beauty is that they probably are if they've bred the likes of you. Where do you plan to cross the line?"

I looked at him, understood that he meant the demarcation line, which separates the occupied north from the unoccupied south but, since I had yet to consider this particular of our journey, I looked down, shook my head. "Our papers are in order. Why would it matter where we cross?"

"Because there is nothing constant about those who guard it. No hard-and-fast rules about who shall be detained, who shall pass through, who shall be taken into the woods and shot. It all depends on what sort of *boche* you find. There are points that are better than others."

"I can't be concerned with that now. The line is still far off. I must think of where we'll sleep tonight."

"Of course."

Moving his hand about his mouth as though trying to wipe away the words he'd just said, he looked at me then, his eyes half beseeching. "Come with me now. I'll get you to Le Puy by suppertime. And I know where you can find what you need. Besides, it's beautiful, high on a plateau, and there are hostels in the churches and lace in the windows and lentils on the table. Your road is long, the war longer."

And as if Aubrac and Le Puy and the lace and the lentils had not been enough, the next morning he sent us his daughter.

Of course I didn't know that was who she was when she whispered something to the woman behind us in the ration queue and then slipped in front of her. A small, thin girl slouching in a long, loose dress, black suede sabots with wooden heels on her tiny feet, smooth black hair cut like a helmet with a short fringe, *she cannot be more than seventeen,* I'd thought. Having barely nodded in my direction, she was attentive to Amandine, complimenting her tartan shirt-waist, her beautiful eyes. The girl seemed to study her. Just as it was our turn to enter the store, she looked at me, said, "There's a bar in the Place du Plot called L'Anis. I'll be there in about an hour."

As though she'd said everything and everything she'd said was understood and agreed upon, she walked quickly away from the queue.

When we arrived, she was already sitting at a small table. Gesturing to us to join her, she spoke softly, quickly.

"If you would like, I can offer you passage to the area near Vichy. Tomorrow. There's room in my truck. For you, your things. If it would help."

"Vichy? Right at the heart of the —"

"I said 'near' not 'in.' We can leave you in one of the surrounding villages, from where you could continue on the smaller roads. I'm not trying to convince you, you understand. Only if you . . . It's just under a hundred and fifty kilometers."

"A month's walk for us."

"Yes. That's what I —"

"I, we have no route in mind, generally heading north."

"I know."

"The man who gave us passage yesterday?"

"Yes. He asked me to look out for you this morning. My father. He thinks your little girl is Jewish."

"She is not."

"Sometimes people believe that a good set of false papers will suffice, will —"

"Amandine is not Jewish."

As though she had neither believed nor heard me, she opened another argument. "We have a place in a village outside Vichy."

"The cooperative government —"

"No, not cooperative, not even collabora-

357

tive. The French veneer is thin on the *boche* machine. But our place is remote enough to be of little interest to anyone but us and our neighbors."

She smiled for the first time, and I saw her father's face in hers. From the pocket of her jacket, she took a single cigarette, tapped both ends on the table, excused herself, walked into the bar, returned puffing hungrily at it. There was a tremor in the hand that held it.

"I will share this with you if you like," she said, holding out the cigarette.

I shook my head.

"The house is in a small village. People stay with us."

"You mean that you hide people."

"We shelter them. Sometimes only for a few days, sometimes for much longer. My mother, five village women. We work with, we work with others to help people on their way."

"On their way?"

"To a place where they can wait out the war. Sometimes to Switzerland —"

"But we're not hiding, and we don't want to go to Switzerland."

"I know. The Champagne. My father told me. He tried to contact some people there last evening, to see if there was a route, a line into which our friends could 'insert' you but . . . nothing. Not right now. Even the government of Reims has established itself somewhere else. In Nevers, I think. Have you communicated with your family?"

"I've heard all this before. I understand that nothing and no one will be as, as before. But that's where we're going."

"How long have you been on the road?"

"Nearly three months."

"Where did you begin?"

"Montpellier. I know, not even halfway yet."

"You cannot be thinking to continue on the road for much longer now. The weather —"

"No, no, of course not. I have a general letter of introduction from my bishop in Montpellier, which I shall present at a convent, a monastery. I will ask to trade work for room and board. Amandine grew up in a convent, and we are familiar with the religious life. I was once a postulant myself."

"A well-trained pigeon returning to the flock —"

"It's not that at all. And what if it were? I don't know what you're after with us but —"

I stood to leave, took Amandine's sweater

from the table where she'd placed it, held out my hand to her.

"You could stay with us. There's room. We pool our rations, we work a small farm outside the village. Everyone helps. Less comfortable than a convent, perhaps, but then again, I've never lived in a convent."

"I don't even know your name."

"I'm called Lily."

"And to cross over into the occupied zone?" I hoped to sound savvy.

"Vichy and our village are in the free zone. On the edge."

"I didn't, I don't know my geography as well as —"

"When the time comes for you to make a crossing, you must go with *passeurs,* men who know the woods. Entry without barbed wire and checkpoints. Without *boche.* But tomorrow we shan't need —"

"Why would you make such an offer to us?"

"Why wouldn't I?"

"Even though Amandine is not Jewish?"

"Even though."

"Where shall we meet you?"

"I've arranged for you to stay again at the place where you were last night."

"But this morning I was told that there would be no room."

"There's room for you. Be outside the house at five. I won't wait."

Five bells ring from the tower of Notre-Dame and, Amandine sleeping in my aching arms, I wait because Lily will not. Tempted to climb back to our little attic bed and forget this adolescent Valkyrie and her offer, I see rather than hear a truck moving toward us. A lumbering beast, its motor spent, it trolls silently over the downward pitch of the cobbles. Stops in front of us. A troupe of agile circus tumblers, Lily and two men descend wordlessly, set to work stowing our rig and us into one part or another of the truck. One of the men climbs into the driver's seat, starts the engine, curses the creaking gearshift, and we are off.

The men speak neither between themselves nor to us three who are settled in a wide, deep well behind the front cab, a makeshift sort of space with a folded-back canvas roof. A hiding place? What had I agreed to this time? I feel nothing of fear though and, from the beatific gaze she throws at me, less does Amandine. Wedged between us, she looks from Lily to me with a closed-mouth smile, trying to contain glee. Lily hugs her repeatedly and, now and then and without looking at me, stretches her arm behind Amandine's shoulders to touch mine. I close my eyes, nod to the Fates, invite them to have their way with us for the next few hours. By afternoon we'll have arrived in this place, this village near Vichy, and I shall resume my sway. We shall thank them for the passage, offer to pay them, be on our way. That is exactly what we'll do.

"If we're stopped at any point, please don't offer information. Answer questions if they are asked. But nothing more. Do you remember the name of the village where we're going?" Lily's soft, urgent voice wakes me.

"I don't know that you've told me its name."

"Lagny. Not on the *boche* map. A group of houses, a church, a few shops. If you are asked, we are going to Lagny. You are cousins. Displaced, in need. That's all."

"Yes, Lagny."

It's nearly nine when the driver turns onto a broken, rutted road and soon after turns again, onto a dirt path that leads into a vineyard. He stops, and the two men descend, walk a bit down among the vines, their somber voices resounding in a monotone chant to where we sit under a stand of chestnuts. From the canvas bag she wears like a bandolier over her sweater and trousers, Lily takes a small cheese wrapped in what looks like a roughly torn length of old sheet.

"Our *bleu.* Bleu d'Auvergne. Cow's milk. We have no sheep."

From the pocket of her trousers, she takes a knife, unfolds it, carves thin, crumbling slices from the wheel, lays the cheese on chestnut leaves, and passes it to us. Two long thin brown pears she peels with finesse, holds out a slice to each of us from the point of her knife, licks the juices from the blade before slicing again. Repeats the rite until the pears are finished. Another round of cheese. Stowing the remains of the cheese, the knife, she rises, gathering the fruit peelings and stamping them into the earth around the trees. She walks between two rows of vines, parts the wide, succulent green leaves at a certain point to find the right bunch of grapes. An expert snap, and she returns, a fat mass of dark blue Gamay dangling in her hand. From her open palm, we pluck them from the stems, crush the grapes between our teeth, the sweet, potent juice filling our mouths. One grape at a time under the chestnut trees, sitting on the stubble and the stones of the Auvergne.

"This next part of the ride will be a bit

different. Off the roads. A little rough. Are we ready?" she wants to know.

As she slips the canvas bag into place over her chest, I see the outline of the Valkryie's pistol under her sweater.

Raised up in a small forest of pines and chestnuts, it is tall and wide and made of stone. Eight chimneys bolt like pillars above the thin slate tiles and give the roof the air of a ruined temple. Faded wine red wooden shutters ornament the three rows of windows, and over the great black door, with its iron handles and knockers, "La Châtaigneraie 1628" is engraved, barely readable, upon what remains of a marble cornice. The Chestnut Grove. Our things deposited on the flags of the terrace, the men having driven off, we stand behind Lily as she enters her family home.

On either side of a long, dark hallway, sweaters, coats, hats of all sizes and conditions are hung on iron hooks while sabots, soft boots, shoes are lined up on shelves below them. I am preparing my exit lines while Amandine is running ahead, her hand in Lily's.

"Everyone will be working. Harvesting, picking. I'll show you where you can . . ."

To her back I say, "Lily, listen, I appreciate your kindness in having given us passage, but I've decided that . . ."

She opens the hall door onto a wood-smoke-scented salon with a hearth great enough to roast an elk.

"Is this a house?" Amandine asks.

"A rather ancient one. Do you like it?"

The high walls of the salon are papered in purple and mustard stripes, and edged in a wide border of red roses and dark green leaves. The colors startle before they please. Like a long, narrow spit of land in a wavy red sea of waxed tiles, a table is flanked by twenty mismatched chairs. Sofas are arranged about the hearth. Yellow-flowered porcelain tureens and pewter pitchers sit on starched lace doilies along the lengths of two wooden dressers and, in the depths of armoires with no doors, there are stone crocks covered in brown paper and tied with string and bottles and jars of fruits and vegetables, preserved. In a corner, baskets of walnuts and chestnuts spill out over a large round table, and dried mushrooms and berries and small, silver-skinned onions are festooned everywhere. As though twilight was shaken down upon it all, there is something both of gloom and of radiance. Lyrical, haunting.

I shall not say how lovely the room is or sit

or even stop to talk, I tell myself. We must go now, or perhaps we never will.

"As I was saying —"

"Why don't you stay the night and get a fresh start in the morning? Some of the people you'll meet might be able to help you with your route. They'll know more than we do about the state of things farther north. And someone will offer passage if they can. Or you could remain."

Standing behind Lily, Amandine looks at me, says nothing aloud.

"Thank you. We'll stay. For a night. Thank you very much."

Lily shows Amandine and me to a cold room on the third floor. Feather beds upon pale blue wooden frames. A hearth with a fire laid, a wood basket, an armoire painted with a country wedding scene. The small rippling panes of a curtainless window give an undersea luster to the treetops and a steeple and the heaped-up roofs of the village, and we sit on the ledge, pressing our foreheads to the glass. We rest.

We are eleven at table that first evening. Nine women, two girls: Amandine and a five-year-old named Claude with small gray eyes and skin the color of caramel just before it burns. And Magdalen, of course. Taller and with a sculpted face perhaps more beautiful than her daughter's, she is pale and blond as Lily is dark. From one of the tureens with the yellow flowers, she ladles soup into shallow bowls already laid with roasted bread.

"Pumpkin and onion and wild sage," Magdalen says and breaks into a round, heavy loaf of dark bread, giving the piece to the woman beside her, then passing the loaf itself to her. The woman then breaks off a piece of the bread and passes it and the loaf to the woman beside her. Around the table. Pewter pitchers of water and wine.

When the soup is finished, Magdalen carries in a tray on which there is what looks like a length of broom handle, a great mound of white cheese, a large pat of butter, a few cloves of garlic still in their purple skins, a small pewter pitcher, and a stone basin filled with boiled potatoes, steaming. With Claude's gentle humming as accompaniment, Magdalen begins pounding at the potatoes, heaving in cheese and pounding again, some butter, then milk from the pitcher, a good whack with the wooden thing upon the garlic, and she slips the cloves from their skins, flings them into the basin. More pounding, more cheese, more butter, three fat pinches of sea salt from the *salière* on the table, more pounding still until she begins to raise the mass from the basin with the wooden thing, pulling it up higher and higher into thick white strings, beating it back down, pulling it up again, and then finally walking about the table to serve it in our bread-wiped bowls.

"Aligoté," she tells me before I can ask her.

She stays seated at the table while the others begin to clear, gestures for me to put down the plates I've taken up, to sit next to her. "Bring your glass, Solange."

She pours wine into it and into hers. Looks at me and smiles. "Lily will take Amandine and Claude up to your room, light the fire. Whenever Lily is home, Claude begs to sleep in her room. I imagine there will be all sorts of strategies about who will sleep where tonight. Are you well?"

"Oh, yes. We're well. And thank you for —"

Shaking her head, fluttering the back of her hand in dismissal, she says, "We grow food for the Résistance. Wheat for bread. Our herds are a good size. We have a small dairy. Bread and cheese. It's what they need most. We grow vegetables and corn. Sugar beet. We keep something for us. My husband, like many of the men who fought in

368

the Great War, never stopped. And since this all began, this latest . . . it's a question of conscience. He must fight. He cannot accept defeat. He's that kind of French. We had this house, the land, he found a way for us to fight with these. Empty bellies can't think, can't rest, can't believe. Instead they begin to believe what the fuller-bellied enemy tells them. Hunger versus satiety, that's really what it comes down to. War. Empty bellies make traitors. We feed people. There is a prison in Clermont-Ferrand. When we're not working in the fields or the dairy, we work in a kitchen near the prison. The Vichy fiends have granted us permission to bring one hot meal a day to the prisoners. Their duty to feed them they'd somehow overlooked. Death by starvation is far uglier than a bullet in the skull. So we cook soup, make parcels, buy soap and wool on the black market, knit socks and scarves. We bury the dead. We do what Vichy doesn't do."

We have moved into the kitchen, where three of the women work without a single wasted motion, sweeping, scrubbing pots, placing dishes and cups and cutlery in their proper places. Magdalen has seated me at the table, where she sets about whacking apart four or five small yellow pumpkins,

369

places the pieces on a metal tray.

"They'll cook overnight in the embers. Soup again tomorrow. We eat what's ripe, and right now that means cabbage and pumpkin. We save the preserved things to bring to the prison. Or to take with us should we have to flee . . ."

She shakes her head, laughs, wipes her hands — small, long-fingered — down the length of her apron, removes a guttering candle from a pewter holder, lights a fresh one with its flame. Sits down again.

"Lily and Jacques are almost never here. They have other work."

"Lily has told me. They take people out of the country."

"If you decide —"

"I won't."

"Stay as long as you'd like. There's work here and on the farm. Choose which would suit you. Amandine can have her lessons with Claude. A classroom in the church. We have a teacher. Three hours in the morning. Sometimes the children sleep in the *colombier,* though I think it's already too cold for that. Three more children are arriving tomorrow. No adults. They're Jews. Claude's mother was Dutch, her father Algerian. Both naturalized French citizens. Jews. All the laws broke down early for the Jews. No

370

rights. They gave Claude over to . . . They put her in the line when she was three. A few months past three. Before the occupation. They knew what was coming. When they left her, they also left her history. Photos and letters, keepsakes. Most parents who leave their children want to believe it will be only for a while, that they shall somehow be spared, reunited. Two wooden boxes locked in a valise, they were sent on to an orphanage in Switzerland, the place where she is expected. Her history will be waiting for her."

"No word from Claude's parents?"

"There is word. Both missing. We'll get her to Switzerland. It wants time. Is that what happened to Amandine?"

I look at her, shake my head.

"It's only that you look nothing alike and she calls you Solange and . . ."

"You're right, she's not my daughter. But her parents, they, their absence from her life has been —"

"I need no explanation. I'd only wondered about —"

"I've told Lily and your husband, Amandine is not Jewish."

"I'll not ask you again."

"But you must allow me to thank you, you and Lily, your husband, for helping us to get so much closer to home."

"Will you stay for a while?"

"You can imagine how tempted I am. A paradise here. On the road we never know, from day to day —"

"Nor do I know. Once inside the Résistance, the only way out is death. It's a mantra we all share. Life expectancy, six weeks. Not so true for people who do what we do up here, but quite true for the others. Those 'in the field.' When I see my husband or Lily, I never know if it will be the last time. Will he or she or one of the others, will they be stopped on the road with one of our 'guests'? Interrogation, torture, execution. Not such a paradise. Oh, inside these walls, the fire and the soup . . . But beyond them . . ."

She fills the silence by rinsing the pumpkin seeds under the tap in the sink, pulling them from the mass of strings and pulp. She dries them in a kitchen cloth, spreads them out in a large skillet, sets it aside. She dries her hands on her apron again, leans against the sink, folds her arms across her chest.

I want to talk longer with this Magdalen but fear she is ready to send me off upstairs.

"Lily. She's so young."

"Nineteen. Most of the women in this business are young. Their men gone, hus-

372

bands, lovers, fathers, brothers, they either take up with the *boche* or fight. Whatever way they can. I think solitude has much to do with it. We, we elders, it's we who have brought down the evils. Made victims of the young. They're lost trying to wander the paths we've laid. To feel less lost, they submit to the romance of danger. The thrill. They deliver packages, they hide arms. They set up transmitters, shelter Jews, arrange for false documents. Lily has a white velvet hat with a white, blowsy rose in the front and the good black suit I was married in twenty years ago and suede sandals with heels thin as blades and, when she dresses in this costume, sits across from some schnapps-bloated *boche* in Vichy, she begets wonders. The prison program in Clermont-Ferrand is hers. Then, in boots and hunting jacket and with a Luger in her belt, she walks children from safe house to safe house across the mountains. There are legions like her. I and the mothers of all of them, we should have given our daughters the same name. We should have called them France. The youngest ones are the students from the universities in the bigger cities, the ones who, tottering about on their high heels, rendezvous with the *boche,* glean names and dates, times and places. Those who are a bit older usually operate more rurally. Crack shots, warrior saints. France's secret weapons. Those are the ones you'll meet up with as you proceed."

As you proceed. Her voice, her words, over and over during that night I felt something like envy, I think that's what it was. Envy of these others, how they are living out the war with purpose. Raison d'être. All my energy was taken up in trying to keep us fed. Out of harm's way. Once we are home, I will be able to help. Of course we could stay here and join them. We could do that. I think that's what Magdalen and even Lily want us to do, expect us to do, and yet, as alluring a prospect as it seems right now, I am too weary of living in other people's houses, living other people's lives. I want to take Amandine home. I think for right now that's my job in this war.

Though Amandine pleaded to take Claude with us, she, too, was ready to return to our journey by the time we'd stayed three nights at La Châtaigneraie. Each in our way, we knew that staying longer would be staying too long. On the evening when I told Magdalen that we'd be starting off in the morning, she said, "As you wish."

She walked about the kitchen, hands on her hips. "This is not bicycle country. Leave it here. Leave most everything here except your clothes. I knew you wouldn't stay. I've found some heavier things for both of you. Coats, boots. From here on you won't need to walk much. Each place where you'll stay, the people will take you on to the next. I can't show you the route on a map or even talk you through it. The shortest, fastest way will never be yours. But you know all that by now. A little progress north, then to the west, back to the south, a better road north. Weather, *boche* movement, changes in our ranks, food and petrol supplies — routes and timing change according to these. You might be driven only a few kilometers one day, thirty or forty another. If the snows come early, you'll have to stay put. For a while. You will not always be warm or even comfortable, but you will always eat. Always be welcome. People will do the thinking, the deciding, the contacting for you. In some way, you're part of us now. You may be asked to take along a parcel to the next place, deliver a verbal message. Nothing more."

"No white, blowsy rose?"

"No Luger either."

"And what if I want to do more?"

It felt strange to tumble into the back of an

auto or to climb up into the bed of a truck driven by someone whose name we didn't know, whose face we saw only in shadow for a morning's desolate expedition. Breasting black volcanic hills one after another until shreds of chimney smoke heralded our destination, we would stop then, leave the auto or the truck in a blind and trek to some ancestral farmhouse or hunting lodge or bunker. The women whom Magdalen said we'd find were always there. Sometimes in groups, sometimes alone with their children, they barely broke stride to greet us, feed us, bed us down. We'd stay for a day, sometimes for a month. I did as Magdalen said I should, I let them decide. Around their oil-clothed kitchen tables, in attics and cellars, and in the hides where they kept grain and aged their cheese, they plotted shelters, organized their stores, made pallets where other people's children could sleep. They worked the fields, stirred the soup, suckled their babies, oiled their guns, nursed the wounded, reddened their lips with the ash of crushed bricks, and rimmed their eyes with a shard of charcoaled wood pulled from the fire.

Chapter XXXIV

April 1941: A Village in Bourgogne

Solange looks about as though she has only just awakened, uncertain of where she is, even with whom she has been talking. Or if she has. She looks then at the woman who sits on the small sofa facing her, a meter or so across the rose and blue carpet from the chaise longue where she lies.

Of course, the woman. This Dominique. Brown curls clipped like the short mane of a carousel horse, pale skin, brownish eyes full of light like tea in a thin white cup. Wide-legged trousers and a jacket, black leather worn to brown, her bare feet tucked under her on the sofa. Dominique.

"What time is it? How long have we been sitting here? I, forgive me, it's only that —"

"Nothing to forgive. You slept a bit. And when you awakened, you began to tell me of your journey. I was content to listen. "

"Our position, I know that we're in Bourgogne, but will you tell me more precisely where we are?"

"Six kilometers from Auxerre. On the river Yonne. A hundred souls live in the village. Our rations are almost always full. The church, the elementary school, and, to some degree, the *mairie,* all function quite normally. The *patron* of this house was the village doctor. A Jew. When the *boche* requisitioned it, he and his wife were, they were 'relocated.' "

Solange rises, walks about the room, takes up a photo from its place on a small table, looks at it, puts it down. Everything seems in order, perhaps just as it was when the doctor and his wife lived there.

"It's beautiful, isn't it?" asks Dominique. "The house. The garden, especially the garden, we'll walk out there later. And down to the river, if you'd like."

"Yes, Amandine will like — She hasn't awakened? All this time?"

"Not a sound from her. I went to check earlier, and she hadn't even changed position. She was, you both were so tired."

"May I ask you something? Our driver, when she left us at the edge of the village this morning, she told us to cross the square, said that, on the other side of a small pinewood, we would find a house. Find you.

It was just before noon, I think, and, as we hurried along we saw what looked like a flower seller's cart overturned under the trees, near the gazebo. Violets and iris and white roses. Amandine ran to where the flowers lay, began to gather them, not to take but to save. She'd righted the cart, you see, and had set about to put things in order, but I told her that it would be best for us to find the house first. That surely someone else would see about the flowers. I'm not certain how to explain it, but I felt fearful there. No, that's not it. . . . It was as though *fear* was all about the place. As though everyone had run away. Loaves set to cool on a windowsill, the flowers strewn on the cobbles, but no one about. I looked up at the windows, nothing. Not a sound. Amandine had to run to keep up with me. I couldn't wait to find you. I was grateful that the house was so close by. What was it there? What happened?"

"Nothing. Nothing at all. It's only that everyone was at table or already under the covers, resting. You've been too long in the hills. Everything is tranquil enough here. A model occupied village. You know they were billeted here for months, the *boche*. Some right here in this house. Most of them in the village center. When they left, the

379

women waved handkerchiefs from their upstairs windows, the men shook hands with them."

"And you, a *résistante,* were you here when they were?"

"I was cook and housekeeper to the *boche.* A good story, which I'll save for another time. Should we meet again after all this is finished."

"You were a *collabò?*"

"I might have given that impression. We shall not speak of anything more about me. Will you agree to that? By now you must be at ease with omissions, silence."

"Yes. At ease."

"The armoires and commodes in the rooms upstairs are full of clothes. Help yourself. Once in a while, I wear Madame's things. A blouse, lingerie, a nightdress. In the room where Amandine is sleeping, you'll find something there. There are some sweaters that might do for her, though —"

"Thank you. I'll wake her so she can bathe. She'll be happy to walk to the river. We'll be down in just a while."

"No reason to rush. We have cheese and bread. A jar of apricots. The kitchen is cold, so I'll stir up the fire and set us up in here. I have some information about the next part of your journey."

"Will we leave tomorrow?"

"I think it will be the day after. Sunday. All the way north from what I understand. The rest of the way. Though you know not to count on . . ."

"I do."

"I hope that you'll rest well here, Solange. Things are somewhat different than they were in the places where you've been staying. The only things anyone hunts around here are wild hares."

"Where are you from? I mean, now that they've gone, why are you still here?"

"Nothing about me. Remember?"

"Dominique said that we might find something to wear. After baths, shall we have a look?" asks Solange.

"I'll choose for you and you choose for me, okay?"

Wrapped in a towel, her hair in another, Amandine drags a small upholstered chair up to the open doors of an armoire, climbs upon it, considers each dress and jacket and blouse, pushing aside the satin-padded hangers faster and faster until, "This is it. Look, Solange. Look here. This is the dress I want you to wear. You'll be beautiful as the ballerinas in *Swan Lake*."

She climbs down from the chair and, over

her arms, carries an icy blue chiffon evening dress. In front of the mirrored door to the bath, she holds it against herself and dances about.

"Solange, you must —"

"What in the world?"

"Say yes, please say yes. Try it, you must try it."

How strange this laughter sounds. Is it us, laughing and screaming as though . . .

"Too big," says Solange even before the dress is settled into place.

"Not so much . . . hold still. . . ."

"It fastens with these little hooks. Be careful or you'll tear it. It is lovely, isn't it, but we're going down to the river and then coming back to eat cheese and apricots by the fire. It's hardly the dress for —"

"Just show Dominique. Please, please."

"And you, what will you wear, little one? Your tulle skirt is practically in shreds, and none of Madame's things will do for you."

"I'll just wear my sweater and the corduroy pants. They're still sort of clean."

Solange says, "I have a better idea. The tulle skirt with my yellow sweater. I haven't worn it since the day we left the convent, and it will cover most of the damaged parts of the skirt. You'll be a vision."

For each satin loop Solange fastens over a

pearl button on the yellow sweater, Amandine kisses another part of her face.

"Hurry, hurry, I want to see."

"Be patient, little one, these loops are so small and you keep moving."

How thin she is. Thinner than she was always? Perhaps not. Taller, though, far taller over these ten months, and what flesh she has is taut and hard, good muscles in her calves, her thighs. But so thin.

"There, go to look."

The yellow sweater falls to Amandine's knees, and a wide ruffle of tulle — shirred by the tight band of the sweater — shows beneath it. The effect pleases Amandine, and she runs to find her well-seasoned socks and the old-fashioned high-top oxfords that Madame Aubrac had given her.

Solange wears her boots and a hand-me-down *résistante* jacket. Still laughing as they descend the stairs, they find Dominique by the fire, and they twirl and curtsy for her approval, then fall upon the rose and blue rug, the chiffon and the tulle bouffant about them.

"I'm honored to be dining with two such splendid creatures. Had I known we were dressing, I would have —"

"You're already perfect," Amandine tells Dominique.

"At least let me put my boots on before I offer you aperitifs. And surely we need music. And I think Amandine should have some flowers in her hair."

Dominique places a record on the gramophone. "Folk songs from the Poitou," she announces as she pours yellow gentiane into two small, thick glasses. For Amandine, cassis syrup and water.

"I'll return in a moment. Just a moment in the garden," promises Dominique.

"Why didn't we have aperitifs in the convent?' Amandine asks Solange. "And why weren't our uniforms made of chiffon? We could have done good deeds and prayed and sung plainsong in chiffon just as well as we did in gray serge, don't you think we could have, Solange?"

"Perhaps. Yes, I think we could have. Can you imagine how chiffon might have changed us all? Who could be cruel in a dress that billows?"

"I think Mater might have tried."

"Yes, she might have tried. If Paul were here, perhaps we would have found a dress for her. Yes, a dress for Paul. You in your tulle and I in my chiffon and she, what dress would you have chosen for Paul?"

Dominique enters holding out a branch of pussy willow, which she is bending into a circle. A wreath. Holding it in one hand, with the other she opens the drawer in a small table, rummages about, pulls out a short length of string. Winds it about to fasten the two ends of the branch together. She bites the string. Holds out the wreath to Amandine. "Let's try it," she says.

A bit too large, it falls to the middle of her forehead, exulting her eyes. Amandine runs to see herself in a mirror, says, "It looks like the crown Jesus wore on the cross."

Amandine begins to pull at the pussy willows already tangled in her hair.

"No, no, leave it, please. It's like the corona that held Beauty's wedding veil, do you remember?" asks Solange.

Dominique has begun to sing along with a sad voice coming from the gramophone, and Amandine, forgetting about her crown, goes to sit next to her.

"*Mon père m'a donné un mari.* My father has given me a husband, but it's you that I love. I love you, don't forget me," sings the unhappy bride of the Poitou. Dominique urges Solange, and Amandine sings with her.

"I love you, don't forget me."

Dominique goes to the table where the gramophone sits, kneels to search about in the case of records that is stored in a cabinet below it. "Ah, here it is. Do you know this one?"

She puts the needle down on a record, sits back on her heels, closes her eyes.

A woman sings in German, and Solange and Amandine close their eyes, too, and Dominique half whispers, half sings the words along with the deep, throaty voice. When it's finished, Dominique opens her eyes, sings the last line one more time.

"Wie einst, Lili Marlene."

"Why do you sing *boche* songs?" Amandine wants to know.

"Tell me the words," says Solange.

"It's not really a *boche* song. I mean, it was written by a German. During the Great War. But the words are not about patriotism or politics or ideology, not about war at all but about soldiers. It's a soldiers' song. The words are about loneliness, about being separated from your love. The same sentiment as the song from the Poitou. *I love you, don't forget me.* German, French, English, American, Russian, the words have been translated into many languages. I heard a Spanish version of it once. In fact, it has become a theme of sorts with, with many of us *résistants.*" She stage-whispers this last, laughs.

"We sing it precisely because the *boche*

386

have banned it, pronounced it sentimental and romantic and inconsistent with the cause of the fatherland. But the *boche* who were here played it every evening. Once, when I was washing up in the kitchen, one of the men came in unexpectedly and heard me singing along in German. When I saw him I stopped, of course, embarrassed, but he motioned for me to continue, and he stood there listening to me. Well, I sang it with all my heart, I sang it as though it was the only song in the world, and when it was over, he came to the sink, placed his hands on my arms, and he kissed me. He went back to the others without telling me why he'd come to the kitchen in the first place. I think many of us who are living through these times understand that there is much that's quite the same about us. Dreams, fears. Here, I'll teach you the words in French."

Cross-legged on the blue and rose carpet, breezes from the wide, unbolted windows blowing the scent of rain-crushed lilacs about the room, they sing and sing until they sing better and better and Dominique rises, turns up the volume.

"Now we're ready to sing with her," she says.

Dominique settles herself back between

Solange and Amandine. "Here we go then."

The three are Dietrich's French chorus, and they sing until tears fall, each one weeping for her own reason. On a late April evening smelling of lilacs during a war in which fifty million people will die for reasons already then obscure, they sing "Lili Marlene."

It is past midnight, closer to one in the morning when Solange awakens. She's been sleeping on the carpet in front of the now waning fire while Dominique sleeps on the sofa and Amandine on the chaise longue. Not wishing their soirée to end, they'd eaten their cheese and apricots and drunk some tea sweetened with the juices from the fruit and told stories until the first, then the second, then the last one fell asleep. The last was Solange. She rises from the carpet, goes to fix the quilt tighter about Amandine. She stirs up the fire, places a log over the red ash. She sits on the floor near Amandine and strokes her forehead where the pussy willow wreath still sits, moving her fingers among the thick black curls smelling of wood smoke.

"Darling, can you hear me? Will you wake up for a moment?"

Amandine sits upright, looks about, "Is it

time to go?"

"No, no, darling, lie down again. I just wanted to tell you that I'm going out to the garden, maybe down to the river if I can find it. Or to the village. I didn't want you to be worried if you awakened and didn't see me. I'm not tired at all and —"

"I want to come, too, wait for me."

"No. Absolutely no. I've just stoked the fire and it will be lovely and warm here in a few moments and I want you to sleep awhile longer. Besides, you must keep Dominique company."

"She snores. Sort of like Philippe."

"You do, too."

"Why can't you sleep?"

"It's hard to explain. We're very close to home now."

"How close? Can we walk?"

"We could, but I think Dominique is arranging things for us. We'll see tomorrow."

"Will things change when we get there?"

"What things?"

"Will you be the same?"

"Of course. Will you?"

"Of course."

"The greatest change will be that we can stay put. No more traveling. And there will be more people to love. More people to love us."

"I know. But I like it when there's only you and me. I like the feeling when there's only you and me."

"We'll never lose that."

"Never?"

"Never."

"Not even when I'm big?"

"Not even then. That reminds me. Your birthday. In six more days, you'll be ten years old. Up into the double numbers. And do you know what?"

"Uh-uh."

"It's possible, it's very possible that we'll be home by then. And Grand-mère Janka and Magda and Blanchette and Chloe will make a cake for you and a birthday supper and —"

"Will they have sugar for a cake?"

"I don't know, but they'll find something."

"Will you give me the package from the lady with the eyes like a deer?"

"What, where did that idea — ?"

"I know I'm supposed to wait until I'm thirteen but —"

"And it's exactly until you're thirteen that you *must* wait. That's the pact."

"Okay. It was fun singing with Dominique, wasn't it?"

"Very much so."

"I love you, don't forget me," sings

Solange in a soft hurdy-gurdy voice.

"I love you, don't forget me," sings Amandine in the unhappy bride's tremolo.

They sing it together, and then each one puts her hand over the other's mouth to stop the laughter.

"Here, I've poured a little more tea into your cup. Are you thirsty?" asks Solange.

"Not now."

"Then try to sleep, and when you wake, I'll be right here."

Solange buttons her jacket, slips into her boots, takes a shawl from a hook near the door, and walks out into the night. She wanders near the lilacs, brushes her face against them, snaps a branch from a bush.

What is it about tonight? A kind of greediness. After all these days of measuring and arranging, accepting mercy, accepting gall in whatever doses they were offered and then today, Dominique said, "The only things anyone hunts around here are wild hares." Another world. The music, the strange yellow liqueur, a chiffon dress, the truth that we are nearly there. Almost home. From Languedoc to Bourgogne. Ten months. Ten times ten lifetimes. I love you, don't forget me.

"I love you, don't forget me," she sings as she walks, swinging the branch of lilac, stepping through the pinewood, down a beaten-earth path and onto the cobbles of the village square. The dark is penetrated only by a wavering light leaking from between the church doors. Somewhere leaves tap on a windowpane.

Strange that the church would still be lit. I'll bring the lilac inside.

Solange runs up the steep wooden steps of the church and opens the doors. Before she registers what she sees, hears, she knows that she must run. Run back to Amandine. Take the little girl in her arms and run and run and never look back.

"*Bonsoir, mademoiselle.* How lovely that you have volunteered."

"Yes, yes, a volunteer . . ."

"An elegant volunteer. You needn't have dressed for the occasion, and look, an offering, flowers for us, ah, you French women are like no others."

Their laughter wet, salacious, three SS strut down the center aisle toward Solange. Two SS take her arms, the other rips off her shawl, unzips her jacket, runs his black-leathered fingers over her breasts. He slaps Solange lightly under the chin. "A buxom angel come to save us, huh?"

Their laughter louder, black-leathered fingers crush the flesh of her arms, drag her

392

into some darker place. A side chapel. One of them slaps her cheek with a pistol butt, throws her down onto the stone floor. She still holds the lilac. The receding stomp of boots on stone. Stillness. Shadows of marble saints quiver in rolling fans of torchlight and the yellow fire of votives. From where she lies, she sees that the same three SS who greeted her surround a man. One SS strikes a match, holds its pointed blue flame to the eye of the man whose arms are held by the other two SS. Closer yet, the SS holds the flame, brushing it across the eye, across the other eye. The SS leaves the flame to linger on the eyes of the man — the lids held open by a fourth SS beckoned to assist in the finale. The flame wavers and is spent in the breath of the man's scream.

In another sweep of torchlight, Solange sees two small boys who sob "Papa, Papa," from the bench where they've been seated to observe the SS at work upon their father. Dark again, quiet again. Back to black. Until, in the next sweep of light, she sees a woman brought out from somewhere to stand where the man had stood a few moments before. One SS holds her by the hair, two by the arms. The Match Man asks her something. In a very soft voice he asks her again and, when she spits in his face, Match

Man laughs, shouts something and shouts it louder, and a uniformed woman holding a child runs to where they stand. The child screams, tries to hold its arms out to its mother, but the uniformed woman restrains it. Match Man holds his flame aloft, leans his face into the child's, nuzzles its nose, gurgles baby words to it, brings the flame down, runs it across its head, singeing the pale fuzz of hair, touching the flame to its ears, its cheeks. The mother screams, "Clovis." Match Man turns abruptly. Asks another question. Choking, begging for her child, she says it again. "Clovis." Match Man takes the child from the uniformed woman's hands, places it in its mother's embrace. The SS watch as both mother and child grow calm. Match Man and the others disperse, leaving the mother to her freedom. As she walks toward the doors of the church, Match Man turns, aims, shoots. He shoots the woman, who has just declared the name of her husband's resistance cell. Its leader. It was her heart that Match Man was after. Where she held the child. At such close range. A single bullet.

On a late April evening smelling of lilacs during a war in which fifty million people will die for reasons already then obscure, on this night when they sang "Lili Marlene" and "I love you, don't forget me," and drank "gentiane" and ate cheese and apricots and slept by the fire, on the night of the day when Dominique told her, "The only things anyone hunts around here are wild hares," on the night when she was certain they were almost home, the same night when she told Amandine to go back to sleep, that she would be there when she woke, this was the night Solange walked into the war. Across the blurred secret edges of it and into the gore of its pluck. This is how it happened.

At twilight, *l'heure bleu,* the blue hour just before darkness falls, a convoy of nineteen SS traveling by auto and jeep and motorcycle on a road north of Auxerre was ambushed by the Résistance. *Je me défend.* A colonel was among the three SS who were killed. Two *résistants* were captured. Preliminary investigation has disclosed that one of the two is a resident of this village. *A model occupied village.* Reprisals will begin at dawn. In Auxerre. And here. Thirty French men, women, and children in each place. The normal reprisal quotient is ten for one. This exalted number is in honor of the colonel. The villagers who are being interrogated in the church were pointed out by *collabòs.* By their neighbors.

Rising from the floor, Solange walks to

395

the two small boys who still sit on their bench. She holds them, says nothing. From their trembling bodies, she takes as much comfort as she gives. One of them touches the gash on her cheek. Kisses it. She thinks of Magdalen Aubrac. When I see my husband or Lily, I never know if it will be the last time. Interrogation, torture, execution. From outside the church, screams, shots, the deafening thud of boots on the cobbles. The boots like hooves then on the wood of the steps.

SS heave open the church doors and, with the noses of machine guns, herd townspeople inside. The doors of the church are barricaded, the outside walls surrounded, the village sealed. The interrogation will continue through the night. Thirty people will be chosen. The others, many of them beaten to the edges of death, will be freed.

Hours pass, and no one has come to where Solange still sits with the two small boys. When the long leaded windows of the church show a yellow-rose light, two SS come to escort Solange. A group of men in long dark coats stand at the front of the church, and they laugh as one of the SS picks up the hem of the chiffon dress. Holds it gingerly in the tips of his fingers. A page for a bride. She and twenty-nine others are marshaled out the doors, down the wooden steps. They are lined up neatly along the length of a deep trench, freshly dug against the front wall of the church. Villagers stand in front of their houses, crowd in the grassy square. Starched pinafores over their dresses, sweaters against the new day's cold, the women stand together, hold hands. The butcher is buttoning his smock, a cigarette between his teeth. The curé and the young Jesuit who was his assistant — they, too, disclosed by the *collabòs* — swing from the branches of an elm tree. The man who owns the café stands on his terrace and weeps. He turns then, bends to some kind of work, fumbles with something, some sort of apparatus, it's difficult to see. A gramophone on a table covered in red oilcloth. The needle spurts, scratches, and then Dietrich sings. The volume so loud, the sound distorted, her voice reigns above the SS captain's shouts to his firing squad. The villagers begin to sing, and their volume, too, is strong, stronger. How Dietrich's chorus has grown. And at that moment, Amandine can be seen.

Right then, right there where the cobbles of the village begin, where the beaten-earth path ends. Having awakened, searched for Solange, she has come to the village to find her. Solange, from her place in line along the trench, faces the square. She sees Amandine, she hears Dietrich.

The gunfire Amandine thinks is part of the play. The pageant. She looks to where the players fall. She sees Solange drop delicately into the trench, the ice blue dress billowing around her.

Amandine thinks, Ah, look how beautifully she falls. I told her she would be just as beautiful as the ballerinas in *Swan Lake,* and there she is, the dying bird. Look at her, my Solange.

The guns are still then, and the acrid white smoke clears.

The play is over. How well the townspeople play their parts, so still they are in that hole. Like the just-killed birds the hunters would leave on the scullery table in the convent, the brown- and green-feathered birds lolling warm and soft, one or two still writhing. Yes, it's the end of a play. She'll get up now and see me. Come running to me.

The villagers are still singing. They sing in French while Dietrich sings in German. *Tous deux, Lili Marlène. Wie einst, Lili Marlène.* The record ends, the needle scratches round and round, the bells in the steeple ring six, and a north wind scuttles low along the cobbles as the squad points its guns downward, turns in formation to leave the square. Others shovel dirt into the trench.

Now Amandine is confused. Why are they throwing dirt on top of the players? Solange is dead.

Barefoot in her tulle skirt and Solange's yellow sweater, the pussy willow wreath raveled in her curls, she runs to the trench, pummels a soldier about his stomach.

"Pourquoi? Pourquoi?"

Another soldier scoops up the strange creature, quickly throws it down so that Amandine lands on her back, kicking, screeching. A village woman from the watching crowd pushes forward to retrieve her, holds her fast. Amandine burrows into the blue nankeen breast of the woman as she rocks her, whispers comfort. Amandine leans back to look up at her. Her tiny open hands she places upon the wide, wrinkled cheeks of the woman and looks into the chasms of horror that are her eyes.

"Madame, pourquoi?"

The woman pushes Amandine's head back to her breast, holds her more tightly, asks, "Who are you?"

"I am Amandine, madame."

"And, and was your mother, was your mother . . . ?"

"No, madame, not my mother, my

399

Solange."

"And where is your mother, sparrow girl?"

"I don't know, madame."

■ ■ ■ ■

Part V
April–July 1941
Letters from
Andzelika to
Janusz

■ ■ ■ ■

CHAPTER XXXV

April 25, 1941
Krakow
Darling Janusz,
I am leaving Krakow tomorrow. After ten
months of waiting for permission from the
latest residents of the Czartoryska palace
to examine Matka's things, I was informed
two days ago that I would be expected
there this morning. Though I was prevented from entering no part of the place,
two soldiers accompanied me at all times.
I was sickened by the state of things, bullet holes in paintings, mirrors shattered,
draperies pulled from their cornices, furniture piled into corners save the pieces on
which they must lounge during their lei-
sure. The smell. Two of Matka's trunks
were still in the dressing room on the third
floor and seemed untouched. I sat on Matka's little blue velvet hassock, where I
would sit to watch her prepare for her

grand soirées and, with the two soldiers standing guard at the door, I looked through piles and boxes of papers. She must have saved every scrap, every letter, every bill, every record. There were two boxes of my drawings, beginning from when I was three. Several hours into the search, I sensed it was an empty one. I proceeded, though, probing, scouring, ransacking. But there was nothing. About the baby there was nothing at all.

Bajka and I will leave for Germany and Switzerland as soon as Vadim can find petrol. I'd been convinced to travel alone by train, but I have since been discouraged, mostly by the colonel. I will say no more so that perhaps the censors shall deem this innocent enough to be sent on to you. Pray for my mission, as I do for yours.

I love you,
your Andzelika

May 21, 1941
Geneva, Switzerland
Darling Janusz,
Many adventures on the road for Bajka and me. Without our Swiss passports. . . . I shall be reticent about the details. We traveled first to the Black Forest, to

Friedrichsbad. You will recall it was in a villa there that Matka and I stayed for seven months and where the baby was born. No longer a clinic, the servant who came to the door claimed it had never been, that it had always been the private estate of a family from Cologne. At first I thought I'd mistaken it, that the place where we stayed must have been another, and so we asked everyone we encountered or whose attention we could capture, but the answer was always the same. No such clinic existed now nor did it in anyone's memory. After days of this, a woman who worked in the hotel where we stayed and who'd heard us talking approached us, told us that there had indeed been a clinic in the area. When she described to Vadim how to find it, it turned out that it was, of course, the same place I'd remembered from the beginning. The woman in the hotel told us that SS and Gestapo used it as a meeting place. What she didn't say, but intimated with gestures and rolling eyes, was that it is used as a trysting place.

We then proceeded to Switzerland to search for the clinic where Matka had brought the baby for surgery. In a way, this turned out to be a much simpler assignment, since the directors of the first clinic on our list contacted every other clinic and private hospital and even public hospital to which Matka might have taken her. Even a list of specialists who might have been consulted or who might have examined and treated the baby were contacted. After two weeks I was told by the clinic director who guided the inquiry that, under Matka's name or any of the other names I suggested she might have used, there were no records. Once the official search was put aside, this clinic official sat me down and told me that he doubted the baby had ever been brought to Switzerland. He said that, apart from both private and public documentation of patient information, there is always someone who will recall a case, especially the death of an infant. As I described Matka to him, he assured me that someone would have remembered her and come forth by now. I asked him if he would be kind enough to keep circulating the plea for some word, but when he patted my hand and nodded, I knew that he was patronizing me. I knew that if Matka had taken the baby to Switzerland, the information — even if she had requested privacy — would have been disclosed to me now that she is dead. And so the second stone wall. We shall make our way into France and, I hope, to Paris. There seems no reason to return to Krakow.

I may soon have a rather grand surprise for you. This time one that will please rather than torture you. All I shall say now is that Colonel von Karajan is helping me.

God keep you safe,
your Andzelika

June 10, 1941
Krakow
Darling Janusz,
As it turns out there was magnificent reason to return to Krakow. I am writing to tell you that you are a father. (Oh dear, as I write this I see my faux pas since I said previously that Colonel von Karajan was helping me. Well, it is not that sort of help that he provided.) But you are indeed a father. What the colonel accomplished (with untold hazard to himself) was to save a twenty-one-month-old boy who had been (here I shall refrain for obvious motives of fear). His name is Aleksy, and he is as blond and beautiful as you. But that's only half the news. There is also Eljasz, who was one year old a few days ago. He is less healthy than Aleksy seems to be, very

thin, but still there is something fierce and even brave in his eyes. Healthy, thin, fierce, they are our sons, they have been saved and they are ours. "Friends" of von Karajan are preparing papers for them. As soon as Vadim can find enough petrol (von Karajan is working on that as well), we'll be on our way back to Paris. I asked him (von Karajan) to not stop at two. He will find us more, I know he will. This is the best way for me to . . . Ah, how to explain this feeling? I believe that adopting these children is the best way for me to become her mother. Our little girl's mother. Can you understand that?

Bajka helps so much to care for them, but I must tell you that I am already a jealous and possessive mother. I hold them both at the same time and, can you imagine this? Aleksy caresses Eljasz and coos to him, and the three of us fall asleep together. Loving them makes me feel closer to you. And to her.

Please write to tell me that you are happy.

with our love,

your Aleksy, Eljasz, and Andzelika

July 1, 1941
Paris
Darling Janusz,
The boys and I and Bajka fare well. When they sleep, we are either sewing nappies from hotel towels or washing the soiled ones or queuing for rations or begging the hotel kitchen for a few vegetables or fruits before they transform them into some wartime abomination. We always have eggs and milk and even cheese, and both boys seem to thrive. Eljasz is walking and running, and Aleksy shadows him so fervently. I am trying, though, to help Aleksy to understand that he must not worry so for his brother. Character is character, though, and Aleksy, I think, has one very like yours.

The colonel writes that there is a nine-year-old boy who witnessed and was very nearly victim of an "event" in Bydgoszcz a while back. I wonder if you've heard about it. I shall not say more about it here, but the colonel says that his "friends" are trying to save this boy. Of course I said that we would take him. I don't know his name. It seems that the colonel has business in Paris, so that he will accompany the boy, bring him here to me. Three sons, my love.

Perhaps another daughter next.
all my love,
your Andzelika

July 9, 1941
Paris
Sergiusz is his name, your third son. My darling Janusz, I am at a loss to tell you how dear he is. Certainly his suffering shows, he is timid and sensitive, rarely speaks except when spoken to. But even after two days, I see him gaining confidence with our little tribe. Bajka adores him, too, and thus we have become rivals in our desire to care for him. He loves music and says he studied the piano from the time he was four until . . . His parents were killed early on, and it was his older brother who cared for him, the same older brother who he saw shot in Bydgoszcz. His life from that day . . . I shall wait to say more.
When will this war end, my love?
your Andzelika

■ ■ ■ ■

PART VI
MAY 1941
THE SAME VILLAGE
IN BOURGOGNE

■ ■ ■ ■

CHAPTER XXXVI

"May I look inside your valise? Just to see that you've taken everything."

Dominique and Amandine are in the salon, the same salon where they sang and danced and ate and slept on the night Solange died. The room they've continued to share for the eight nights since. Amandine on the chaise longue, Dominique on the sofa, neither has slept nor, for the first three days, spoken more than half sentences. When Dominique tried to soothe Amandine, encourage her to talk, Amandine would open her eyes, shake her head, sometimes she would smile as though to comfort Dominique. Always, then, Amandine would retreat into her thoughts. And for hours, Dominique would sit beside her, caress her back, her arms. Try to feed her.

It is Amandine's thoughts of Claude, the little girl, the five-year-old Algerian girl who'd been staying with Madame Aubrac when Amandine and Solange were there, it is her thoughts of Claude about which Amandine first speaks.

"Maybe I should go back to Madame Aubrac. I could help with Claude. Her parents are lost and she was going to live in an orphanage. If I go to help, maybe she won't have to go to an orphanage."

"That was a while ago," Dominique says, "and I would think that Claude has already gone from Madame Aubrac's. But I think it's wonderful that you . . . Will you tell me some of the other things you're thinking about?"

"I don't know."

"No words?"

"No out-loud words."

"Do you want to tell me some of the words that you say only to yourself?"

"Alone. Scary. Maman. Solange. Sometimes I say *boche.*"

"It's strange but, these past days, I say the same words to myself. The same ones. I also say Amandine."

"I guess we're not so different."

"Not at all. No matter how different we may *seem* to one another, the truth is that we're not. None of us are. So different from one another."

"Not even the *boche?*"

Dominique smiles, shakes her head but doesn't speak.

"I think I'm hungry," Amandine tells her.

Among Solange's things, Dominique finds the brown-paper-wrapped parcel tied with white string. Attached to it is a small white card on which is written a single word: "Amandine." Dominique turns it over in her hands, wonders about it. Finishes the task of looking through Solange's clothes, folds them neatly, replaces them in the valise. She puts Solange's identity papers in an envelope, seals it, places it, too, in the valise. She picks up the parcel and carries it downstairs to the salon, where Amandine sits by the fire.

"I found this in the valise. I thought you might like to put it away yourself, so you'll know where it is."

She brings the parcel to Amandine, sets it down on the table near the chaise longue.

Amandine picks it up, studies it as though she does not recognize it. Then "I'm not supposed to have this until I'm thirteen. I don't know what it is, but it's something that was left for me with Solange."

"That was left for you? A gift?"

"Like a gift."

"From whom?"

"A lady with eyes like a deer. That's what Solange said."

"Eyes like a deer. Beautiful. And you have no idea what's in it?"

"No. Do you think it would be okay to open it? I promised, but . . ."

"I think it would be okay. I think you should open it."

Amandine looks at the parcel, looks at Dominique, begins to untie the string.

Dominique reaches out to take the parcel. "Here, let me help you."

"I can do it. I want to do it."

Amandine slides the string, first off one corner, then another, slips the parcel free. She sits up straighter, unfolds the soft brown paper to reveal a small black velvet envelope with a stiff back, the three corners of it fastened with a velvet button. She loosens the button and, one by one, opens the flaps. Held against the stiff part of the envelope, a pendant is hung. To her it looks like a small bottle made of some purple stone. She notes that the tiny bottle has a stopper made from a lilac-colored pearl. Still hung on the stiff board, she turns the bottle over, holds its weight in the palm of her hand.

"Oh," she says. She says it again.

"May I see it?"

Not noting Dominique's request, Amandine continues to turn the tiny bottle over and over, looking at it from every angle.

"It's attached to a ribbon," she says, lifting the ribbon from its hooks, difficult to see since it is made of the same black velvet as the envelope.

"Is it a necklace?"

"I think it is."

Dominique kneels by Amandine's chair, looks at the piece, which Amandine holds up, letting the pendant swing on its ribbon.

"Yes, a wonderful necklace. Very old, I think. Splendid, actually. Shall I fasten it for you? You hold up your hair and I'll tie it in the back. . . . Go ahead. Wait, let me tie it more tightly so the stone falls right, wait, right there."

Dominique rises, stands back to better see the effect.

"Amandine, it's wonderful. Who was the lady who left it for you? The lady with the . . ."

"Solange said she didn't know who she was. A lady who came to visit her grandmother one day. She wasn't my mother. Solange said she wasn't. She said she was someone who knew my mother. At least that's what she thought."

"It's a magnificent gift."

"Solange called it a symbol."

"Of course, a symbol."

"I don't understand. But I like it."

"I think that Solange must have meant it was a symbol of your mother's affection. Her love."

"I guess. Claude had *symbols,* too. She had letters and photographs waiting for her at the orphanage. I heard Madame Aubrac telling Solange."

"Another sort of symbol but —"

"Do you know one of the reasons why I want to go home? I mean to Solange's home."

"Tell me."

"So that I can ask her grandmother about the lady with the eyes like a deer."

"Yes, well . . . Do you know what I think?"

"What?"

"That also you have eyes like a deer."

"Amandine, I've been asked, my friends have asked me about your school. About the convent. I told them what I know about it. Of course we don't know yet even if it would be possible for you to return to live there, that is, we have yet to make contact and so don't know if the school has remained in operation. But it does seem the best place to begin . . ."

In the garden, sitting in a metal chair, her cheek laid down on a small cloth-covered stone table on which there is a cup of tea and a plate of bread, Amandine stays quiet.

Dominique tries again. "Madame Aubrac, I mean if the convent school is . . . Well, we think that surely she, that Madame would . . ."

Amandine raises her head from the table, looks up at Dominique. "Not the convent. Not Madame Aubrac. I want to go home."

Dominique walks from where she has been standing in the doorway from the salon to the garden, kneels on the spring-softened ground, on the new-sprouted weeds and grass, tries to take Amandine from the chair into her arms. Amandine resists. Dominique rises, paces near the table.

"You know that you can't stay here. I can't stay here. I should have been gone —"

"Can you take me home? Jouffroi is their name. Avise. A farm near Avise. Solange told me that we were close enough to walk."

"Solange's papers, I've looked at them. I know the family name, where they live, and we have been trying to reach them, to tell them —"

"About Solange?"

"Yes. And about you. But so far, we have not been able to —"

"If you show me the road, I can walk —"

"Foolish girl, do you really think that I would . . . It's only that they might have gone away. You know that so many people have left their homes and —"

"Solange said they would never leave."

"I know that's what she said, what she believed. But her mother, the family, they may not have had a choice."

"Please, Dominique, please keep trying. Jouffroi."

"There is another possibility. There is a person who is connected to us. He lives farther north. Not nearer to Solange's family than we are here. Northwest. But still north. This man lives in the center of a village. A big house, a garden surrounded by a stone wall. This man, he has land just outside the village. He keeps goats and he makes cheese."

"Solange's mother keeps goats and makes cheese."

"I didn't know. . . . This place that I'm talking about, it's on the river Oise. In the Val-d'Oise. Have you ever heard of it?"

"How close is it to Avise?"

"I don't know the number of kilometers but, as I said, it's north of here. Close to Paris. You could stay with this man and he would continue to, he would keep trying to reach them. The family. And then, in time, perhaps he could help you to . . . He's my father, Amandine. His name is Catulle."

"And your mother?"

"My mother died when I was a child. I have two brothers."

"Two brothers? What are their names?"

"One is Pascal. The other is Gilles, but both are . . . they were taken by the *boche* at the beginning of the Occupation. They work in Germany now."

"Are you going home to your father? Could we go together?"

"No. I'm not going home. Not yet. Some-day I will, but for now I have —"

"You're like Lily, aren't you?"

"Lily?"

"Madame Aubrac's Lily. She's a kind of soldier. She carries a pistol. I saw it once."

"Yes, I suppose I'm a bit like Lily. And that's why, that's one of the reasons why I can't accompany you now, not to the convent or to Madame Aubrac or even to the Val-d'Oise. You must understand that it will not be up to us to decide, not up to you to say where you want to go. Others know more than you and I know, and so it's they who will say. But no matter where you go, friends will help you."

"What's he like? Monsieur Catulle."

He's, he's, I don't know, he's a farmer, tall and broad. He speaks softly. I look like him, everyone says that. Our eyes, amber. Sometimes green. He will, he will be pleased, very pleased if you stay with him. I know that. There may be other people staying there. From time to time. He will take good care of you."

"Is he old? He wouldn't be going to die while I was there, would he?"

"No, no. And no, he's not very old. He fought in the Great War."

"There was a war greater than this one?"

"So they say. He's past fifty, fifty-three I think. He's handsome. Madame Isolde, she is our housekeeper but has always been like a mother to me, she is in love with him. And a Polish woman, a widow who is the grande dame of the village, well, she's rather in love with him as well. Madame de Bazin. Her first name is Kostancja. I love to say her name. When I was a little girl, I would always go to play with the children of her maid. Her maid was Polish, too. You'll meet Madame Isolde *and* Madame de Bazin. If you go to stay with Catulle."

"What's a Polish woman?"

"A woman who was born in Poland. Poland is a country east of here."

"Why does she live in France?"

"Because a long time ago she married a Frenchman. And she left her home to be with him. It happens all the time."

"Do you mean that people don't stay in the same place always?"

"Yes. That's what I mean."

"How long will it take to get there?"

"To get where?"

"To Monsieur Catulle."

"It depends. You see, this next journey of yours, no matter to what destination, will be a little different from the ones that brought you, you and Solange, here to me. Once it's arranged, once I know more, I'll explain things to you. As best I can. Won't you drink your tea now, Amandine?"

Dominique's first thought after the execution had been to take Amandine and leave the village. She'd thought to leave that same morning. No plan, no destination; her instinct was to disappear with the child. She was good at that. At disappearing. But word had come almost immediately that she and the child should stay put. They should wait. Then, last evening, the directions were communicated. A member of a cell not connected to Dominique's would be waiting for Amandine at a specified time and place the next day.

Today. This person will take Amandine to Catulle, to Dominique's father, while Dominique herself will proceed to Paris, to work that has been assigned to her there. No complications are anticipated. They will travel together for the first part of the journey and then separate.

Dominique has instructed Amandine. What to say, what not to say should they be stopped by the *boche*. The single awkward moment of the transfer will be when Dominique must leave Amandine to walk alone over a short expanse of countryside to the place where she will meet her next *convoyeur*.

"But why can't you walk with me?"

"Because the person who will come to fetch you and who will take you to Catulle, he or she is part of a different operation than mine. Another group. It's a rule among our groups that we never see one another. For the sake of safety. A protection for all of us, so that should any one of us be questioned about another by the *boche*, we'll be telling the truth when we say we don't know them. It's difficult to understand, I know. . . . I can hardly . . . too much for a child of ten . . ."

"How long will I be alone?"

"About as long as it takes to walk from

here to the village. A few minutes."

"How will I know if it's the right person? What if there's more than one? Who am I looking for?"

"I don't know the person. I can't describe him or her to you. But the person will say this to you, he or she will say, 'I have the cheese for you.' "

"That's kind of strange."

"Perhaps. But that's what he or she will say. Now let's get you ready."

"I *am* ready."

"Are you convinced to wear that sweater? You've not had it off except to bathe since . . . for all this time."

"Please, it's what I want to wear."

Solange's yellow sweater over brown corduroy pants, her high lace-up shoes, the valise packed with the rest of her clothing, Philippe's straw hat, Solange's things, her pussy willow wreath. The tin of walnut oil. Over her wrist, the old blue velvet pouch, its only contents a half bar of German ration chocolate which Dominique had tucked into it. Amandine is wearing the necklace under a kerchief that Solange often wore over her hair. Twice protected, she's told herself. But against what, she is unsure.

"Would you consider wearing this hat?"

Dominique holds up a simple brown wool basque.

"Here, let me put it on for you. Let's tuck all your hair up inside it."

"Why?"

"It's to make you look less, I don't know, less *foreign*."

"What is *foreign?*"

"Something that is or someone who is a bit different. *Insolite.* You are *insolite.* A grand compliment, you know. To be unusual. There, just like that, with only a few curls showing. Would you care to see in the mirror?"

"It's so I'll look less like a Jew, isn't it?"

"What?"

"I heard Solange and Madame Aubrac talking. Madame Aubrac told Solange that I looked like that. Like a —"

"That has occurred to me as well, with your dark eyes and dark hair, and it's only that, you must understand that the *boche* are especially —"

"I'll wear the hat if you like. If someone asks me if I'm a Jew, I will say that I don't know. Because I *don't* know. I don't know at all. I don't know anything about myself or about anyone else, and that's why I keep saying those words to myself. You know, *scary, alone.* Those words."

Dominique lifts the kerchief from around Amandine's neck, touches the amethyst. "This is proof that you are not alone. Try to remember that. Try to remember what Solange told you about this. Will you do that?"

"Yes."

"And don't be foolish about the *boche*. Should you be asked if you are a Jew, you must never answer *I don't know*. You see, your papers, since they do not list the names and birth dates and places of birth of your parents, well, someone who is checking your papers, he might consider you *suspect*."

"Sus—— ?"

"*Suspect* means that someone might not believe you. In this case, might not believe your papers. A controller might think that your papers are false. The truth is that they are false. You had no papers, according to what Solange told me, and so your bishop had papers made for you. Some of the people who will look at your papers will readily accept them. Others may not. Those who don't will undoubtedly ask you if you are Jewish. They will ask you if you are a Jew. You must always answer that you are not. *No sir, I am not a Jew.* That's what you must say. Over and over again, as many times as you are asked that question. Will you promise me that?"

"Yes."

"All right. Let's go over this again. What is your full name?"

"Amandine Gilberte Noiret de Crécy."

"And where were you born?"

"In Montpellier. May third, 1931."

"Your mother's name?"

"I am an orphan, sir. I do not know the name of my mother."

"Your father?"

"Also unknown."

"Good. Now let's go."

It is just after eleven in the morning, less than half an hour after Dominique had helped Amandine to step out from the auto onto a narrow, unpaved road cut through a field of low brush. The upward winding road is all that Amandine sees.

"Are you sure it's here where I'm supposed to be?"

"Yes, I am."

Dominique checks to see that all of Amandine's things are in order, hung from and strapped and clutched to various parts of her.

"Now please wait for me to drive away. Count to one hundred. Count slowly. And then begin walking up that road. At the end of it, you shall meet your *convoyeur.* Just keep walking until a person appears before you and says . . . I have —"

"I know what the person will say."

Dominique holds Amandine close to her, says, "We shall see one another again, my darling. I believe that we shall. And meantime, I ask you to whisper this in my father's ear. Say, 'Your little girl loves you.' Will you do that for me?"

"I'll tell him. I'll —"

"I'm going to run off now or else I may forget my duty and take you with me. . . . *Au revoir, Amandine.*"

"Au revoir, Dominique."

"I have cheese for you."

"How did you know it was me?"

"Well, the truth is that not so many lovely young ladies have passed by this way today and so I —"

"Bonjour, monsieur."

"Bonjour, mademoiselle. Please follow me. Right here, this path to the left. Up the hill a little way. Are you hungry? I really do have cheese for you and bread and . . . Not such a long trip ahead of us now . . ."

"There we are. Let me help you to gather up your things. Good. Shall we take a last look? Your purse, your valise."

"Are you leaving me here, monsieur?"

"Not leaving you but asking you to wait. I must go now. In ten minutes, more or less, you shall be met by . . . It's comfortable enough here, and you are quite protected. Out of sight of the road but very close to it."

"No one told me that I would be alone again, I mean after I walked to where you —"

"I must go now. All will be well. I assure you."

"But who am I waiting for?"

"Au revoir, mademoiselle."

Amandine sits on the patch of ground indicated by her *convoyeur*. Again, yet again, she consents. She settles her belongings about her, positions the valise as a pillow, lies down, her face in the shade of an elm, her legs stretched out to the sun. She breathes deeply, as Baptiste taught her to do long ago. She tries to quiet the words inside. She touches the necklace, the kerchief. She hears something. Someone crunching over the stones of the road. She sits up, wonders, waits — as we all must wait — to see who will appear over the rise.

Amandine thinks, He is tall. And his hair is like hers. Curly like the mane of a carousel horse. That's what Solange said of Dominique's hair that night when we were dressing. She said that Dominique had eyes the color of tea in a thin white cup. So does he.

His voice a soft rasp, he is saying, "*Bonjour, p'tite 'zelle.* I am Catulle."

■ ■ ■ ■

PART VII
MAY 1941–
NOVEMBER 1945
VAL-D'OISE

■ ■ ■ ■

Chapter XXXVII

Doors slam, people call to one another. Cold air flaps heavy lace curtains against a windowpane, and she throws back the covers, runs to lift them. To see where she is. Milk cans clatter in a wheelbarrow pushed by a boy in a blue smock and a white basque. Wearing a man's shabby clothes, a woman with a strident voice is asking Monsieur Catulle if he will barter three *banon* for a hare "still quivering" and a small jar of its blood. He tells her that he can shoot his own hare, and she says, "Of course you can but not one like this, no, never again one quite as handsome as this —"

"Let me have a look at him, madame. He and a small truffle and I'll give you four *banon.*"

All this while it's still dark, she thinks. Wind shudders the rimed panes, and she wonders if it's still May. It was May yesterday when I left Dominique and met the man with the

435

cheese and then the other man. Bonjour, p'tite 'zelle. I am Catulle. She looks out to the high stone wall around a garden patched like the one at the convent. A bed of purple cabbages, one of the green crinkly kind. Lettuces, leeks, flowering peas. Apple trees, cherry, apricot. The largest tree is a fig. Wild iris have pushed up here and there; it must still be May. Solange must still be dead. Dominique, where is she? I am here but where is that?

Though her corduroy pants are folded neatly upon a chest of drawers, she has worn her yellow sweater as a nightdress. Her shoes are set near the bed. She dresses quickly, opens the door to a dark corridor and a steep wooden stairway, which she descends with no memory of ever having climbed it. Another dark corridor and soft voices from the other side of a small green door. She knocks.

"Entrez, entrez. Bonjour, Amandine."

He seems larger than he did yesterday. A fresh white shirt, Dutch blue braces, his small, pointed, curly beard and mustaches — how could I not have noticed his beard and mustaches yesterday? — still glistening from his morning bathe. He is spooning up what looks like wet, purplish bread from a large white bowl. He rises.

She walks to him, offers her hand to greet him formally. He gives her his.

"*Bonjour, monsieur.*"

"*Bonjour, bonjour, petite, et bienvenue.*

"Sit, sit, and here is Isolde. Madame Isolde, may I present —"

"*Bonjour, chérie.*"

Her hair pulled up on top of her head into a small graying brown pastiche, Madame Isolde is thin and tall, with war-sunken cheeks, brown liquid eyes with thick lashes, which she flutters like a fan, and teeth so white they seem blue. Her breath smells of anise seeds, and her hands feel rough as she holds Amandine's face, looks at her with a wide smile. "You were sleeping so soundly last evening when Monsieur brought you in that I carried you up to bed, made you comfortable as I could, and left you to your dreams. Of course you're hungry."

"Not very. I ate quite a lot of cheese yesterday . . ."

"Bread, some bread, and the milk is warming. This morning's egg with a few drops of marc. You need to be strengthened, I can see that."

She sets about cracking a large brown egg into a cup with no handle, beats it furiously with a fork, pours something into the cup from a tall green bottle, beats again. Hand-

437

ing the potion to Amandine, Isolde nods her head, urging her on with it. "All in a gulp. The only way to do it."

Amandine drinks, begins to choke, but quickly restores her calm. She smiles tentatively at Catulle, who is laughing. "Your initiation into the Val-d'Oise, *ma petite*. We have very little, as you will see, but we do have a few good hens. A fresh raw egg every day makes up for much of what we don't have. Well, then . . ."

Amandine is tearing a piece of bread into small pieces, arranging them on the white embroidered tablecloth. When Isolde puts down a cup of hot milk, she wraps her hands around it. Sips at it. Smiles at Catulle, sips again.

"Tomorrow I shall prepare your breakfast, one that you shall much prefer. Red wine–soaked bread. It's better with sugar but . . ."

Wiping her hands on her apron, Isolde sits down at the table. The three are silent, each one looking and nodding at the others, until Catulle says, "Madame Isolde is our housekeeper, Amandine. Our commander, to put it better. But she will see to whatever it is that you —"

"First thing is to find her some clothes. And shoes."

"Yes, yes, of course. The market —"

"The market has nothing, I'll take her home with me this afternoon, and we'll look through what I have in my trunks. Always something."

"It's very kind of you, but what I have will do nicely. I expect I'll be leaving soon and —"

"Leaving?" Catulle asks.

"Yes, monsieur. Dominique told you, didn't she? That I'm on my way home."

"I have not spoken to my daughter in more than a year, Amandine. But it was communicated to me that you have some friends up north. Toward the Belgian border."

"Avise. Near Reims. Their name is Jouffroi."

"Yes, well I did, I do know that, but you see, listen, why don't you and Madame Isolde go about the morning together while I get to my work? And after lunch, we shall speak about this."

"About my going home?"

"About why it's best for you to stay here with us. For now."

Madame Isolde heats water in a cauldron over a woodstove in a shed behind the house where a great deep zinc tub sits. Towels, a brush like the ones the convent sisters used

439

to scrub the stairs, Amandine tells her, a cake of blackish soap. Isolde goes to work on Amandine's slender limbs. Washes her hair, rinses it with water gone cold. Almond oil, purple capsules that make lilac foam. Solange is still dead.

"Pardon, madame?"

"I was saying, 'There we are, all finished.' Until we fix up some other things for you, I found these in your valise. I've ironed them. They'll do for now."

Amandine buttons up her old tartan shirtwaist and pulls her black market sundress, dark blue and white stripes, over it. Both are too small and short for her lengthening body. Their effect raises a gasp from Madame. "I'll get things ready for Monsieur's lunch, put that hare to soak, sweep up a bit, and do the beds. Then we'll be on our way. The queue will be shorter nearer to ten, so there's no rush. Sit in the sun to dry your hair, won't you? Such lovely hair, Amandine."

Catulle has invited Amandine to sit with him in the garden. He has set out two heavy iron chairs under the apple trees. Though it's still light, he has lit a small lantern, hung it from a tree branch.

"Amandine, I understand your wanting to

440

get to Madame Jouffroi. Though I don't know all of your story, I know that, well, I know enough to understand why you would like to see her."

"Do you know about Solange?"

"Yes. I know that she was your guardian, that you and she were traveling north to her home. I know that she was killed."

Catulle waits. Amandine, satisfied that he knows this much, at least this much, waits for him to proceed.

"But it isn't possible. Not now. It's not the imprudence of trying that I'm against but the futility of it. There is no way to get through. There would have been no way for you and Solange to get through. Their village lies in what the *boche* have designated 'the forbidden zone.' It's an area that has been, well, it's been cut off from the rest of France. No one can get out, no one can get in. Not without authorization. Not without permission."

"How do I get permission?"

"You don't. You can't. I meant military permission, authorization. And those do not apply to you. Please listen. Just as I believe Dominique and her friends did, my friends and I have done our best to contact Madame Jouffroi. We've even tried to contact people who might know her, people who

441

live nearby. The search has been an empty one, Amandine."

"Do you mean that she's dead?"

"No. Not at all. It's likely that Madame Jouffroi and her mother, her daughters, it's likely that they were displaced by the *boche.* That means that the *boche* could have taken over their house, their farm. That's probably what happened. Until the war is over, until people begin to return to their homes, to their villages, there's not much to be done. Can you try to begin thinking of this as your home? Not for a week or a month. Perhaps for a very long time."

"How long?"

"I don't know. As you've come to realize already in this brief, inconceivable life of yours, no one of us knows very much at all."

"It seems to me that everyone is either dead or hiding. Or lost or waiting."

Catulle is quiet. He looks at Amandine, looks away. "You've just about covered all the possibilities. But I am not dead. And Madame Isolde is not, and all the —"

"I know, but you could be by tomorrow, and Madame Isolde could go for a walk and not ever come back because the *boche* decided to shoot her, let her fall into a ditch, and then cover her up with dirt. And where is Dominique, and where are your sons?

Where is Solange's mother? Where is mine?"

This is the most that Amandine has spoken since Solange's death. Perhaps it is more than she has ever spoken. The most she has given voice to the words that stay inside. Philippe and Baptiste, Paul and the convent girls. Josette. They march past her now. Solange is there. Hedy Lamarr, who impersonates her mother, she is there. She looks at this man sitting near her. Wonders why he is crying.

"That's the part of your story that I know less of, Amandine. I know that you're an orphan. That —"

"I don't know much more than that, myself, monsieur. Just as it says on my papers: mother, unknown; father, unknown. I worry so much about her. Not so much about my father. I don't know why I've never wondered about him, but I think it might be because of Philippe. Père Philippe. He was a priest at the convent. I used to think that he was my father. That was when I was very little. And so he sort of became him. You know, became my father. But even though I used to think that the abbess in the convent was my mother, when I learned that she wasn't, well, eventually I was glad. Glad that she wasn't my mother. Do you understand?"

"I think so. Because she wasn't, she wasn't . . . ?"

"Like a mother. Solange was. I guess I've had two mothers. One is dead, and one is lost. I miss the one who's dead and I worry about the one who's lost."

"You worry about her?"

"Of course. Wouldn't you worry about your mother if she was lost? I don't even know her name. How shall I find her, how shall I begin?"

"Maybe it's she who must find you."

Built of round gray stones, it is long and low, Catulle's house. Endlessly turning corners and forming small river-shale-paved courtyards from which curved wooden doors — each painted with an appropriate fruit or vegetable — open onto root cellars and pantries and a wine cave, it would be the typical mid-eighteenth-century village house of, perhaps, a prosperous merchant or, in his case, a prosperous farmer who prefers the convenience of village life to the isolation of living on his land. When his sons and his daughter were at home, when they were growing up — albeit without their mother but in the care of a revolving procession of devoted aunts and cousins and always Madame Isolde — the house was ripe with cheer. Under the low-beamed ceilings against the annually whitewashed walls, hearths smoldered in every room, the curtains were starched, the heirloom mahogany glossed, the tile floors waxed to peril. Masses of flowers and blossoming branches and fruits spilled from vases and jugs and bowls, and there were cupboardsful of green-and-yellow faience plates and silver and crystal and some tiny jot of old lace was everywhere there was a space for it, that's how it was, Catulle's house. And the smells of supper and wood smoke, of some voluptuous potion — a brace of fine putrid birds, the haunch of a boar — shuddering away in a bath of noble wine perfumed with a faggot of wild herbs in Isolde's great black iron casserole at the back of the stove. For the epoch of those twenty-odd years between the wars, that's how it was. The village, too.

Close enough but not too close to Paris, the place thrived from the overnight carting to the city of bounty from its rich earth — vegetables and fruits, which were sold each dawn at Les Halles. At least as much did the village thrive by its own essential frugality. There were cafés and *pâtisseries,* wine shops, *épiceries,* bakers, butchers, little restaurants with wide *guinguettes* cantilevered out over the river where, on a summer's evening in the light of pink and yellow lanterns, people would dance. If one was careful, one could partake of all of this and still put something aside in the wooden cigar box in the bottom drawer of the kitchen armoire. But now, life with the *boche*, under the *boche*, the villagers have adjusted. *Jours maigres* to be sure, yet often there are good days. Another kind of *good days*. The houses, the park, the school, the *mairie* show only a mild embattering from early *boche* strafing. Unlike in the Great War, this time France saved herself. In some ways, she saved herself.

Up and down the main street of the village, much seems as it was. The pastry shops are closed, of course, and the butcher hands out what the *boche* give him. Likewise the *épiceries*. Though in the bars the *café* machines are quiet and the only offerings are thick glass tumblers of watered wine or some unrefined homemade poteen that the *boche* didn't want, the old men still play cards at the oilclothed tables, still cheat and challenge, if with less voice and less heart.

The restaurants survive in an interesting way. Villagers bring some part of their rations to barter with the cooks for a plate of soup, some sort of braise or stew. A sweet concocted from salvaged fruit, a piece of honeycomb, yesterday's bread, an egg, some cream. And then, next morning, the foods that the villagers had brought the evening before to barter are put to use for that day's menu, a self-sustaining concept that flourishes upon French culinary ingenuity and the truth that says: A good cook can make a good supper from nothing. And though one of the old men might strap on his accordion and play for a bit, no one dances on the *guinguettes* stretched out over the river. No one save the girl whose fiancé was shot on the first day of the Occupation because he moved too slowly into roll call to suit the *boche*. She dances sometimes on the terrace of one little place, her arms an arc about his ghost.

The effect of the Occupation on the village is like that of a Vermeer left to the ravages of sun and rain and the slashing of a small, sharp knife. Still recognizable, even still good, certainly still precious. Perhaps more precious to one who has known it as it once was.

Catulle and a troupe of older village men work his land. The vast portion of his crops is requisitioned, as are those of his neighbors. And those of most of France. What he manages to set aside or glean helps. There are rations. There are the forests, the river. Among his treasures he counts three goats, a bevy of hens, a gallant rooster, a rabbit hutch. Madame Isolde. He waits for his children to return, opens the doors to their rooms each day, more than once a day, walks to their windows, touches their beds. Beds where *boche* slept and might sleep again while his sons and his daughter slept, sleep . . . where? He thinks of the girl. This Amandine. Her ancient little soul. Nothing more than a scuffed valise and someone else's shoes to call her own, still she worries for her mother.

Though she's been with Catulle and Isolde for two months, she still shakes hands with both of them as she enters the kitchen every morning. Still thanks them before she sits down at table and again when she rises. She has grown fond of them, of how they look and speak, what they do, the simple ceremonies of their life. She thinks what she feels is something like the happiness she felt with Solange. Something like it. She wonders if it's terrible that hours pass without her thinking of Solange. Or is it that she never stops thinking about her? Is it that Solange is always nearby? No, not nearby but rather inside her. Yes. Inside her.

or walks anywhere near them, even on the other side of the street, Isolde turns her shoulders inward, pretends to peer into some shop window, or drags Amandine into a café and orders a glass of water. Amandine observes, too, that whenever this happens, Isolde smoothes her hair, pats her topknot, takes a few anise seeds from her pocket and chews them nervously. Her lashes, which flutter like a fan, move in double time.

"Who is that woman?"

"Which one?"

"The one over there talking to the man with the dog. The pretty woman."

"Pretty? She's a lurid cow strung with pearls."

Though Amandine laughs, she will not be deterred. "I think I know who she is. Dominique told me about her. She's from another country, isn't she? And she likes Monsieur Catulle."

"Everyone likes Monsieur Catulle. And yes she's from another country. Her name is Madame de Bazin."

"Why does she make you so nervous?"

"She does no such thing. I just don't like her and so I avoid her."

"Oh."

"That's all," Madame Isolde says, pinching anise seeds into her mouth and chewing them with her front teeth. The lashes move in a blur.

When it's five minutes before noon and Amandine hears Catulle opening the gate, she walks — she does not run — down the path to greet him. He bows to her, she nods her head, and, side by side, they go into the house to lunch. Amandine praises Isolde's food, drinks the "single finger" of wine that Catulle pours for her, and after the meal, when Catulle goes to rest and she and Isolde have put the kitchen and dining room in order, they walk the hundred meters to Isolde's little place above a café in the rue Lepic. A tiny kitchen with a stone sink and a two-burner gas plate, a sleeping room with a narrow cupboard bed, an open hearth, and a zinc bathing tub set up in the middle of the wooden floor, a bathroom painted chartreuse, which is down the hall and to which Isolde has the only key. The two lie in the cupboard bed. Sometimes they sleep a bit, but often they just stay quiet, rest. When they do talk, it's about food. About what they shall fix that evening, the next day, about what they would fix if they only had . . .

Isolde talks about chicken poached in cream set over sautéed apples and onions

452

splashed with Calvados. Though she has been twenty-five years in the Île-de-France, she — a born and bred Normande from Dieppe — is always spiritually hungry for her native cuisine. She speaks of buckwheat crepes — thin and delicate — rolled with applewood-smoked ham and Camembert, then gratinéed under a flame with good white Norman butter and more of the cheese. She longs for a stew of mussels — just harvested — poached in their own sea-salted liquors with cream and bay leaf and the buds of dried wild thyme rubbed between the fingertips.

"But I do like working with river fish, with whatever the boys and the old ones bring to me — carp, catfish, pike, once in a while a salmon lost from his school. I bone them, salt them, lay on branches of bay and thyme, and cover the whole mess with a plate weighted with a stone. In a few days . . . Ah. With a sauce of pounded mustard seed and cream . . . And what about the peas? Let's make a soup tomorrow. We'll poach the pods with mint, and when they're tender, we'll pass them through the *mouli* and add the tender peas whole — poached for two or three minutes in sea-salted water — to the puree. A knob of butter if the rations are full, a fistful of crisp *lardons,* and fried bread.

"I can taste the mint. And the *lardons,*" Amandine tells her in a dreamy voice.

"It's late for wild asparagus, but sometimes a few shoots come up near the river. An omelet —"

"I used to make stone soup when we slept in the woods. A potato and hard bread, wild herbs, and, if we had one, an egg stirred in. It was good, madame."

"In September if you'll find me some *chanterelles, morilles,* a handful of *trompettes de mort,* along with a few *noisettes,* I'll make the most luscious . . ."

Neither speaks of her life before they knew one another, though Isolde inquires.

"There might come a moment when you want to tell me something, you know, something about you. Or about others. Should that happen, I want you to know that —"

"I do know."

In the evening after supper, after Catulle pours some wine into the last spoonful of soup, raises the shallow bowl to his lips and drinks from it, after he cracks a few of the walnuts from the basket of them by the hearth and warms the kernels over the fire in a copper pan, after he pours out a small glass of marc and tips it down his throat and pinches up some of the leaves and weeds and whatever else it is he keeps in the tobacco tin next to the walnuts and tamps the stuff down into his pipe, lights it, sucks hard to keep it going, once the foul smoke spirals into a fine white cloud, he stands up, thanks Isolde and Amandine for his supper, goes to take his sweater from the rack by the garden door. Drying a dish or putting away the silver, Amandine watches him. In the same way she likes seeing the kitchen table set for three when she comes to breakfast in the morning, she likes seeing the three sweaters on the rack. She likes that hers hangs on the lower peg between theirs. Her yellow one — the one with the little pearl buttons and the satin loops, the one that belonged to Solange and, before that, to Solange's mother — her yellow sweater between Isolde's white and his gray and brown tweed.

As he is putting on his sweater, that is the moment when she wants to ask if she might go with him. She knows it's to the river he is headed, to the bridge at the edge of the village, the one with the high wooden walls that curve like the hump of a camel. She knows he will look down at the water and smoke his pipe and stay there till the light

455

changes. From her window at the top of the house, she always goes to watch him down there on the bridge. Some evenings other men come to join him, and she sees them nodding their good evenings, lighting one another's pipes if they are spent, shaking hands sometimes or patting one another on the shoulder. Mostly he's alone there, though, and she wonders what he thinks about as he leans on the high wooden wall.

One night after she helps Isolde with the washing up, Amandine takes her yellow sweater from its peg and follows him.

He hears her before he sees her, hears her mincing steps on the wooden floor of the bridge, and he straightens up, turns to her, smiling, as though he'd been expecting her, which, of course, he had. Neither one needing to talk, they both look down at the river then. After a while, Catulle says, "I like the sound of the river beating on the stones, bent on the sea. I like how small I feel under the stars."

"You feel small?"

He puts his spent pipe in his pocket, raises his chin toward the heavens. "Small in a good way, small against the greatness of all of this."

"I like to bend backward so that I can see more of the sky. I bend farther and farther back until my head spins and I feel as though I am surrounded by the sky, like I'm inside it. Is that how it feels when you die?"

"It might be."

"Not sure, though?"

"Not sure."

"Why do you come here every evening?"

"I like to stay here and consider the day. I think about my children, and I guess I talk to them, ask them how they fare. Then I ask myself if I think to have done a good job with the day."

"Did you today?"

"Do a good job with it? Fairly."

"How can you tell?"

"You know how it feels when you've been very cold and then you come indoors to sit by the fire? If I have that feeling, then . . ."

"What if you don't have that feeling? What if all you feel is the cold? Only cold. What if you can't find the house with the fire?"

"I think of what I can do the next day so I might have the feeling then."

"I've tried that, but sometimes I can't think of what there is to do. What might make things feel less cold."

Catulle relights his pipe, takes a while to get it going. He lowers his left arm from the ledge of the bridge then lets it hang loose by his side, his palm turned up. Noticing what he's done, Amandine looks up at him, looks down at his hand; all the while Catulle keeps his eyes forward, the pipe stump between his teeth, the smoke swirling about him. When she puts her hand inside his, he curls his fingers around it, stays still. Smokes, looks ahead. After a while, Catulle can feel her hand unfold from a fist, feel her tiny fingers insisting between his. They talk awhile and then they walk back across the bridge, down the road past the café and the baker and the restaurants with the empty *guinguettes* stretched out over the water, past the shops and the other houses. They walk all the way home.

CHAPTER XXXVIII

"She's waving to you, Madame Isolde. Don't you see? She's just there by the baker."

"Who?"

She knows very well who it is but, once again, Isolde will turn a blind eye to her rival. Or she would have if Madame Joubin hadn't come up just then and detained her with news of a winter coat. Red wool with a green velvet collar, which will be quite lovely for Mademoiselle Amandine. There's a hat, too, a small Scottish cap in green velvet with a feather.

Upswept, faded blond hair, pale skin taut across the wide bones of her face, darkish eyes that might be blue in sunlight, a small mouth with an upper lip that seems to slant — like a triangle — from a single point to join the full, pouting lower one, Kostancja de Bazin is more sinuous than plump. Black silk dress, faille pumps with high slender

459

heels. Not a single pearl about her, pear-shaped diamonds drop from Kostancja de Bazin's ears and another one, hung from an almost invisible chain, sinks into the hollow of her throat. A newspaper cone of purple tulips in her hand, she stands quietly behind Isolde, smiling at Amandine and waiting for Madame Joubin to finish her story.

"Ah, madame, you are well enough I see, but who is this dear little creature?"

"Madame de Bazin, may I present Amandine Noiret de Crécy."

"I would have thought as much. Beautiful *and* aristocratic."

Amandine curtsies as she has been taught to do. Says, *"Enchanté, madame."*

Also as she has been taught to do, she looks directly into the eyes of Madame de Bazin, answers her questions.

"How old are you, Mademoiselle Amandine?"

"I am ten, madame."

"And do you, by chance, play a musical instrument?"

"In the convent, I studied the pianoforte."

"Wonderful, wonderful, and your preferred composers?"

"I don't know very many of them, madame, except Beethoven and Brahms. Just before I left the convent I'd begun to practice my first Chopin Étude. Opus ten, number two. My right hand is weaker than my left and my *maestro* said this would strengthen it, but I —"

At the mention of Chopin, Isolde rolls her eyes, folds her lower lip in upon itself, and shifts from foot to foot. "Amandine, we must be going, still some commissions and —"

"Chopin. Frédéric Chopin is my compatriot, you know, and he, too, lived much of his life in France but, as we Poles do not matter where we live, he remained true to his blood."

She bends down toward Amandine's upturned face, speaks more softly. "I shall play the Nocturnes for you someday soon, my dear. All of them."

"Madame de Bazin, we must wish you a good day and be on our way. Amandine?"

"Au revoir, mademoiselle, au revoir, madame. À bientôt."

"Not if I can help it. *À bientôt.* Why did you have to say 'Chopin'? Now she'll never let you be."

"What's wrong with Chopin?"

"Absolutely nothing, according to her. Obsessed. Obsessed with him. She speaks of him as though he's her darling older brother. She organizes music appreciation classes for the villagers and musicales in which people are invited to play piano or violin or cello, but the truth is, it's she who plays the whole program, Chopin, Chopin, Chopin, and only when the audience is exhausted does she call up the others to perform."

"I would like to hear her play. Actually, I would like to play again. If there was time, I mean. When I've finished helping you in the afternoons, might I go to her so that I could practice? It's been a year since —"

"I'm sorry, Amandine. I wasn't thinking of you but of myself. Of course you may go to Madame de Bazin to practice. I'm certain she would be quite thrilled to instruct you. We must talk to Monsieur, of course, but . . ."

Kostancja de Bazin, born and raised in Poland, married an older Frenchman, a rather celebrated violinist of his time who died when Kostancja was not yet twenty. A series of love affairs — most often with her piano teachers — kept her in Paris until, after visiting the village one Sunday afternoon soon after the Great War had ended, she met and weeks later married the local squire. Alas, he, too, passed on before their first anniversary. This history of the

462

swift and violent demises of her husbands earned for Madame de Bazin the title *l'Empoisonneuse.* Some thought she did it with mushrooms, most believed the men died willingly in her boudoir. Thus, having inherited — from this second valiant — the grandest house in the village, a château, really, its furnishings worth a ransom, its lands vast by local standards, Kostancja de Bazin settled into country life with her maids and her peasants and her pianoforte. While still in her widow's weeds, she'd set her darkish eyes on Catulle la Fontaine. After a slow simmer of a seduction that had endured nearly twenty years, Madame de Bazin — war or no war — would now seize upon this child, this Amandine, perhaps not unlike Isolde had done, as a means to unite herself to him. Amandine, wise as she was, understood this.

"What's this that Madame Isolde tells me about your meeting Madame de Bazin? Do you wish to study the pianoforte? You might have told me. Surely there's an instrument to be had somewhere . . ."

"No, no, Monsieur Catulle. It was only for a moment, I mean, I've been thinking and I'd rather . . . You see, I was being polite to Madame de Bazin and, really, I don't miss practicing at all, in fact, I was rather tired of it and —"

"Well, until I can see about finding a pianoforte, I can arrange with Madame de Bazin for you to practice there for a few hours each week. I will ask what would be convenient for her and —"

"No, please, no. I've changed my mind. I would like it best if —"

"All right then. We'll leave it for the time being."

"Yes, monsieur. We'll leave it . . . ."

But Madame de Bazin leaves nothing *for the time being.* When the invitations to her "afternoons" are returned "with regrets" over the signature of Madame Isolde on Amandine's behalf, she finds motive to visit Monsieur Catulle, to bring a large egg-glossed Polish cheese bread one Sunday morning when she knows that he will be at home.

"My Teckla made two of these, and since I couldn't possibly . . . I do hope you'll enjoy it, Monsieur Catulle."

She turns abruptly from her exit and stops very close to where Catulle stands by the open door, tilts her head, the darkish eyes laughing through her short black veil, says, "Oh, and while I'm here, please do tell me of Mademoiselle Amandine, such a well-bred child. She is well, I trust, has adjusted to our little school, though after her instruction in the convent I can hardly think it suits her."

There are more cheese breads and, once, a whole head of cabbage stuffed between its leaves with bread and eggs and cheese and tied with string and poached in the broth of a hen. It was her maid who stopped by with a *zvarlotka* filled with apples and, on another Sunday, an oval porcelain tureen of *uszka,* tiny buttery, wild-mushroom-stuffed pastries, which Catulle and Amandine — Isolde having claimed disinterest in the delicate little things — devoured with a pot of strong tea. It might have been the *zvarlotka,* or perhaps the *uszka,* but, in time, Catulle was duly softened and so asked Amandine, "Are you certain you have no interest in studying with Madame de Bazin? She does seem sincere in her desire to know you better."

"No. Well, I wouldn't mind if you would accompany me to one of her musicales. You and Madame Isolde together. I would like that."

"I doubt that Madame Isolde would agree, but I shall ask her. I shall tell her that when the next invitation is received, she should accept for three."

Despite that she is so close to being beautiful this Sunday afternoon and that Catulle gives her his arm as they walk the kilometer or so along the main road to the de Bazin château, despite even that Catulle tells her she is superb in her camphor-smelling yellow wool dress and coat, and that her creamy white satin cloche makes her eyes look like ripe hazelnuts in the sun, despite all of that, Isolde chews her anise seeds and bats her lashes and repeatedly asks no one in particular why she had been fool enough to agree to the outing. Amandine, pretending it was to be helpful to Madame de Bazin that she had gone on ahead of them, hopes that some scintilla of romance might strike them along the way.

"*Alors, mes amis,* reversing the history of his father, who had fled France for Poland during the Terror, Frédéric Chopin left Russian-dominated Poland, barely a man, in 1831 so that he might study and perform in Paris."

Madame de Bazin, the pear-shaped diamonds swinging from her passion-reddened ears, stands by the pianoforte in her salon and speaks of Chopin to her audience of children and adolescents and their Sunday-primped, war-worn mothers. On and on over the foot shuffling and the throat clearing and the murmurings of the house, she tells them that Chopin, with his fellow exiles in Paris, lived life in a B-flat minor lament, embittered by Russian dominion over their beloved land. They suffered as only Poles can, she says, by tapping their feet, clapping their hands, and grieving in the heartbreaking *robato* of the mazurkas. This was Chopin's genius, Kostancja de Bazin tells them, to recast the melody of a folk song. To gift his compatriots their past.

By this time the house is benumbed to Madame. Insensible to Chopin. Even to the sweets that sit on silver trays an arm's length away, piles of chaste pink and green chimeras. Children sleep against the shoulders of their mothers, the few old men who'd come for the sweets sleep, too. At some early point Catulle had risen, walked quietly away to smoke his pipe in the garden. When Madame begs pardon and leaves the salon for a moment, one woman asks another, "If she loves Poland so much, why is she here? Why doesn't she go home?"

One of the old men, fresh from sleep, leans forward to look down the row of chairs to where the woman sits. He says,

"Because there is no home. No Poland. All carved up by the Russians and the Austrians and the *boche* in the Great War and then, when the Poles had only just begun to put things back together again, Hitler —"

"Well, she lives in France now and rather well, I might say, and I think all this talk about Poland is . . . well, why should we care?"

Amandine, sitting in the row in front of the woman, turns to glare at her. Amandine wishes to tell the woman why she might care about Madame de Bazin, about Poland, about Chopin, and searches for a particular word but can't recall it and so, in lieu, puts her finger to her lips to ask for silence. When Madame resumes her place, Amandine turns to her, rests her chin on her fist, and listens.

On the way home, Amandine asks Isolde, "What is the word that means you can feel what someone else is feeling?"

Isolde looks at her, thinks a moment. "Do you mean *empathie?*"

"Yes. *Empathie.*"

So charmed was Amandine by Kostancja de Bazin on that Sunday that she would spend the following Tuesday afternoon and all the foreseeable Tuesday afternoons hence at the château with her. With Chopin and the pianoforte and Madame Teckla's cheese bread.

Each week Amandine practices for an hour or so under Madame's gentle observation and eventually refines, perhaps minimally enhances, lost technique. Madame supplies her with exercise books and sheet music and great verbal stimulation and, after a month or so of these Tuesdays together, Madame also supplies her with a pianoforte.

A spinet, painted white, low and triangular in shape, its tone more like a clavichord than a true pianoforte, it is delivered one evening to Catulle's home on a horse-driven cart, pushed along the walkway to the house by three of Madame's farmers, and put into place in the salon under Catulle's direction while Isolde stands by, arms folded across her chest, and Amandine tries to contain her glee.

On one Tuesday, Kostancja de Bazin announces, "Today I shall dance for you. I shall show you the dance I learned as a child. I haven't thought about such things in years and years, but today, today . . ."

At the word *dance,* at the sight of Madame fussing with a gramophone, Amandine thinks of Solange and Dominique and hears the German lady singing the soldiers' song. She wants to ask Madame if they might wait for another day, but Madame has already struck her pose, the music begun. As Madame moves, sways tenderly, Amandine's pangs dissolve, or could it be that they change form? Amandine hums softly to the music. A few moments pass and, from the chair where she sits, Amandine begins to move her feet, her arms. She rises, begins to dance. As though she knew the dance, as though she remembered it. Could it be? How can it be? Surely it cannot. And yet she dances. What does she hear in the music? Can she sense that it's hers? this music? this dance? Eyes half closed now, Amandine dances — hands, palms up at her waist — *reckless and nimble,* as her mother danced on the night she fell in love with Janusz. If one who had seen Andzelika dance then could see Amandine dance now, one would know. Like mother, like daughter. One would know.

The glass shivers into a pattern, discernible, to Kostancja de Bazin as she watches Amandine in wonder. Each on her own part of the dark marble floor, they dance.

When the music ends, Amandine opens her eyes, walks to where Madame stands, smiles at her, curtsies, thanks her. Madame brushes the nearly dried tears from Amandine's cheeks, curtsies back to her.

"*Dobrze zroblony, piekna dziewczyna.* Well done, beautiful girl."

"Is that your own language? Polish, I mean?"

"Yes."

"I like the way it sounds. I like all the *z*'s. You look different when you speak in Polish. I've heard you speaking to Madame Teckla. You look even more pretty. Also I like the way you speak normally. You know, in French. I like the sounds you make. Does the music make you cry, too?"

"Yes, it must be the music."

From a heavy crystal bottle, Kostancja de Bazin pours a transparent liquid into a silver cup. Sits on the sofa, pats the place near her, beckons Amandine. "You've never told me about yourself. About your family."

Amandine looks down at her hands, folds them, opens them. "I don't know about my family. Solange Jouffroi was my guardian, and she was —"

"Yes, I, Monsieur Catulle has told me about that. I've never mentioned it to you because I'd thought it more genteel —"

"Yes, someday I think I shall be able to talk of Solange. I would like to talk to Madame Isolde and to Monsieur Catulle about her, and to you, perhaps. But for now . . ."

"And your parents?"

"Unknown. To me and to everyone who has ever been near me. Monsieur Catulle says that my mother must find me because I have no way of finding her. When he told me that, I felt better somehow. Ever since I was little I'd been wondering how I would begin to look for her and never thought that it might be she who —"

"Your name? Surely your name . . ."

"My name was given to me by my bishop. When we were at the convent. Solange named me Amandine, and later Bishop Fabrice gave me his mother's name, Gilberte. And his own name, Noiret de Crécy. I've never tried to tell anyone about what I remember, from the beginning I mean. You know, memories. Solange was always there, and since she knew everything that I did and since I never knew anyone else very well, I'm not used to talking about things."

"I understand."

"Monsieur Catulle and Madame Isolde are my first friends. Well, the first ones that haven't died yet. Dominique was, too, but I only knew her for a few days. Oh, and you, too, madame. I'm sorry that I can't tell you more about me, but I don't know —"

"It is in unfamiliar places where we find ourselves, Amandine."

Kostancja de Bazin, still sitting on the sofa, still sipping slivovitz from the silver cup, thinks,

If she is not in some way Polish, then I am not. The shape of her hands, the delicacy of her touch on the keyboard, the way she holds a book, arranges flowers, how she holds her fork. Even in her wretched clothes, she has some bond with elegance. Yes, yes, of course her convent school, her finishing school . . . still, there is something more at work in that child. How she moved to that music. The tenor of her still babyish voice. Not so rare this phenomenon of race memory, though. Tolstoy told us it was that when Natasha danced. Instinct, birthright. The cut of one's eyes. Why cannot it be true for Amandine? All that comes to mind now is *zal*. Even if I desired to, how could I explain *zal* to her? The condition of a Polish soul. Regret, mourning, grief, melancholy. Those threads of guilt. All there in her. She wonders if it's her doing that this Solange was killed. She struggles with that. She likely thinks it was somehow she, herself, who caused her parents to leave her. God knows what other weight she carries. *Zal*. And yet she compresses it, holds her head erect, works and studies and smiles. And if she is

Polish? What would my knowing or her knowing, what would that change? Another orphan, highborn and abandoned. Not uncommon. Someone's shame. Such an exquisite thing she is. Before long I shall have convinced myself it's I who was meant to raise her, meant to take care of her. Did her dance today, did it brush against my own *zal*? God help us, I think it's true. As she grows older, Catulle cannot possibly continue to . . . When, if Dominique comes back, she would help, but . . . And that foolish Isolde could never give her what I can. The answer is that Catulle and I should marry. He dotes on her. He is alone and I am alone. She is alone.

That she and Monsieur Catulle should marry held aloft as her cause, Kostancja de Bazin dispenses with the Sunday bagatelles, proceeds toward intimacy more directly. Inviting him to walk in her garden, she speaks of her impressions of the child, of her talent, which merits nurturing, of her "way of being," which calls for sensitivity. "What would you say if I told you that my fondest wish is to devote myself to this child? Because I have no other commitments, shall we say, I can do that as you cannot. Just as — for yet another set of reasons — your housekeeper cannot. Let me have her, monsieur."

"No. The *boche* have spirited away three of my children, and I shall not have you making off with my fourth. That's how I've come to think of her. She is my child."

"It is exactly because I know that you've come to think of her as yours that I ask."

"What do you mean?"

"Of course, you would come with her. Or, more deftly put, I would come to both of you."

"What are you saying? That you would surrender your little fiefdom here to come rule over my far more humble one. Is that your plan, madame?"

"Not to rule over it but to grace it. You must admit that's what it lacks, monsieur. My presence would serve as complement."

Catulle touches her cheek, barely touches it at first, testing it, wondering if all the womanishness of her might blemish under his farmer's hands.

"Are you truly prepared to give up all of this to —"

"I think, monsieur, that I have been preparing for this all my life."

As though Monsieur Catulle had agreed to her proposal, Kostancja de Bazin begins to arrange things. She and her household set about packing, separating goods and chattel that might make the voyage two kilometers down the road to Monsieur Catulle's home from that which might stay packed away in the storage rooms of the château. She sends to Paris for whatever bits and pieces of clothing are to be found to supplement Amandine's wardrobe. She plans little teas and luncheons, and always Amandine is by her side. Her magnum opus, however, is to be a supper — as grand as her wits and her stores will allow — for twelve townspeople. A modest gala during which, Madame de Bazin is confident, Monsieur Catulle will announce that he and she, with the blessing of their darling Amandine, are engaged to be wed. Though she has not been thoroughly precise in explaining her plan to Monsieur, nor has he been thoroughly precise in accepting it, she trusts his comprehension, his moral sensibility. Despite the truth that Monsieur possesses these in abundance, he refuses his chair at the head of the table, sits among his neighbors and, when he stands, it is only to raise his glass to Madame's generosity. Kostancja de Bazin bows her head, waves her hand against the praise, lifts the long oval sapphires of her eyes to her guests, and, through them, smiles all around the table. The moment lost, perhaps the battle, it is *zal* of which she thinks as she rises, leads her guests into the garden.

Chapter XXXIX

"What does it mean that the Americans have declared war?"

"It means we're less alone with the *boche*. It means that the *boche* won't have such an easy time of it any longer. Less smug they'll be about it all. Yes, less smug. And don't ask me what *smug* means. Not right now. I must . . . I have something I must do . . ."

Catulle bends to kiss the top of Amandine's head, puts on his coat, his muffler, his basque. "Stay here this evening, please. It's very cold and —"

"I will. You didn't have your walnuts, so I'll crack them for you, set them in the pan. Okay?"

"Okay."

For the past month Catulle has frequently been absent from home. A few days, sometimes longer. He leaves without notice, returns just as abruptly. When Amandine asks Isolde where he goes, what he does, she says, *He is doing what he must do.* And when Amandine asks, *What is it that he must do?* Isolde doesn't answer but says only: *the war.*

What Isolde does not tell Amandine is that Dominique has been imprisoned in Paris. In the prison de la Santé. That her trial is set for early January and that Catulle has been meeting — openly or via the auspices of others — with those who might be willing and able to effect her case. Bribes, reason, Catulle is trying all of it. She has been accused of participation in the writing, printing, and distribution of Résistance pamphlets, work of which she is indeed guilty. Her sentence will likely be forced labor in Germany until, after she has been starved and worked close enough to death, she will be rewarded with a quick execution.

Today, only days after the Japanese spectacle in the Pacific, Catulle has received news via Dominique's group that her trial has been postponed, that she is being sent directly to a work camp in Germany. That she and eighty others from la Santé as well as Cherche-Midi will be sent to the labor camp in Germany called Krefeld. They will travel first by train and then by truck. And then they will walk. On average, thirty percent of the prisoners die of starvation and exposure along the last stretch of the journey.

Though his own subversive work is muffled by layer upon layer of cover, Catulle is not wholly without notoriety among the *boche,* and thus the hazards, to himself and to Dominique, that his presence in the capital would present, he has examined. And discarded. Catulle will go to Paris this evening to ask permission to visit her. Now the *bribes* and the *reason* he will use to cause her escape.

What will happen, though, even as he arrives in Paris, is that he will be detained. He will learn that he had been betrayed, marked out to the *boche* by members of his own group, those who had used the story, the true story of Dominique's plight to lure him. Aided then by double agents, another Résistance group intervened, and it's they who will take Catulle as he leaves the train in the Gare du Nord, they who will save him from the betrayal and set him on the next course of his life, lead him away — the tip of a pistol held in a paper sack against his spine — skulking into the dark belly of the station, out through some camouflaged door into a waiting van on the evening of December 10, 1941. The only way out of the

Résistance is death.

Later, when he is able to take in these events and, in some part, their significance, it is of Amandine he thinks.

But I am not dead. And Madame Isolde is not . . .

I know, but you could be by tomorrow, and Madame Isolde could go for a walk and not ever come back because the *boche* decided to shoot her, let her fall into a ditch, and then cover her up with dirt. And where is Dominique, and where are your sons? Where is Solange's mother? Where is mine?

"He may not return for a very long time."

Amandine does not look at Isolde as she speaks but, her head resting on her upturned palm, she moves the torn pieces of her breakfast bread about on the white embroidered tablecloth. More than three weeks have passed since Catulle went away, and it was only this morning that Isolde was visited by a woman, ostensibly wanting to buy cheese, who informed her that Monsieur's absence would be a long one, that he was well enough, that she and Mademoiselle should expect no further word, that she should close the house and take Amandine to stay with her in her village flat. There were a few words about practicalities. Now

Isolde looks at Amandine, the child's pallid face washed pink in a slant of January sun and, though she wants to take her in her arms, she says, "It's no use mooning. This is what war causes. And we're among the fortunate. You know that perhaps better than I."

No response. The pieces of bread are moved into yet another pattern.

"Here's what we must do. While you're at school, I'll begin covering the furniture, storing the silver, that sort of work. The field workers have nothing to do in this weather, so I can ask their help. We shall decide together, you and I, if there's anything that we need or want to bring with us to my place. Certain valuables I shall store elsewhere. Then we'll pack up our clothes and settle ourselves in the rue Lepic."

"Why do we have to leave?"

"Efficiency. We can keep warm in my place with far less wood than we can stay barely clear of frostbite here. Safety. If the *boche* come by again, want to set up another time in the village, this house will be as attractive to them as it was in the summer of 1940. If we're here, they'll send us away or, worse, we'll be requisitioned along with the house. Made to do their bidding. No *boche* will be interested in my little flat. But it doesn't matter if you or I understand or agree, it's what he wants us to do."

One by one Amandine puts the pieces of bread into the cup with the now-cold milk, mashes them together. Begins to eat the pap with a spoon. "What about the garden?"

"Nothing but six cabbages are left, and we can come to take one whenever we need it. We'll wash the windows once a month, dust and scrub whatever and whenever, according to need. In the spring, we'll work the garden just as we always do. We are not quitting the house but simply going to live elsewhere for the time being."

"Why don't you tell me now that he's never coming back?"

"Because it wouldn't be true. Don't you think that I miss him, too? Everyone is missing someone, Amandine. Every last one of us. Eat your breakfast, do your work, and be off to school."

Amandine looks up at Isolde, perhaps shocked, perhaps hurt by her brusqueness.

Isolde says, "When I look at you, I wonder if Madame de Bazin, her frilly snobbishness, has not deluded you. Parties and dresses and piano playing can't make the war disappear."

"I never thought they would. I was —"

"By the way, I shall see that your pianoforte is placed in the little salon, where the sun will warm it each morning. I shall wrap it in quilts. It won't be harmed. Not by the cold, anyway."

Amandine rises, goes to where Isolde stands holding on to the back of Catulle's chair.

"Don't you look at me with those eyes or . . ." Isolde sits in Catulle's chair, pulls Amandine down upon her lap, rocks her.

That winter of 1941–42, Amandine and Isolde pass in a quiet temperament of sympathy.

While Amandine is at school, Isolde works either in the little flat or in Monsieur Catulle's house. She milks the goats, makes the cheese. Feeds the hens and the rooster, takes the eggs, feeds the rabbits. Dispatches one every now and then to barter or stew. She queues for their rations, cooks and sews and, in a zinc pail wrapped in red and white cloth, she carries soup or an omelet or a cabbage pie to Amandine for her lunch. For nearly every supper, Isolde stands in front of the two-burner gas plate to cook her Norman *galettes,* consolation of her childhood. The traditional buckwheat long finished, she makes them with whatever flour or meal she finds or ferrets. Rubbing a trencher of lard — the same precious trencher she keeps for weeks at a time — across the hot pan, she pours in the batter from a small blue cream pitcher. Thin, lacy, crisp, she rolls them up with a smear of their own chèvre or some mash of vegetables. Sometimes they eat them with a whisper of sea salt and drink a tumbler of wine and, always and without telling one another, they wish that the others were with them.

Each day when she returns from school Amandine takes from the hook by Isolde's door the long, flat black iron key to Catulle's house and walks the hundred meters to it from the rue Lepic. She walks through the house, tries to find the scent of his pipe smoke, climbs up to the bedrooms and walks through them, pats the beds, looks out the windows, practices the daily rite that he practiced, wonders what the house will feel like when everyone returns. Sometimes she uncovers her little spinet, takes off her mittens, leaving the black fingerless gloves she wears under them, plays a few scales, part of an étude, and then closes the lid, puts all the quilts back in place, locks the door and pulls it tight. On her way back to the rue Lepic, she stops on the bridge with the high wooden walls that curve like the hump of a camel. Standing where she and

Catulle used to stand, she looks down at the water and up at the sky and considers her day.

Evenings, Isolde and Amandine sit by the stove, where Amandine studies or reads aloud and Isolde — in preparation for their return — knits with the unwound wool of sweaters she'd knitted years before for Dominique and her brothers. They speak of Monsieur as though he was in the next room.

Amandine visits Madame de Bazin on Tuesdays, if not every one of them. They talk and drink tea and often leave the pianoforte closed under its ruby silk shawl. Less lustrous her eyes, less curvaceous her form, Madame tells Amandine she goes often to Paris. The reasons she leaves unsaid. And there are people about, guests perhaps — ghostly and half glimpsed — who pass in the halls. Amandine understands that Kostancja de Bazin, too, has taken on some quiet work in the name of France.

One day there is a large package, a box wrapped in white paper, sitting on the table in front of the sofa where Amandine and Kostancja de Bazin like to sit. "Open it, *ma petite,* it's something I made for you from something made for my . . . Well, it's a long story, but do open it."

"What is it? It's so heavy and —"

"Oh, don't be so careful, tear the paper, there, slide it off, ah, I can't wait to know if you'll —"

"Oh. What is . . . It's so beautiful. Is it really for —"

"Of course it's for you. Here, let's try it. Slip your arms through, there. Come to look in the glass in the hall . . ."

Kostancja de Bazin has made for Amandine a *kontusz,* a small replica of the many-colored coats that Polish nobles once wore as emblems of sympathy for their peasants. It is like the *kontusz* that Amandine's maternal grandfather — Antoni Czartoryski — once wore. Count Antoni Czartoryski who, some twenty-five years before, on his estate hunting lodge near Krakow, murdered his baroness mistress, sister of Amandine's young father, Piotr Droutskoy, and then shot himself. Madame de Bazin has fashioned Amandine's *kontusz* from an heirloom bedcover embroidered in a folkloric country scene depicting the Mazur region of Poland near Warsaw, the place where Madame de Bazin's mother was born. Green and red on a black ground, its length falls to Amandine's knees, its full split sleeves end at the elbow.

Amandine turns round and round in front of the glass, runs about the halls and then out the main door and onto a veranda, letting the wind make a sail of the coat's fullness, laughing, skipping until she sees that Madame has come outside, is gesturing that she should stop. Amandine runs to where Madame de Bazin waits, falls into her arms.

"I knew you would love it, that it would be just right for you," Madame tells her.

"Oh, I do love it, and it is just right, but I won't wear it until Monsieur returns and *then* —"

"You know, it's not necessary that you wear it ever. I just wanted you to have it. Perhaps someday I'll tell you the story of —"

"The story of the coat?"

Kostancja de Bazin looks at Amandine, smoothes back the curls from her forehead, looks deeper into her eyes. She thinks, There is such a pure beauty in her loneliness. Soon she will begin to hold it tight to her, to understand that her sort of solitude is not caused by loss nor can it be relieved by discovery. It's there, the *zal,* always there. Most especially when she smiles.

"Well, yes, of the coat but another story, too, or maybe it's not a story so much as

488

some thoughts that I'd like to tell you. Someday."

Chapter XL

And the somedays passed. And the weeks and months. Three years' worth and more, though the *boche* never returned nor did Monsieur Catulle, nor did Kostancja de Bazin tell Amandine her story or her thoughts.

Isolde and Amandine lived much as they'd lived that first winter after Catulle had gone away and, each spring and summer, they went back to open up Monsieur Catulle's house and planted the garden and helped the old men who worked the fields and they scrubbed and polished and washed the linens and the curtains, left them to dry in the sun. They never stopped talking about Monsieur as if he were in the next room or across the meadow, coming up the road, a tall, burly angel sauntering through the dusk.

Amandine went to the bridge each evening, crossed her arms over her chest, whispered to Solange how she loved her.

Back in the rue Lepic, she studied and read, helped Isolde to cook. After supper, after baths in the old zinc tub, after prayers, after all, they would lie, holding hands, in the little cupboard bed and tell one another they were living the life they were meant to live, and both of them knew it was true.

And on that day in May 1945 when villagers began screeching up and down the road and old men danced and young women wept and laughed with their heads thrown back before they wept again, on that day when the war was over, Isolde and Amandine began to worry about Monsieur, about Dominique and Pascal and Gilles in another way. You see, while the war raged, one could tell oneself that everything would change when it ended, and so now that it had, what was it that they would tell themselves?

Trains came from Paris and from other parts of the country more often, and men who'd been boys five years ago stepped down into the arms of women who'd been girls. And with as much of their hearts as they could put back together, they celebrated.

Amandine and Isolde put the house in order, planted the garden, washed the curtains, ironed the sheets. They waited. But it was on that day in May when the war ended that they stopped talking about Monsieur. Stopped altogether.

It is a Tuesday morning in September 1945 when Amandine opens the door from the dark hallway into the kitchen and finds him sitting there in his chair at the table with the white embroidered cloth, tearing bread into a bowl of wine. His face long and thin, his mustaches and beard as much white as brown, he looks up at her, squeezes his eyes as though the sight of her was too bright.

"Bonjour, monsieur."

"Bonjour, Amandine."

He stands to shake her offered hand, then touches her face. Something like the men who stepped from the trains, Catulle sees before him a young woman whom he'd left as a little girl. Amandine is fourteen years old. In a rose-colored dress above coltish legs, she is a long-stemmed flower. Her hair she'd never cut in all those years and, pulled tight off her face now, the thick black plait of it hangs to her waist, the high, broad bones of her cheeks showing and her blue-black eyes, where had he seen those eyes? Like the eyes of a deer.

Isolde has the water heating for his bath, the soup on the burner for his lunch, Amandine goes to school and, like the others in the village, like the others all over Europe, they set about to cure the misery and begin the rescue that each one must do for himself.

Though Isolde had asked immediately as he walked through the door that first morning while she was setting the table and though he'd answered her, plain and simple — *no, no word* — that was all Catulle said about his children. And then, in November, the telegram — cryptic, glorious — Dominique will be arriving in Paris from England in four days' time.

DO NOT MEET TRAIN. WILL FIND MY WAY HOME. WAIT FOR ME.

"England. How did she manage . . ."
Sitting at the worktable peeling carrots and chewing anise seeds, Isolde pushes aside the chintz curtain that separates it from the kitchen. She swallows, says, "Let's all go to Paris, we must be there . . ."
Catulle looks at her. "Yes, of course we will, but she doesn't say —"
"We'll meet every train arriving from the north on Friday, we'll wait for every train, every last train —"
"And what if she finds her way here while

we're waiting for her there?"

"Then you go. Take Amandine and go to Paris and I'll stay here —"

"Yes, perhaps that's . . ."

Amandine has been watching one, then the other, silently listening.

"Shall we go to Paris to fetch Dominique on Friday?" Catulle asks her in a tone he might use to ask who will take tomorrow morning's eggs.

Miming his reserve, "Yes, monsieur. We shall go to Paris to fetch Dominique on Friday."

That same evening, when they walk to the bridge, Amandine is quiet while Catulle, his own reticence unbound, gushes forth nostalgia, tests the sound of dreams.

"Ah my darling girl, your big sister is coming home. My beautiful daughter, she's safe and she's coming back to us and . . ."

Catulle looks at her then, sees the rift in her cheer.

"What is it, my girl? Tell me."

"I guess it's, well, I can't help but think about Madame Jouffroi. You know. Her *beautiful daughter.* Solange is not going home. I want to go to Madame Jouffroi. I want . . ."

"In time, in time . . ."

"It's not so much that I want to go for myself. At least not as I thought I did all those years ago. But just because I'm, you know, I'm *better* now, that I *feel* better, well it doesn't mean that I don't miss Solange. Oh, monsieur, why aren't they both coming home, why isn't everyone coming home, why . . ."

"Please forgive me my . . . I hadn't thought about . . ."

"No, no, it's only that because Solange can't go back to her mother, I must. Don't you see that? I can tell her about Solange, about our life in the convent, about our journey. I can tell her my memories. Solange can't tell her but I can. Sometimes I think it was my fault that Solange died. If she hadn't come to the convent to take care of me, if she had stayed at home, if —"

"I'd noticed how lovely you are becoming, but I hadn't noticed your conceit."

"What?"

"Do you think you are so powerful? Powerful enough to have caused the death of Solange?"

"It's not powerful that I feel but —"

"Guilty, is it?"

"Something like guilt."

"You did not cause the death of Solange

any more than you caused your parents to —"

"I used to think that must have been my fault. And my fault that Philippe died and that the abbess was cruel and the convent girls, too. When I was little I did think that way, but this is —"

"It's quite the same thing. Don't mistake this feeling of yours for something less. Now, look at me, answer me. Let me show you something of my own fear. Is it because you'd like to go to live with Madame Jouffroi that you wish to find her?"

"No. No, I want to find her for the reason I've already told you. I must find her for Solange. But there is another one. Another reason. Maybe she or Grand-mère Janka will tell me something. About who it was, about the lady who left my necklace with them. I don't think I ever showed it to you, but it's all I have that might have come from my mother, my family. It's all I have."

"Long ago I promised that when the war was over I would help you to find Madame Jouffroi, and so I shall. Meanwhile, please try to believe me when I tell you that all our lives are made of some epic search. Mostly we search for a thing or a person or feel a longing, unnamed, and what happens while we're searching, while we're longing, is that

496

we lose the life we already have. Neither the beauty nor the pain of your life can depend upon your finding your mother, Amandine. I confirm what I told you all those years ago —"

"*It's she who must find you.* I remember."

"I dearly hope that you can go to Madame Jouffroi so that you can say the things you desire to say to her, spend time with her as you wish. But I, Madame Isolde and I, and Dominique, and someday, with the help of God, Pascal and Gilles, we would —"

"Like me to stay with you."

"Yes. We would like that."

"Have you decided which one of them you're going to marry?"

"Which one what?"

"Isn't it time that you chose?"

"Ah, Madame Isolde and Madame de Bazin. I believe that all three of us are past our game. I've decided to wait for you. That is if either Pascal or Gilles doesn't beat me to it. How enchanted they shall be with you."

■ ■ ■ ■

PART VIII
NOVEMBER *1945*
ON A TRAIN TO PARIS

■ ■ ■ ■

Chapter XLI

Though the war has been over for nearly seven months, the distinction among first-, second-, and third-class cars often still falls into confusion. Passengers take seats or compartments as they find them. Amandine and Catulle sit in an undesignated car, which they chose because it is the least crowded. Though they breakfasted well and their journey will be less than two hours — local stops and inevitable delays calculated — Isolde, in the same zinc pail she carries to Amandine at school, has packed a *goûter* for them. They sit now, unwrapping it.

It is perhaps half an hour before they are due to arrive in Paris when a man and a woman shepherding four children are ushered through the car where Amandine and Catulle sit, a conductor leading the way. Two people — likely servants — carry baggage and coats and follow close behind.

"Where are they going?"

"I would think to some more private place in the train."

"She's beautiful, don't you think? That woman."

"I didn't notice her."

"And what do you think of that woman across the way? Third row ahead on the left."

"I can see only her chignon, which is nice enough but —"

"Do you think Madame de Bazin is beautiful?"

"She is of a certain type of beauty, I'll say that. Yes, I think she is beautiful."

"And Madame Isolde?"

"Yet another sort of beauty, but a beauty nevertheless."

"As much as I am fond of Madame de Bazin, if you were to ask me who I thought you should marry, I would choose Madame Isolde."

"Why must I marry at all? I want only for the children to come home and to be of some help to them as they resume their lives. I want that you and I and Madame Isolde live as we have lived and that —"

"But if you love her —"

"I never said that I loved her. Yet I suppose I do."

"Well, then . . . ?"

"Let us wait until the boys come home. And Dominique, you know she will be changed. I think more changed even than I."

They are quiet then until Amandine says, "Do you know why I like trains, monsieur?"

"Have you had so much traffic in your life with trains?"

"When I was little, Solange would take me to the station in Montpellier so that I could watch the trains arriving and departing, and I loved that more than the ballet. I remember that when we boarded the train in Montpellier at the beginning of our journey to Avise, I never wanted that ride to end. I like trains for different reasons now."

"Such as?"

"Into a dark tunnel, back out into the light. The cornfields slipping by —"

"Cornfields slipping by fast as life does? Is that it? I know how old I have grown . . ."

Amandine looks at him, shakes her head and smiles, turns to look out the window. Still looking away from him, she asks, "Where were you all the time when you were away? Are you ever going to tell me about that?"

"I don't know if I can. Certainly I cannot now."

Catulle wants a change of subject. "Your

necklace, let me look at it more closely. Yes, it's lovely." He reaches to touch the pendant, runs his finger across the stone.

"It's old, it looks to be very old. The one that Solange had kept for you?"

"Yes. The only other time I've worn it was on the day when I came to you."

"And that jacket, what did you call it?"

"A *kontusz*. Madame de Bazin says the word differently, but it's something like that."

Catulle studies her. Under her coat of many colors, Amandine wears a black wool skirt and sweater, thick black stockings and ankle boots, black fingerless gloves. Her plait Isolde has tied with a black velvet ribbon like the one around her neck.

"I fear your *mise* is far too elegant for a day to be spent in the Gare du Nord but —"

"I wore the necklace and the coat for good luck."

A long, piercing whistle sounds their approach to the station.

"Here we are then. Let me wrap the rest of the bread. Stay close so we are not separated."

As the train slows Amandine stands, watches their entry into the station from the window of the empty seat across the aisle. She notices a tall man in chauffeur's livery who walks along beside the slowing train. The man stops flush with one of its farther doors as the train shudders into its berth. The conductor heaves open that door, leaps to the ground, pulls down the metal steps, greets the chauffeur. The man and the woman and the children whom Amandine had seen escorted earlier through their car wait at that door to descend. The man, holding the hands of two young boys, is first in line, while an older boy, who looks to be about twelve or thirteen, stands behind him. Carrying a baby girl in her arms, the woman stands third in the family line. The chauffeur moves closer to the steps, bows smartly, offers his hand.

"Good evening, milord. And my young lords."

"Ah, good evening, Vadim. Thank you, thank you. . . . Now you two, please stay right here with your brother while I help Mummy . . ."

Once on the ground and having settled his sons, the man turns to give his hand to the woman. "Watch your step now, darling. There we are."

The woman stands at the top of the metal steps, moves her right wrist to and fro, adjusting the position of the cord of a black satin pouch. Wearing a short silver fox jacket, the sleeves of which seem rather too short on her long white arms — as though the jacket had been meant for a woman more petite than she — she looks down at the sleeping baby held in the crook of her other arm, kisses her. She raises her head then, pauses a half moment. Her smile is wide and sweet and directed somewhere beyond the man and the chauffeur and the others who await her on the ground. As though she has forgotten what to do next, she, looking out at the platform, hesitates. She looks down then, extends her hand to the waiting chauffeur. "Vadim, good evening."

The chauffeur removes his hat. His bow is deep and slow. He rises to take her waiting hand, bends to brush his lips a centimeter above it, then guides her down the metal stairs, "Welcome home, Princess Andzelika."

EPILOGUE

As Amandine and Catulle pass by the train door from which the woman holding the sleeping baby girl is descending, Amandine looks up at the woman, smiles. Holding Catulle's hand, Amandine lags so she might look longer at the woman. She lets go of Catulle's hand and, turning so she nearly faces the woman, Amandine smiles again, and the woman smiles back. Amandine moves faster then to catch up with Catulle's pace and, as she passes through a glint of morning sun, the stone in her necklace catches fire. The woman's eyes are drawn to the bauble that swings about Amandine's throat as she runs by.

ACKNOWLEDGMENTS

For the comfort of her hand over a decade of my wandering the shoals of a writing life, I thank my agent, the splendid and beautiful Rosalie Siegel.

For her quiet, steady brilliance, her graceful ways, I feel humbly appreciative that Jillian Quint is my editor.

For being there, Erich Brandon Knox.

per Fernando Filiberto-Maria, sempre di più l'amore mio

ABOUT THE AUTHOR

Marlena de Blasi lives in Italy with her Venetian husband. She is the author of four previous memoirs — *That Summer in Sicily, A Thousand Days in Venice, A Thousand Days in Tuscany,* and *The Lady in the Palazzo* — as well as three books on the foods of Italy.